W9-BFV-009

ISLAND OF FIRST LIGHT

A Novel by Norman G. Gautreau

Cover art: Painting by Richard Myrick, who lives on Deer Isle, Maine, and in Washington, D.C., and exhibits his works at the Deer Isle Artists Association during the summer. From the collection of Margaret and Peter Allen.

MacAdam/Cage
155 Sansome Street, Suite 550
San Francisco, CA 94104
www.macadamcage.com

Library of Congress Cataloging-in-Publication Data

Gautreau, Norman G., 1941 —
Island of first light / Norman G. Gautreau.
p. cm.
ISBN 1-931561-71-0 (hardcover: alk. paper)
1. Community life–Fiction. 2. Islands–Fiction 3. Maine–Fiction. I. Title.

PS3607.A98I84 2004
813'.6–dc21
2004000792
Manufactured in the United States of America.
10 9 8 7 6 5 4 3 2 1

Jacket and book design by Dorothy Carico Smith

ISLAND OF FIRST LIGHT

A Novel by Norman G. Gautreau

MacAdam/Cage

To my ancestors

AUTHOR'S NOTE

The principal islands mentioned in this book are fictional, as is String of Pearls. The setting is far Downeast Maine near the Canadian border. Visit www.nggautreau.com for a Reader's Guide and more.

Passamaquoddy words (and two Mi'kmaq)

Accihte aht-CHEE-teh (Changing Color Moon—roughly July.)
Apsqe AHP-skweh (Feather Shedding Moon—roughly August.)
Kelotonuhket gel-duh-NU-ked (Freezing Moon) *the 'g' as in gull.*
Kji-niskam kchee-NEE-skahm (A Mi'kmaq word meaning the Great Spirit.)
Koluskap GLU-skahb (According to Passamaquoddy legend, the first man.)
Mi'kmaki meeg-MAH-gee (A Mi'kmaq word meaning Mi'kmaq Territory) *the 'g' as in gull.*
O'zalik oh-zeh-LEEK (a Passamaquoddy pronunciation of Angelique.)
Passamaquoddy pas-sa-ma-KWA-dee (Tribe of the Wabanaki Confederation.)
Punam BU-nam (Frost Fish Moon—roughly December)
Putep BU-deb (whale.)
Siqonomeq ZEE-gwuh-nuh-megw (Alewife Moon—roughly May) *the 'gw' as in Gwendolyn.*
Toqakiw duh-GWAH-gee-u (Autumn Moon—roughly September.)

'People can't die along the coast,' said Mr. Peggoty, 'except when the tide's pretty nigh out.
They can't be born, unless it's pretty nigh in—
not properly born, till flood.'

—Charles Dickens, *David Copperfield*

~

What is the world, O soldiers?
It is I:
I this incessant snow,
This northern sky;
Soldiers, this solitude
Through which we go
Is I.

—Walter de la Mare, *Napoleon*

SIQONOMEQ

Alewife Moon

On the day Caitlin Gray left her husband, the sky was a deep blue. Englishman Bay flashed a million spikes of sunlight; the Christmas scent of spruce and the tang of sea salt filled the air. On the horizon, the dark, serrated tops of the spruce trees on Alabaster Island and its neighbor, Snagged Anchor Island, stood sharply against the bright backdrop of sea and sky.

Caitlin huddled against the window of the Downeast Trailways bus as it negotiated a curve overlooking the bay; soon they would be arriving at the ferry terminal. At first, she'd thought of taking the car but ever since the accident she was afraid of driving. Besides, she knew Alabaster Island was small and she would have no trouble getting around. What use would the car be? It would only serve to remind her, as it always did, of the accident. And the little boy.

Jeremy had been his name.

She remembered how he appeared so suddenly from between two parked cars; how he stopped in the middle of the road staring in child-fright at her onrushing car; how she had no time to do anything but register horror before hitting him. She remembered the rush of people to the boy as she sat shaking in her car, her mind electrified at the roots; the police opening her door, helping her from the car, questioning her. The strobing blue-and-white lights of the police car sweeping across her face. Had she not been drinking coffee; had she not hit a speed bump; had the coffee not been too hot when it spilled onto her bare legs; had she not been going a little over the speed limit;

had all these things not happened, she might have seen the child and been able to avoid him. A chain of cause and effect she'd unwittingly set in motion.

There had been no charges. There didn't need to be. Just an accident. For her trial she faced the boy's parents and grandparents at the hospital, said how sorry she was, cried, was consoled by the parents.

But then the grandparents said, "You took our Jeremy from us."

Her reflection in the bus window, waves of muted light, floated over the bay intermingling her face and the sea. Her swan like neck was emphasized by short-cropped, brown hair tousled by the seat back. Studying her refracted image, she patted her hair down. Still attractive, she thought, especially for a woman in her forties. But she also saw sadness in her face, a sadness that had been there since the accident.

And since she began to suspect something between Nigel and Ekaterina Valerovna.

In the distance the ferry for Alabaster Island, scarves of foam at its bow, approached the mainland. It appeared to merge into her transparent face. She looked forward to boarding the ferry and leaving the mainland behind. It would be the break she had been planning for months.

Leaving Nigel was wrenching, made only slightly more bearable by the fact that Dylan and Ellen were grown and had their own lives to live. She would be losing only her husband, not her children…or they, her. A shiver passed through her lips but she refused to cry. Let the reflection cry. She let her thoughts stray to Alabaster Island where she'd spent a summer twenty-seven years before—when she was single and free and in love with Garret Webster. She thought of him, tried to remember what it had been like those summer afternoons when they made love in his attic studio, when she posed for him as he worked on his sculpture. Was he still on the island? Would he remember her?

Once, he took her up in a small plane over Englishman Bay. Alabaster Island and its mate, Snagged Anchor Island, gave the appearance of taffy being stretched into two pieces, connected only by an elongated reef thin as a baby's drool. From that height, the reef, called String of Pearls, seemed curdled in cream. But at ground level, she knew, the cream would become ocean waves snarling at the rock, etching into its surface crags and crevices. Her last time on the island, she'd often watched the reef appear wraith like out of the moist belly of the shrouding fog as though, that moment, being painted by the finger of God. Would it be the same?

Of the two glacial drumlins only Snagged Anchor Island was uninhabited. It was at the easternmost reach of the United States, where sunlight first rose from the sea. Often, she'd sat on the cliffs of Alabaster Island with her lover to watch the sun swell the horizon and send shafts of light to ignite the tips of the tall spruce on Snagged Anchor Island. It was the beginning of her fascination with the place.

The memory of her long-ago lover brought a nagging thought back to her, another name, one rooted in the present. She mouthed the name Ekaterina Valerovna, the roll of vowels falling like droplets of venom from her tongue. She was certain Nigel was with her at that very moment. How long had it been going on? Should she have left long before?

ekaterina valerovna

She imagined the beautiful blond, legs splayed, skirt immodestly hiked to her knees, cello vibrating against her thighs, gazing with doe eyes at Nigel as he led the quartet with little nods on the downbeats. When Caitlin had the accident Nigel was performing a concert in Santa Fe with that woman. She remembered they were supposed to close the program with Beethoven's opus 130, a piece she'd heard them play before at the New England Conservatory. She remembered how throughout the fifth movement, the expressive cavatina, Nigel and Ekaterina fixed their gazes on each other, overhead lights sheening in the tears streaming down their cheeks.

cavatina...ekaterina

No doubt that's what they were doing at the very moment the boy, Jeremy, chased a ball from between parked cars...and she killed him.

She wondered if Nigel, even then, also vibrated between Ekaterina's legs.

The bus carrying her to the ferry rounded another turn and the ferry terminal came into view.

~

Freddy Orcutt sat on a bench in the ferry terminal on the mainland. He cradled his pipe in his bony, macula-spotted hands looking forward to when he would be on the ferry's deck and he could light it. He was still not used to the new rules about not smoking indoors in public. Scanning the faces of the people in the terminal, he tried to imagine which of them might be the person who would be renting Jimmy's cottage. Helen Underwood only said she'd rented the cottage to someone over the phone without mentioning if the person was a man or a woman, young or old. Helen wasn't even sure which ferry the person would be catching. He hoped it would be a later one because he wanted to give the cottage one last check before meeting the person, whoever it was.

He frowned, thinking how he'd damn near sold the place. He remembered how Helen Underwood was shocked but delighted, the previous month, when he said he was ready to sell. Beginning twenty or more years before, she seriously suggested once a year that he sell the place. "After all, I can't imagine why you want to keep a vacant house like that."

"Just do. That's all," he would say each time. Perhaps he simply refused to give up hope that his daughter-in-law would someday bring the grandchildren back. He remembered how he'd helped them eat breakfast cereal, emptying the box so they could get the prize.

Helen would press him for a day or so before giving up until the following year. The rest of the time it was a friendly standing joke between them. If she was in Pauline's Coffee and Bake Shop when he entered, she would ask, with a smile, "Ready to sell?" and he would answer "Nope," and that would be it, much as if they shared a comment about the weather.

So when he entered her office the previous month—a shingle-sided, freshly painted, one-room building with a closet bathroom—and said, "I'm ready to sell Jimmy's cottage," she was stunned. She lifted her eyeglasses, which hung from a gold chain around her neck, to her eyes. Links of the chain clicked against her large earrings. "Are you serious?" She had a bark-stripping voice as though she'd learned to speak over a bad phone connection. Her complexion, like unbleached linen, gave the impression her voice had shunted the blood from her face. That, and her graying hair, gave her a ghostly appearance. As long as he'd known Helen, she always seemed to be the same age. She'd never married and, so far as anybody knew, never had a lover. Perhaps Morgan Fludd was right when he said, "What with her goldang voice, ain't no man would not be ascared at what she might sound like if he ever got her off."

When Freddy nodded, Helen asked, "How come?"

He shrugged his shoulders. "Getting old. Guess it's time to start settling accounts. Get my affairs in order."

Helen came out from behind her desk, walked up to him, and took his hands in hers. She gazed into his eyes. "I hope you're not sick or something like that. Angus Macleod hasn't given you some bad news, has he?"

"Nope. Ain't been to see him 'cept for my annual physical. Said I'm likely to be bothering folks around here for some years to come."

"Well I'm glad to hear that. But all the same, Freddy, you look annoyed about something."

"Now you know that's just my natural look. When I was born my father took one look at me and asked my mother what I was so pissed off about. Been like that ever since." At least that's the story he told himself. However, the grim expression had fixed permanently in April of 1945 at Dachau.

Helen Underwood laughed. "So why the sudden change of mind about Jimmy's place?"

"This year it'll be twenty-five years since Jimmy died. Guess that's time enough."

"I understand, Freddy," she said, squeezing his hands tightly before letting go. "What are you hoping to get for it?"

"Don't matter much."

"Surely you have some idea."

"Don't need the money. I ain't spent any of the insurance money for me and Jimmy's boat yet," Freddy replied. "Nothing to spend it on since Agnes died."

Helen walked to her desk and took up a clipboard, which held a real estate form. Her heavy legs were like corncobs, riddled with cellulite and varicose veins. "Why don't you take a cruise somewhere? You know, one of those big cruise ships. You'd be bound to meet some attractive widow. You could use a woman around the house." She started to make entries on the form.

"After spending a lifetime on the sea, why would I want to do that?"

"For the company."

"Books keep me company. The Red Sox in the summer."

"Baseball is no substitute for a woman."

"They're gonna win come next season. I feel it in my bones."

Helen laughed, a grating sound. "You say that every year. They haven't won the World Series since before I was born. Since before *you* were born, for God's sake." She paused, looked intently into his eyes, and said, "Are you sure?"

"Good pitching and this guy, Ramirez—"

"Freddy, you know what I mean."

He averted his eyes and looked out the window. "Eyuh, I'm sure." He felt his eyes begin to water so he went to the window and made a show of peering down the street. "Speaking of Angus Macleod, I see him walking into Pauline's. Think I'll go have a cup of coffee with him."

"Okay, Freddy, you do that. I'll come by later to look at the cottage and figure what we can get for it. I'm going to get you a good price, Freddy. Then I'm going to get Martha Roberts to show you some of the cruise brochures she has in her office on the mainland."

"Once is enough. Ain't going on one of Martha's trips again," he replied, slipping out the door.

Now, in the ferry terminal, he thumbed through the pages of the book he'd taken a taxi to the mainland library to find, a history of early settlements in Downeast Maine. It hadn't been at the island library. Turning to the index, he found the name "Orcutt" listed several times. He flipped to one of the pages indicated and started to read but his thoughts kept wandering. Only in his reading chair at home could he truly concentrate. Once again, he surveyed the people in the terminal. He knew most of them; May was still early for island visitors. No one appeared likely to be the person who would be staying in Jimmy's cottage.

He sighed. It was difficult, but he persuaded himself again that renting the place was the right thing to do. He looked out the window and saw the ferry approaching the mainland. It was still a good mile away. Late. He went outside to smoke his pipe, nodding to O'zalik and Quentin Moseley as he passed.

~

O'zalik Moseley—long-legged, slim-hipped—gave her husband a reluctant greeting. She was disappointed to find him standing in the mainland ferry terminal when she returned from a visit with her grandparents at Pleasant Point Reservation near the Canadian border. Her return to the reservation was timed to coincide with the annual run of the alewife on the St. Croix River. For both her and the alewife it was a kind of homecoming, a return to the place of birth. She spent several days listening to her grandfather's stories and it reaffirmed her passion for her Passamaquoddy heritage. But seeing Quentin standing with Garret Webster when she came through the door deflated her. She'd been expecting she wouldn't have to see him until the ferry arrived at Alabaster Island.

"Angelique, it's good to see you," said Garret with a pleasant smile.

"Did you have a good visit?"

"Yes, thank you, Garret."

it's o'zalik

A few years back, she decided to change her name to O'zalik, the name her grandparents and everybody on the reservation used. Some of the residents of Alabaster Island accepted her new name; some didn't.

O'zalik turned to Quentin. "What are you doing on the mainland?"

"Just keeping Garret company," he replied in a tone that suggested he need not explain.

Garret said, "I came to talk with a man about some new furniture I'm having built for the inn." They exchanged some small talk before Garret excused himself. He went over to chat with two women, always playing the role of the cordial inn keeper. She liked him, enjoyed cleaning rooms for him occasionally at the Spruce Cove Inn. Soon, she heard laughter coming from Garret and the two women.

Their Passamaquoddy heritage was not the only thing O'zalik and her grandparents talked about. They also talked about her marriage to Quentin Moseley.

"I don't know if I can stay with him," O'zalik said as they sat around the kitchen table drinking coffee.

"Oh, dear…" said her grandmother.

"O'zalik, what are you saying?" asked her grandfather.

"I'm saying I think I made a mistake marrying him."

"But you must give it more time."

"I've given it plenty of time, Grandfather. He's not the same man I met."

"But his father died not long ago. He's upset. Perhaps when he gets over it he'll come around to being the man you first married."

"I doubt it, Grandfather. I seriously doubt it."

Things started to go badly between them from the day O'zalik first mentioned going out to explore Snagged Anchor Island. Her grandfather told her that it used to be a sacred place for the Passamaquoddy and she ached to visit the island, to see if she could feel the presence of ancestors. But Quentin seemed to resent being reminded of her Passamaquoddy heritage. Or, she thought, it could be he hated being reminded the only woman he could attract was an Indian.

bastard

She thought when Quentin's father died, things would be better. The man hated her to the point of refusing even to acknowledge he had an Indian as a daughter-in-law. She couldn't remember the last time the old man said a civil word to her. Now he was rotting in his grave up on Cemetery Hill. *Good.*

It was shortly after the death of Quentin's father when the man from the Fisheries Service showed up with form copies from Quentin's logbook. All New England fishermen were required by the National Marine Fisheries Service to keep logbooks with quadruplicate entries detailing where they fished, how much they caught, what they threw away, what kind of gear they used, and twenty or so other items of interest to the government. Armed with that information, the Fisheries people would close off areas they thought were being overfished. All fishermen complained of the burdensome paperwork and, even more, of the closures which threatened their livelihoods. And they fought back any way they could. Quentin's way of fighting back, however, soon caught the attention of the government.

"I'm afraid we have a problem with your log entries, Mr. Moseley," the young man in the business suit said, standing in the doorway. He stared at Quentin's beefy arms.

O'zalik looked at her husband. Quentin said nothing. His neck veins were like ropes, a swollen square knot near the collar bone looking angry enough to erupt. He was round-shouldered with soft, pale skin and blond hair so thick and tangled it would have snapped a plastic comb.

"Please come in," O'zalik said. "Tell us what the problem is. I'm sure we can straighten it out."

She led the way into the kitchen. It was small with an old Sears Roebuck stove, cabinets with peeling paint, a fifteen-year-old refrigerator, a wobbly, chrome-legged table O'zalik had covered with a tablecloth to hide the torn contact paper underneath, four plastic-covered chairs, a single lightbulb dangling over the table, and a floor covered with linoleum that was cracked and curling at the edges. Despite all O'zalik's efforts, the room still stank of the cigars her father-in-law, old Ben Mosley, had smoked incessantly.

O'zalik poured water into a kettle and placed it on the stove. She joined Quentin and the Fisheries man, who were already seated at the table. The man pulled out a stack of forms held together by a heavy metal clip. He snapped the clip off and lifted the top form. "You give the coordinates of where you were fishing as forty-two degrees forty-eight minutes north and seventy-three degrees, fifty-six minutes west."

"So?"

"That's Schenectady, New York, Mr. Moseley. A shopping center, to be precise. And I don't even think they have a fish market."

"So I made a mistake." His words came coarse-grained, like hacking hot sand from his throat.

The man lifted the next form. "Rutland, Vermont." And the next. "North Conway, New Hampshire."

O'zalik gave her husband an incredulous look.

The man continued. "And this one," he said with a laugh. "Colorado Springs, for Chrissake." He looked up, shook his head. "Shall I go on, Mr. Moseley?"

"So what's your point?" Quentin asked sourly.

The man slid a form toward Quentin. "See where you put your signature? What does it say there?"

Quentin read in silence, his neck veins visibly throbbing.

Reading from another form, the man said, "With your signature, Mr. Moseley, you certify the information is true, complete, and correct…and made in good faith. Now we know the regulations are a pain in the ass and we expect you fishermen to try to wiggle out of them any way you can. In fact, you know goddamned well we turn a blind eye to lots of stuff because we know how hard it is. But we won't be taken for fools, Mr. Moseley."

"What are you telling me?"

"I'm telling you, you have a choice: you can voluntarily shut down for a few months or you can face a charge of perjury."

Quentin blanched. "I can't shut down. It'd cost me a fortune."

The kettle started to whistle. A rope of steam gushed toward the ceiling. O'zalik gave Quentin another incredulous look and moved to the stove, shaking her head. She listened while she prepared tea.

"Not nearly as much as lawyers' fees for defending yourself. Besides, how are you going to go out fishing if you're in some lawyer's office in Bangor or in a courtroom?"

O'zalik pressed her lips together. Out the kitchen window, she watched a seagull hover for a moment, tilt its wing, and soar off on the wind. She smiled with longing, rising to her toes, an urge for flight pervading her muscles. It was a sensation that, ever since a child, she'd experienced whenever she saw a bird.

Over tea, they talked a bit longer. In the end, Quentin agreed to shut himself down. And when the man left, O'zalik remained silent for a while. She looked past Quentin into the living room, where a bookcase housed her collection on the Passamaquoddy. Among others, there was *Restitution: The Land Claims of the Mashpee, Passamaquoddy, and Penobscott Indians of New England*, a Passamaquoddy dictionary, *Handicrafts of the Modern Maine Indians*, *Birch Bark Canoe Building*, *Passamaquoddy Stories and Legends*, and a Passamaquoddy language course on audio tape. She'd recently bought several more books at the Abbe Museum in Bar Harbor and she was aching to get to them. She looked at Quentin and said, "Jesus, Quentin...Colorado Springs?"

He shot her an angry look. She walked out the door.

Since then, Quentin seemed to resent his wife more than ever. It was obvious he knew she thought he was stupid and had cost them a lot of money, making it necessary for her to get a second job.

Maybe she'd only seen what she wanted to see in those early days—a charming, vulnerable man who seemed kind. It was hard to believe she ever saw him that way, but then again she'd been searching for a way off the reservation. As much as she loved her grandparents, who had brought her up after her parents died in an auto accident, she found life on the reservation too constricting. Like most young people, she had no future there. Then she met Quentin. Perhaps, out of her need, she made up stories about him, eventually believing her own stories rather than the evidence before her eyes. From her upbringing among her Passamaquoddy relatives, she knew the power of story.

Initially, she was patient with his fits of anger, wondering if their roots didn't go back to his time in the Gulf War. Shortly after they were married he'd told her how he'd enlisted for the war because he missed out on the action in Vietnam, being sent over just before the fall of Saigon. He was, in his words, "a sanitation engineer" in the desert. In a voice tight with tension he told her how on the first day of the ground war his job was to follow the assault wave with a plow and fill in the trenches where many thousands of Iraqi soldiers had been killed. "They didn't want the press and the public to see all the shit and the blood and the pieces of bodies, so I buried it all," he'd told her. "Even the ones who were still alive and firing their weapons. I buried those sons of bitches, too. When I finished a pass, I would go back and smooth away any arms or legs still sticking out. It was like the slaughter never happened. I hid the whole friggin' mess."

She told her grandparents all these things but they saw it only as evidence that she should show more patience and they made her promise to give it more time. But now O'zalik wondered if she had been right to make such a promise.

She sat coolly beside her husband waiting for the ferry, which she saw in the distance, to arrive.

~

The bus pulled up to the ferry terminal. Caitlin Gray gathered her bags, walked into the building and to the ticket counter where she picked up the ticket she had reserved and paid for over the phone. As she started to settle into a seat near the window, a young boy working off energy by running across the room, bumped into her.

The boy's mother grabbed his arm. "I told you not to run. It's too crowded. Now apologize to the lady."

"It's all right," Caitlin said. "He didn't do any harm."

The boy, looking sheepish, said, "I'm sorry," then followed his mother to the other side of the room.

jeremy

The day of the accident, she drove home and poured herself a drink. Searching through a desk drawer, she located the slip of paper on which she'd written the number of Nigel's hotel in Santa Fe. She called his room at the hotel. No answer. She left a message: "Nigel, please call. There's been an accident. I need you."

She settled back in the comfortable, overstuffed couch in her living room, waiting. And as she waited, she surveyed the room, the scene of so many happy moments. It was a way of reestablishing a grasp on her life.

Or was it too late? Would he call? Was the marriage over?

ekaterina valerovna

Dominating the room was the one big luxury they'd permitted themselves years before on a limited budget—a Steinway grand. It was tucked in a bay window, various scores and a handsome, walnut and brass metronome sitting on its polished surface. A framed photograph of her, Nigel, Dylan, and Ellen, taken on a ski vacation in Vermont, their expressions radiant, also sat on the piano. Against the far wall was a fireplace surmounted by an entertainment center where the television, always on in those days, flickered. A top-of-the-line audio system completed the entertainment center. Another wall was taken up with floor-to-ceiling bookcases surrounding the door to the dining room. Most of the shelf space housed books on music theory, musical biographies, and an untidy pile of music scores. One section, however, belonged to her and it was here that she had her personal library, a visible record of her unfocused college years. It held a collection of works by Dylan Thomas, T. S. Eliot, Emily Dickinson, W. H. Auden, Robert Frost, Sylvia Plath, and a variety of more contemporary poets including Robert Pinsky, Sandra Cisneros, Denise Levertov, and John Ashbury. Many of the hard-bound volumes were autographed. Often she would sit in her spot on the couch and stare at her collection, gaining inspiration from it. Next to them was a row of books on archaeology, her other passion during her student days. Writing and archaeology—both concerned with digging, with exploring what lay hidden. Excavating.

For as long as she could remember, she'd wanted to write, to create. From an early age her parents, Aristide and Yvette Babineau, had encouraged her. They taught English studies at Emerson College in Boston and were particular fans of Dylan Thomas. Indeed, they gave their daughter the name of Thomas' wife, Caitlin. In high school she was the editor of the school newspaper, frequently contributing poems. And while still in high school she'd even managed to get a few of her poems published in obscure poetry reviews. This helped her gain admission to the Boston University writing program, where she mingled with other writers and where she thought her career as a writer was about to take off. She found herself associating with artists of all sorts, painters, writers, musicians, sculptors.

Then she met Nigel at a party. They fell hard for each other, were soon married. Caitlin quit the writing program and accompanied Nigel to New York, where he attended Juilliard. She devoted herself to supporting Nigel's studies by finding a job as a technical writer. Nights and weekends she took courses in archaeology, especially the archaeology of Native Americans. Within a year, Dylan was born and the following year she gave birth to Ellen. Caitlin settled into two decades of happy family life. Now, with Nigel consumed in his work and Dylan and Ellen living on their own, she had a renewed, burning desire to write.

But in the end, it was the Steinway that crowded out everything else.

At last, just before four in the afternoon, he called. "Got your message, Love. What's up?"

"Thank God you called," Caitlin said. "Nigel, There's been an accident."

"That's what your message said. Are you all right?"

"Yes…yes, I'm fine. I mean, I'm not hurt."

"The car totaled or something?"

"No. Maybe a little dent. That's all. Nigel, I—"

"So what's—" He stopped, then he said, "Hold on a minute." Caitlin heard his voice muffled as if he'd covered the mouthpiece with his hand. She couldn't make out the words. After a moment, he came back on the line. "Listen, Caitlin, I've got to go. We played Beethoven's Fifth cello sonata last night and we're playing it again tonight. The *adagio con molto sentimento* didn't go the way I wanted it, so we're going to give it another run-through."

cavatina ekaterina

All at once, Caitlin didn't want to tell him about the little boy. It would feel too much like competing for his emotions, like begging. She was afraid he would see it as a drain, an intrusion, even while he outwardly comforted her. Besides, the boy was dead. There was nothing Nigel could do from Santa Fe to alter that stark reality. "Okay, go ahead with your rehearsal. I'll see you when you get back."

"But are you sure you're alright?"

"Yes…yes, I'm fine."

"It sounds like a pretty minor accident if you're not hurt and the car only has a little dent."

"Yes, a minor accident." A tear snaked down her cheek.

"So you'll be okay?"

"Yes."

"Right, then, I'll call you later. Gotta go."

"Yes. Talk to you later."

And at that moment Caitlin knew she would leave him. The only question was when.

~

Freddy Orcutt watched the ferry slide past the bell buoy at the outer limit of the channel and turn for the terminal building. The foam at the ferry's bow diminished as it slowed for its final approach. Casual onlookers might think the ferry was off course as it aimed somewhat to the south of its slip, but Freddy had confidence in Morgan Fludd, for the man knew the set of the currents and the state of the tide and would undoubtedly have the ferry's bow positioned at the mouth of the slip at precisely the right moment.

Morgan was another person who thought he should sell Jimmy's cottage but Freddy would have none of it. Not sell. Renting had less finality to it.

The previous month he crossed the driveway from his own cottage to the vacant one an hour before Helen Underwood and her prospects were due to arrive. Though he was in his mid-seventies, he walked tall and with a negligent ease, having retained much of the vigor and agility of his earlier years. He was lean and loose-limbed. A pair of reading glasses rode in the vest pocket of his shirt. The tip of his right index finger was calloused and blackened from tamping burning pipe tobacco, an aromatic cross-cut blend of Cavendish and Latakia redolent of the tar in old ship's rigging. People said he carried a dignified bearing about his loneliness. However, if Helen Underwood at the real estate office or O'zalik Moseley at Pauline's Coffee and Bake Shop asked him, he would admit to being stiff with aching joints some mornings, particularly if a southwest breeze was blowing. But on that day, only occasional zephyrs ruffled the sea. It undulated slowly with long swells coming from a storm hundreds of miles away. Like the rise and fall of an old man's chest under a heavy blanket.

They built the cottage many years before, he and his son, Jimmy, to match his own cottage overlooking the ocean. He'd built the first cottage some years before when he married Agnes. Before that he lived with his parents in the house on Front Street that was in his family for generations. When his parents died, Freddy sold that old house (with Helen Underwood's help) to the new island doctor, Angus Macleod.

He and Jimmy did much of the work on the second cottage themselves with only occasional help and Freddy remembered them as wonderful, sunlit days. An image came to him of the two of them balanced on scaffolding, the sun warm on their bare backs, he holding in place the long board that would form part of the soffit for the roof overhang while Jimmy drove the nails home...or another time when they were hammering shingles on the roof and a gust came up lifting loose shingles and sending them sailing into space. Freddy and Jimmy, laughing like kids, scrambled on the slanting roof to prevent more shingles from blowing away then climbed down the ladder with the salvaged shingles cradled under their arms and retrieved the ones scattered all over the yard.

"Some of them shingles probably blew clear over to Snagged Anchor Island," Freddy muttered to himself with a chuckle as he entered the vacant cottage.

He found himself often thinking of Jimmy...and of his wife, Agnes. But it was scant companionship. And he found himself thinking of Miesko, the little Polish boy at Dachau...the Germans he'd killed when his unit liberated the camp. That day in April 1945 a bright sun palpated the land from a cloudless sky as though nothing was wrong on the earth. But then he saw the rude, naked face of evil. He'd participated in it. And ever since he wondered about his own blame.

In the years since, he'd often call Miesko, who was now a rabbi in New York. With Agnes and Jimmy gone, he wanted the comfort of talking with someone who was like family to him.

Once inside the cottage, Freddy closed the door behind him and repeated, "Eyuh, clear over to Snagged Anchor Island." He gave a little laugh. He turned to look at the door he'd just closed and remembered when they were hanging that door and had so much difficulty getting it to swing properly. He and Jimmy cursed so loudly, Agnes came across from the other cottage and insisted they take a break and have some lemonade.

her voice…peaceful like wind chimes

the sharp taste of the lemonade…ice cubes clinking in the glass

He looked into the living room to check that everything was clean and orderly. He was glad he paid O'zalik to straighten up the place. He paid her in advance, saying, "Now don't you go telling your husband about this. You use the money for yourself."

She'd nodded with a conspiratorial smile. "Yes, Freddy."

And, later, when she came to his door to say she'd finished, he said, "Now don't forget. Keep the money for yourself. Quentin should go out and earn his own drinking money instead of letting you earn it all for him."

He stepped into the living room. The afghan Agnes knitted for Jimmy as a house-warming gift three decades before was neatly folded on the chintz sofa. He sat down and felt the wool between his thumb and forefinger, pleased to note it was still in good shape even after all that time. He lifted a corner of it to his nose and sniffed. O'zalik had left a hint of her scent behind. Once when he asked her what it was, she replied, "Abenaki Moon. My uncle sells it in his Native American gift shop. He sends me some every once in a while." She told him it contained sweetgrass, sage, and other scents and ever since, if he went into Pauline's Coffee and Bake Shop when O'zalik was working, he allowed himself the romantic thought it was the scent of North America before the Europeans came. It was a good thing her uncle sent perfume instead of money, he thought, since Quentin Moseley would have no interest in taking it from her.

They'd installed skylights—Jimmy loved light—and now Freddy heard a tiny clattering sound. He'd heard it before, crows dropping pebbles and watching them skitter along the glass. It was a sense of playfulness that almost brought tears to Freddy's eyes, an innocent joy, one he wished he could experience.

He looked out the large window. A mile or so out he saw a lobster boat rising and falling slowly under long swells, a motion like breathing, faint clouds of seagulls hovering and flitting above it. He figured, given the dark color of the hull, it was Ernie Botham and Burle Ledyard tending traps and he experienced a momentary yearning to be back out on the water.

How Jimmy and he argued about that window! Jimmy wanted it as big as possible for the view but Freddy thought if it was too big, it wouldn't stand up to a good nor'easter. "Besides, most times all you'd see is fog," Freddy said. In the end, though, he gave in and they installed the biggest window they could find at the building supply place on the mainland. In more than twenty years and countless storms, the window had never broken. Jimmy was right after all.

Freddy was so engrossed in his memories he didn't hear Helen Underwood's car pull into the driveway. He was startled when she opened the front door and called his name.

He bolted to his feet and rushed to the front door. "Sorry, Helen, I didn't hear you pull up."

"This is Arthur and Julie Kimball. They're from Bangor."

Arthur Kimball extended his hand. He was a burly man and his grip was hard. "We figured it's about time we got a summer place."

"I see."

Julie Kimball, trim and petite, went straight to the window. "Arthur, come here and look at this view."

As the couple started to explore the cottage, Freddy experienced a twinge of violation. It was something he hadn't expected. He told Helen he would be waiting in his own cottage.

He passed the time smoking his pipe on the back porch of his cottage, the blue smoke rising and fanning out along the ceiling of the porch in the still air.

There were days when he and Jimmy would spend entire mornings on the porch studying the fog. It was a frequent presence on Alabaster Island, sucking the colors from things, turning the world various shades of gray. And it had a thousand faces. Sometimes it was warm and moist and it seemed to inhale the sunlight that was burning it off the way a dying man inhales a last breath. At other times it came as a drizzle of gray, heavy with the smell of fish, living and dead, filaments of fog curling lazily about the island's buildings like the vaporous arms of a hydra, mizzling droplets of moisture on every surface. Then there were times it couldn't quite establish itself and left only faint-hearted shreds of mist that quickly capitulated to the sun. Sometimes it stayed out to sea, appearing as a scrim of gray on the horizon like an army waiting for the call to advance. But most times it rolled in from the sea cold, impenetrable, thick as dark cotton, so heavy it pressed down on the waves, flattening them. It presented so many faces that Freddy wondered why they didn't have more words for it the way Eskimos have many words for snow. Perhaps because they didn't like it, didn't want to honor it.

Ernie Botham and Burle Ledyard, their boat trailing scarves of foaming wake, were proceeding south to lay out more strings of traps. He watched them nearly disappear into the troughs for several long seconds before riding up high again on the next swell. It was a respirating rhythm that always made him think of the sea as a living thing. But the same swells that were so gentle out in the open water became steep waves when they dragged over the shallow bottom as they approached String of Pearls. He watched the thuggish waves breaking over the reef. From years of such watching, he could tell precisely the state of the tide by the way the waves broke around the permanently exposed outcroppings of Big Pearl and Little Pearl. Now, it was nearing low water, exposing much of the reef. It glittered whitely in the sun, earning its name.

Yet he, like many others on the island, could never look at String of Pearls without experiencing a deep sense of unease, especially when the waves were breaking over it and throwing up spray as they were now. Because people had drowned there.

And it was where Jimmy's boat washed up.

A mile away, at the other end of String of Pearls, spruce-studded Snagged Anchor Island slipped under the shadow of a passing cloud.

More than half an hour passed before Helen appeared on the porch. "The Kimballs sound very interested," she said. "I'm going to take them back to my office, where I think they'll make an offer."

Freddy said nothing because he was thinking of the time he and Jimmy planted the maple that stood between the two cottages. Then, of course, it had been a mere sapling supported by stakes. But now its branches overspread the two houses.

"I'll call you?" said Helen, an inquisitive look on her face.

He turned to look at her. "I'm awful sorry, Helen …"

She gave him a look of suspicion. "Second thoughts?"

"I ain't gonna sell. I can't."

He saw a shadow of anger pass across her eyes. "I see."

"You gotta understand."

"I think I do."

"Agnes never wanted to sell it neither. Always said we should keep it."

"Diana and the grandchildren ain't coming back. You know that, Freddy, don't you?"

"I suppose." He remembered his daughter-in-law saying she had to leave the island because the associations were too painful. She couldn't live in the place where she and Jimmy had been so happy. Where Jimmy died. She could not bear to ever see the place again.

"But you're still not going to sell?"

"Nope. I'll rent, but I ain't gonna sell."

"So, we're back to the same old thing."

"Guess so."

She looked at him for a long moment, gave him a weak smile, and said, "I didn't think you could go through with it."

"Guess not."

"You have to let go sometime, you know."

"Ain't the time."

"I could have gotten you a good price."

"Ain't the time, Helen," he repeated sharply.

She gave a resigned nod. "Okay, Freddy, it ain't the time." She paused, gestured toward the driveway, and asked, "What in heck do you expect me to tell them?"

"I'm awful sorry, Helen."

"Yeah…I'll see you at Pauline's tomorrow." She chuckled. "I'll ask if you're ready to sell and you'll say, 'Nope,' and everything will be the same as it's always been. Okay, Freddy?"

"Eyuh."

"Except tomorrow I'm going to make you buy me a cup of coffee."

He nodded. "Figure I owe it to you."

After Helen Underwood and the Kimballs left, Freddy sat on his porch for a long time, rocking in his chair, smoking his pipe, staring out to sea. Remembering. He didn't come in until he saw Ernie and Burle racing back toward the entrance to Spruce Cove, their boat throwing sheets of spray to the sides and leaving a roiling wake. The sun dazzled the foaming water. Freddy saw flashes of light as the men threw crabs and undersized lobsters pinwheeling back into the sea. Though the men were a good quarter mile away, Freddy imagined he could hear their laughter.

high pitched…like a loon…infectious

He levered himself up from his rocker, went into the kitchen, and turned the weather radio on. He'd forgotten it earlier in his anxiety about Helen Underwood bringing prospective buyers. He figured he'd go into town and have dinner at the Boat Shed rather than prepare something for himself. Undoubtedly there would be somebody he knew there, somebody he could sit and wait for the end of the world with.

There always was.

~

When Caitlin left the ferry terminal she felt a familiar terror. It was a bloom of breath trapped in her throat as she hurried toward the long metal ramp to the ferry, a congealing of guilt heavy in her chest. As though only by hurrying, by giving herself no time to think, could she resist the urge to turn back, forget this escape, return to her husband, her children (grown as they were, she still thought of them as her children). She remembered the phrase "escape velocity" from some recent program on public television—perhaps *NOVA*—and knew it applied to her in this moment. *Escape velocity.*

With Nigel and Dylan and Ellen all away most of the time, there seemed little else to do but watch television. No family to turn to. She watched television to keep her mind from wandering to Ekaterina Valerovna. Why hadn't she confronted Nigel with her suspicions? Why did she confine herself to secretly sniffing his clothes for lingering traces of perfume? Did cavatina-Ekaterina even wear perfume?

A shuddering, metallic crash brought her back to the moment. The boarding ramp had been lowered, connecting the ferry to the access roadway. She hoisted her backpack onto her shoulder, lifted a valise with her left hand, and grabbed the handle of her rolling suitcase with her right. She hurried toward the ferry, the wheels of the suitcase chattering on the rough surface. She scurried past the other passengers and was almost to the ferry when her shoe caught a protrusion and, with a small cry, she stumbled to the metal grating, landing hard on her right knee. She grimaced. The pain came in waves of silent sound—a high-pitched, outraged shriek, a sharp, stinging sensation. She saw a tear in the right knee of her blue jeans and remembered vaguely how a quarter century before in college she'd deliberately torn the knees of her jeans because that had been the fashion.

"You all right, Miss?"

Caitlin saw a hand extended to her. It was bony and veined, mottled with spots. She looked up to a dour, weathered face framed in short white sideburns. The man helped her to her feet. He chided her about rushing as though she were a little girl. "Ferry ain't gonna leave for fifteen minutes. Ain't no point in hurrying." He said it with a sudden genial smile, tipping a worn, woolen cap.

She blushed. "Thank you…ah …"

"Name's Fredrick Orcutt." His smile faded and his features settled back into a dour expression.

"Well, thank you again, Mr. Orcutt. I can't imagine—"

"Folks here call me Freddy."

Caitlin gazed at him. "Oh, yes...Freddy." She smiled, extended her hand. "I'm Caitlin Gray."

Though his hand was rough and calloused, the hand of a man who worked outdoors, his grip was surprisingly soft; a hummingbird would have felt secure within its grasp. "Pleased to meet you," he said, before quickly withdrawing his hand. He folded his left hand over his right, and held them, with awkwardly bent elbows. Caitlin saw how big his hands were and the way they were all ridges and valleys of bone and muscle. He wore a wedding ring on his left hand.

She started to walk again toward the ferry. Freddy Orcutt walked alongside her, carrying her wheeled suitcase.

"Do you live on Alabaster Island?" Caitlin asked.

"Eyuh."

"Have you lived there all your life?"

"Not so far."

Caitlin raised an eyebrow and smiled when she saw the mirthful creases around his eyes. "I see. Well, this is my second time to the island. The last time was about twenty-seven years ago. I can't wait." She wished that was as true as she made it sound, but the undercurrent of terror was still there.

"Suspect you'll find it pretty much the same. Most folks do."

"Yes, I think I will. I'm staying indefinitely." *What courage it took to say just that much.* "I'm to meet a real estate agent about renting a small cottage."

"That'll be Helen Underwood," Freddy said off handedly.

"Yes. Do you know her?"

"Eyuh. Voice like a lawn mower." Caitlin waited for him to say more. But he fell silent, apparently feeling he'd said all that needed saying. He gave the impression words had to pry open his lips to escape into utterance.

After they boarded the ferry and climbed to the upper deck,

Freddy Orcutt unhooked a chain stretched across a flight of metal stairs from which a sign hung. It read, "Authorized Personnel Only." Freddy tipped his cap, and said, "Nice talkin' with ya. Need to give my regards to the captain." He mounted the steps and rapped on the door of the pilot house. Caitlin watched as a man nearly as old as Freddy opened the door, gave a curt but friendly nod, and said, simply, "Freddy." She heard Freddy reply, "Morgan." The door closed with a metallic click.

She remembered he'd called her "Miss." She smiled.

Twin shadows of seagulls swept the deck. She heard their *kree-krees*, and looked up. One had a crab in its beak, and the other was attempting to get at it. The first gull dropped the crab and its shell cracked on the hard surface of the deck. The gulls dove for it.

That she picked May for her journey back to Alabaster Island was no accident. The last time she arrived on the island it had been in May. She recalled stopping on the way in Damariscotta Mills on the mid-coast of Maine to view the alewife run. The sky was filled with ospreys, eagles, seagulls, and other birds circling above the wriggling and thrashing mass of silvery fish making its way up the run that lies over the mill dam to reach the pond in which they were born. She watched as time after time an osprey made a sudden downbeat of its wings, a flutter, and plunged into the squirming fish. It would snatch up a single fish, rise, rearrange the fish in its beak, and fly off toward Great Salt Bay. Many of the fish were caught, but some of them made it back to their place of birth. She also remembered the truck carrying lobster bait that was on the ferry, because the main use of the alewife was as chum for the lobstermen.

Caitlin moved to the stern of the ferry's top level where several rows of molded plastic benches were bolted to the deck. Her knee still stung. She bent down to examine it and saw tiny beads of blood where skin had scraped against metal. How could she have been so awkward? She attributed it to the nagging sensation of terror and the lightheadedness it produced—a trembling of the spirit, which was now mimicked by the low rumble and vibrations from the ferry's engine room.

She grabbed the paint-flecked railing where droplets of moisture shivered in sympathy with the ship's power plant. The white bulkheads of the ferry were interrupted here and there by brilliant orange life preservers and red fire extinguishers. A line of cars and trucks trundled down the loading ramp into the open belly of the ferry. The stink from a truck loaded with rotting bait fish for the lobstermen on Alabaster Island assaulted Caitlin's nostrils. The name painted in bold red script on the side coaxed a reluctant smile from Caitlin:

Chum, Chum, Cheney

Albert Cheney, Prop.

A second truck, heavy with building materials, rolled onto the ferry and the ship settled another inch deeper in the water, its sides squealing against tires protecting the pilings. Caitlin thought it must be near low water because the pilings shone wet for half their height. Also, before the stench of the bait truck overpowered it, she'd noticed the peculiar fetid smell of low-tide decay. She studied the ridged and runneled mud of the exposed harbor bottom outside the ferry dock channel. It glistened in the noon sun. Several small rowboats sat askew, stranded on the bottom, their idle anchor lines coated with sea slime.

Overhead, the sky was a deep cobalt blue. But in the west it was an impasto sky, clouds the color of bruises—a gruel of gray, white, pink, blue—smeared across a pewter gray background as though applied by some celestial palette knife, all hard edges and definitions. A rancorous sky. Even from so far away, the heavy clouds lent their harsh light to where the ferry waited for straggling cars to be loaded. Though it was spring, it was almost like a late afternoon winter light.

She'd known terror before. Hadn't everybody? Once, not long after their wedding, she and Nigel were on a plane landing at Logan airport in Boston. As usual in the final seconds of a flight, they fell silent, both of them anticipating that reassuring sense of the plane sinking softly the final few feet before touchdown, like a seagull settling to a perch. But instead of the gentle bump of landing gear, they heard a roar and felt the plane shudder violently. The pilot had applied full power. Some people screamed. Caitlin and Nigel clasped hands. It was several long seconds before they saw the ground gradually recede below them. The pilot came on to say another plane had crossed the runway just as they were about to land. It was only afterward, as they walked through the terminal to baggage claim, that a delayed reaction set in and she started to shake. Nigel held her until the trembling stopped.

Caitlin jumped when the ferry's horn buckled the air. She gripped the rail more tightly. There came a deep shudder and she saw the pilings of the ferry slip start to slide away. She saw the water, churned by the ship's propellers, sluice brown with turned-up mud against the dock. Beads of moisture on the rail started to dance as the engines sent mechanical convulsions through the ship.

like a cello vibrating against the flesh of long thighs

Another time, almost twenty years before, she was watching her son Dylan in the public playground when she became distracted by something. A passing couple? A man jogging? And when she turned around, she saw Dylan running into the street after a ball. In the same instant she saw, from the edge of her vision, a truck bearing down on him. Even now, she could only vaguely remember what happened. Had she screamed? Did Dylan freeze as she thought she recalled? The truck screeched to a stop just in time and she shook for the next half hour.

you took our jeremy from us

As they passed a point of land, Caitlin felt a cold wind bully her hair. Smoke from the one stack stretched out straight like a slash against the sky. The flag whipped and snapped, pulling its halyard into a strained catenary, its sound like hundreds of tiny detonations.

Out beyond the protection of the harbor, Englishman Bay was marbled with whitecaps and black troughs, a piebald sea. It had a menace to it. She'd heard a storm was tracking across the Gulf of Maine toward Nova Scotia and guessed she was seeing its long fingertips probing shoreward.

And what about the time she thought she'd driven Ellen away for good after they fought about that boy Ellen was dating? What was his name? Ricky? That was a different figure of fright, a different tint. It took weeks before Ellen talked with her again.

She studied the marbled surface of the water where the wind decapitated whitecaps and sent spindrift into the air. As the ferry lurched against the bruising waves of the bay, Caitlin heard a man shout. She looked over to where two people stood at the rail not far from her. The man wore a lumberjack shirt, half untucked where it rode over a beer belly. His blond hair waved thickly in the breeze and he gesticulated angrily at the woman. He yelled, "I don't give a shit!"

Caitlin, embarrassed, looked to see if anyone else heard him. But no one seemed to take notice. She returned her attention to the couple. The woman leaned toward the man and spoke softly near his ear before backing away and giving him a menacing smile. The woman was beautiful in an exotic way. Her skin was dark and her features seemed made of carved and polished mahogany. She was like the image of an ancient Egyptian princess on the matching bookends Nigel insisted on buying during their trip down the Nile before the kids were born—one of the few real trips they'd managed to take together.

As her thoughts returned to Nigel, she frowned.

~

When O'zalik leaned close to Quentin to let him feel her hot breath and said, softly, "You'd better give a shit because I'm not giving up until that island is turned over to my people," she thought she saw her husband flinch. Armed as she was with the information she'd received the previous day from the French translator, she felt nothing could stop her from getting Snagged Anchor Island declared a Passamaquoddy burial ground. Least of all, her husband. The thought gave her a new confidence. She even felt ready to declare her new last name, completing the transition from Angelique Thomas Moseley to O'zalik Tomah. Freddy Orcutt, the only islander she trusted, was the only one she'd told beforehand. It was a month earlier, when she told him she'd decided to adopt her full Passamaquoddy name, that he gave her the journal he'd found on Snagged Anchor Island many years before.

"But why would you want to change your name?" he asked. They were in Jimmy's cottage, which she'd just finished tidying up.

"I'm Passamaquoddy. It's who I am. You know I've never been happy as a white woman."

"But to change your name? What about Quentin?"

"I don't care what he thinks. What matters to me is that I honor my Passamaquoddy roots. Becoming Angelique Moseley was the real change. All I'm doing is going back to what I was."

"I know about all your books on the Passamaquoddy...and the language tapes," Freddy said. "But I had no idea you felt so strongly."

"Freddy, it's everything to me." A tear slid from her eye. "Living so close to Snagged Anchor Island where my ancestors worshiped their gods, as my grandfather says, and not being able to get out there...It, it hurts."

Freddy wiped the tear from her cheek. "Eyuh, a person's heritage is a mighty important thing." He paused as if considering something. "You wait here; I have something for you." He left Jimmy's cottage and crossed to his own. Moments later he returned, holding an old, battered book. He held it out to her with both hands. "Here, I want you to have this."

"What is it?"

"Some sort of journal. It's in French. I think it talks about the Passamaquoddy."

She took the book. "Where did you get it?"

He told her he found it on Snagged Anchor Island. "That's what made me think of it, when you mentioned the island."

"You never had it translated?"

"I found it when Jimmy died. Later, I thought about it from time to time, but I never did anything with it. Maybe you want to get it translated."

"Freddy, I don't know what to say."

"No need to say anything. Just tell me what it says. I'd be mighty curious."

Now the journal was safely at the University of Maine, where she left it the previous month, and she carried its translation with her. She never told Quentin that, after visiting her grandparents, she stopped at the university and met again with Robert Blanchard, an expert in early Native American history. And she couldn't tell Freddy. Not yet, anyway.

Taking a new last name, renouncing her husband's surname, would be like what she'd read about ancient Roman men. They divorced their wives simply by uttering, "I divorce you, I divorce you, I divorce you." It would be even more satisfying than a real divorce.

She fingered the bundle of translated sheets in her knit bag. They were her power.

When, a month before, Freddy gave her the journal, she turned to the first page and read:

Relation de ce qui s'est passé de plus remarquable dans la mission d'un père de la Compagnie de Jesus des Wabanaquis à L'Acadie, les années 1755 et 1756 par Père Jérôme Dalou

O'zalik knew just enough French to tell it was written by a Jesuit. *La Compagnie de Jesus* she knew is French for the Jesuit Order, the Company of Jesus. She also guessed it concerned the Wabanaki, a confederation to which the Passamaquoddy belonged.

people of the dawnland

It was only after she read Robert Blanchard's translation that she understood the full power of what she had; only then did she appreciate how devastating it might be to the islanders who never let her forget she was an outsider—an Indian woman. She could only imagine what Quentin and the other white-man inhabitants of Alabaster Island would think when she revealed their ancestors to them.

~

Freddy Orcutt stood beside Morgan Fludd in the wheelhouse, shifting his balance to the easy roll of the swell, a familiar feeling, one he missed since retiring from the sea. As he watched the Welshman grip the wheel, he longed to be at the helm of a fishing boat again somewhere out over Georges Bank, but he could never do it—not after Jimmy died the way he did. Besides, he was well past the age of retirement. He looked out the starboard window of the wheelhouse and saw the woman, Caitlin Gray, leaning on the rail. He watched her for a while.

"Helen Underwood said you almost sold Jimmy's cottage a little while back," said Morgan Fludd. His eyes sparkled with characteristic mirth from a suety face. It was a face that emerged from his hunched shoulders like the head of a turtle from a shell. He had a fireplug of a body and stood slightly bowlegged, his shoulders square.

"Was thinking of it."

"Fetch you a goodly amount, what with prices summer people are paying these days."

"Don't wanna sell."

Morgan altered course slightly to port to avoid a string of lobster pots. "I'm hearing ya, but I'm also thinking what I'd do with that kind o' money. Maybe take a fancy cruise somewhere."

Freddy turned to look at him. "Now that's that busybody Helen Underwood talking with her godawful voice and you know it. You spend your life driving a boat and you ain't gonna take no cruise. That's for damn certain."

"Eyuh. Guess you're right."

"Damn certain," replied Freddy. "Dude ranch maybe make more sense for you. Change of scene and all."

"There you go," Morgan said brightly. "You oughta go to some dude ranch in Wyoming or someplace."

"Was talkin' 'bout you, not me." Freddy turned away and looked out the window again. "I don't need no more traveling."

He'd been to New Orleans once. Martha Roberts, the travel agent on the mainland, found a special deal and persuaded him, with Helen Underwood's help, to go. She said it would be good for him to get away for a while. So he went and on the second day he'd walked along beer-swilling Bourbon Street, incomprehensible music blaring from every bar and club, and he saw some guys in football jerseys and orange wigs beating up on a woman and he was outraged and he stepped in to help the poor woman and the guys turned on him and started beating up on him. He was only saved when the cops showed up. That's when he learned the woman he'd tried to rescue, the woman who'd aroused the gallantry in him, was a transvestite. Hurting and confused, unsure any longer what was real, he'd returned to the hotel where he sat in his room staring out the window at the full, fat moon with filaments of a horse-tail cloud streaming under it, the same moon hanging over Alabaster Island at that very moment. After a half hour he went downstairs and checked out early and took a taxi to the airport where he slept in a row of seats until he could book a flight out.

"Don't need no traveling, no how," he repeated to Morgan Fludd.

He fell silent. Alabaster Island, Snagged Anchor Island, and String of Pearls appeared on the horizon. A familiar, empty feeling came to him. As he had done so many times over the years, he wondered how it was possible that Jimmy's boat could have drifted onto String of Pearls that day some twenty-odd years before. It would have had to be against the current. The only explanation was there had been a freak eddy to the current, something Freddy had never seen at the reef before. He remembered clearly his reaction when he learned Jimmy's boat was on the rocks. It was Garret Webster who first told him.

He was sitting in Pauline's—it was known simply as the "Coffee Shoppe" then and Freddy was pleased when the pretentious extra "pe" disappeared—he was sitting there when Garret barged through the door and said, "Mr. Orcutt, I'm afraid I have some bad news for you. We found your boat washed up on String of Pearls and there was no sign of Jimmy."

Freddy stared at the man a few moments before saying. "What are you, crazy? Jimmy would never leave our boat." He rose to face Garret.

"Maybe he was washed overboard somewhere out to sea and the boat drifted in without him," replied Garret. "I'm only telling you what we saw."

"Who's 'we'?"

"Me and Quentin Moseley. It was when we went out to make one last search for that Chatfield girl."

Freddy and the others had returned from their own search for the missing teenage girl about three hours before. There hadn't been a boat on String of Pearls then, for they would certainly have noticed it. And the Coast Guard, which had been searching the waters of Englishman Bay for the Chatfield girl while Freddy and the others searched Snagged Anchor Island, never reported a disabled boat. On much younger legs and galvanized into action, Freddy rushed for the door, his heart pounding. "Show me."

Garret Webster and several other men followed him out the door. Together, they ran down to the dock, where they found Quentin Moseley standing in a motor launch. Its engine was rumbling and water was spurting from its exhaust. As soon as the men were aboard, Quentin shoved the throttle forward and the launch shot away from the dock toward the opening to Spruce Cove. Behind them, boats started rocking at their moorings, one after the other all the way out to the mouth of the cove, in the wide "V" of the wake thrown out by the heavily loaded launch.

It took them fifteen minutes to get to the stretch of String of Pearls between Big Pearl and Snagged Anchor Island. Freddy's heart sank when he saw the boat sitting near Big Pearl at an awkward angle. It was the attitude of a boat in distress. As Quentin eased the launch against the reef with a small jolt, Freddy leapt off the bow deck. He ran, slipping on the wet rocks, toward the boat. Several other men—Ernie Botham, Burle Ledyard, and Morgan Fludd—followed him while Garret Webster and Quentin Moseley kept the launch positioned against String of Pearls.

Freddy climbed aboard the boat. He clambered across the awkwardly tilted deck to the companionway and swung himself below. Contrary to what he'd expected, the cabin was orderly, everything in its proper place. A tide-reference book was lying open on the chart table. There was no sign at all of a boat that had passed through a storm, an observation Ernie Botham was quick to make. "Everything's too neat for a wave big enough to fling Jimmy overboard."

"That's what I'm thinking," replied Freddy.

"Eyuh," said Burle Ledyard. "Must have just slipped. Maybe fish juice or somethin'."

Morgan Fludd put a hand on Freddy's shoulder. "Goldang it, Freddy, I'm awful sorry."

"Me, too," said Ernie Botham.

"Goldang it to hell," said Burle Ledyard, shaking his head.

Freddy gazed at the three men, a hard look on his face. "I don't believe it," he said. "Something ain't right here."

"What're you thinking, Freddy?"

"I'm thinking about that there hole," Freddy replied, pointing to a ragged hole in the hull more than a foot in diameter below the waterline on the starboard side. "Ain't no way the boat would stay afloat with a hole like that in her if it happened somewhere out to sea."

Morgan Fludd nodded, "Which means she was holed right here."

"Meaning she was driven on the rocks," said Burle Ledyard.

"Now you see why I ain't buying it?" asked Freddy. "In the first place, Jimmy would never do something like that, and in the second place, even if he did for some reason—sick, maybe, or heart attack—"

"He's too young for a heart attack," said Morgan Fludd.

"I know that, Morgan. All I'm saying is *if* something like that happened, then where the hell is he?"

Everyone was silent for a few moments. Finally, Ernie Botham said, "Maybe he was hurt but he was able to get out to Snagged

Anchor Island before the tide came in."

Freddy's hopes soared with this thought and he clung to it in desperation. They climbed out of the boat and rushed back to the launch. "Let's get our asses over to the island," Freddy said to Garret Webster and Quentin Moseley. "Maybe Jimmy made it there."

"That's the first thing we thought of," said Garret. "We already looked. There was no sign of him."

"Well, we're gonna look again."

When they nosed the launch onto the beach at Snagged Anchor Island, they all piled out and discussed how to proceed. In the end, they split up into teams the way they had when looking for the girl. Freddy and Morgan Fludd searched the northeastern end of the island, Ernie Botham and Burle Ledyard took the middle, while Garret Webster and Quentin Moseley took the southwestern end. They searched for more than five hours, finally giving up and meeting again on the beach. Freddy and Morgan Fludd were the last to arrive.

"Anything?" asked Freddy, already knowing the answer.

Everyone mumbled "No."

Back in the launch, they coasted slowly back to the wrecked boat, parallel to String of Pearls, looking for any sign of Jimmy.

Hope dies a lingering death and it was weeks before Freddy could bring himself to even consider the one theory that made sense. It was Morgan Fludd who said, "Only way it could happen is Jimmy slips and falls overboard while the boat is moving; the boat goes on without him; and drives itself up on the rocks."

"But that don't make no sense, Morgan," said Freddy. "You know as well as me a boat with no one at the helm is gonna turn in big circles one way or the other depending on the spin and pitch of the propellers."

"Eyuh, ordinarily, but—"

"But what?"

"I guess what Morgan's saying," said Burle Ledyard, "is it could be the rudder on the boat was stuck just enough in the other direction to make the boat go straight."

"Or at least in circles big enough to run up on String of Pearls before running out of gas."

"That would be real peculiar," said Freddy.

"Eyuh, but not impossible. A piece of line stuck on the rudder shaft..."

"Sure, that's it," said Morgan Fludd. " That's how it could've happened. A piece of line caused the rudder to stick suddenly, throwing Jimmy off balance—"

"Or else, it didn't throw him off balance," said Ernie Botham, "but he was leaning out trying to fix it when he fell overboard."

Freddy waved his hand dismissively. "With the motor running? Jimmy ain't that stupid."

"Well, yuh...maybe he just slipped."

"And the boat steered itself like some freak onto the rocks."

When they returned to Alabaster Island the day Jimmy disappeared, Freddy was not satisfied. He borrowed a launch from Crenshaw's Marina and went out to Snagged Anchor Island on his own. He planned to search every inch of the island for himself because there was something that bothered him. Though no one would say anything to his face, he knew people must be wondering about the coincidence that Jimmy and the girl disappeared at about the same time. Already, he knew, there must be rumors about a possible relationship between Jimmy and the girl. They'd known each other because the Chatfield family stayed on the island each year for at least ten summers. Before Jimmy and Diana married, the girl used to hang around with Jimmy, Garret Webster, and Quentin Moseley on occasion. Even Freddy was forced to wonder if there could be anything to the rumors despite being convinced that Jimmy was happy in his marriage. He swore he would do everything possible to quell any such gossip before it got to the ears of Jimmy's wife, Diana. And, of course, there was Agnes and the grandchildren to consider.

Besides, he knew the radio on the boat was out. He should have had it fixed days before. And Jimmy? He never was good at maintaining things and (this part hurt deeply) he wasn't a careful seaman. Freddy remembered the shame he felt when they found the boat washed up and holed. No one said a thing to him, but he could imagine what all the men were thinking: is that the way Freddy Orcutt taught his son to work a boat? Could there have been a storm that Jimmy didn't know about? Was he, Freddy, partly to blame?

By the time he got back to Snagged Anchor Island, the light was already beginning to fail. He took a flashlight from the launch and started to explore, determined to stay the night and resume his search in the morning. Before two hours had elapsed, the batteries of the flashlight grew weak and he settled himself under a huge, east-facing overhang. Since the wind was from the southwest, he was well protected and he spent a reasonably comfortable night. He slept on and off until the rising sun found the entrance to the overhang. He was just about to set out again when he noticed a mark on the back wall of the open cave. It was the rough shape of a cross apparently scratched into the rock with a knife or a stone. He ran his fingers across the shallow incisions. As he did so, his right foot bumped against a boulder. He looked down and saw that it was one of several. On closer inspection, they appeared to have been placed there purposefully, as if to build a cairn which had since collapsed. Bending down, he started to move the boulders. After a few minutes, he uncovered a small package—something wrapped in what appeared to be many layers of oilskin. Filled with curiosity, he unwrapped the oilskin and found a small, black, leather-bound book, a gold cross embossed on the cover. He opened the book, careful not to tear the fragile pages. In neat lettering, on what appeared to be a title page, were a few lines in old-fashioned handwriting:

Relation de ce qui s'est passé de plus remarquable dans la mission d'un père de la Compagnie de Jesus des Wabanaquis à L'Acadie, les années 1755 et 1756 par Père Jérôme Dalou

It looked to him like French. After pausing for a time to consider his discovery, he tucked it into his belt and resumed the search he began the evening before.

All day he searched. But he came up with nothing and was forced to conclude that he would never find any sign of Jimmy or the girl. Finally, his shoulders slumped in despair, he boarded the launch and returned to Alabaster Island.

That was twenty-five years before and in all that time Freddy could never bring himself to accept the explanation Ernie Botham and the others offered. The only thing he was forced to accept was that Jimmy was never found. But, that sometimes happens with fishermen, he told himself.

Part of the reason Freddy never accepted the explanation Jimmy had fallen overboard was his desperation not to kill all hope for Diana and Agnes. If he had trouble accepting Jimmy was gone, they had even greater difficulty. Together, they clung to the slim possibility Jimmy had been picked up by some passing ship or, since they heard nothing from any ship, that he had somehow made his way to one of the many deserted islands in the vicinity and that he would soon be rescued by a boat or a ship that happened to pass by. There was enough traffic in and around the islands for it to be a real possibility. But in the days that followed, Freddy and some of the others methodically searched all the possible islands, even dipping into Canada, with no results.

First days, then weeks passed, and gradually they were forced to come to terms with their loss. He remembered the way Agnes suddenly doubled over one afternoon as though she'd been hit in the belly by a baseball bat and he'd come running to her and asked, "What is it, Dear? Is there some sort of pain?" and she'd answered, "Jimmy's dead," as though she had just that minute received the news. The sight of her bending over and gasping for breath—that was one of the scenes that haunted him.

Weeks after she'd reconciled herself to the fact of Jimmy's death, Agnes looked at him and said, "How can you live with yourself, knowing you were supposed to get the weather radio fixed and you didn't?" The question, coming as it did with a hate-filled glance over the top of a newspaper and a trembling hand holding a coffee cup, ambushed him; it helped fuel his own guilt and the suffering that went with it. Instead of grieving together, instead of supporting each other through their agony, Agnes laid down a different set of rules, one in which they could only endure if she had him to blame and if he played his suffering part.

Which he did, he thought. Which he did for all the years she had left to live in bitterness as their marriage settled into a steady state of unspoken acrimony and guilt. Yet, for all that, he still remembered Agnes as she was before Jimmy's death—the two of them sitting on the porch drinking coffee, planning Jimmy's house, talking about the rose bushes.

Morgan Fludd interrupted his thoughts. "You're awful quiet there, Freddy. Something wrong?"

"What? No...no, not a thing."

"Eyuh."

The book he discovered remained tucked away for years. In fact, in the grief following Jimmy's disappearance and the effect it had on Agnes, he'd totally forgotten about it until one day a few weeks ago O'zalik Moseley talked at length and passionately about her Passamaquoddy heritage. It reminded him of the book and, remembering that the title contained the word *Wabanaquis*, he gave it to her as a gift. She had been delighted and immediately took it to the mainland to have it translated.

~

Caitlin stared, mesmerized, at the churning wake of the ferry. It folded in upon itself to form a foaming rooster's comb.

When she told Nigel she was leaving, she said it was only for a while to give herself some time alone, time to think, to gather herself. She said nothing about Ekaterina Valerovna because what if she was wrong in her assumption of an affair between them? So, lacking the courage to make a clean break, she made it a half measure.

It was a cold day in February and Nigel had started a fire in the fireplace before sitting at the piano to continue his work on a new composition for string quartet. He was consumed with the composition and with preparing for the concert he would be giving at Tanglewood that year. It was the summer home of the Boston Symphony, and the opportunity to play there might well be the break in Nigel's career for which he longed.

Caitlin patiently waited until he went into the kitchen to pour himself a cup of coffee. She'd been planning—dreading—this conversation for several months and finally decided she could wait no longer. She felt weighted down by her devotion to her family. It was something she'd refused to admit to herself until she talked with a psychiatrist and complained vaguely of a sensation of sinking. All her adult life she'd supported their ambitions, encouraging them, sacrificing her own aspirations to their dreams. She'd become little more than their cheerleader. And they came to depend on her. She was like a trick mirror, reflecting Nigel and Dylan and Ellen back to themselves larger than life. And it was from this self-fulfilling, larger image of themselves that they acted. Believing their own reflections, they grew to fit them. But, consumed by their own ambitions, their needs fulfilled, they acted less and less like a unit. Her family was disintegrating.

Meanwhile, Caitlin sank.

The psychiatrist said daughters of alcoholic fathers—which, God knows, she was—tend to feel themselves hyper-responsible for others. They do just what Caitlin had done—sacrifice themselves out of an exaggerated sense of responsibility for the ones they love. The psychiatrist advised her to "carve out some personal space, some place in your life where you can devote yourself only to yourself." The advice was vague and it ran against the grain of her longing for family, but it sat with Caitlin until, remembering the pleasures and joys of summers on Alabaster Island when she was young—especially that last summer with Garret Webster—she decided to take the recommendation literally and return to the island. If only for a little while. She owed nothing more to them. Nigel's career was adequately established, the children were making their own way. She owed nothing and the thought was both liberating and frightening.

She never mentioned Ekaterina Valerovna to the psychiatrist. There seemed too much shame in it.

When Nigel returned to the living room, she spoke before he had a chance to return to his composition. "There's something I want to talk to you about, Nigel," she said, hearing the slight tremor in her voice.

"What is it, Dear?" He slid the sleeves of his customary black turtleneck higher on his lean arms.

"Why don't you sit on the sofa and drink your coffee."

"That serious, eh?" he asked with an amused smile. He sat, placed his cup on the coffee table, leaned back, and asked with exaggerated British cheeriness, "Right then, what's up?"

"I'm going to take a place for myself."

He gazed at her, bewilderment in his face. "I don't understand."

"I need some time to myself." She felt out of control, as though she had taken a plunge and was in free fall. No way of going back.

Nigel held up a hand. "Whoa, whoa! Stop. Back up a little bit. What's this all about?"

"Nigel, I've been feeling stifled. I want to do some writing, get to know myself a little. And I can't do it here."

"Why not?"

"Because as long as I'm here, I spend all my energy cheering you and the kids on. I spend all my time supporting you."

"We never asked you to do that."

She gazed at her husband. *How dishonest of him.* "No, but you accepted it. And I can't help myself. As long as I'm here, I'll never get some time, some space, to myself."

Nigel stared at her a long time, apparently trying to comprehend exactly what she was saying. Finally, he asked, "How long?"

"I don't know. A couple of months. The summer."

"What about Tanglewood? I was hoping you'd be there with me."

She thought: *For* me, is what he meant to say. She said, "Jacob's Pillow is only a few miles away. Ellen will be there." It was a dance school Ellen was attending.

also there was sweet cavatina ekaterina…con molto sentimento d'affeto

They talked for another half hour, Nigel raising objections and Caitlin dismissing them. Caitlin saw how wounded he was. Selfishly wounded. Yet, how worried, too. She tried to reassure him. "Look, I'm not asking out of our marriage. That's not what this is about at all. It's just for a few months." She wished she were as certain of what she said as she made it sound.

"Is there someone else?"

Bastard. "Nigel, how can you even think that?" As his question echoed in her mind, she became increasingly angry. "How like a man—"

"Oh, let's not get into all that gender stuff again."

"You're the one who asked the stupid question."

"Well, what am I supposed to think? You casually announce you want to take a few months vacation from your marriage, your family—"

What family? "It's hardly casual and it's certainly not a vacation."

Nigel said nothing. He pressed his lips together, folded his arms across his chest, and turned his head to look out the window. It was a series of gestures that had always annoyed Caitlin. *Pouting, that's what it was.*

"Look at me," she said sharply.

He glared at her.

She felt her anger building anew. "Look, damn it, I intend to give myself some private time to *write*. There's no one else. Christ, there's more to a woman's creative urges than…than…" She whirled and stomped out of the room.

than what lies between her vibrating thighs

In the next few days, they hardly spoke. But gradually, reluctantly,

Nigel seemed to accept her plan, as well as her reasons, and the customary surface civility returned to their marriage. And he stopped protesting. Was it a sign? Was he looking forward to free time with Ekaterina Valerovna?

~

O'zalik saw Garret Webster approaching from the other side of the ferry. He was a tall man, square-shouldered, with dignified salt-and-pepper hair tied back in a ponytail, giving him the look of an artist. Just as he reached them, the ferry hit a wake. His gait faltered as the deck rolled under him. He smiled at his awkwardness. "I've never had sea legs and I guess I'm too old to get them now," he said. "How long were you on the mainland, Angelique?"

"Just four days," O'zalik replied. "I stayed with my grandparents."

Though on occasion she filled in by cleaning rooms for Garret at the Spruce Cove Inn, O'zalik knew little about him. He was perhaps the most respected person on Alabaster Island. Everybody thought he was the perfect citizen. Part of it, of course, was that he was so good looking and so pleasant to be around—always considerate of others. Another part of it was his generosity. For example, each year he threw a huge lobster bake for all the resident islanders. She knew he and Quentin grew up together, but she could never understand why Garret seemed to pay so much attention to Quentin. They were so unlike one another. Garret was sociable and well mannered. Quentin was a loner with gruff ways.

Garret turned to Quentin. "Buy you a beer?"

"Sure."

"Angelique? How about you?"

"No, thanks. You two go ahead."

After they left, O'zalik took out the little notebook she'd used in her meeting at the University of Maine, started to flip through it, modifying notes. She planned to write an article about the journal for the *Island Gazette*. That is, if she *could* write the article. And if she could bring herself to write it, she was certain revealing its contents would be equivalent to dropping a bomb at Sunday church service.

Bob Blanchard said as much the day before when they met at the Fogler Library on the University of Maine campus. They were sitting at one of the long wooden tables positioned at right angles to the wall. A grid of sunlight and shadow lay across the table from the tall, multi-paned windows. Bob had spread papers all across the table. A French Canadian from Prince Edward Island who was also one quarter Mi'kmaq, he spoke fluent French and taught in the university's Native American Program. He was jogger-trim with eyeglasses and a dark, academic beard. When, a month earlier, O'zalik made inquiries, he was the one person everybody had recommended.

"First, O'zalik, let me tell you some odd things about what you brought me. This clearly is a journal kept by a Jesuit priest, but it's styled in the fashion of a *Relation*."

She nodded. "I remember that word from the title page, but I couldn't make out what it might mean in this context."

"It's one of those annoying words whose spelling is identical in French and English but with utterly different meanings. In French, a *relation* is an account or a report—a relating of something."

O'zalik rolled her eyes. "I should have thought of that."

"But in this context, *relation* has a special meaning. The Jesuit *Relations* were sort of annual reports the missionaries sent to their superiors back in France informing them of conditions among the Native American tribes and of the progress of their efforts to convert them. But, in addition to informing superiors, the *Relations* had another purpose. They were designed to entice readers to contribute money to the missionaries' work. For this reason, they were published and distributed throughout France and they contained entertaining narratives usually depicting courageous Jesuits and the virtuous character of the Native Americans who were baptized."

"So they were advertisements?"

Bob Blanchard nodded. "Among other things. Especially when

you consider they also took great care to describe the land. The reports were almost travel narratives in that way, almost novels."

"You said it's styled *in the fashion* of a Jesuit *Relation*," O'zalik said. "Does that mean you don't think it actually *is* one?"

"That's what is so odd about it—it couldn't be an authentic *Relation*."

"Why not?"

"The date, 1756. It's far too late."

"Why?"

"Because the Jesuit *Relations* stopped in 1673. What happened is Pope Clement X issued a papal brief instructing that all writings about foreign missions had to have the approval of the Vatican before being published."

"He didn't like what was coming out of North America?"

"Actually, it had nothing to do with North America. It was aimed at reports coming from missionaries in China. From what I gather, the problem was the Jesuits wanted to permit their Chinese converts to continue worshipping ancestors as practiced in Confucianism but the Dominicans objected and persuaded the pope of their position. Basically, the pope required approval of all reports from the field in order to squash the debate in China."

O'zalik gave a disgusted look. "Because the Dominicans didn't want the Chinese to continue to worship ancestors?"

Bob Blanchard smiled. "Sound familiar?"

"So if the problem wasn't with the Jesuits here, why didn't they just submit their reports for approval?"

"They were caught between a rock and a hard place. The government of Louis XIV didn't recognize Vatican authority in French territory. Therefore, the Jesuits figured if they went ahead and got Vatican permission, they would then be denied permission to publish by the French government. If they got permission from the French first, then the Vatican would deny them. So they just stopped."

O'zalik pondered this for a moment. "Don't you just love when religion mixes with politics?"

Blanchard shrugged his shoulders. "Welcome to the real world."

"So, why did this Father Dalou want to make his journal look like a *Relation*?"

"An interesting question to which I don't have the answer," said Blanchard. "I can only guess he learned about *Relations* when he was studying to be a Jesuit priest and liked them well enough to imitate them. Maybe he hoped to bring them back. Who knows?"

O'zalik nodded. "And the contents of the journal…the *Relation*?"

"I'll let you read them for yourself. I don't want to spoil your pleasure. But this I guarantee," said Blanchard, "you're going to experience a lot of emotions…and you're going to be pissed off. I was." Blanchard arranged the translated sheets neatly and handed them to O'zalik. "You know, this is an important find, O'zalik. You ought to see about publishing it in some academic journal. I can give you some recommendations."

"Maybe. But first I want the people on Alabaster Island to read it."

As she watched Quentin and Garret Webster emerge from the cafeteria carrying tall paper cups, O'zalik pondered what Bob Blanchard said the day before. From what little she'd read, she'd already seen what he meant about being pissed off. She would, if at all possible, find a way to force herself to write the article. She would explode her bombshell on the complacent, self-righteous people of Alabaster Island who treated her like a second-class citizen.

Shadows of seagulls undulated over the waves. She looked up with a frisson of pleasure to see one dip a wing and shoot off downwind.

~

As she leaned on the rail of the upper deck, Caitlin saw a man she thought might be Garret Webster. He emerged from the cafeteria along with the man who had been arguing with the beautiful woman. They were carrying cups from which liquid spilled onto the deck as they walked to where the mahogany woman was standing. Caitlin edged away from the rail and sat down next to an older woman who stared over her eyeglasses at the couple and gave a tsk-tsk shake of her head even as her knitting needles flew furiously. With a sideways glance at Caitlin, the woman said, "Always arguing like they was, those two. Can't for the life of me imagine what Quentin Moseley was thinking when he brought her to the island."

"Is that the man?" Caitlin asked. "Quentin Moseley?"

"Eyuh. And that there's Angelique." The woman shook her head and added, almost with a sneer, "Indian." She returned to her knitting.

Caitlin leaned back to watch the mainland recede in the distance, wondering what Dylan and Ellen were doing at that moment.

She told them about her plan at Nigel's birthday party in April and it was agonizing because she was as much a bulwark for her children as she was for Nigel. Over the years she wove a fine web from the filaments of her love and support, a web into which Nigel's hopes nestled, in which Dylan's dreams and Ellen's desires took refuge. For more than a decade, while Nigel earned little money and struggled to build his music career, and the kids went to school, Caitlin worked at a soul-crunching job in a large corporation. Only her income kept them afloat. With honest intentions and motivated only by love, she made it easy for them to entangle themselves in a lacework of dependency by always being ready to support, console, encourage, cheer, cajole—by being so much a part of everything they did that they came, in strange ways, to depend on her for their success. And by being so much a part of everything they did, she pulled that fine web around herself like a cloak until it was a chrysalis enclosing her own creativity, forever quiescent, inchoate.

What dangerous comfort it had been when she saw her family happily engaged with their pursuits—what a trap of complacency. How it used to warm her to see Nigel in one of his familiar long-sleeved turtlenecks that emphasized his leanness, with the sleeves pushed up to the elbows, intently studying a score and moving his mouth silently to the sounds he heard in his head. Or Dylan, in one of his rebellious heavy-metal T-shirts (Nigel hated that music), poring through an issue of the

New England Journal of Medicine or some anatomy textbook. Or Ellen practicing dance moves, barefoot on the bare wood of the hallway. Such scenes would leave Caitlin balanced precariously on a precipice of contentment and gradually, innocently, and ever filled with love, she would come to see how they took her away from herself. And how she allowed it. And now, the joy had slipped away like past Christmases and she didn't know how to recover it.

She'd thought Nigel's birthday would be a good time because Dylan and Ellen would be there together—they never missed their parents' birthdays. That way, she could tell them both at once and be done with it. Unfortunately, Ellen brought her current lover, a black man named Turell Tyler who was a dance instructor at Jacob's Pillow in western Massachusetts where Ellen studied dance and performed in a modern dance troupe. But Caitlin refused to allow Turrel's presence to weaken her resolve. She waited for a break in the story Nigel was telling.

"...so just as we enter the quietest part of the adagio, the lead violinist hits an A-flat instead of an A," said Nigel. "I tell you, I was never so shocked in my life; this man is bloody Mr. Perfection." He laughed heartily and the others joined him.

When the laughter faded, Caitlin said, "I have something to say—" She heard her voice emerge thin, brittle—like a schoolgirl pussyfooting from the wings at the class play. She hated herself for it. She remembered her mother, how the astringent years with an abusive, alcoholic husband had corroded her voice, made it a tiny cobweb of a voice. His evil had been a needle piercing her like an egg, sucking out the yoke and the fluids, gaining his own sustenance, leaving an empty shell. Caitlin felt her own creative being was inside a brittle shell and she refused to allow Nigel to do the same to her through his self-centered ambition. And she thought of the many writing seminars she'd attended and all the half-done, man-wrecked women and their shy, skimpy voices and their timid, therapeutic writing—all he-dids and I-saids and he-saids and I-crieds. She'd kill herself if she became like that. She swore it.

"One minute, dear," Nigel said, placing his empty wine glass on the table and gesturing to Dylan for a refill. "There's more to the story."

Caitlin bit the inside of her cheek and slid her own wine glass toward Dylan.

a cobweb of a voice

"Now, you have to understand, he's this immensely fat man and his face is puffy and red as Santa Claus. So when he looks at me with these big round eyes and with his mouth open in horror like he'd just let fly a fart, well it struck me as so funny I bloody near lost it. In fact I almost busted out laughing and I could see all the violins, violas, and cellos—the entire string section—were just barely containing themselves." He laughed again, lifting his glass to his lips. "Ekaterina was red in the face."

with the cello vibrating between her splayed legs

Caitlin waited three heartbeats, gave a sideways glance to Turrel Tyler, and said, "As I was saying, Dylan…Ellen—"

"—in the middle of a goddamned Requiem."

Pause. Three heartbeats. "I want—"

"What do you think the audience would have thought? They come to hear a sublime Requiem and the whole orchestra is laughing like a bunch of school-kids."

Caitlin waited.

Nigel's laughter faded from guffaws to chortles to snickers like a drawn-out diminuendo. His manner of laughing always infected everyone. Dylan, Ellen, and Turrel Tyler had to put their wine glasses down and force-swallow the wine in their mouths. A reluctant smile came even to Caitlin's face. It was one of Nigel's more engaging characteristics. She loved him for it one time, she reminded herself.

She wiped her lips with a napkin, sighed, paused, and wiped her lips once again. She placed her hands on the table and leaned forward with a smile. In a voice raised artificially high and loud with what she intended as simulated anger, she said, "As I was saying—"

"I'm sorry, dear. I've not let you get a word in edgewise," said

Nigel, looking at her but not holding her gaze.

"Yes, well I understand."

"Right, then. What is it you want to say?"

"Yes, Mom, what is it?" asked Dylan.

Caitlin's heart quickened. Why was she feeling so guilty about this? It was only her right. They have all found their creative outlets, why not she? She looked into her husband's eyes. She turned to Dylan and Ellen. "You know that Dad's career is starting to flourish. Guest conducting jobs. Some even around the world." She glanced again at Nigel.

He shrugged. "Out-of-the way places. Second and third-level cities. Not much money in that."

"There was London."

"That was once."

"And Tanglewood this summer. Your career is starting to take off."

He gave her a defeated look. "Well yes, Caitlin, but I see it as *our* career. You've helped me every step of the way. Without you..."

She felt a blush of anger. "That may be so, but it's still your career."

"Now, Caitlin, don't—"

She held up her hand, turned to Dylan and Ellen. "And the same goes for you two. Dylan, you're doing well in medical school and you can look forward to a fine internship."

Dylan laughed. "Just like Dad said, you can take a lot of the credit for—"

"Let me finish," snapped Caitlin. The flame on one of the dinner candles guttered. They stared at her with silent, surprised expressions. She tried to ignore Turrel Tyler's presence, but he occupied a small field in the corner of her vision. Though she couldn't see his face, she sensed he shared an embarrassment with her—he for finding himself awkwardly in the middle of a family affair, she for bringing it all up in the first place. She turned to Ellen. "And as for you, Ellen, I've never seen you so happy. I think Jacob's Pillow was exactly the right choice for you." She watched Ellen's gaze shift from her to Turrel Tyler and back again.

"What are you getting at, Mom?" Ellen asked.

"What I'm trying to say is that I need to do something on my own."

"But, Caitlin—" Nigel began.

Caitlin held up a hand. Her heart raced. "I want to write—you know it's what I've always wanted to do." She was speaking now directly to Nigel. "All my life...you know that." True, she thought, but never before with the burning intensity she now felt. It was as though she were responding to an impulse from somewhere deep within her, something she couldn't name but she could feel urging her on. A withered impulse. Or was it external? Was it, perhaps, the moon, now that she was approaching menopause, drawing on some deep-seated creative urge related to her menstrual cycle? It was a curious idea, one that had the power to seduce her. She had always felt tied in some intimate way to the larger forces of nature.

"You mean you want to go to one of your writers' conferences?" asked Dylan.

Her anger deepened. She was convinced they saw her as little more than a dilettante. "No. I've tried that. It doesn't exactly kindle the embers in my spine. I need to devote myself to writing for a good long while, not just for a few days or a week." She'd lost count of the number of poetry and other writing courses and seminars she'd taken. They were all good for a short time, but it was too easy to avoid the hard, butt-in-the-chair discipline of writing once the conference was over.

"But are you saying you can't do it here?" asked Nigel. He was repeating some of the arguments he'd used when she first broke the news to him.

She could see he was hurt. He was sensitive. It made him a wonderful musician. Often, she'd seen him weep openly when conducting something like the fourth movement of Mahler's Fifth Symphony. And, of course, that Beethoven cavatina. Now, seeing his reaction, she was reminded yet again how he'd relied on her presence in his life—how all of them relied on her. Why couldn't that be enough for her?

She bit her lip. "I need to get off by myself for a while." The way Nigel was reacting, she thought, maybe he wasn't screwing Ekaterina Valerovna after all.

cavatina

She just wasn't sure. She just wasn't sure, and the uncertainty of it disturbed her almost as much as the sure knowledge of it would.

ekaterina

Caitlin became aware of Turrel Tyler, head bent, twirling his wine glass slowly by the stem. The wavering candle flame, reflected in the glass, drew her attention. She felt sorry for him, that he had to be thrust in the middle of a family drama. But, then again, maybe he was soon to be family. She glanced into Ellen's eyes, shocked by the sudden thought.

Turrel Tyler cleared his throat. "I suppose it's none of my business, but seeing as I'm here, would you mind terribly if I said something?"

"No," said Nigel. "By all means, please feel free."

"Well it just seems to me that, of all of us around this table, there's only one who still has something left to begin. The rest of us are on the move, as it were."

Caitlin loved him for it. She turned to look directly at him for the first time since starting this conversation and smiled. He returned the smile.

She turned her gaze to Nigel. He was so clearly shaken, she wanted to take it all back. She was about to say something, to back away from the precipice, to relieve the pressure, something like, "Well, it's only something I've been thinking about; we can talk about it some other time," when Nigel asked, "Have you found a place?"

It was a small sign of acceptance, but more than he'd shown before, and she moved quickly to take advantage of it. In a strong voice she said, "Yes, I've tentatively...I've *agreed* to a place on Alabaster Island."

"Isn't that Maine?"

Caitlin nodded. "Downeast Maine." Of course, she wasn't about to tell them she'd been there before. A long time before.

"When?"

"Beginning next month."

"For how long?"

Caitlin paused. "How long would it take you to write a piece for string quartet?"

"It depends on how it went."

Caitlin gave a nervous smile. "It's the same. It depends on how it goes." She paused, looked at Dylan and Ellen, and said, "I need this, you know I do."

Ellen rose, moved behind Caitlin's chair, and embraced her. But Caitlin felt an insincerity in the gesture. Worse, a condescension. Nevertheless, she accepted the embrace.

In the weeks that followed, Nigel broached the subject of her leaving only three or four times and each time only half heartedly. He spent nearly all his time at the piano or in his easy chair with a score studying the music he would conduct at Tanglewood.

Meanwhile, Caitlin quietly made preparations of her own.

~

In the wheelhouse Morgan Fludd said, "Way you're looking at that there lady, I'd say you was some stemmy."

Freddy tore his gaze from String of Pearls, whirled, and asked, "What lady?"

"The one you helped up when she fell running down the ramp. I saw the whole thing from here."

"What about her?"

"You been lookin' at her for the last two minutes," answered Morgan. "And before that, too."

"I been looking at the ocean."

Morgan laughed. It was a smoke-cured cackle of a laugh, high in his throat, brought on by the cigarettes he'd quit only a few years before. "Ocean's all around us. How come you're looking only in that direction?"

"Just happen to be."

"I'm thinking you got a little stirring or something going on. Eyuh, that's what I'm thinking."

"She's young enough to be my daughter," said Freddy, his voice raised artificially high.

"Lots of geezers forget how old they are."

"You're almost as old as me, Morgan Fludd."

"Eyuh, but I ain't staring at no woman thirty, thirty-five years younger than me."

"No, but you're the one going on about her longer than a hard winter."

"Only 'cause you're staring. Everyone knows how stemmy you are."

Freddy would never forgive Angus Macleod for spreading the word about what the urologist he'd sent Freddy to told him. It was after minor prostate surgery and the urologist, Doctor Grabow, gave Freddy a sheet of postsurgical instructions. On it was the admonition to avoid sex for four weeks. In the recovery room Freddy asked the doctor to pull the curtains around the bed and, in a low, whispered voice, said, "Four weeks it says here. Is that necessary?"

"I just want to make sure everything heals properly," said Doctor Grabow.

"But, Doctor, see…it's like this. Me and my wife, we ain't quite finished yet, if you know what I mean." He lowered his voice even more when he heard a nurse pass outside the curtain.

"But it's only four weeks. After that you can—"

"No, no. You're missing my point. You see, we're getting along in years and the urge don't come that often anymore. Maybe once every three or four months."

"I'm sorry. I don't understand what you're telling me."

"It's this, goldang it. What if the urge comes three weeks and six days from now and because of you I can't do nothing about it? What's happened is a whole month has been added to this avoidance thing."

"I still don't get the point."

"Just do the arithmetic. Four weeks because of your instructions plus another twelve weeks because the urge ain't there and before you know it you got sixteen weeks. That's a long time."

Doctor Grabow laughed. "Okay, I see what you're saying. Look, it's not precise. Three weeks is good enough."

"What if the urge comes in two and a half weeks?"

"That's cutting it a little close."

"But you know, confidentially, we ain't that energetic about it no more. More peaceful like, if you know what I mean. Sorta like taking a warm bath."

"And?"

"Well, I'm suggesting it probably won't do no harm."

But in the end the doctor refused to allow any more slack and Freddy went home hoping the old urge would keep its distance.

Of course, that was some time ago, before Agnes' troubles began. But it still pissed Freddy off that the doctor told Angus Macleod and Angus told others, giving Freddy a reputation for horniness.

He turned to Morgan. "It ain't *me* talking like I was obsessed or something. I've a good mind to tell Gladys. Seems to me you're the one talking like you was stemmy."

Morgan Fludd laughed again, his laugh ending in a cough. He looked at Freddy with a reddening face. "Now that's something you ain't got a chance in hell of convincing my wife about." He turned the wheel to starboard as they approached the red bell marking the outer limit of the channel into Alabaster Island. South of the channel, Ernie Botham and Burle Ledyard were pulling traps. Both men looked up and waved as a trap broke the surface of the water and bumped against the dark green hull, shedding cascades of water. They were laughing at some private joke.

"Poor Ernie," said Morgan Fludd. "Don't know how the man can be so goldang cheerful all the time, living with what he's got to live with."

"Eyuh. It's something."

"Burle's awful good to him."

"Burle's a good man," replied Freddy. The sight of Ernie always brought a lump of sadness to Freddy's chest. It was like the sadness he felt every time he looked at the mile-long String of Pearls where Jimmy's boat washed up. For a long time, Freddy said nothing.

"You gone silent again all of a sudden," said Morgan.

"Just seeing Ernie put me in mind of them's that's gone."

"Eyuh, know what you mean." As the ferry slid by the buoy and the lobster boat, Morgan punched the button for the ship's horn.

~

The ferry's horn bellowed a resonating, bass A such as only a team of tubas could equal. Caitlin jumped. A shudder passed through the ferry as the engines slowed and the ship began to turn. Caitlin saw they were passing a red bell buoy and entering a channel bounded by two long breakwaters. The buoy rocked with the wash of the ferry's bow wave, its bell clanging fitfully.

She saw they were approaching Alabaster Island. To the left was Snagged Anchor Island, the pointed tops of its spruce trees serrating the sky. A thin line of breakers stretched, she guessed, a mile from the small island to Alabaster. Streaks of spume shot downwind from the breaking waves. At two spots along the line, outcroppings of rock rose perhaps ten or twenty feet above sea level. Waves crashed furiously against them. It was a menacing scene. Caitlin leaned on the rail, studying the water and the island.

"That there's Snagged Anchor Island."

She turned to see Freddy Orcutt standing beside her. She smiled. "And that line of water?" she asked, pointing to the reef that tethered the two islands. She remembered, but she asked anyway.

"String of Pearls, we call it. Dangerous reef." She thought there was a bitterness to his voice.

Caitlin stared at the line of foam and roiling water for a few moments. "I always associated reefs with the Caribbean or the South Pacific," she said absently. "You know, coral." Some weeks later, talking with a geologist who was visiting Alabaster Island, she would learn the reef was a ridge of pegmatite connecting the two granite islands and that its name, String of Pearls, came from the quartz and muscovite, a silver-gray form of mica, embedded in it. Depending on the light, the rocks would sometimes glow light yellow, sometimes white. Caitlin turned her attention to Alabaster Island. About a mile to the left of the ferry dock was a low cliff of exposed rock as bone white as moonlight. "I always wondered, is that cliff why they call this Alabaster Island?"

Freddy shrugged.

Caitlin gazed at the large house perched on the top of the cliff. She knew it well. The Spruce Cove Inn. She wondered if old Gertrude Webster still ran it but decided that, after almost three decades, the woman was probably dead and the place had been sold. More than likely, the name had been changed. Once more, she wondered if the man she saw was Garret Webster. Probably not. Chances are he was married, long gone from the island, and living in New York City. How many times had he told her he wanted to see if he could break into the art scene there? And she never forgot his strange behavior the last time she'd seen him. He acted frightened of something, almost panicky, and she got the sense things were not going well between him and his imperious mother. The woman frightened everybody, even guests of the inn. Caitlin could only imagine how overbearing she must have been with her son. No wonder he'd seemed so anxious; it was probably desperation to leave the island.

A salt-sharp breeze fingered its way into the open neck of her blouse. It raised goose bumps on her skin, caused her nipples to distend. It dragged the blouse across them with an exquisite, almost painful sensation. Like someone nipping them.

Like Garret Webster that time many years before.

She had been standing naked in an oblong of morning light that filtered through skylights in the inn's attic, which Garret used as a studio. Behind her, from a dormer window, a curtain fanned out with a breeze and brushed the skin of her buttocks. Across the room, Garret stroked and prodded the wet clay on the armature, fashioning a figure that was her own, familiar body rendered in clay. She said to Garret, her voice tremulous with arousal, "Thine hands have made me and fashioned me...Remember, I beseech thee, that thou hast made me as the clay."

Garret laughed. "What are you talking about?"

"It's from the Book of Job."

"You study the Bible?" He passed his thumb softly along each inner thigh of the sculpture, shaping them, smoothing them.

At first, she didn't answer him. She was distracted by a sea breeze that licked at a wet spot on her own thigh. Periodically, Garret looked from her to the sculpture and back again. She averted her eyes, afraid he would see her embarrassment. She focused on a desk across the room. An open sketch pad sat under the pool of light from a small lamp. From time to time, Garret walked over to the desk and studied what she assumed was one of the sketches of her he'd done the previous week. She ached to look at it, but knew he'd be annoyed if she broke her pose.

Garret walked to the desk, studied the sketch for a moment before crossing the room to her. He gently adjusted the angle of her arm.

His touch reminded her he'd asked her a question. "I took a course last year. One of my literature courses," she said. Her heart was racing. She was breathless.

He nodded, returning to the sculpture.

"It was called 'Literature and the Joban Tradition.' "

He smiled. "I see."

"Professor Wilcox."

"Uhmm," he replied absently. He lifted a small pallet knife from his work table and moved around to the back of the clay figure. Carefully, he formed the crack between the buttocks.

"I wrote an essay."

"About Job?"

"I used that quote." She wondered if he could see she was shaking.

"About clay." How could he not notice? She saw him looking at her now. Appraising? "That's why I remember it. About the impermanence of life."

Perhaps it was the tremor in her voice that made him stop what he was doing and stare at her. She saw him looking at her nipples and between her legs. A tingling sensation. Her nipples puckered. She was exquisitely aware of the secretion on her inner thigh. She was afraid to look, but she guessed it must glisten in the sunlight she felt warmly on her body. In a voice at once fearful and pliant, she asked, "What? What are you looking at?"

He walked toward her. She saw the swelling in his pants.

Outside, far below on the sloping inn lawn, several people chatted idly—old women, probably. Caitlin recognized Gertrude Webster's voice. She couldn't make out what was being said. She pictured the women sipping coffee and gazing out at the sea from their Adirondack chairs. Or else knitting sweaters.

Garret was standing close. She smelled the clay from his hands. She leaned slightly toward him—only slightly—but it was enough. He read the invitation and lifted clay-wet hands to her breasts. His thumbs brushed across her distended nipples. He kissed her. He sucked in his breath when she reached between his legs. He took her hand and led her across the room to a sofa nestled in the large dormer and, there, they made love urgently at first, and then slowly, and then tenderly, before lying back naked on the bed.

Garret lit a cigarette. Caitlin watched the blue smoke rise and fan out along the low ceiling. Garret sighed deeply and said, "Contentment is the cool air on a man's dick as he lies on his back smoking a cigarette by an open window."

Caitlin rolled her head, looked at him. "Really?" She wanted to lash out at him, punish him for the selfishness the comment implied. Instead, she held her silence and they fell asleep in the lambent light with the sea breeze brushing across their sweat-damp, naked bodies.

She woke before he did. Lying on the outside of the sofa, she propped herself on her elbow and studied his body for a long time. She rose and wandered over to the sculpture. Of her *body*, she thought, not of *her*, because she'd only loaned him her body to transform it into his own through a work of art. The work was his.

She crossed the room to the desk and the sketch pad. It lay open to a drawing in which she immediately recognized herself. It was the same pose he was using for the sculpture. She thumbed through the sketch pad, fanning the pages from back to front quietly so as not to wake him. There were more studies of her, some in the same pose, others in different poses, one or two frankly obscene. A number of pages further on, she found several sketches of another woman—a girl really—with tiny breasts, in various poses. She studied the sketches one after the other. On one, in left-handed writing, was the name Cindy followed by a telephone number. Elsewhere in the margin was the cryptic word, in block letters, "ACCIHTE." A sting of jealousy rose in her. She flipped back to one of the sketches of her, the one to which the pad had been open. She held it under the small lamp and studied it closely. Unlike the girl, her breasts were more rounded, more of a woman's breasts. And there was a greater fullness to her hips and buttocks.

"What are you doing?"

Caitlin jumped to the barked question. She closed the sketch book and replaced it on the desk.

"I said, what are you doing?" His voice was harsh. He rose and advanced toward her.

"I'm sorry," she said in a small voice. "I was…I was being nosy."

"Well, don't you ever poke around in my things again, understand?"

She gave a half nod.

"I said, do you understand?"

"Yes," she replied indignantly. "I only wanted to see what you've been working from."

"Well now you've seen. No artist ever likes people to see his rough work."

In an attempt to steer them away from their mutual anger, she asked with sincere interest, "Why do you work from life when you have the sketches of what you want to do?"

He gave her a mischievous smile, his anger dissipated. She had seen his moods change abruptly before. It both frightened and excited her. "Because, I wouldn't have your naked body in front of me all the time." He took her face between his hands and kissed her. He ran his hands over her body, arousing her all over again. He slid between her thighs.

Now, years later, Caitlin couldn't remember how many times they spent the entire morning or afternoon in his attic studio that summer. All she knew was that being there, posing for Garret Webster in that room, her blood should have run in her veins hot as magma. But she remembered it only as a half-lived time. As though she'd been holding back. As though something in Garret's demeanor chilled her blood most of the time rather than heated it.

She felt a presence at her shoulder. It was Freddy Orcutt. She'd forgotten he was there. She turned to him and asked. "How was your friend, the captain?"

"Kicked me out. Getting too old to bring her in with a distraction like me in the wheelhouse."

Caitlin glanced up at the wheelhouse to see the captain leaning close to the windshield, eyes squinting, gazing intently ahead. She was glad Freddy joined her; it forced her thoughts away from Garret Webster and the terror of leaving her family, of losing her husband to a blond cellist. Suddenly she felt a lurch which caused her to stumble against Freddy.

He caught her, shook his head. "Only that dumb Welshman putting her in reverse. Coming in like some kinda cowboy. Thinks he's riding a horse at some dude ranch in Wyoming or something."

"You seem always to be catching me," Caitlin said with a laugh.

"Eyuh. Leastwise you didn't fall this time."

"What's his name?"

"Who?"

"The captain."

"Morgan Fludd," replied Freddy with a glance up at the wheelhouse. "And he's gonna run this here ferry right up into town someday, he keeps driving her like a cowboy. Right up to Pauline's Coffee and Bake Shop on Front Street."

"My favorite poet was Welsh. Dylan Thomas."

Freddy gave her a puzzled look.

She smiled, leaned on the rail, and watched as the ferry slowly approached the terminal. Below her, on the loading deck, passengers started to gather near the exit. Among them was the man who resembled Garret Webster and whom she'd seen with the couple who were arguing. Suddenly, with a closer view, she was struck by a jolt of recognition. She couldn't be certain over the span of two decades, but she thought it just might be he after all. The man had salt-and-pepper hair and his hairline was receding, but the nose and the chin were the same. He wore his hair in a ponytail, but men can change hair styles. Also, the panicked look in his eyes when he saw her, much like the last time she'd seen him twenty-seven years before. Yes, it definitely could be him.

The man moved through the crowd of people alongside Quentin and O'zalik Moseley. He grabbed Quentin Moseley by the arm, pulled him away from the woman, and whispered urgently into his ear. Quentin Moseley glanced up at Caitlin. A shiver passed through her and she moved away from the rail, out of sight of the people below.

As the ferry eased into the slip, Caitlin's nostrils were filled with the mingled smells of metal, diesel, and balsam. The diesel fumes made her feel nauseous.

Once the ferry stopped and the loading ramp was lowered, Freddy said, "I'll help with your bags." He lifted two of Caitlin's three bags. Caitlin slipped into the straps of her backpack and followed him to the stairs leading from the upper deck.

"Careful how you step now," said Freddy over his shoulder.

A small crowd mingled at the end of the loading ramp. Even as Caitlin wondered which one might be Helen Underwood, a prim, ghostly woman advanced directly to her and said, proffering a hand, "You must be Caitlin Gray. I'm Helen Underwood." The woman had a splintering voice.

Feeling conspicuous—it was apparently too early in the season for an unfamiliar face not to be noticed—Caitlin held the woman's hand lightly. "Pleased to meet you."

Helen Underwood turned to Freddy. "I see you're being the knight in shining armor once again, Freddy," she said with a smile.

Freddy nodded and said, only, "Eyuh."

Caitlin followed Freddy and Helen Underwood to the parking lot. As they walked, Caitlin glanced to the left and right, looking for the man she thought might be Garret Webster. There was no sign of him.

They were loading Caitlin's bags into the trunk of Helen's Chevrolet when they heard a commotion several cars over. Quentin Moseley was yelling at his wife as she leaned against a battered old Ford Fairlane. She had a defiant look, as though waiting for him to stop. Quentin raised his hand as if to strike her. With a contemptuous smile, she turned her back to him and began walking away. Rust stains from the car showed on the back of her pants. Quentin followed her, hand raised.

Freddy rushed toward them, grabbed Quentin's wrist, and said, "See here, Quentin, that ain't a right thing to do."

"Ain't none of your business, Freddy," said Quentin. "She just said something I didn't like, is all."

"That ain't no reason for hitting a woman. Besides, knowing you, you probably deserved whatever she said. Now leave her be or I'll report you to Richie Comine. I'm guessing he's probably feeling awful lonely over at the jail with nobody locked up at the present time."

Quentin stared at Freddy for a long moment before slowly backing away from his wife.

Freddy asked, "You all right, O'zalik?"

She nodded. "Yes, Freddy. Thanks. I'm grateful."

Freddy turned to Quentin. "I'm expecting you to behave yourself.

Hear?"

Quentin mumbled a sullen "Yuh." He stole a glance at Caitlin.

"See to it," Freddy replied as he turned and headed back toward Caitlin and Helen Underwood.

Caitlin turned to Helen. "Freddy's more than twice as old as that man," she said, incredulously.

"Everybody thinks an awful lot of Freddy. Nobody wants to stand in his disapproval."

Freddy returned, lifted the last of Caitlin's bags into the trunk, and bid the two women good-bye with a tip of his cap. He climbed into an old Toyota pickup with salt-corroded bumpers that glinted dully in the sunlight. Caitlin watched him drive carefully out of the parking lot, stopping at the exit to look both ways before taking off down the road. The right tail light continued to blink until the truck disappeared around a turn.

Caitlin and Helen climbed into the Chevrolet. As she drove out the parking lot, Helen said, "I just need to make a quick stop at my office. I forgot some papers."

Within minutes, they were in the center of town. Helen pulled to a stop opposite a small cape-style house with gray, weathered shingles, left the car in idle, and said, "I'll only be a minute."

As Caitlin waited, she studied the town she remembered clearly even after more than two decades. The buildings were weathered and pitted from salt-laden winds. Alabaster Island, adrift in the Atlantic off the extreme eastern seaboard of the continent, was so at the mercy of the scouring winds and the sea that its circumstance influenced the selection of hymns. On any Sunday, she remembered, a person passing by the Congregational Church might hear the words "From every stormy wind that blows, from every swelling tide of woes…" or "Oh hear us when we cry to Thee for those in peril on the sea…" issuing from the church. Inside, during all but the warmest months, the singing would be accompanied by the hisses and clanks of the steam radiators. The islanders lived in fear of, in respect for, the sea. They knew they lived a marginal existence humbled far out into the domain of the ocean. This was brought home to them by the nor'easters that often lashed the island with rain or snow or ice crystals. Perhaps that's why the buildings on Front Street—the church, the coffee shop, the gift shop, the drugstore, the tiny library—seemed to hunker together as if seeking comfort in each other's company. All the buildings were salt-burned. It was just as Caitlin remembered it.

As promised, Helen Underwood was gone only a short time. When she returned, she pulled into the street and made a U-turn through an unpaved parking lot. Caitlin saw a building with the words "Crenshaw's Marina" painted in white over the doorway. Most of one wall was covered by a huge American flag. As Helen brought the car back onto the street, Caitlin saw the Moseleys' Ford pulling away from the curb.

They were opposite Pauline's Coffee and Bake Shop and Caitlin saw, through the window, O'zalik Moseley standing behind the counter tying on an apron. She raised her eyes and stared at Caitlin with nut-brown eyes, expressionless, until Helen accelerated down the street.

~

Freddy had to grip the steering wheel hard to keep his hands from shaking. He was too old for run-ins like he just had with Quentin Moseley. There would have been no need if the man just behaved himself, but that would never happen. Even when Quentin was a boy, he was a troublemaker. How many times had Agnes asked Freddy to talk with Jimmy, tell him not to play with Quentin Moseley? And she was right—she usually was—but how can you tell a kid who his playmates should or should not be? Better to teach him how to be a judge of character for himself.

And Quentin seemed to get worse after the Gulf War. O'zalik once told Freddy how Quentin's job was to bury the evidence of the slaughter, something Freddy thought was dead wrong. "Seems to me," he'd said to O'zalik, "soldiers should be made to tour the battlefield after it's over, see what they done. Keep 'em humble. Let 'em know ain't none of us are saints."

How he and Agnes worried every day Jimmy was away fighting in the Vietnam War. The agonized letters they'd received. The descriptions of slaughter. The self-recrimination. For Freddy, it peeled a scab from the old Dachau wounds. He should have told Jimmy about the liberation of Dachau, about the Germans he gunned down, about the partially snow-covered bodies in the gondola cars. But he couldn't. All he could say was "Hang in there, Jimmy. It'll be over soon, and you'll be home. Then you can forget about it all." In the end he wrote a long letter filled with news about the island; about how Helen Underwood overheard Ben Moseley making a nasty comment about her voice and they'd had a spat; how Gertie Webster was so mean to some guests, they called Richie Comine who refused to intervene; how Ernie Botham and Burle Ledyard were still conducting their ongoing feud. But as to consolation, he could not find the words. "Ain't none of us are saints" seemed too lame.

jimmy

With a quick glance as he came to the Island Cemetery, Freddy located the solitary maple that shaded Agnes's grave. It was in the section reserved for founding families. He lifted two fingers from the steering wheel, a slight nodding gesture, the kind Downeasters use, and turned his attention back to the road. But something else in the founders' section caught his eye. It was old Ben Moseley's new, gleaming headstone not far from the simple monument that marked Doris Crenshaw's grave. He'd died during a howling nor'easter when a rotting tree limb snapped, exploded through the window, and caught him sitting smoking a cigar. The limb knocked him unconscious even as a shard of glass sliced through his carotid artery. O'zalik found him slumped in his chair, the cigar on the floor where a pool of blood extinguished it.

Freddy thought: *the descendants of the founders are dropping like flies*. He experienced a strange sensation of envy just like the one he'd felt at Ben's funeral. It wouldn't be so bad, especially if he could go quickly the way Ben had. If what people said was true—that there was an afterlife, a heaven—it would be good to be with Agnes again.

And Jimmy.

He had no intention of drooling away the long, unwinding years of his life on his porch staring at Snagged Anchor Island and spitting stem juice on the stained floorboards. He came to believe nothing good ever happens. Nothing good except, perhaps, once in a while like a perversion, an eclipse of the sun. Once, speaking with the candor of alcohol, he said to Morgan Fludd, "Happiness is like a bottle of perfume. If it's dropped and smashed on the floor, ain't no way of putting it back together again, getting the perfume back in."

The problem was, he wasn't at all certain he believed this whole business about an afterlife. Maybe this was all there was. This small island. This ocean. This sky.

He glanced into his rearview mirror for a last peek at the solitary maple. He pressed his right foot harder on the accelerator and soon came to an intersection where he turned right toward his cottages. He slowed to allow a spruce grouse to cross the road.

As he pulled into his driveway, Freddy thought of the woman, Caitlin Gray. He'd thought he detected a deep sadness behind her eyes, something that wouldn't easily go away. But although she appeared troubled, perhaps even afraid, there was also a kind of enthusiasm in the way she asked questions. She had a lively curiosity, this woman, that reminded him of Jimmy, the way he would ask a ton of questions when he was a boy. It might be good, having her around.

He went into Jimmy's cottage to make sure everything was in order.

~

Caitlin and Helen Underwood reached the edge of town. The road, bordered by tall spruce on both sides, followed the coast. They were on the windward side of the island. A parade of ragged cumulus clotted the sky west to east. Caitlin saw ranks of large waves angling to the shore, their tops ripping away in spume and spindrift. The line of white she knew as String of Pearls was ahead of them. The waves broke even more furiously over it now, leaving behind a frothy scum in areas where the water was trapped by the jagged contours of the rocks.

Helen said, "Whatever possessed that man to bring an Indian woman here is way beyond me. Nothing but trouble will come of it. That's what I said at the time. I mean, think of the poor woman; she should be with her own kind on that reservation at Pleasant Point where she'd be much more comfortable." She shook her head. "That Quentin, he was never the same after the Gulf War. How can an Indian woman feel at home on a Yankee Protestant island?" Her voice was like fingernails dragging across a blackboard.

"How did they meet?" It seemed a fair question since Caitlin gathered from what Helen implied, they had not met on Alabaster Island.

"I think Quentin was doing some work over to Machias. Met Angelique in some bar, I suppose. Now don't get me wrong, Angelique's a sweet woman and all that, but..."

"Freddy told me her name was O'zalik."

"Well, that's the Indian version of Angelique. Seems she's taken a fancy to calling herself that. Going native, I guess. Probably a way of getting under Old Man Moseley's skin."

"Is that Quentin's father?"

"Eyuh. And, Lord, was the old man mad! Said he didn't want no Indian woman in his family."

"Have they been married long?"

"Only a few years."

"Then his...Quentin's...father must have died recently."

"Just last year. Died during a storm. If you ask me, Ben's death is what has Quentin behaving so badly these days. They were close, his father and him."

They were passing the island cemetery. Caitlin saw a new, gleaming black headstone. She assumed it was where old Mr. Moseley lay. The island had only a few hundred permanent residents; how many funerals could there have been in recent months?

After passing the cemetery, they turned right and climbed a hill. At the top, the road curved left to follow the ridge of a cliff overlooking the ocean. A cluster of small cottages huddled near the edge of the cliff as though hunkering down for the next nor'easter. At several places flights of stairs led down from the cliff's edge to the pebbly beach Caitlin remembered from twenty-seven years before. She prayed her cottage was one of these.

Helen slowed and turned into a gravel driveway. Caitlin was surprised to see, at the end of the driveway, Freddy Orcutt's battered Toyota pickup. The driveway was shared by two cottages, a larger one on the left and a smaller one on the right, both sheathed in weathered gray shingles.

"That's Freddy Orcutt's truck!" Caitlin said.

"Seems only fitting, seeing as how that's his house," replied Helen, pointing to the larger cottage. "The other one's yours. Also belongs to Freddy."

"You mean I'm renting from Freddy and neither of you said anything back at the ferry dock?"

"What's there to say? Seems like one landlord's as good as another."

Caitlin opened the door and stepped from the car, shaking her head in amazement. She looked around. Her footfalls made tiny crunching sounds in the gravel as she walked to the end of the driveway where a recently mowed lawn led to the edge of the cliff. As she passed, she felt a shimmer of heat from the hood of the truck, heard the clicks of its cooling engine. She stopped a few feet from the edge and looked out over the water. From there, she had a perfect view of Snagged Anchor Island and String of Pearls. The waves breaking on the reef seemed less ferocious, perhaps because the water was rising over it with the incoming tide, or perhaps due to the effect of the twin perspectives of distance and height.

"Pretty view," said Helen who came up behind Caitlin. "Comes free. Now let me show you the cottage."

As they walked back toward the cottage, Caitlin heard the crackle of a radio coming from Freddy Orcutt's cottage. "*...from Stellwagen Bank to the Bay of Fundy, including the entire Gulf of Maine, seas two to four feet, winds southwest ten to fifteen knots increasing to twenty knots in the afternoon...*"

"What's that?" Caitlin asked.

"Marine forecast radio. Came from Freddy's fishing boat when he sold it. He always has it on."

Helen opened the front door to the cottage and motioned Caitlin inside. Mildly surprised the door hadn't been locked, Caitlin passed through a narrow hallway and emerged into a small room that took her breath away. A sofa and coffee table and one stuffed chair surrounded an oval Colonial rug—a perfect arrangement for reading. But the focus of her attention was a table with two chairs that sat in front of a large picture window overlooking the ocean. She went to the window and looked out. Snagged Anchor Island and the reef connecting it to Alabaster Island dominated the view. That, she decided, was where she would write. Without question. She could always eat off the coffee table. "It's perfect," she said.

"I'm glad you like it. Let me show you the bedrooms." Helen led Caitlin into a small bedroom large enough only for a full-sized bed, a bureau, a night table, and one chair. "I'm afraid it's not very big. And the other one, where Freddy's grandchildren slept, is even smaller. It has only a child-sized bed and a crib. I don't know what you'll do when your family visits. Of course the living room—"

"My family won't be visiting."

"They won't?"

"No."

"Oh...Well in your e-mail you said you wanted the phone removed. Are you quite sure...considering?"

"Yes, I'm quite sure."

"I see. I'll have somebody come out and remove it. I would have done it before, but I was sure you'd change your mind once you...I mean, once—"

"There's no need to call somebody," said Caitlin with a smile. She went to the night table where the phone sat, knelt, unplugged the chord from the jack, rose, and handed the phone to Helen.

Helen stared at the phone in disbelief.

"Don't worry, it'll be fine," said Caitlin.

"But what if—"

"It'll be all right."

Yet as she watched Helen leave, the telephone cord trailing behind her in the gravel, Caitlin wondered if it truly would be all right. What if something happened to Dylan or Ellen? She forced herself to stop worrying, remembering she'd given them Helen Underwood's address and telephone number. Just in case.

After she unpacked her laptop computer and placed it on the table, she sat staring out the window wondering how long she would be able to hold out. The waves breaking on the reef formed a ragged white line. Big Pearl and Little Pearl sent off white and pink flashes in the sunlight. She remembered how, back home, she helped Dylan with a school project about rocks and minerals. She guessed the pearls were granite imbedded with quartz and feldspar.

A wave of anxiety washed over her. Her role, what had given her purpose, had been to hold her family together and to raise her children. She'd failed at the one and completed the other. Now everything was invested in the computer screen sitting black and waiting on the table.

ACCIHTE
Changing Color Moon

O'zalik waited until Quentin left the house before she pulled out the typed pages of the translated journal and started to reread. When she told her grandfather about the journal, he reminded her the Jesuits were European. She should not get upset if what she read betrayed a biased view of Indians. "The French Jesuits were far better than the English in accepting certain parts of our way of life," he said. "But in the end, they were still trying to make Christians of us. That required they denounce some of our ways."

Yet, despite her grandfather's admonition, when she first read the journal she had taken an instant dislike to Father Dalou's haughty, self-important, airs. His only redeeming virtue, she thought, was the obvious sincerity with which he took his mission and the genuine love he had for both the Acadians and the Indians for whom he felt responsible.

A REPORT OF REMARKABLE EVENTS OCCURRING DURING A MISSION OF A PRIEST OF THE COMPANY OF JESUS AMONG THE WABANAKI OF ACADIA IN THE YEARS 1755 AND 1756 BY FATHER JÉRÔME DALOU.
Translated by Robert Blanchard.

(Translator's note: Where both French and English place names are given for a location, I have used the French name, including the English name in parentheses only on the first occasion of its use. I have also chosen not to edit the text in any way, though Father Dalou has an annoying penchant for hurling adjectives like spears at his enemies. Unfortunately, it is a practice that may amuse contemporary ears and thus rob the narrative of some of the seriousness with which it should be taken.)

I, Father Jérôme Dalou of the Company of Jesus, record these pages so it may be known what perfidies and treacheries the English anti papists have perpetrated on an entire people, namely the Faithful of Acadie (Nova Scotia in this context—R.B.) *who are numbered among the most devout of God's children.*

For as long as I have lived the godless English have disputed France's rightful claim to New France and have waged war upon us. Some forty years ago (when, as it happens, I was born) the non-repentant English succeeded in wresting Acadia from the French through the deception and dishonor of the so-called Treaty of Utrecht. Yet the Acadians are a peaceful and innocent people and have lived among the English settlers and not caused any difficulties for their foreign overlords in all these forty years. Therefore, it is with great vexation of spirit that I endeavor to understand the recent truculence Governor Lawrence has shown toward the Acadians and also toward my children, my Christian Savages, the Mi'kmaq Indians. I can only conclude that the catastrophic defeat of the French this June past at Fort Beauséjour emboldened him to the point of lunacy, an affliction too often found among the crazed English. For, despite the fact that the Acadians have lived these many years under oppressive English rule without causing any problems whatsoever, he has seen fit to deny them boats and arms (implements they need to earn a Christian living in this land) for fear they might be used to aid their French compatriots. Furthermore, he has required that every Acadian take an oath of loyalty to England and agree, as part of that oath, to bear arms on the side of the loathsome English. The Acadians agreed to the oath of loyalty on the condition that it exclude this last provision.

What, then, of Lawrence's lunatic response to this reasonable and peaceable stance? He instructed John Winslow who commands four com-

panies from Massachusetts (which, at that time, included Maine—R.B.), *this colonial who is Lawrence's lackey, his valet-a-pied* (flunky in this context?—R.B.), *his sycophant, his puppet—all character traits I can certainly vouch for since I, myself, have tried to reason with the man—he instructed this puppet of his to assemble, on September 2nd past, all the men and teenage boys of Grand Pré into the churchyard and there read to them an edict that could only have been composed by Satan himself. The edict (my hand trembles even to write the vile words) announced that since the Acadians have refused the full oath of loyalty, their homes and their lands, their cattle and other livestock, their barns and their outlying buildings, are all forfeit, and moreover that the Acadians would be expelled from the province which has always been their home. The men thus assembled were all arrested and eventually loaded on ships to transport them away.*

It was a most heartbreaking sight as, slowly and heavy with sadness, the doleful men and boys marched to the harbor, a distance of some two kilometers. As they marched, their sabots (wooden shoes—R. B.) *created an ominous tapping rhythm like the roll of drums at an execution. All along the path of tears they were met by the women and children they were being forced to leave. Madame Bernard, who, with her husband, had in the past often given me shelter, and who now was gravid with child for the ninth time, clenched the sleeve of her dress between her teeth as Monsieur Bernard shuffled toward her arm-in-arm with Marcel, their oldest son. It was most heartwounding to see the family embrace, father and eldest son bidding farewell to Madame Bernard while all six other children clutched at the legs of their father and brother.*

All day long there was much lamentation as this scene was repeated many times—entire families embracing each other for the last time amidst a torrent of tears—enough tears, indeed, to float Noah's ark. I fell to my knees and raised my agonized voice in prayer. Many of the women and children joined me, murmuring their prayers piously until a father or a son appeared whereupon they would jump to their feet, embrace their soon to be departed loved ones, and cry loudly. O, the horror of it!

The Jesuit explained how he came to believe God instructed him to save the remaining Acadian families by enlisting the help of the Mi'kmaq Indians of Cape Breton Island whom he had visited on several missions. After rereading his description of his journey north and his meeting with the Mi'kmaq leader, Edmond, O'zalik unfolded the map she'd bought at the university bookstore in Orono. She located the places mentioned. It was her idea that Bob Blanchard retain the place names Father Dalou used but include their English translations so she could reference them on contemporary maps. Using the spread of her thumb and forefinger, she measured the distance from Grand Pré to Cape Breton. She came up with roughly one hundred and fifty miles.

When, after a week's journey during which I was forced to evade the evil English several times, I arrived in the Mi'kmaq camp, the Savages greeted me as usual with the words, "Our Father, our Father, how obliged we are to thee for giving us the pleasure of seeing thee!" I embraced Edmond and announced I would celebrate Mass that very evening. After Mass, Edmond and I sat with a group of noble men and I told them of my plan. As I expected, they immediately agreed and the next day we set off in a flotilla of canoes for the south.

After four days and six portages, we arrived at a deserted place some ten kilometers from Grand Pré where we were easily able to hide the canoes for later use. It was already October and I was eager to begin the work of the Lord before the bitter winter set in. But when I entered Grand Pré the next day, I had cause to fear I was too late. I saw a score of ships already sitting at anchor in Bassin des Mines. Most of the families had already been loaded aboard the ships and there was no hope of saving them. Alas, this included poor Madame Bernard and her family.

It was sadly apparent I could no longer accomplish my original mission, so I turned my attention to trying to rescue those who had already eluded the damnable English. It was God's apparent will that my proposed mission would also be an unexpected act of desperation.

O'zalik spent the next hour marking the map so she would be better able to follow the narrative of the escape.

an unexpected act of desperation

~

Shortly before dawn, Freddy eased himself from the left side of the bed. It was a practiced movement formed during a lifetime as a fisherman. Even now, with arthritic joints, he accomplished it so gracefully that, had she been there, Agnes wouldn't have been disturbed. As he had done every day of his married life, he went into the kitchen to start the coffee before stepping out onto the porch to check the weather. The only difference was these days there was plenty of coffee left at the end of the day. He'd never been able to adjust the amount he brewed; it would have been a kind of acceptance.

When he opened the door to the porch, a chill wind greeted him. Fifteen knots from the southwest, he estimated. He guessed a front had passed in the night, though why he didn't waken as usual when that happened puzzled him. Looking at the southwestern sky, he saw a splay of stars. A gibbous moon, waning from full four days previous, was several hands high in the south. Directly above him, and clearly visible in the vault of the heavens, were the Little Dipper and the Northern Cross. The stars in the eastern sky, however, were already fading into the brightening dawn. A rim of bruised rose started to show itself on the eastern horizon, a slight blistering of first light. Freddy glanced at his watch: a little before 4:00. He scanned the sky one more time. No sign of weather. The boys should have an easy day of it. Ernie Botham, Burle Ledyard, and the others would be heading out soon. Already he heard the distant cough and sputter of an engine being started. It soon settled into an even thrum and he saw a lone running light glide toward the mouth of Spruce Cove. Probably Ernie and Burle, best friends who always fished together.

Freddy chuckled to himself. Of course, they weren't always close. Before Ernie got cancer they'd been feuding, it all beginning with an argument over who was encroaching on whose fishing territory. But instead of cutting each other's trap lines—the normal recourse in lobster disputes—they preferred more inventive ways of getting at the other. Burle acted first, approaching Ernie's boat at high speed and turning at the last moment to inundate Ernie with sheets of spray. A week later, Ernie went to the mainland, bought a "Taunting Tammy 3-hole inflatable sex doll" using Burle's name, and had it delivered to Burle, c/o Pauline's Coffee and Bake Shop. Burle waited a month to retaliate, then went to the mainland to buy several books on cross-dressing that he conspicuously placed in the wheelhouse of Ernie's lobster boat after Ernie left the boat at Crenshaw's for minor repairs. It went on like this for years, keeping Richie Comine busy with fruitless investigations. It included a wide variety of both imaginative and mundane uses for spray paint, urine, bilge water, dildos, sheep droppings, expandable foam, obscene bumper stickers, butter, women's underwear, rocks, cat litter, rotten fruit, chum, ropes (around propeller shafts), Vaseline petroleum jelly, ruby red lipstick, more urine, counterfeited summonses, garbage, and even once, a live cow. Gradually, it became as much a game of confounding bug-eyed Richie Comine as it was of taunting each other. All this had the effect of increasing their respect for each other's ingenuity and restraint. Even the spray paint caused no real damage. Ernie used it only after Burle's boat was sitting on a cradle at Crenshaw's waiting for a new paint job. And, in fact, Burle, along with the other islanders, took great delight when Ernie misspelled "pervert," spray painting "prevert" instead. Angus Macleod, the learned doctor, said that, based on the French roots of the word, it meant "pre-green," upon which Burle changed his mind and instructed Crenshaw to paint the hull a dark green so that Ernie would be perpetually reminded of his error.

Then, not long after Ernie received his cancer diagnosis, they sold their boats, pooled their resources to buy a larger and better one (painting it dark green). They named it *Taunting Tammy* and began to fish together.

Freddy waved in case Ernie and Burle could see him in the moonlight then returned to the kitchen. He poured himself a cup of coffee and turned the weather radio on. As he did every morning, he went back out on the porch and packed tobacco into a meerschaum pipe that had a crazed and cracked stem, lit it, and settled into his rocker. A port running light, glowing red, glided across the water of Spruce Cove. He tried to guess who would be the second boat out. Walter Peake? He watched until he saw the white stern light, which told him the boat had turned to starboard. Whoever it was, he was going to fish off Spindrift Ledge this morning. Soon, a half dozen other running lights appeared, sliding toward the mouth of Spruce Cove and the waiting sea. Above the faint grumble of the engines, he heard a ripple of laughter. Could *that* be Ernie and Burle? Maybe they weren't the first boat out after all, as was their custom. He wondered if Ernie had trouble getting out of bed again. All the same, he liked to hear the two men laughing. It was good for Ernie.

In years past, the smell of coffee invariably woke Agnes. She told him it was like being stirred gently by the shoulder. So it was always that sequence in the morning for him: coffee first, then the weather radio, then a quiet smoke on the porch watching the cove come alive until Agnes, sleepy-eyed, joined him.

On some mornings—worse than others—he would take out the old bottle of Fidji by Guy Laroche. No one knew he still had a bottle of Agnes' perfume, the one she'd worn only for big island events. He'd bought it for her one Christmas. He would occasionally take it out, unscrew the cap, and sniff it.

The pipe was a gift from Jimmy. He had brought it back from Germany, where he spent a couple of weeks recovering from slight wounds at the U.S. base in Ramstein. The bowl was an elaborately carved representation of Father Rhine and Lorelei, the young maiden entwined in the embrace of the bearded, sad-faced old man. When Freddy first took the pipe from its box, it gleamed white like the back of a swan. But meerschaum ages with each bowl of tobacco and now it had a soft, golden glow to it. Each morning Freddy studied the darkening color, marking the inexorable slip of time from that long-ago Christmas. As he sat in the gloom of early morning, the beam of Sheep's Pasture Light swept across his aged face every ten seconds, further measuring off his life six times each minute. And in the sweep of light he saw String of Pearls and, faintly in the gloaming distance, Snagged Anchor Island. A shiver passed through him. It always reminded him of the people who had disappeared over the years.

And of Jimmy.

And of the ghosts out there.

Funny how the mind works, he thought. That the sight of Snagged Anchor Island always made him think of Jimmy was understandable to him. But why did it invariably bring him back to that day at the Dachau concentration camp? Maybe it was because he'd decided, for lack of a better place, to consign everything evil in the world to the little island. Just a place to lock it away, keep it at bay. As though if it had a place of its own, it wouldn't come calling again as it had so often in the long unspooling of his years. At least not as frequently. Maybe it was because he could never talk with anybody about it, not even Agnes or Jimmy—maybe that's why he'd found a special place to lock his ghosts away, to cast them into the pit.

He'd lied about his age to join the army and ended up as a replacement in the Third Battalion, 157th Regiment, of the U.S. Forty-fifth Division, the "Thunderbird" Division. He made friends with many of the American Indians from Arizona, New Mexico, Oklahoma, and Colorado who had been original members of the division. His first experience of combat came when, off the coast of Sicily, he and others scrambled into a landing craft that then broke free of its davits and dropped onto another boat loaded with soldiers, crushing twenty-one of them. Later, after a landing at Salerno, his battalion was bombed by American planes. The earth erupted all around him; he saw bodies of his friends blown apart; he was struck in the face by human intestines. Still later, he landed at Anzio, where Germans killed many more of his friends in a night attack. Another time he saw the carnage—the shattered, bloody results—where German tanks had come up to the lip of a foxhole line and fired their main guns directly into the foxholes. He helped liberate Rome. He shot down German soldiers escaping from a destroyed tank. He landed in France and plodded up the Rhone valley, killing Germans every chance he got. He was in a bayonet fight in the woods of the Vosges. He still remembered the shock of his bayonet entering a human body, the gush of blood that blinded him for an instant, the anger with which he slashed upward, working the blade through organs. A short time later he was surrounded with his battalion near Reipertswiller by an SS Mountain Regiment, saw more of his Indian comrades slaughtered; he himself slaughtered more Germans.

But nothing, none of the carnage, none of the broken bodies, none of the endless nights of bombardment, none of the constant shrill of shells, the outraged screams of men, none of it wounded him so deeply as what he saw—and what he did—when his battalion liberated the concentration camp at Dachau. After seeing a trainload of dead prisoners on the outskirts of the camp, thousands of them, their bodies half buried by snow as though, he thought, God were trying to hide something but ran out of snow; after penetrating the barbed-wire-encircled inner compound; after seeing the crematorium with its piles of ashes and the gas chamber with its piles of emaciated dead bodies; after seeing the haunted faces of the broken, starved, near-death, living prisoners; after seeing these same enraged inmates kill their former guards, ripping and tearing at their throats and eyeballs and genitals with their bare hands; after seeing all this laundering of the human soul, Freddy Orcutt and his fellow GIs lined up captured German soldiers, Waffen SS, many of them boys, and in a frenzy of horror and revulsion and anger mowed them all down.

In that moment he'd recognized in himself the hatred, the urge to demonize others in order to permit what he'd done, to permit what he'd seen in the concentration camp. It had been a journey into the nether regions of the human soul. Each German soldier who fell varnished his soul with a layer of indifference, layer upon layer.

When he approached the dead Germans, he'd seen a young soldier, blood running red and diluting to pink in the snow.

He remembered the Polish boy, Miesko, he'd befriended, ribs erupting from his drum-tight skin; how he tried to console the boy who'd lost his parents, his sisters, to the gas chambers; how the boy ended up consoling him for the killing of the Germans. Consoled him for the terrible journey he'd been compelled to take. And Miesko's gesture of sympathy, his subordinating his own physical needs to Freddy's spiritual needs, was a solvent that started to peel away the layers of varnish.

For Freddy, Dachau had a new geography and its geography was Snagged Anchor Island and String of Pearls, which tethered it to Alabaster Island. He could never see the island, the reef, without thinking of Jimmy. And it was within this sadness that he consigned everything else that saddened him. When he looked at the island, he saw the mutilated bodies of his comrades, the bodies of his bayonet victims, the shattered humanity of the prison camp, the mowed-down German soldiers—they were all out there.

And Jimmy.

How he'd tried to talk Jimmy out of joining the army. How he'd tried to protect him from the things haunting his own memories. How he'd tried. But Jimmy joined and then his letters showed how he'd been forced to look into the same pit.

jimmy

they're all there consigned to snagged anchor island

Freddy hated the place.

~

Caitlin slept poorly, overcome by a sense of loneliness. Though she had been on the island several weeks, she mostly kept to herself, feeling very much the outsider. Freddy Orcutt may have been next door, but she seldom saw him. He seemed to value his privacy as much as she did hers. Or was it, for both of them, shyness? As for Garret

Webster, she'd seen him here and there, mostly at a distance, and they'd never talked. She wasn't even sure she wanted to talk to him. Or he, her. Probably not, judging by the look he gave her on the ferry and also by the cool distance that had grown between them the time twenty-seven years before, when he caught her rifling through his sketch book.

All night she heard the faint snore of waves breaking on the beach fifty feet below her open window. When at last she was fully awake, a shaft of moonlight lay across her face like a satin sheet. It fell on the bureau giving it a ghostly glow. Caitlin rose and went to the window. The moon was full and fat as it brooded over Snagged Anchor Island. A broad band of moonlight formed a silken ribbon leading from the island to her. The light shimmered turbulently along the median of the band. Big Pearl and Little Pearl stood out clearly in the milky radiance. From somewhere below, she heard the harsh *braaak, braaak* of a great blue heron. It was probably fishing in the still, shallow waters of one of the small coves along the coastline. From across the cove, the beam of the lighthouse swept the harbor repeatedly.

She went into the living room, sat at the table, and started her computer. Two hours later, she had three short fragments of a poem:

On the fifteenth night of the moon,
in the forest, the halves of tree trunks
are moonsilvered as silk
and wolves begin a howling spree…

Moonlight sizzles on the water and
shines bone white through a shroud
of passing cloud…

A woman wallows in the depths
where the light puddles…

But the fragments wouldn't come together to form a complete

poem...or even the first draft of a complete poem. She sat at the table staring out the window. The sky was turning from black to blue black and the stars were fading. On the eastern horizon, a dark rim of blood red heralded the rising sun. With the moon and the brightening sky there was just enough light for her to see waves beginning to break over String of Pearls, spilling foam. Incoming tide. A shaft of light from the lighthouse at Sheep's Pasture Point swept across Spruce Cove flaring one boat after another in the anchorage.

She dressed and went outside to feel the morning air. The faint murmur of the weather radio came from Freddy Orcutt's cottage. A rich aroma of pipe tobacco mingled with the salt air. Putting aside worries about being intrusive, she strolled around to the back of Freddy's cottage to wish him a good morning.

Though the sky was brightening, Freddy's porch remained in darkness. She could barely make out his profile in the rocking chair. As she approached, he rose so fast from his rocker that it kept on rocking without him. He called out an enthusiastic, "Good morning."

"Good morning, Freddy."

"You're up early."

She smiled. "I think it's the sea air."

"Have a seat," he said, motioning her toward a second rocking chair. "I'll bring you a cup of coffee."

"Oh, I don't want to be a bother."

"No bother. Brewed a whole pot. It'd go to waste elsewise."

He disappeared into the kitchen. Caitlin sat in the rocking chair. Moments later, Freddy emerged, handed her a cup of coffee, placed a bowl of sugar and a carton of milk on the table between them, and sat. He took up his pipe and sucked on it a few times to get it burning again. With his blackened right index finger he tamped the tobacco.

"That's quite a fancy pipe," said Caitlin.

"Eyuh," Freddy replied, holding it out and looking at it. "Meerschaum. Gift from my boy Jimmy back when he returned from the army."

"Who are the figures supposed to be?"

"This here's old Father Rhine and this here's Lorelei. Card came with it describing everything and saying it was an old German legend."

"I know it. Lorelei threw herself into the river because her lover abandoned her and she became a siren who lured fishermen to their destruction."

Freddy nodded. "Eyuh, goes about like that. Jimmy always did have a funny sense of humor." The sweep of the lighthouse beam momentarily showed Freddy's dark expression.

"That stem has seen better days," said Caitlin.

Freddy withdrew the pipe from his mouth and examined it. The black stem, crazed and cracked, had turned yellow in places where his teeth had bitten into it. "Eyuh," he said.

Beyond the porch, the sky was brightening to a deep cobalt blue. Freddy pointed the stem of the pipe toward it. "According to the radio, there's a storm out over George's Bank, but no sign of it here."

Caitlin squinted toward the east. "No. It's lovely here."

"Boys will be having a good day of it," Freddy said.

"What boys?"

"Ernie Botham, Burle Ledyard...the others. They're all out lobstering."

"Is that what you used to do? Lobstering?"

"Nah. I fished deeper waters. George's Bank kind of stuff. Bottom dragging."

"When did you quit?"

"Back some fifteen years ago, or so." He looked out to sea. "Ernie and Burle, they're always going out together. Inseparable. That's them in the distance now. The dark-colored hull."

"Are they related?"

"Nah. Just friends. Don't know what Burle's going to do, though, come the winter."

"What do you mean?"

"Ernie will be dead by then. Doctors give him no more'n six

months."

"Oh..." Caitlin didn't know what to say.

"Guess that's the way life works," said Freddy, staring at the bowl of his pipe.

Caitlin felt a deep sadness. She squinted into the dazzle of the spangled sea and the sky with its rose-fringed clouds. Across the cove, houses were drenched in a buttery light. Several windows flamed reflections of the sun. Finally, she said, "I used to think most of the world was created by apprentice gods who only got it half right—that the true God only created Hawaii and the others could only manage poor imitations—and in some cases they botched it completely. But it's so beautiful here I think it must be the work of the Master."

Freddy peered at her, his eyebrows raised quizzically. After a moment in which he seemed to be wondering if she was finished, he said, "Eyuh."

Caitlin laughed. "Is that all you have to say? 'Eyuh?'"

He nodded. "Eyuh."

For a long while they stared at the sea in silence. Finally, Freddy turned to her and said, "Guess I'll be needing some groceries. You?"

"Yes. I've run out of some things."

"Basket's not big enough," said Freddy pointing his pipe at the bicycle leaning against the wall of Caitlin's cottage.

Caitlin looked at the bike. It came with the cottage and, though it was a modern mountain bike, it sported on the handle bars the kind of basket reminiscent of a half century ago. Though she'd used it several times, it limited what she could purchase. "No, I guess not."

"I'll drive you in."

"That's very kind of you."

"We'll sit here, enjoy the coffee for a while, watch the sea. Then we'll go."

Fifteen minutes later they pulled out of the driveway and headed toward town. Keeping one eye on the road, Freddy turned toward Caitlin with a mischievous smile and asked if he could buy her breakfast. "Be fun. Cause a flap, me with a younger woman." He gave a quick, impish chuckle. "Gladys Fludd—she's the wife of Morgan, the ferry captain—will have a field day with it."

Pauline's Coffee and Bake Shop was a small one-story building nestled between a drugstore and a clothing store featuring vacation wear. Freddy held the door for Caitlin and she entered an embrace of pleasing smells—bread, sweet rolls, and other things baking. And there was brewing coffee. She also recognized the sweet aroma of chocolate chip cookies. Of the five tables, four were occupied. Most of the round stools at the counter were empty, revealing the splits and cracks in the plastic covering the seats. The tiled floor was faded, evidence of countless days when salt water dripped in puddles from the foul weather gear of the lobstermen and fishermen.

As Freddy guided Caitlin to the one free table, the people at the other tables greeted him by name. They gave a wary smile to Caitlin. Morgan Fludd, in particular, shot Freddy an eyebrow-raised look and a teasing smile, his eyes dancing in his round, yeasty face.

Freddy asked another man with at least two days of stubble, "How they crawlin', Walter?"

"Ain't," the man replied. He wore yellow slicker pants supported by crossed suspenders.

"How come you ain't out there? Ernie Botham and Burle Ledyard went out bright an' early," said Freddy.

Several men nodded, saying, "Eyuh."

Wayne Crenshaw, who owned the marina, said, "Always the first ones at the gas pump, poor Ernie Botham and Burle Ledyard."

"Eyuh, always the first," said his son, Jasper Crenshaw, a young man with shifting eyes.

"They sound like hard workers," Caitlin said.

Jasper Crenshaw gave Caitlin a suspicious glance. "Who are you?"

"Now, son, that ain't polite," said his father. "Behave yourself."

Jasper's expression turned to a sulk, but he said nothing. He turned and looked out the window. Caitlin thought he had the vacant expression of a cat who looks into the distance to locate an itch in its tail.

"I'm Caitlin Gray," she said, but he gave no response.

O'zalik Moseley approached the table. "How're you doing, Freddy?" she asked as she placed knives, forks, and spoons wrapped together in a paper napkin before them. She turned the coffee cups that were already on the table right-side up.

"Gettin older."

"Oh, stop your complaining," O'zalik said softly with a warm smile. "You'll outlive us all."

Freddy turned to Caitlin. "This here is O'zalik Tomah. She's always like this—just slightly ironic." He emphasized the long "i" sound. He turned to O'zalik who was pouring coffee for them. "This here is Caitlin Gray. She's from Boston and has been staying at Jimmy's cottage to do some writing."

Caitlin wondered why Freddy gave Tomah as the woman's last name. She thought it was Moseley.

O'zalik flashed a smile at Caitlin. Her teeth, set against her light-mahogany skin, sparkled white. "So, you're a writer?"

"I try."

"I can't write worth shit. Never could." O'zalik pulled an order pad from her apron. "Think you could teach me?"

Caitlin hesitated. She was reluctant to commit herself, but O'zalik fascinated her. How could she, of all people, refuse someone's desire to write? The woman reminded her of herself, and she felt an instant bond. "I'd be happy to," she said. "Just let me get settled a little, okay?"

O'zalik beamed. "Sure. When do you want to start?"

"I…I don't know."

"Anytime's okay with me. Next month, maybe?"

O'zalik's persistence charmed Caitlin. All the same, she had to remind herself why she came to the island. "I want to do some of my own writing first."

"No problem. I can wait."

Freddy said, "Ain't the time to ask for favors, O'zalik. Woman's only been here a few weeks or so."

"Okay, okay, Freddy. I said I'd wait. Just thought I'd ask."

"Well, you did your asking. Now bring me my usual and bring Mrs. Gray, here, whatever she wants." He turned to Caitlin. "I'd recommend a scrid o' their hash browns, too."

Caitlin ordered two eggs sunny-side up. O'zalik turned and disappeared through a swinging door into the kitchen. As the door swung inward, Caitlin saw Quentin Moseley working at a grill. The man looked over his shoulder at her.

While she waited, Caitlin amused herself listening to Freddy banter with everybody in the room. It was good to be among people; her solitude had begun to weigh heavily on her.

Moments later, O'zalik returned. She set a plate down before Caitlin. One of the eggs was cooked just right; the yolk on the other egg had broken. "One eye opened, one eye closed," O'zalik said without apology.

"That's okay," replied Caitlin. But O'zalik was already placing Freddy's pancakes before him. "And listen, I'd be happy to talk with you about writing sometime."

O'zalik's face brightened. "I'll take you up on that," she said. "You can be sure of it."

Caitlin and Freddy ate mostly in silence. They were almost finished when Quentin Moseley burst in from the kitchen through the swinging doors. He gave Freddy a nod, threw a quick glance at Caitlin, and went up to O'zalik. He whispered something into her ear and she followed him back into the kitchen. Within moments, Caitlin heard him shouting.

Freddy gave a sad shake of his head.

"I wonder why they stay together if they don't get along?" asked Caitlin.

"Man's always jumpin' down her throat like that. Ever since his pa died." Freddy slid his chair back, stood, and said, "Eyuh, be trouble something awful between them two some day. Mark my words."

"She seems unhappy."

"Eyuh, suppose so. Don't think she feels much like she belongs here, her being Passamaquoddy and all."

"And living with that man Quentin can't be much fun either."

"You got that right. Man's a zero. Funny, though, sometimes she seems happy as can be and other times she's downright sad. Can't never predict her moods."

They arrived at the market. After Caitlin filled a shopping cart with groceries and paid for them, Freddy helped her load them into the pickup. As they drove back toward her cottage, they made small talk about the island people and especially about Quentin and O'zalik. Finally, Caitlin asked, "Tell me about the Spruce Cove Inn. I notice it's still in operation."

Freddy gave her an quizzical look. "You mean Gertie Webster's place?" He paused. "That's right, I forgot—you been here before."

"A long time ago."

"Eyuh. Well, she's long gone, same as a lot of folks. Her son's running the place."

"Oh, her son. Ah…"

"Garret's his name."

She felt a slight breathlessness. "The inn is a big place. Surely he doesn't run it by himself?" she asked.

"He has help."

"His wife?"

"Ain't married," Freddy replied. "Has a few widows working for him and in the summer gets some college girls to help out. O'zalik also does some work there."

"I see. Was he ever married?" she asked, trying to make it sound as casual as possible.

"Not that I recollect."

Five minutes later, they pulled up to the cottages. Freddy helped Caitlin carry the groceries into the kitchen then, saying it was time for his morning nap, left. Caitlin set a kettle of water on the stove and lit the burner. After storing the groceries, she made a cup of tea, started up her computer, and sat down for a morning of writing.

She stared out the window. Much of String of Pearls was exposed now, only the middle section was roiled by row after row of shallow waves breaking over it. It glittered in the diffuse sunlight. Overhead, a gossamer-thin sheet of clouds made for a scumbling sky.

When she first arrived, it surprised her that Garret Webster was still on the island after twenty-seven years. She wondered why he never married; whether he'd remember their times together. Of course, he would, she thought. People don't forget that kind of thing. But would he remember the good times they had or the hostility that had grown between them after he caught her looking at his sketchbook? And the real question was, would she dare go over to the Spruce Cove Inn and reintroduce herself? Wouldn't that, in a way, be a kind of betrayal of Nigel? And did that matter?

cavatina ekaterina

She scrolled down to the last fragment of the poem.

A woman wallows in the depths
where the light puddles...

~

Snores told O'zalik that Quentin was asleep in their bedroom. She rose from the sofa. She had begun sleeping there months ago. Slowly opening the screen door so not to make a noise, she went out of the house and down the road to where it intersected with Front Street. She turned left, went to a bench on the pier at Crenshaw Marina. A large security spotlight flooded the area with light. Halyards slapped softly against the aluminum masts of the dozen or so sailboats in the harbor. Masthead lights freckled the sky, blending with the sprinkle of stars overhead. A soft breeze ruffled her hair. She thought of the Jesuit's journal and tried to imagine how she would write an article about it.

My mission reduced to saving but few families from among the many Acadians living in Grand Pré, I set out on the first day of December in the year of our Lord 1755, from a hiding place near the village where I had gathered three families of Faithful and an escort of twelve Mi'kmaq.

The Faithful, being the families of Messrs. Babineau and Leclair and now including the poor, fatherless family of Madame Plamondon, have been for these several months past sheltered from the dreadful English by me and my most wonderful Christian Savages. Since September when Governor Lawrence's perfidious Deportation Order was read to the poor Faithful, families have continued to be split apart. Men, and in some cases even women and children, have been murdered by the reprobate English who think not of Christian virtues or of the compassion of Jesus but only of the land they now confiscate from the original Catholic settlers. They have been burning all the homes and barns of the Catholic Faithful. Even churches have fallen to the torch. Almost every night of our seclusion among the Savages we could perceive the reddish glow from raging fires. It is like an apparition of Hades. It put me in mind of the passage from Revelation in which it is said that after a thousand years in the pit the devil will be loosed a little season.

There are with the vicious English some two thousand troops from Massachusetts and these men have caused untold grief to the Faithful. Madame Plamondon had the misfortune, since there was no man in the house, of being required to board a certain Captain Webster who violated her purity and made her his concubine much against her Catholic will. But it seems Roger Plamondon, Madame Plamondon's husband, who died in prison at the hands of the diabolical English, was well liked by the Mi'kmaq and when they learned of the defilement of Madame Plamondon, they resolved to avenge her by dispatching Captain Webster to his Judgment. They accomplished their noble deed by slipping into Grand Pré in the middle of the night and making their way to Madame Plamondon's house. There, while Captain Webster slept, they spirited Madame Plamondon away then returned to cut the captain's throat. It is truly unfortunate they thought it necessary to return with his scalp as proof of their deed. I have tried to instruct them against this brutish practice, but they insist it is a just reward for every fiendish Englishman who participates in the great theft of Mi'kmaki which is their word for Acadie.

Of the Faithful, altogether there are twelve, they being Aristide Babineau; his wife and three children, a boy aged five, and two girls aged seven, and six; his elderly mother; Jean Baptiste Leclair; his wife (childless); his father, August Leclair; and finally Madame Plamondon and her two children of which one a boy aged fifteen and one a girl aged twelve.

The band of Christian Savages now numbered ten after their brothers returned north. Their sakom is Edmond of previous mention. The eight other Mi'kmaq all have proper Christian names.

After prayers, we left in the middle of the night. Our immediate plan was to make our way to the canoes waiting for us on the shore of Bassin des Mines and be past Cap Fendu (Cape Split—R.B.) *by first light. Edmond told me we would be accompanied on our journey by the voice of the moon singing loudly. When I asked what he meant, he only smiled and said I would see soon enough. This proclivity the Savages have for sport is often vexing.*

The canoes (in number, five) were waiting for us exactly as promised by Edmond. A spirited discussion began concerning the allocation of people to canoes but, seeing there was no time to waste if we were to use the outflowing tide of Bassin des Mines, I was forced to assert my authority as leader—and as man of God—and make the assignments myself. Of course with five canoes and ten Savages, I had already determined there would be two Savages per canoe. This was necessary because of the skill required to negotiate the turbulent waters on which we were about to embark, especially around Cap Fendu. Then, to assure decisions were made in one place only, I assigned myself to the canoe paddled by Edmond. It would not do to have Edmond making choices without my immediate supervision. As for the rest, and in the spirit of Christian compassion, I endeavored to keep families together as much as possible. Only in three instances was this not possible. The Babineaus, obviously, were too numerous to keep together so I distributed them among two canoes. Guy

Plamondon, a young man aged fifteen, made it clear to me he did not want to travel with his mother (having, unfortunately, witnessed one of her liaisons, however unwilling, with Captain Webster) so I assigned him to the second canoe in file after mine. Since Madame Plamondon and her daughter, a winsome young girl of twelve named Lisette, were to travel in my canoe, this arrangement kept them as close as possible while still honoring the young man's wishes. And finally, I prevailed upon Auguste Leclair, Jean Baptiste Leclair's father, to travel with the young Mr. Plamondon. In that way, the old man would be in a position to curb the young man's anger, and the young man would be in a position to assist the old man who had difficulty getting about.

The moon was nearly full when we took to the waters. My children, the Passamaquoddy Indians to whom we were going, call this moon of December "Punam" or the frost-fish moon. The waters upon which we embarked had a strange appearance, like diluted blood, caused by the churning up of red soil by the extraordinary tides and the turbulence they create. In the Bassin des Mines the tides can rise as much as sixteen meters so one can only imagine the ferocity with which the water flows in and out of the small opening at Cap Fendu. Especially with the sun and the moon in alignment as they would be, the difference between the tides would be greatest, making for even faster currents. (He of course is describing a spring tide, the term for which in French is "marée de vive eau." However, in his text he used the term "marée de morte eau" which is the opposite, i.e., a neap tide. I have made the assumption that his description is correct and only his knowledge of oceanographic terms is faulty—R.B.) *With such an inflow and outflow of water, the currents can reach eight knots which is why ships and boats tend to avoid this passage and which, in turn, is why we chose it as we were unlikely to be spotted. But it would require all the skills of the Savages to keep us from disaster.*

As we paddled quietly into the basin, "Punam" lit the waters with a heavenly radiance. Soon, I heard a strange roar unlike anything I had ever heard. I turned to Edmond and asked what it was. He laughed, saying it was the "voice of the moon." In fact, it was a roar made by the rushing water which, being drawn, of course, by the moon, made the phrase an apt one indeed. Nonetheless, it is an example of the infuriating superstitions of my Savage children.

To our chagrin, it was not the only sound we heard that night. Above the roar, we heard the gush of a leviathan exhaling mist from his blow-hole. He came as a great shadowy bulk, moving slowly past us, and sending his terrible vapor high into the air. He was so close we could even smell the horrible stench of his breath, and we were terrified. I made the sign of the cross and uttered praise for the Lord, for this leviathan was truly one of His great creations and, as the Lord said to Job, "so great is this beast that we had not the power to put a hook into his nose or bore his jaw through with a thorn. Nor could we imagine he would make many supplications unto us, nor speak soft words unto us." That said, I was moved to imagine his gush of breath as his word and it was like the equally malodorous English. As he passed, his great eye beheld us and at the sight of it we trembled. Josette and Georges Babineau, ensconced in the fourth canoe with Madame Babineau and being of the ages five and six, cried fearfully and could only be quieted after long moments in their mother's arms.

We paddled on, moving ever more swiftly as the current gained speed. At last, as a first hint of light appeared like a blessing from God, we slid past Cap Fendu. By now, the current was weakening and preparing for its reversal so we turned the canoes across the current and toward shore where we would hide for the day. It was imperative we make the shore because once the current reversed itself we would be drawn irresistibly back into Bassin des Mines in broad daylight. Venus and Jupiter were both low in the southeast sky and, with the first light of dawn, Mercury rose above the horizon. Truly, God's Heavenly acolytes were witness to our travails.

The lead canoe (in which I traveled) was nearly to the shore when we heard a fearsome cry. We looked to see one of the canoes upended and its hapless occupants flailing for their very lives. Leviathan raised his flukes from the water like the great hand of God and brought them down again on the poor, desperate innocents. Moving swiftly and with great God-given energy, Edmond and the other Savage paddled furiously toward the victims. I implored the Lord to have mercy on us and took Madame Plamondon in my arms and comforted her since she feared the distressed canoe was the very one in which her son was riding. She trembled in my arms and told me her son, Guy, could not swim. When we arrived at the scene of the catastrophe, we found only Baptiste and Auguste Leclair. Guy Plamondon and the other Savage were nowhere to be seen. Baptiste had a severe laceration on his head where the splintered canoe had apparently struck him. Nevertheless, he held Monsieur Leclair under the arms thus preventing him from sinking into the abyss while his own blood dissipated into the water. Monsieur Leclair struggled, it seemed unreasonably (until we later learned the source of his distress). Of Guy Plamondon, alas, there was no sign. Madame Plamondon, driven mad by grief, plunged into the turbulent waters in an effort to find her cherished son while her daughter, Lisette, wailed in agony and fear and called for her mother to return to the canoe. Valiant Edmond leapt from the canoe, causing it to rock fearfully, and swam after Madame Plamondon. With his superior strength—she being of course a weak female—he brought her back to our canoe. He did not try to lift her aboard but instead held onto her with one arm while he grabbed the stern of the canoe with the other. He instructed Baptiste to do likewise with Monsieur Leclair and the canoe which carried Jean-Baptiste Leclair and his wife. The two Savages started to kick their legs and, with the help of the paddlers (I, myself, had assumed Edmond's paddle), propelled the canoes toward the shore.

Immediately upon arriving, and despite the great risk of being discovered, we made a fire. The souls who had been immersed were suffering greatly from the cold and, unless we warmed them quickly, there was more than a small possibility they would die of the chill. Those of us males who had remained dry vigorously rubbed the naked bodies of the victims to restore their circulation while Mesdames Babineau and Leclair, Grandmère Babineau, and the girl children remained at a discreet distance, drying Madame Plamondon and the unfortunate victims' clothes.

The Savages and Madame Plamondon recovered quickly, but it was another matter for Auguste Leclair. His advanced age nearly did him in and it was, I am convinced, only my prayerful intercession with our Lord which returned the old man to the living. When at last he had recovered, Monsieur Leclair allowed as he was in the process of rescuing Guy Plamondon when he lost his grip on the hapless, struggling boy. He was about to dive beneath the surface to resume his rescue attempt when Baptiste, over his vigorous protestations, grabbed onto him. It was only after hearing this that we understood why he had struggled so in the stronger Baptiste's arms and why he told his story with tears of frustration staining his cheeks. He apologized to me, saying I had placed him with the boy to be of aid and he had failed in his charge. I assured him he did all that was possible and that God had ordained it was time for the boy to return to His Glory and there was nothing we mere mortal men could do about it. We cannot expect to be saints.

Madame Plamondon, of course, was inconsolable. She wept softly throughout the requiem service I performed for poor Guy Plamondon.

We were a dispirited group as we hid among the rocks and waited for the sun to complete its circuit so we could be off again. Edmond said when the legs of the Boy Spirit sank in the northwest sky, we would have to move out again if we were to keep to our plan. He pointed to the stars and I saw he was referring to the constellation Cygne (Cygnus or the Northern Cross—R.B.) *I wondered if he chose that constellation, the Boy Spirit, because of what happened to Guy Plamondon or if it were an entirely circumstantial choice. I decided it was God who had put the idea into the Savage's head, for God ordains everything and derives, it seems, great satisfaction from providing us with an abundance of meaningful signs.*

Thus it was, with tired bodies and vexed spirits, we witnessed the majesty of God's ever-revolving firmament. Orion rose in the east and chased the full moon westward while Cygne slid foot first toward the northwestern horizon, signaling the continuation of our forlorn journey.

Shortly before we were to depart, the stars became obscured and a new worry came to me. Would the weather turn against us?

Only that morning Jolene Baxter—the owner and publisher of the *Island Gazette*—asked O'zalik again about the article, causing a wave of anxiety to surge in her. It was always the same when she was faced with the prospect of having to write something. The words simply wouldn't come. It was that way all through school. She saw no reason why it should be different now. Despite Jolene Baxter's encouragement and the obligation she felt to share Father Dalou's story, she wasn't sure she could do it. She already had procrastinated several days.

~

Freddy eased his body out of bed with an enthusiasm he hadn't felt in a very long time and made his way to the bathroom. Usually he waited until midday to shave—that is, if he shaved at all—but this morning he filled the sink with hot water, lathered his face, pulled out his Gillette, and with careful strokes shaved away the stubble. After rinsing off the remaining lather and drying his face, he brushed the back of his hand upward against the grain of his whiskers to test his work. It was something Agnes always did after nuzzling his neck. She said she loved the smell of his shaving soap. Of course, that was before her decline.

In recent days he and Caitlin Gray had spent much time together and he found her conversation both fascinating and entertaining. He wasn't used to so much talking—certainly not since Agnes died—and it surprised him how much he enjoyed it. And Caitlin also seemed to enjoy their conversations. At least, most of the time. Some days, she clearly preferred to be by herself and he was too much of a gentleman not to respect her wishes. So far, he wasn't quite able to predict which days she would appear on his porch and which days she would rather be left alone. But as long as he was going to make a full pot of coffee, he might as well make a good one. Just in case.

Freddy went into the kitchen. He glanced out the window toward Jimmy's cottage. There was no sign of activity. Feeling the chill of the kitchen tiles on his bare feet, he crossed to the refrigerator. He was reminded of the time he and Agnes decided to replace the old, worn-out, curling-at-the-edges linoleum floor with hand-laid tile. He thought it extravagant at the time, even more so when they took the ferry to the mainland and went into a building supply store and he learned just exactly what Agnes had in mind. Despite his protests that it was too expensive, Agnes stubbornly insisted on imported Italian tiles. And after they were laid in the kitchen by old Elwood Palmer, who was good at that sort of thing, Freddy had to admit they looked wonderful. He was so pleased with them, in fact, that he took to walking around the kitchen without his slippers except on the coldest of winter days.

As he opened the refrigerator, he tried to remember how long it was since Elwood Palmer died. It was before Agnes, he knew, because he could remember going to his wake and funeral with her. But how long before? It was getting more and more difficult to remember such things.

He pulled out the bag of French Roast beans he'd bought the day before at the Island Market. It had been years since he'd bothered grinding coffee beans fresh, preferring instead to use preground simply because it was quicker. But there was a definite difference in the freshness.

After grinding the beans and starting the coffeemaker, he turned on the weather radio. It was a necessary habit, a ritual, even if it always stirred up a familiar anger—an indignation at having outlived his wife and his son. And, with it, a generous amount of guilt. Had he not overslept that day, twenty-five years before, because he'd spent half the night caring for Agnes who was fighting a bout of pneumonia; had he, knowing the radio on the boat was broken, turned the home weather radio on; he would have been able to warn Jimmy if there was rough weather on George's Bank before his son left the dock.

The news hurt Agnes deeply. And, although she recovered from her pneumonia, she was never quite the same again. In a way, Freddy felt he lost the two people he loved in this world at the same time. Jimmy's death made Agnes old and ill and that was part of the bargain,

Freddy supposed. Nothing good ever happened. The minister had said that's what life sometimes hands out. But Jimmy? So young? It left Freddy with an ever-present dry taste of anger. A hatred for anything that would allow it to happen. A hatred that was always stirred up when he looked at String of Pearls or Snagged Anchor Island.

Jimmy's memorial service was the last time Freddy stepped inside a church except for funerals. Regular churchgoing had been mostly Agnes' idea anyway. It was also the last time he'd seen his grandchildren. Shortly after the service, Jimmy's wife, Diana, said she could no longer live on Alabaster Island and she took little Jimmy Junior and Catherine away. Only once since had he seen his daughter-in-law. At Agnes' funeral. She hadn't brought the children with her.

When Jimmy died and when Agnes died it was as though his soul was being varnished all over again. This time with the varnish of bitterness. Only occasional letters and rare visits from Miesko Heilprin helped.

Shortly after the war, he'd managed to track down Miesko at Feldafing, a displaced persons camp southwest of Munich and not far from Dachau. He gave Miesko enough money to travel to the United States on the promise the boy use the money only for that purpose. When he returned stateside, he arranged a job for Miesko, a necessary condition for sponsoring his immigration. It took almost a year, but eventually he was able to send for him. In the meantime, he'd located relatives of Miesko in New York, so when the boy arrived, Freddy drove him to the city. Once there and settled, Miesko, who attended a Talmud Torah at Feldafing, continued his studies, eventually becoming a rabbi.

Over the years, and with Miesko's help, the varnish peeled away from Freddy's soul layer by layer. All the same, the deepest layers were still there and they had grown hard, brittle, cracked. But even these recently started to peel away, leaving raw spots for which Caitlin's companionship promised to be a balm.

In the bedroom he unscrewed the cap from the bottle of Fidji by Guy Laroche. He sniffed and vague memories of Agnes came to him.

It saddened him, though, that the memories became weaker over time.

The coffeemaker beeped the end of its brewing. He strode into the kitchen, screwing the cap onto the perfume bottle as he went. He placed it on the table and poured a cup of coffee. He went out onto the porch just in time for sunrise. The sky was clear. A half arch of sun rose from the horizon. There was no sign of the fog mentioned on the weather radio.

~

Caitlin woke to the squawk of the marine forecast floating across the narrow gap between the cottages. She looked at her watch; it was already seven-thirty, two hours later than she was accustomed to getting up. She attributed it to the insomnia that kept her fidgeting under the blankets for several hours between midnight and sometime in the darkness of early morning. She rose, went to the bathroom, made a cup of instant coffee and, clutching its warmth between her palms, stepped barefoot onto the grass to look at the water. There was a slight, pleasing chill to the dew-soaked grass. In the distance, she heard the insane laughter of a loon. And, closer at hand, came the melodious plaint of a mourning dove—*ooAHH-coo-coo-coo*—which Nigel always said sounded like "Oh, no! Please don't go."

jeremy miller

The ambulance had rushed the boy to the Newton-Wellesley Hospital. After answering questions for the police and giving them her phone number, she'd driven to the hospital. She found the parents in the waiting room, told them she was the driver. They stared at her for a long moment before the father said, "It was good of you to come. Not many people would do that."

"How is he?" she asked, afraid of the answer.

"They're still in there," the father said, nodding toward the ER. He extended his hand. "My name's Adam Miller. This is my wife, Sally.

She told them her name.

Sally Miller's parents arrived. After they hugged Sally and Adam, they looked at Caitlin. Adam told them she'd been the driver and how courageous it was of her to come to the hospital. They nodded coolly.

A half hour later, a doctor emerged, slipping his rubber gloves off. "We did everything we could," the doctor said.

Sally Miller collapsed into a chair. Her husband sat beside her and held her.

Caitlin said, "Oh God, I'm so sorry."

Sally Miller's father said, "You took our Jeremy from us."

you took our jeremy from us

Although a scrim of fog obscured the horizon, Snagged Anchor Island was plainly visible, a sash of mist around its midsection. String of Pearls was completely covered, giving no indication of its existence save for the exposed outcroppings of Big Pearl and Little Pearl. Water rose and fell easily around their wrack-skirted bases, a rhythm like breathing. The sunlight was angled too low to ignite the mica imbedded in the granite, so the Pearls appeared dull in their sea-green surroundings, as filled with an unfilled potential for glistening as jewels in a tomb. As she gazed at them, she heard a rhythmic creak coming from Freddy Orcutt's back porch and realized his rocking was precisely synchronized to the sea swells at the base of the pearls—three slow rocks to every swell. Waltz time. She wondered if it were intentional.

She decided to go over and say "Hi." As she mounted the stairs, she gave a cough to alert him to her presence. Apparently he didn't hear her, for he continued to rock, staring out to sea.

"Good morning, Freddy," Caitlin said softly. Freddy glanced over his shoulder at her. She saw a hard look on his face. Feeling a surge of embarrassment, she said, "I'm sorry. I'm interrupting you," and turned to go back to her own cottage.

She got to the bottom of the stairs before he said, "No bother. Was just thinking of them that's gone."

"Your wife?"

There was a long pause before he said, "Eyuh..."

"I do apologize. You'd like to be alone."

She turned again, but he said, "… and my son, Jimmy—"

"I see."

"—and them that's goin', like Ernie Botham. Just saw him and Burle Ledyard out there."

Caitlin was unsure what to say. She waited, silent. At last, Freddy rose and, heading for the kitchen door, said, "Coffee's hot. Want some?"

She held out her cup. "Already have some," she said with a smile.

"Instant?"

"Yes."

"I have freshly ground coffee," he said, reaching for her cup.

She released the cup. "Yes…sure, that sounds wonderful."

He hurled the cup's contents over the railing. She watched him go into his kitchen. He was wearing hiking shorts and she noted how fit his old legs appeared. A moment after he disappeared inside, she heard him blow his nose several times. While she waited, she listened to the marine forecast.

…heavy fog extending from George's Bank north to Cape Sable. Visibility generally a mile, down to half a mile or less in areas of greater density.

From her previous visit she knew of such days—many of them—when the Labrador current would mix with warm air to produce nearly impenetrable fog that rolled in from the ocean to swallow Snagged Anchor Island, String of Pearls, and the far shore of Spruce Cove. The islanders would feel they were in the cold, soupy, big-bellied embrace of a higher power. On such days, the beam from Sheep's Pasture Light would appear as a faint blooming in the undifferentiated gray curtain. Lobstermen and fishermen would feel their way out of Spruce Cove on years of experience and mumbled prayers, sounding their foghorns to alert others of their presence, to persuade each other their solitude was only illusory. It was a condition of life at the murky margin between land and sea.

She looked up at the sky. Two vapor trails, airplanes too high to hear, stretched across the sky northeast to southwest. The end of the trails were already shredding, but at their leading ends she saw bright flashes moving across the sky, the low sun reflecting off aluminum fuselages. Planes coming in from Europe to Boston or New York.

"Fog's out to sea," Freddy said when he returned with the cups of coffee. He handed Caitlin her cup. "Careful now, it's awful hot." He sank heavily into his rocker.

As they sat staring out over the water, Caitlin said, "Last night the reef was exposed for nearly its entire length out to Snagged Anchor Island. Is it ever completely exposed?" She watched three seagulls tracing spirals of flight, screeching "kreee, kreee."

"Eyuh. In two days it'll be spring tide. Be high and dry then."

"Spring tide?"

"Ain't got nothing to do with the season. It's a tide happens after a new moon or a full moon when the difference between low and high water is greatest. Around here, that's 'bout fourteen feet or so." He paused as if recovering from such a long speech. "Then, there's a *perigean* spring tide..." He emphasized every syllable, smiling as though the word—and his command of it—gave him a special pleasure. "That's when a spring tide occurs because the moon is closest to the earth in its orbit. When a spring tide happens, you can walk out to Snagged Anchor Island."

"What's out there?"

Freddy shrugged. His countenance turned dark. "Been there only a couple times, long time ago. Some say they've seen shearwaters fly to the island. Claim there's a nest there. But I think it's only a legend. Almost never see a shearwater at the coast; it's a bird for the open ocean." After a long pause Freddy said, "... and maybe the remains of some Passamaquoddy."

"What?"

"Over there, on the island. Passamaquoddy remains. At least, that's what O'zalik thinks."

"You don't think it's true?"

"Don't know one way or the other."

"Hasn't anybody searched?"

"O'zalik keeps talking about it but she always runs up against Garret Webster."

"What's he got to do with it?"

"Owns the island," Freddy replied. "Doesn't want people going out there and disturbing it."

That didn't seem to Caitlin a good enough reason to prevent what could be an important find. Her old interest in archaeology surfaced. "I'd like to go out over the reef and see for myself," Caitlin said. "You say I can do that the day after tomorrow?"

"You can do it, but I wouldn't advise it."

"Why?"

"Dangerous. Something awful. As low as the water gets at low tide, it's also higher than usual at high tide. It's what's *meant* by a spring tide." He looked at her with an intense expression. "Few summers back a boy drowned on String of Pearls. Parents warn't watchin' good enough. Went on out and got trapped when the tide changed. Same as happened to others, too. Many others."

"It must have been awful for the parents."

Freddy said nothing, just nodded slightly with that dark expression. "It maybe also happened to a young girl some time ago. Twenty-five years...'bout the same time Jimmy died."

"That was only two years after I was on the island. Why do you say maybe?"

"Big mystery. Never found the body. Just disappeared. Possible the currents took her out to sea. Garret Webster found a girl's sneaker lodged in a crack on Big Pearl. We had a big search party."

"Did you go?"

"Eyuh. That was the one time I been out there. Don't want nothing to do with the place, elsewise. We split up into a bunch of different two-man search parties. Found nothing 'cepting that sneaker."

Caitlin placed the coffee on the wicker table between them. "So you figure they got swept out to sea?"

Freddy nodded. "The way I see it is the reef got them like it's got too many others…The damned inrushing tide; that's the way people disappear around here." His words seemed to come with great effort.

Caitlin saw the hard look she'd seen earlier return to his eyes. She'd been told they never found Jimmy Orcutt's body. She wondered if the disappearances were related but decided it wasn't a good question to put to Freddy.

"Snagged Anchor Island. Ain't nothing good ever happened out there," Freddy said. "Ain't even a good place for whales. They beach there like it's something irresistible. Stinks to high heaven. Ain't nothing but evil out there."

But regardless of what Freddy said, Snagged Anchor Island held a strange attraction for Caitlin. She tried to judge how long it would take to walk the length of the reef and back.

"Besides," Freddy said, continuing to stare out at the reef. "There's the ghosts."

Caitlin glanced at him. "Ghosts?"

"Eyuh, the Passamaquoddy ghosts, maybe…others."

Caitlin tested the coffee again. Still too hot. She took a careful sip and returned it to the small, round table. "Surely, Freddy, you don't believe in ghosts."

Freddy nodded toward Snagged Anchor Island. "Ghosts are out there," he said matter-of-factly. "It's another reason nobody ever goes out there."

Caitlin gave a tolerant smile.

After a few moments Freddy said, "Jimmy's wife—she ain't never called. Ain't heard from little Jimmy Junior and Catherine in a long time. They're in their twenties now."

"Do you try to contact them?"

He remained silent for a while before finally saying, "Well, no use chatting all day. Got to spread some fertilizer."

Caitlin had seen the small, rectangular garden plot out back. "Can I help?"

"Don't see why not."

They spent the next hour spreading wrack weed Freddy had gathered from the shore at low tide.

After a long silence Caitlin asked, "Really? Ghosts on Snagged Anchor Island?"

"Eyuh."

Caitlin enjoyed the earthy smell of the wrack weed she spread with a hoe. It was a fetid smell hinting at the wildness of life at the boundary between ocean and land. She thought of how, here, in Downeast Maine, the sea plays with the land as a cat plays with a mouse—full of fun…and finality.

When they finished spreading the wrack weed and returned to the porch, Freddy said, "Got lemonade in the 'frigerator. Want some?"

"Sounds great. You put the tools away, and I'll get the lemonade." Caitlin went into the kitchen. When she emerged a few minutes later with two tall glasses of lemonade, she said, "There's a bottle of perfume on your kitchen table."

Freddy looked at her. "Eyuh."

"Your wife's?"

Freddy nodded.

"It must be pretty weak by now."

He frowned. "How's that?"

"Fragrances rest in a base of volatile oils. Over the years they break down, lose their potency." She wasn't sure she should be saying this; she could only guess what significance the perfume held for Freddy. But instinct told her he already was aware the scent was fading. Indeed, maybe there was no scent left at all, only the memory of it. Maybe if he knew the reason, it would be better.

"Is that the case?"

"I'm afraid so. I guess nothing lasts forever." She handed him a glass of lemonade. The ice clinked against the side.

Freddy stared at the lemonade for a moment then said, "Nope. Guess not."

~

In our silent canoes—silent, save for the rhythmic splash of the paddles—we were no more than two hours into the continuation of our grim journey when the snow started. I feared with the loss of the stars to guide us we would be unable to find our way, but Edmond assured me we would have no problem. He told me although it is true the Savages are superb navigators who use their great knowledge of the heavens to guide them, they are equally good seamen who could employ the set of the waves, the angle and smell of the wind, and the feel of the current to obtain assurance of their course. I regarded this boast with some skepticism as the Savages have a habit of trying to please me, yet there was no choice in the matter but to trust him.

God sends trials to test us and to make us stronger in our Faith. The trial He now deemed fit to send us came in the form of an increasing snow storm and a howling wind. The snow was more like minute pinpricks of ice, so bitterly did it sting our skin. It became difficult to keep all the canoes in sight. Along with the growing waves which were encouraged by the wind, the poor visibility threatened to separate our party. We were forced to use shouts to stay in contact, a method which caused me great trepidation since I knew not how close to the shore (and thus to the debauched English) we might be. By my best guess, we were not far off Port Royal (Annapolis Royal by the time of this narrative—R.B.) *where, according to my latest information, a sizable contingent of degenerate Englishmen and their Massachusetts cohorts reside. I was even more alarmed when Edmond stopped the canoe and, after sniffing the air and trailing his hand in the water, confirmed my suspicions. Speaking softly, Edmond told me we must stop paddling and allow the current to carry us away from danger.*

It was less than an hour later when we faintly heard ugly English voices, confirming our worst fears. Indeed, we were just off the coast near or at Port Royal. Furthermore, we were so close inshore that we were in danger of being caught up in a reverse eddy of the current and driven not to safety, but into the hands of the enemy. As silent as we were before, we became even more silent now. There came not a sound from the five canoes which, since we were drifting with the current, we had tied together in a column. I say no sound, however that is not entirely accurate. There was, of course, the continuing sound of the wind and the whisper of the snow crystals against our persons. But there was also another sound which caused me great distress. It was the ageless sound of a woman weeping softly. Several times I looked to see if it was the miserable Madame Plamondon. But she was utterly silent, indeed so silent it would be a wonder if she ever spoke again. I deduced the weeping must be coming from Madame Leclair, Madame Babineau, or Grandmère Babineau. I concluded it must be Madame Babineau since both Madame Leclair and Grandmère Babineau had adult males in the canoes with them who undoubtedly would have consoled them and, in the consoling, hush them. But though the canoes were tied together, I was unable to confirm my reasoning without causing a great stir that might have alerted the dissolute English to our presence. So I waited and prayed while the current carried us onward.

I say carried us onward, but I must also observe that our speed was becoming distressingly slow due to the imminent reversal of the tide. I calculated we had another hour left before we would be forced to make an encampment or be carried back along the hostile coast. Once again I raised my voice to merciful God in silent prayer that in His manifest blessings He would guide us to a safe haven where we could pass the following day. Fortunately, my prayers were answered when, just as the current went ominously slack, there was a brief cessation of the storm and the clouds parted for but a short time to reveal to us, by the light of the too long absent moon, a low, deserted shore. I was convinced by its appearance that it was the long, narrow arm which encloses the western side of Baye St Marie (Saint Mary's Bay—R.B.)

It was only when the last canoe touched the shore that my previous sus-

picions confirmed. It was, indeed, Madame Babineau who was weeping. She wept because she held the lifeless body of innocent Georges Babineau, all of five years old, in her lap in the same manner Mary once held the crucified and dead Jesus. I must confess that so wet were my eyes with tears, so overwhelmed with pity was I, that I raised my eyes to the moon, it having appeared for us like the veritable eye of God, and asked Him why he had caused this guiltless woman to suffer so and why he had taken so pure an innocent as little Georges (with whom I had often played in our days of seclusion among the Mi'kmaq). I asked Him (in a silent voice so as not to agitate the others whose weaker Faith might not have withstood so urgent a question) why in our most difficult of journeys, He had chosen to make it more difficult to the point of insufferability. Why does He make good people suffer so?

My imperiled soul, so placed at great risk by such a bold and defiant question, was shaken to its very core by what happened at that moment. For no sooner had I given voice to my question, than the clouds closed to obscure the moon once again. There can have been no clearer sign from God and I hastened to ask His forgiveness and to assure Him of my unquestioning Faith in His mysterious ways.

Madame Plamondon, herself inconsolable, consoled Madame Babineau.

The rest of our party of Christians, ourselves inconsolable, consoled the two, and we passed the hours of daylight and the reversed tide in that manner and without a fire to warm our chilled spirits. For, we knew, the enemy was close.

When she read again that last passage, O'zalik was shaken. Her eyes were wet with tears as she forced herself to sit down at her computer and try make a beginning for the article she had promised Jolene Baxter. But after more than an hour of trying, she slammed her fist on the table. Tears of frustration stained her cheeks. She had an image of her high school composition teacher, Mister Francis, standing above her with her latest attempt at an essay on Wabanaki land claims, and tsk-tsking. He had a way of doing it that both shamed and angered her. And not for that moment only, but permanently. She could never, after spending two painful years with that man, even think about writing without the thought bringing a shudder and a shiver of nausea to her.

It just wouldn't do. She could not write the article.

On the other hand, she owed it to Father Dalou and to the people he shepherded—and particularly to her Passamaquoddy ancestors—to tell their story. Especially knowing as she did from her first reading of the journal that, in the end, it bore so tellingly on the self-satisfied, upstanding people of Alabaster Island.

Of course, she could again offer Jolene Baxter the source manuscript as translated by Bob Blanchard. But Jolene had already made clear she didn't want that. "That would certainly be interesting to my readers," Jolene said. "But what interests me more is the story as told by *you*, someone we know, and with your point of view. I would like to see your take on it, the view of a modern day Native American. O'zalik, you also owe it to your people because it will help build better bridges of understanding between the Passamaquoddy and us Yankees. And, heaven knows, that's something that's needed around here."

O'zalik remembered what Caitlin Gray said—that she would be willing to work with her on her writing any time. All O'zalik had to do was ask. Well, O'zalik decided, she would ask all right, but it wouldn't be quite the question Caitlin was expecting.

madame plamondon, herself inconsolable, consoled madame babineau

~

fragrances rest in a base of volatile oils…over the years they break down

Freddy had not known that. When Caitlin mentioned it to him, his first reaction was one of anger. He'd felt she was intruding on his private memories. But after thinking about it, he decided she was only trying, in a subtle way, to tell him it was time to move on. And maybe she was right. Maybe he, himself, had been thinking the same thing. Isn't that why he almost agreed to sell Jimmy's cottage? But it was hard to give up something he'd lived with for so long; there was such a finality to it. Perhaps hanging on this long to the memory of Agnes…and of Jimmy…was unhealthy, even a bit strange, but it somehow comforted him and eased the burden of guilt. Agnes never wore the perfume after Jimmy's death, so every time he caught its fragrance, it brought him back to a time before everything began to fall apart. Now, Caitlin Gray had come along to upset the uneasy balance he'd made of his life and he wasn't sure he liked it. It wasn't only her comment about the perfume, it was also her company—the way her presence gave him pleasure, the way he had come to rely on her visits. As pleasant as her companionship was, he found it caused his grip on his memories to slip. But was he ready for that?

That morning an inflamed rim of sun blistered the horizon, a bubble of molten slag. It came with a cold rustle of wind that swept into Spruce Cove. Halyards chimed hollow in the harbor. Waves rasped at the reef, throwing columns of spume into the air. As Freddy watched, Ernie Botham and Burle Ledyard were bounced around in their boat as they plowed into the waves at the mouth of the cove. The islands were shrouded in mist.

Caitlin was outside waiting for him. The previous night they'd made plans to go to Pauline's for lunch. However, before leaving the cottage, he went into the bedroom and took the perfume bottle from the dresser. He had to test it, to see if he'd only been imagining the scent all these years. He lifted the bottle to his nose.

Only a faint trace.

He sat on the bed as a wave of sadness overwhelmed him. Then, with a deep sigh, he rose, got the keys to his truck, and went out to meet Caitlin.

over the years fragrances lose their potency

"I killed a little boy."

Freddy stared at Caitlin, unsure what to say. She'd asked if they could sit on his porch for a little while before going into town. The wind had died, leaving behind an annoyance of mosquitoes. He'd poured some lemonade and after she had a few sips, she said, "I killed a little boy. His name was Jeremy Miller."

"How did it happen?"

She told him.

After a long pause, Freddy said, "Ain't none of us are saints, Caitlin. Not a damned one of us. I killed some boys myself."

"You?"

"Eyuh."

"How? When?"

He'd gotten himself into a trap. Never once had he talked about it, not even to Agnes. He struggled to find a way to stop, to say nothing more, but once he uttered those words it was like a boil had been burst. It started to drain out of him and he couldn't stop it. "It was during the war."

"World War Two?"

"Eyuh."

"Aren't you too young to have been in the war?"

"Lied about my age. Lot's of us did. I don't know…guess 'cause we was eager to do some killing."

"But you can't hold that against yourself. Soldiers are supposed to—"

"It was a place called Dachau." He pronounced it the German way, as though expelling something toxic from his throat. He told her about their arrival at Dachau. "First thing we come to was this here train. It was stuffed with bodies. Lots of the cars was open gondolas and the bodies was piled up. Thousands of them. But not one was completely exposed; every body was partially buried by the snow like as if God was trying to hide something but ran out of snow. I threw up. Right there and then, I threw up. In all my years on the sea getting seasick I never threw up like that."

"Freddy, you don't have to—"

"But that warn't the worst of it. We went through a gate with a big German eagle. We saw piles of bodies outside the gas chamber—just so much human trash with no fat on their bones lying every which way on top of each other. And then there was the crematorium…"

He paused for a moment. He shuddered. His eyes were moist.

Caitlin remained silent.

"This German guy comes out to meet us all spic-and-span and wearing his decorations and saluting and saying, 'Heil Hitler.' The bastard. An officer spit in his face, called him a *Schweinhund.* Had him shot. Then we rounded up more than a hundred or so of the Germans—Waffen SS—the worst kind." He told her, haltingly, how they gunned the Germans down. "Then we gave some of the inmates pistols and shovels to finish off the ones who wasn't dead yet. We even shot the damned dogs. And that ain't the whole of it. We turned some of the German guards over to the inmates who stripped them and killed them with their bare hands. The place was the worst kind of death hell."

"God, Freddy…"

"And you wanna know what got me the worst? It was after the camp was liberated and the gas chamber and the crematorium was all shut up, more than a hundred inmates a day went right on dying. The war was over for them. They was liberated. But they kept right on dying. I figured it ain't right for them to die after they was liberated." For a long while he remained silent, staring out to mist-enshrouded Snagged Anchor Island. Finally, he said, "Ain't none of us are saints, Caitlin. Not a goddamned one of us." He felt tears slide down his cheeks.

Caitlin put a hand on his wrist. "It must be horrible to have such memories."

miesko

"There was a little Polish boy named Miesko. I gave him some food because he looked like he was gonna die, he was so starved. We couldn't speak each other's languages but I swear he could read my heart. Someone told me how his parents and his sisters died in the gas chambers and I tried to help him, to comfort him. But do you know what he done?"

"What, Freddy?"

"He starts to comfort me, goldang it. *Me*. With his eyes he says he saw how we shot them Germans and how it shook me up and he brushed his bony finger under my eyes to tell me not to cry no more because it was all over. It was all over." Freddy shuddered.

Caitlin squeezed his wrist. "Did Miesko make it?"

"Eyuh. Writes to me from time to time. He's a rabbi in New York. Speaks perfect English now, better'n me, even."

"I'm so happy."

"Came to Agnes's funeral. Miesko came to Agnes's funeral."

Caitlin said nothing.

"I ain't never told nobody this about that place," Freddy said. "In almost sixty years I ain't never told nobody. Not even Agnes. Miesko's the only one I ever talked with about it."

"I'm honored you told me."

"Eyuh." He sighed deeply. "Times I want to ask God why he permits such evil. Seems there's gotta be a reason."

like as if god was trying to hide something but ran out of snow

"I don't think he'd answer," said Caitlin. "Probably too embarrassed."

Freddy gave a sardonic laugh. "Eyuh…too embarrassed."

"I'd be satisfied if he simply explained mosquitoes," Caitlin said, slapping at a mosquito and laughing. "What was the idea behind that?"

like a wind chime

Freddy gazed at her a long moment. Finally, he took a deep breath, rose from his chair, and said, "Time to go to lunch."

~

Caitlin heard a knock on the door. She opened it to find Wayne Crenshaw standing with a Red Sox cap in his hands.

"Mr. Crenshaw…"

"Call me Wayne." He fidgeted with the cap.

"Please…please come in."

Wayne Crenshaw followed her into the living room. At her bidding, he sat on the sofa. She pulled a chair over to face him.

"What's up?" Caitlin asked.

"It's my son, Jasper. He ain't too bright and he gets himself riled up something awful. Can't stand strangers…or people like Angelique Moseley."

"You mean Native Americans?"

"Eyuh. Always thinking they want to take the land back. And now with that woman talking about Snagged Anchor Island and all, how there might be Passamaquoddy remains out there…"

"But why would he care about Snagged Anchor Island? It's a deserted place. Nobody goes there."

"He has some kinda fantasy me and him could lease some of the land from Garret Webster and build a bigger marina out there. Do lots of extra business while at the same time keeping the folks with their yachts at arm's length from us here on Alabaster Island. He talks kinda violent about it sometimes."

"Oh, I'm sure his talk is harmless. I— "

Crenshaw shook his head. "I know him a lot better, if you don't mind my saying. Ever since his mother passed away he's been awful difficult."

"I'm sorry to hear you lost your wife."

Crenshaw nodded. "Eyuh. But that was some time ago. I been trying to…sort of keep him pointed in the right direction ever since, if you know what I mean."

"I've seen what a loving father you are," replied Caitlin.

He continued to fidget with his cap. "Eyuh. But there's only so much a man can do. That's why I've come to see you."

"I don't understand."

"They say you're a writer."

"I do write some. Mostly poetry."

"Poetry..." he repeated as if the word itself were foreign to him. "I got to thinking, if Jasper learned how to write out his thoughts it might take some of the sting out of them—kinda get it out of his system."

Caitlin was silent.

"Do you think so?" asked Crenshaw.

"I don't know. I suppose so."

"So I was wondering if you would help him. Teach him something about writing and such. I'm thinking it would be good for him."

Caitlin was taken aback. She came to the island to free herself to write and suddenly she was presented first with O'zalik, now with Jasper, as potential students. It wasn't at all what she had in mind and she wasn't sure she wanted to involve herself so intimately with two of the islanders. After all, wasn't that a part of what she was trying to escape? Having people depend on her? Even her growing closeness to Freddy had begun to worry her. On the other hand she'd seen on a few occasions at Pauline's how volatile Jasper was, despite her assurances to Wayne Crenshaw. She couldn't be at all certain the young man wasn't headed for trouble. Yet, she didn't believe in writing as therapy; she saw it as a purely creative act. Although, she knew, many people wrote therapeutically. She certainly saw enough of them in the writing seminars she'd attended. Perhaps it *would* help Jasper gain control of his anger.

After a long pause, she said, "I'll be happy to work with Jasper. If he's willing, that is."

Crenshaw smiled broadly. "Oh, he'll be willing all right. The other day he talked about you all the way back to the marina. That's what gave me the idea."

After Crenshaw left, Caitlin sat for a long time thinking about how she would work with Jasper.

you took our jeremy away from us

~

Instead of waiting for the turn of the tide, we set out again before slack water, giving us several extra hours to cross to a suitable place on the western side of Baye Françoise (Bay of Fundy—R.B.). *We did not want to be caught in the middle of the crossing when daylight came since every enemy ship carrying poor Acadians would perforce sail south out of the bay before altering course for the open Atlantic. And since it was a minimum of a hundred kilometers across, we would need all the time we could manage. Moreover, as Edmond informed me, by setting out during the last of the inflowing current, which we would be crossing at right angles, we would be carried some distance northward thus compensating for the southward drift we would inevitably experience after the current changed. I said a prayer of thanks to God for making the Mi'kmaq such good seamen and for permitting me and other missionaries of the Company of Jesus to make good Christians of them.*

No stars shone when we slid the canoes silently into the water. The moon also was absent. It was impossible to see the other canoes and we could only know of their presence by the soft splash of the paddles stirring the water. No one spoke. One or two of the children wept quietly as the cold caused them to suffer miserably.

My Mi'kmaq children paddled bravely into the night as only Savages can. They knew as well as I, or better, how long the passage would be and that we must make it as expeditiously as possible lest our charges start freezing to death.

I accepted the terrible pain in my hands as a burden God had given me to test my piety. My only recourse was to pray. Mercifully, God heard my prayers and took the pain away. (At the beginning of this entry I noted the handwriting was more ragged than before. It became clear at this point the man was suffering the first symptoms of frostbite. The loss of sensation in his hands would be a prelude to the excruciating pain he would later feel when his hands thawed—R.B.)

It was sometime in the middle of the night that we heard the ship. It came first as a salt whisper, the familiar hissing of water along a hull. I gave a signal to Edmond and he stopped paddling.

We heard clearly the crash of a bow wave and the creaks of a ship working its timbers against one another. The sounds were becoming louder and I became frightened that, even worse than the blackhearted English seeing us, they might fail to see us and run their ship right through us.

There also was a strange slapping sound I could not place, like a whip indifferently employed. I wouldn't have put it past them.

I peered into the darkness in the direction of the sounds. Snow crystals sissed against my face making it difficult to keep my eyes open for very long. I knew as surely as I knew all the names of all the saints of France that if I could not see the ship, nobody on board the ship could possibly see us. And even if they saw us and wanted to avoid running us through (an unlikely assumption concerning the baseminded English), they wouldn't be able to alter course in time.

I saw a red lamp—the port running light. The ship was already upon us. The hiss of the hull through the water became louder and all at once I heard the sound of weeping. Quickly, and with whispered instructions, I beckoned the Acadians to lie in the bottoms of the canoes and pull furs over themselves.

The hull slid by like a giant specter, a different, darker shade of gray. I could now identify the slapping sound I earlier heard as an untrimmed jib flapping in the wind, for I perceived a shadowy figure crawling along the bowsprit to tend to it. And as the ship slid past us, we heard the weeping once more. It was the sound, no doubt, of many children crying for their fathers and for their homes. I also heard a woman's voice reciting the Hail Mary. Then came Madame Plamondon's voice from under the fur saying, "Mon Dieu, I recognize that voice. It is my neighbor, Madame Arsenault." Madame Plamondon started to cry so loudly I was forced to press my hand against the fur where it covered her mouth.

Aboard our canoes, the children all started to cry softly in sympathy with the children on the ship. But the ship was already passing and receding into the night. If the enemy heard our children, they would only have assumed the sound came from their ship, so much a ship of soulful lamentation was it.

I am compelled to admit that at the very moment of the ship's passing and upon hearing the pitiful plaints of the lost children, I turned my eyes to Heaven and prayed fervently that God would, at that very moment, separate the shameful English from their captives by means of a terrible shipwreck in which all aboard would perish and in that way the Faithful would be liberated and carried into Heaven and eternal bliss by the hand of God and the Mephistophelean English would plunge into the Inferno and the eternal perdition which, for all their cruel and iniquitous deeds, is their just due. It was a rash thought. A moment after thinking it, I unthought it and asked God's forgiveness.

Downcast in spirit, we pressed on. Many hours passed. I noticed the Savages were paddling with less vigor than before and concluded the effort was beginning to wear mightily on them. They no longer wore their usual confident, smiling appearance but instead stared absently straight ahead into the dark and the snow. Indeed, Edmond presented a most frightening and vexing appearance. He apparently was no longer able to control his fluids, for his spit was now frozen on his lips and jaw, and slobber from his nose was frozen around his mouth. His stare past my shoulder was vacant. If, as I was certain, Edmond was the strongest of the Savages, I could only imagine what state the others might be in. Yet, hour after hour, they paddled on in total silence. It was a heroic effort the like of which I had never seen.

I must have dozed, for I had not noticed the snow had stopped. My first indication was the sudden appearance of the moon, faint and fuzzy, through what I concluded in the darkness must be lingering but shredding clouds. The moon was bright enough, however, to reveal the shadowy hulk of land ahead and to our right. We had made the crossing. I made this point to Edmond, but he said nothing. He merely continued to paddle, digging deeply for a few strokes to redirect the canoe to the right.

Soon, we were on land and had a small fire going. After a while, with the warmth of the fire, my hands started to thaw. The warming was accompanied by an excruciating pain which perplexed me. I had assumed that warming could only bring greater comfort, not greater pain. That my plight was not a solitary one was born out by the whimpering of the others as they must have experienced the same pain. Even some of the Savages, though not crying, grimaced with discomfort.

But this did not include Edmond. He sat expressionless against a tree, saying nothing and making no effort to warm himself by the fire. I tried to speak with him but he refused to answer, or even look at me. Baptiste, his companion, placed a hand on my shoulder and motioned for me to accompany him some distance away from Edmond whereupon he told me that Edmond was preparing to journey to Grandmother God. In other words, to die.

My heart was deeply pained. If Edmond was to die, he should be preparing his journey to Jesus Christ, not to some Grandmother God which was a vestige of the ignorant beliefs the Savages formerly held. I went straight back to Edmond to set him straight on this matter before it was too late. He was murmuring something I could not make out. I said to him, "You must pray to Sasoo," using the pronunciation for Jesus the Mi'kmaq employed because they have no equivalent for our sound of "J" in French. "You must not pray to a Grandmother God." But I might as well have been speaking to a deaf person. His attitude did not change in the least. As I stood before him, I began to recognize his murmuring as a kind of chant. I even recognized some of the words. One, in particular, caused me deep pain. It was "Kji-nisgam," the word for the Great Spirit in primitive Mi'kmaq beliefs. I asked Baptiste what the meaning of all this was and he replied that Edmond was chanting his death song.

I was appalled.

For hours, I pleaded with Edmond not to abandon Jesus Christ, but I got no response. He even refused all offers of food. He stayed as he was throughout that night and all of the next day, staring into the distance and chanting his primitive song. I began to fear we might have to go on without him and I worried that, without him, we might never find our Passamaquoddy brothers.

~

On the day of Garret Webster's lobster bake, Caitlin held her first session with Jasper Crenshaw. When she heard his knock, she went to the door. "Come in, Jasper."

"Miss," he replied with a shy half bow.

"Your father says you would like some coaching with your writing."

"I don't write much, but my father says it might help."

"I think it would. Have you thought of what you would like to write about?"

Without hesitation he replied, "My mother."

"I see." Caitlin motioned for him to sit on the sofa. "How old were you when your mother died?"

"I don't know. Twelve, I guess."

"Do you think of her often?"

"Eyuh."

"I have some beer in the refrigerator. Would you like one?"

"Guess I will."

Caitlin went to the refrigerator and retrieved two beers. She opened them and handed one of the bottles to Jasper. "What would you like to say about your mother?" she asked.

He took a swig of the beer, stared at the bottle, and said, "I guess about how beautiful she was."

"I never had the opportunity to know her. What was she like?"

"Beautiful. Warm. She had a nice voice, too. Not like Helen Underwood."

"Then you should start by writing those things down in detail."

"I go to her grave a lot."

"Do you?"

"Eyuh." He paused a long while before asking, "Do you want to see her grave?"

"You mean now?"

"Eyuh."

"Is that what you want to do? Show me her grave?"

"Eyuh."

She thought about it for a moment. "Okay, we can finish the beers later. Show me her grave." She experienced a wave of joy at the thought he already trusted her enough to involve her in something so personal. Here was a person who was in need of her help, and not just her supportive help, but her creative help. She began to sense a new purpose. Perhaps this is what she'd needed all along. Once her children had grown and Nigel's career seemed secure, she'd felt almost useless.

daughters of alcoholic fathers feel themselves hyper-responsible for others

But if there was no one for whom to feel responsible...

At the cemetery—a small clearing surrounded by spruce trees with a few maples here and there—Jasper pulled some wild flowers and placed them on his mother's headstone. "She was beautiful like these flowers," he said.

"You should put that in your writing." Caitlin looked at Jasper. He was gazing at the headstone. Past his shoulders, she saw massive clouds building over Snagged Anchor Island. Their dark bellies suggested the possibility of a thunderstorm.

"And she smelled good, too."

Caitlin said nothing. A gust of wind soughed through the spruce trees. A colloquium of seagulls appeared above the rim of the cliff and hovered near them. Jasper turned to face in the direction from which the wind came. "Southeast. It's the afternoon sea breeze," he said. He nodded toward the clouds over Snagged Anchor Island. "Convection clouds." He enunciated each syllable of "convection" as if it were an effort.

"I'm not sure what that means."

"When the land is hot, the air rises and builds those clouds. The colder air over the ocean comes in to take its place. That's what makes the sea breeze. Happens almost every hot day after one o'clock." He recited it as if from rote. Caitlin had the impression the words were not his but his father's.

"I see."

"When Mom died, we had a nor'easter."

"Do you think you could write about that? About all the details? About how you felt?" Caitlin suddenly felt unsure of herself. Was she doing the right thing by encouraging him to relive such a moment of grief?

"Eyuh."

"I mean, I think it would help."

"Old Ben Moseley died in a nor'easter."

"I heard. Will you write about what we said?"

He nodded, absently rearranging the flowers on the headstone. Apparently satisfied, he backed away from the grave.

"Shall we go back?" asked Caitlin.

"Eyuh."

As they walked along the path in the cemetery, Caitlin noticed another headstone under a large maple. It read: "Agnes Orcutt. Born September 2nd 1925—Died February 12th 1998." A fresh bouquet of flowers sat at the base of the stone.

Caitlin frowned. "Jasper, this says Agnes Orcutt died only a few years ago."

"Eyuh."

"But I thought she died many years before."

"Nope. Just a few years ago. Me and Dad went to the funeral."

A flash of light caught Caitlin's eye. She raised her head to see String of Pearls through the trees of the cemetery. It glittered, almost fully exposed. A spring tide was approaching. She pondered her discovery.

"Be completely out of the water in a few days," said Jasper.

"It almost makes you want to walk out there, all the way to Snagged Anchor Island," replied Caitlin.

"Eyuh."

"But I'm told it's dangerous."

"Nah, done it dozens of times."

"You? You've crossed over there?"

"Eyuh. First time was after they said my mom died. I didn't see her and didn't believe them, so I guess I was hoping she went out to the island. Was looking for her."

Caitlin gazed at him, saying nothing.

"Then when I saw her in…in the box, I went over there to get away from them."

"All the other people?"

"Eyuh. Real peaceful there. Go there lots."

"And you never had a problem…with the tide, that is?"

"Nah. Be careful, don't stay too long, everything's fine."

"What's it like?"

"Like walking on water…all the way to heaven."

Caitlin shifted her gaze from Jasper to String of Pearls. The sunlight ignited the imbedded mica into a million flashes.

"I get to talk with my mother when I'm there."

She turned to look at him again. "You talk with her?"

"Eyuh. Then I come back."

"What do you talk about?"

"Things."

"What things?"

"I tell her what's happening. Like Ben Moseley dying while smoking a cigar. How it was during a nor'easter just like her."

"What other things?"

"Just things."

"Is it difficult…crossing the reef, I mean? Is the footing okay?"

"Piece of cake."

Back at the cottage, they finished the first beer and had another while they talked. They spent almost two hours and with every passing moment Caitlin felt Jasper's trust in her deepen and she felt her own sense of responsibility grow. She wondered what she had gotten herself into, but it was too late to back out. She could see she was already committed to using whatever measure of creativity she had to help Jasper deal with the loss that had obviously so unsettled him. Her conviction was strengthened when, toward the end of their time together, he said, "I also want to write about them."

"Them?"

"Them that took my mother."

Caitlin's brow furrowed. "Who?"

"Them."

She probed a little, she couldn't get him to be more specific. He rambled on about many things and she suspected he was simply trying to avoid answering her directly.

~

By the time Freddy arrived at the Spruce Cove Inn for Garret Webster's annual lobster bake, most of the islanders were already there. As far as he could tell, only Caitlin and O'zalik were missing. He hoped it wasn't because they felt out of place—outsiders. He'd stopped by Caitlin's cottage to offer her a ride, but she wasn't there.

The weather being perfect, the inn staff had set things up on the sprawling lawn. Dozens of folding tables and hundreds of metal chairs sat in parallel rows under a large, open-sided tent. Though the lobsters wouldn't be ready for at least a half hour, some of the older people who didn't like to stand were already scattered at the tables. A tendril of steam wafted under Freddy's nostrils, drawing his attention to the cooking area several dozen yards from the tent where some of his friends gathered. He approached them.

Though the inn staff was in charge of preparing the feast, they were being secretly supervised by a gaggle of lobstermen each one of whom, Freddy was certain, thought he knew the perfect way to prepare a lobster bake. Ernie Botham and Burle Ledyard, standing together, greeted Freddy. Wayne Crenshaw, who was also with them, nodded. Jasper Crenshaw stood at his father's shoulder.

"Boys," said Freddy. He turned to Ernie Botham. "How're yuh doing, Ernie?"

"Feelin' fine. Wouldn't know I got this cancer thing."

"Ernie's able. Works the stern real good," said Burle Ledyard.

"Ain't lost a step."

"That's good to hear."

"Me and Ernie was telling Wayne here the best way to make a fire for a lobster bake," said Burle.

Freddy looked at one of the fire pits. It was two parallel rows of cinder blocks, two courses high, onto which a sheet of iron about four feet by six feet had been placed. Under the iron, a fire roared. On top of the iron plate the cooks had placed a six-inch layer of seaweed on which they mounded foil-wrapped potatoes and onions, partially husked corn, lobsters, clams. A glimmer of early-evening sun caught the lobster and clam juices, which, dripping down, would help cook the potatoes, onions, and corn. A gas pocket burst with a snap, telling Freddy the fire was made from split logs. That being the case, he knew Ernie Botham and Burle Ledyard would argue for charcoal, maybe butane. But if charcoal or butane had been used, he knew they would have argued for split wood.

Freddy gave Ernie and Burle a frown, "They're using wood," he said. "I'd have gone with charcoal."

Ernie Botham gave a smile of surprised delight. "Eyuh, that's what we was saying. Makes a hotter fire."

"Or maybe butane," said Burle Ledyard.

Freddy nodded sagely. "Maybe butane."

"But not wood."

"Not wood."

The complex savory smells coming from the baking lobsters, clams, corn, and potatoes caused Freddy's mouth to water and persuaded him wood was just fine. A slight breeze came up, sending a cloud of steam from the barrel a few paces away where mussels were being steamed in wine for appetizers. His stomach growled in anticipation.

Morgan Fludd waddled over to them, a beer in his meaty fist, looked at the fire pit, and said, "Shoulda used charcoal. Hotter fire."

Ernie Botham and Burle Ledyard gave twin nods.

"Freddy, where's your lady friend?" asked Morgan Fludd with a wink.

"Don't know. Was wondering if her and O'zalik would show."

"Don't need no Indians here," said Jasper. "Just want to take our land."

"Jasper, I told you to stop that," said Crenshaw. "Snagged Anchor Island don't belong to us anyhow. Belongs to Garret Webster. Now, come on, let's get a couple of beers." They walked off, Crenshaw's arm around his son's shoulders.

When they were out of hearing distance, Morgan Fludd said, "That Jasper, he ain't too bright."

"Number than a pounded thumb," replied Burle Ledyard.

"Eyuh," said Ernie Botham.

Freddy gave a dismissive wave, "Ahh, he's harmless, just like Caitlin Gray says. She's taken a liking to the boy. Teaching him to write stuff."

"That's nice, but don't know about him being harmless, though," said Morgan Fludd, shaking his head. "He's got it in his head that Angelique Moseley means to turn the island into a Indian place and it don't sit well with him."

"She sure talks about it a lot," said Ernie Botham.

"Wayne keeps him in line. Besides, what happens to that island is Garret Webster's business."

"Eyuh," said Ernie Botham with an enigmatic smile.

"What's more," said Morgan, "ain't any of us would take kindly to it being turned over to the Indians."

"Nope. In that sense, Jasper may be slow but he ain't wrong."

After a pause during which all four men seemed to be contemplating Jasper Crenshaw's mental capacity and instability, Burle said, "Time for another beer. Lobsters're almost done."

They each got a beer and took seats at a table that also included the Crenshaws and Richie Comine. Most of the places at the other tables were already filled with people anticipating a good feed. Garret Webster appeared at the opening of the tent and raised his arms in a gesture that called for quiet. When he had everyone's attention, he gave a short speech in which, as usual, he thanked the island lobstermen for providing the lobsters that, he said, rubbing his hands, were just about ready. Freddy knew however that, as in every year, Garret generously paid full market price for every single lobster, which was one of the reasons he was so well liked on the island. At the conclusion of Garret's speech, everyone applauded enthusiastically, pushed their chairs back, and began forming a line at the serving station.

When he returned with a paper plate piled high with a lobster, an ear of corn, and a potato, Freddy saw that Morgan Fludd was already busily dismembering a second lobster. Morgan's prodigious appetite was legendary, but Freddy was still amazed at how the man could have gone through a lobster so quickly. As he cracked a claw of his own lobster, Freddy shook his head in disbelief. "You're the biggest gannet-gut I've ever seen, Morgan."

Morgan glanced up, drawn butter glistening on his chin. He was about to reply when he stopped and said, "There's Angelique Moseley now, Freddy. She's coming this way. And the Caitlin Gray woman is with her."

Jasper Crenshaw, sitting across from Freddy, became suddenly alert.

Freddy stood. "O'zalik, Caitlin, I'm glad you could make it."

O'zalik glanced to the other side of the tent where Quentin was standing with Garret Webster. "I'm not staying, Freddy. I just came to see if you'd put in a word with Garret for me."

"What kinda word?"

"I've been trying to persuade him to let me bring some people from the tribe to help me explore Snagged Anchor Island, but he won't budge. I thought you could have a word with him. People listen to you."

Freddy glanced at Jasper who was giving O'zalik a hostile stare. He looked back at O'zalik. "It ain't the proper time, O'zalik. We should talk about this privately."

"It's never the proper time."

"There'll be trouble if you keep pushing this."

"That doesn't bother me. I'm used to trouble."

Quentin and Garret appeared at the table. "What's going on?" asked Garret. "You seem to be having a mighty serious discussion."

No one said anything for a long moment. Finally, O'zalik said, "I was just talking about Snagged Anchor Island."

"Are you still going on about that? I told you, I'm not giving you and your folks the run of the place."

"Give me a good reason why."

Quentin murmured, "Bitch."

O'zalik shot him a hate-filled glance.

Garret stepped between them. "Because I want to keep the place like it is. Unspoiled."

Freddy saw Jasper exchange a worried glance with his father.

"That's not a good enough reason," said O'zalik. "Not when there are remains of my ancestors out there."

"But you've got no proof of that."

"How can I get proof if you won't let me bring some archaeologists out there?"

"Angelique, I'm finished talking about this. I don't want to hear any more."

O'zalik stared at him a long moment then said, "You'll have your proof. Before I'm done, all of you will have all the proof you need." She glanced at Freddy, turned abruptly, and left.

~

Alabaster Island lounged in the fold of a dazzling morning, the sun glancing off the granite cliffs, the sea shimmering with a million flashes, windshields on lobster boats in Spruce Cove flaring—first one, then another, then another, strobing all the way across the cove. It was a baptism of light, a bluing of the water that, later, as the sun arched higher in the sky, would turn Atlantic sea green. Caitlin felt the sun warmly on her shoulders as she descended the path leading to a small beach, which, in turn, led to String of Pearls. Approaching the shore, she heard the clatter of pebbles in the suck of retreating waves. A streak of sunlight caught in the curl of a wave angling toward the reef—light slowed by the slower medium of water so you could see it move, pulse after pulse of light streaking along the length of String of Pearls. Seagulls carved the air with swirls and swoops, occasionally diving for a clam or a crab. A light breeze ruffled the water.

Caitlin glanced at her watch. *9:25.* Low tide—a spring low—would occur in fifteen minutes. Already she saw the reef was completely exposed, gleaming wetly in the full, perling glare of the sun. She walked steadily toward it. As she came close, she could make out details of its composition not visible from a distance. On the seaward side of the reef, where it was fully exposed, was a band of blue mussels and, in places, yellow-brown bladder rockweed and some green kelp. On the more protected side, there were patches of bright green algae. She stepped onto String of Pearls and started to walk. She walked on the left—the protected side—to avoid the splash of waves crashing into the reef. Here and there, were patches of sand where tiny trails, barely impressed into the surface, meandered—some creature of the margin that had dragged itself toward a purpose Caitlin couldn't discern. Here, the carapace of a dead crab. In the distance, beyond the pearls, Snagged Anchor Island beckoned.

Were there Passamaquoddy remains out there? When Freddy and O'zalik talked of the possibility, Caitlin's imagination was stirred; she felt an almost irresistible urge to discover if it was true. Ever since her archaeological studies at Boston University, she'd been interested in the ways of Native Americans, especially their relationship to the earth and the elements. It was a way of looking at the world, of being in the world, that caused a resonant response deep within her. Going out to Snagged Anchor Island felt like a kind of homecoming in ways she didn't yet understand.

Walking along the ridge of the reef, she felt like Moses parting the waters. It was just as Jasper said. After about ten minutes she was approaching Little Pearl. It bore a clear high-water mark beyond which the outcropping was always exposed. Above the line of blue mussels continuing from the ridge, a white band of barnacles clung to the rock and, above that, a band of black periwinkles. On the crest of Little Pearl a great cormorant spread its glossy black wings, drying them.

It took her five minutes to scramble to the top of Little Pearl. When she was about halfway up, the cormorant lifted into the air with hoarse squawks. As she approached Little Pearl, the outcropping obscured her view of Snagged Anchor Island. Now she could see the island clearly. It looked surprisingly close, Big Pearl closer still. She would have to ask Freddy if String of Pearls was truly almost a mile long or if that was an exaggeration.

She pressed on towards Big Pearl and soon found her estimate of the distance between the outcroppings was an illusion. Moving slowly because of the uneven and slippery surface of the ridge, it took her almost a half hour to reach Big Pearl. She found the going very difficult. Jasper Crenshaw said it was a piece of cake and she guessed now he was simply in better condition.

She had already been on the reef almost an hour. She would have to hurry if she was going to get to Snagged Anchor Island and back before the incoming tide started to cover the reef. She looked on the left and on the right for a way around Big Pearl, but there was none. She would have to climb it. She started climbing and soon came to a short, five-foot, nearly vertical pitch. Pausing to catch her breath, she searched for handholds.

Again, she thought of Freddy. He said the spring tide provided more opportunity for exploring but also more danger. It was a long time since she had challenged herself in such a way. Always, it was Nigel and the children who were exploring their limits and she who stood on the sidelines rooting them on. But now she began to wonder if what she was doing was just a stupid, selfish experiment. What if she overstayed on the island and became trapped on String of Pearls by the inrushing tide as others had before her? Would that be fair to Dylan and Ellen? Had she the right to risk walking out of their lives that way? Out of her own life?

She turned.

A wave of terror broke over her. Suddenly, she felt the distance back to the beach on Alabaster Island stretch out surrealistically before her. Her knees started to shake—like those times when she was a child and found herself in the dark at the bottom of a flight of stairs, the inescapable sensation of some presence looming behind her. And just as, back then, she bounded up the stairs to escape whatever it was, she now quickened her steps back toward Alabaster Island. By the time she reached Little Pearl, seawater was already licking at the low points of the reef. She quickened her pace, scrambling over Little Pearl much faster than she had on the way out. When she got to the other side of Little Pearl, she stepped into a shallow depression already filled with seawater. Her sense of panic grew. Now, with no more outcroppings between her and Alabaster Island, she could see waves already sluicing over the low sections of the reef. Once more, she quickened her pace. She scurried only a small distance when her legs suddenly seemed to have a will of their own. It was as though somebody else was controlling them and she felt herself lurching to the right. She was disoriented, confused. She stumbled and fell, scraping her left knee painfully. She looked at her knee and saw blood. A brutish wave crashed onto the seaward side of String of Pearls and she was inundated with spray. Diluted by the seawater, her blood ran thinly on the granite. She felt a sharp, stinging sensation as the salt water invaded her wound. She cried out.

Realizing the water was coming higher all the time and she had to move quickly, Caitlin forced herself to her feet and started walking again. At the low spots, she waded along the granite ridge ankle deep in water. An occasional exploding wave threw spray at her, stinging her knee all over again. She had the sensation the reef was sinking under her.

She looked to see how close the beach was but could scarcely see it for the salt spray on her sunglasses. She whipped them off and threw them away. Now she saw the beach was close and she almost gave a shout of joy. She forgot the pain in her knee as she scrambled the last hundred yards.

She struggled onto the beach, breathless, cleared away some pebbles, and sat in the sand. Gently, she pressed her hand to her left knee, examining the wound. The skin wasn't broken, but there was a silver-dollar-sized abrasion.

Gradually, her breathing returned to normal, matching the slow push and pull of the waves. A low-skimming seagull swept over String of Pearls. She watched it rise with a current of air.

"Ever want to fly like that?"

Startled, Caitlin turned to see O'zalik standing behind her. "Oh, you surprised me. I didn't see you coming." She stood and faced the woman. She brushed the sand from the seat of her pants.

"They say we injuns can sneak through a forest of undergrowth without being heard," O'zalik answered with a small laugh. "Just as silent as those seagulls. God, I love to watch them fly."

"They are beautiful," Caitlin replied.

"Every time I see them, I want to fly, too. What about you?"

"I guess it never occurred to me."

"Well it does to me. All the time." She spread her arms as though to take flight herself. With a sigh she tore her gaze from the soaring seagull. She looked at Caitlin. "Scrape your knee?"

Caitlin gave a sheepish expression. "Slipped on the rocks."

"Going out there is dangerous stuff, you know."

"Yes...yes, I've been told."

"All the same, it's kind of tempting, isn't it?"

"Have you ever been out there?"

"To the island? Yes. I never crossed the reef, though," O'zalik said. "But I sure as hell plan to."

"Why?"

"There's a legend that some of my ancestors are there. I figure the only way they got there was by crossing String of Pearls. I need to see what it was like for them."

"Why do you think they crossed String of Pearls?" asked Caitlin. "Wouldn't they go by boat like normal people?" She laughed, implying that normal people didn't include herself.

O'zalik gave a sardonic laugh. "I have reasons to believe the people on Alabaster Island weren't about to help them with boats and probably even destroyed any canoes they might have had."

"Why?"

"They didn't belong here," said O'zalik. "Even the name of the island means white."

"I see."

"You're surprised at my bitterness," said O'zalik. "But why shouldn't I be bitter? Even today I sometimes feel we're not welcome in our own land. How would you feel?" O'zalik fixed Caitlin with an intense stare. "God, I hate this place and the self-righteous, pretentious people who live here."

Caitlin saw the fire in the woman's eyes. "I apologize if I'm being too nosy, but why do you stay?"

"Don't apologize. I'm just bitching. It isn't often I get a chance. Nobody seems to want to listen much…except maybe Freddy Orcutt." O'zalik glanced at Caitlin's knee. "You should wash that out." When Caitlin said nothing, she continued. "I ain't leaving this place until I find out for sure about Snagged Anchor Island."

"So your husband has nothing to do with it?"

"Not any more, he doesn't."

Caitlin nodded her understanding. She hesitated. "How did you two meet?"

"You mean how did an Indian like me get involved with a Yankee Protestant like Quentin?"

Caitlin blushed. "I'm sorry. I didn't—"

"It's okay," O'zalik said, holding up a hand, smiling. "It's a good question and deserves a good answer. I was going to Bowdoin College in Brunswick and he was a civilian cook at the naval base there. We met at a pizza joint. When I graduated, I was bored, wanted to get away. As much as I love my grandparents, I didn't want to return to the reservation. Too confining. I wanted to see what the rest of the world was like. It was as simple as that." She started to walk toward the path leading up away from the beach.

"All the same, coming to Alabaster Island must have been a shock for you," Caitlin said.

"I had no idea it was so different. Except for Bowdoin, I'd never really been off the reservation. I had no idea what small-town Maine could be like."

"Small-town anywhere," said Caitlin.

O'zalik looked at Caitlin. "What kind of name is Caitlin?"

"Irish."

"With brown eyes and dark skin…for a white American, I mean?"

"My name's Irish, but I'm French. My maiden name is Arsenault. But my mother loved Dylan Thomas, the poet, and his wife's name was Caitlin. I also learned to love Dylan Thomas."

"Never heard of him. Only poet I ever met was Leroy Bop-Tootty-Bop. He was a black classmate who recited poetry at Bowdoin."

Caitlin smiled. "I'm afraid I don't know him."

"Did you say your maiden name is Arsenault?" O'zalik asked.

"Yes."

"When you say you're French, do you mean French as in from France?"

"Oh, no. I'm French Canadian…or, as some would say, Franco-American."

"But there are two kinds of French-Canadian, the Québécois from places like Montreal and Toronto and the Acadians from Nova Scotia, Prince Edward Island and so forth."

"I'm Acadian. My ancestors come from P.E.I and New Brunswick."

"Hmm," replied O'zalik with a thoughtful expression.

"That seems to interest you," said Caitlin, a little bemused.

"Oh, it's nothing. Genealogy just always fascinates me. We

Indians have always been interested in ancestors."

They had arrived at the top of the path where it connected with the coast road. A pair of spruce grouse, came toward them clucking. Islanders called them "fool hens" because they were so completely unafraid of humans. Caitlin's cottage was about a mile to the right. But when O'zalik turned left toward Spruce Cove, Caitlin followed. "Do you mind if I walk along with you?"

"No. But I'm not going far. I'm due at work."

"But...," said Caitlin, confused, looking over her shoulder. Pauline's Coffee and Bake Shop was in the opposite direction.

"My *other* job. I help out at the Spruce Cove Inn. Quentin is useless as far as making money goes. Only cooks at Pauline's part-time while I work two jobs...You said Arsenault is your *maiden* name?"

"Yes."

"Then you're still married?"

"Yes." She knew what the next question would be, so she answered it. "My husband, Nigel, is a music conductor. He's busy preparing a program for Tanglewood and I wanted time on my own to write, anyway."

They bid each other good-bye and walked in opposite directions. Once or twice Caitlin turned as if to accompany O'zalik to the Spruce Cove Inn. Since she arrived on the island, she avoided talking with Garret Webster. Perhaps it was time. But she resisted the temptation and continued on her way toward Jimmy's cottage.

~

Freddy found Caitlin at their customary table in Pauline's. "You look lost in thought," he said, at the same time nodding a greeting to O'zalik.

She smiled. "Nothing, really. I was thinking about Jasper Crenshaw."

"How's it going with the writing?" He nodded when O'zalik gestured to his coffee cup.

"We've met a half dozen times so far, but I don't think I'm getting very far. Every time I get him to write something, it starts out about his mother but then it drifts to things that make him angry."

"He ain't had an easy time of it, what with his mother dying."

Caitlin nodded. "Yes, that's obvious, but he seems to blame phantoms for his mother's death. He keeps going on about strangers and Native Americans. I can't seem to get through to him that these people had nothing to do with his mother's death. I'm thinking of giving it up."

Freddy frowned. "Think that's wise?" O'zalik poured coffee into his cup. He wrapped both hands around it.

"What choice do I have. I'm totally ineffective."

Freddy remembered all the conversations with Caitlin on his back porch. "Sometimes, talking's enough. Don't need no writing."

"Perhaps..."

"Wayne says the boy's a lot less agitated."

Caitlin gave a sardonic smile. "Wish I could see that for myself." She paused, looked into Freddy's eyes, and said, "Freddy, I hope you don't mind my asking, but when did your wife die?"

"A long time ago," he answered. Why was she asking? He was relieved to see O'zalik coming toward them again.

"Coffee hot enough, Freddy?" asked O'zalik.

Wayne Crenshaw, Richie Comine, and Morgan Fludd burst through the door and greeted everyone. Morgan Fludd lifted the dome over the pie keeper and took out a slice, which he carried to an empty table. Wayne and Richie sat at the same table. Crenshaw had a downcast look.

"You're looking like the ocean just dried up, Wayne," said Freddy. "What's up?"

"If Morgan here is right, maybe it has."

Morgan Fludd looked to where O'zalik was working behind the counter. He leaned forward and in a soft voice said, said, "I was saying that if Angelique there manages to persuade the gov'ment or something about there being Passamaquoddy remains on Snagged Anchor Island, then that puts the caboodle to any plans Wayne has of building a marina out there."

"Why?" asked Freddy.

"Because they'll just take it over by imminent domain."

"*Eminent* domain."

"Same thing. Wayne still ain't got his marina."

"Why would they do that?"

Freddy turned to Wayne Crenshaw. "What's this about building a marina? I ain't heard you mention that before."

"It's been a dream of mine…and my boy."

"But you already got a marina."

"There ain't no good accommodations in Spruce Cove for *big* yachts. You know that. A good blow and anything bigger than fifty feet is coming off the mooring sure as fish jump. Ain't that right, Morgan?"

Morgan nodded.

"Damn right," said Wayne. "And more and more of them yachts is coming here. When you consider the nearest place can accommodate many boats like that is Bar Harbor, well then…"

"Makes sense to me," said Richie Comine.

Freddy shrugged.

"It'd help everybody on Alabaster Island. More business," said Crenshaw. "But if them Indians take over the island, ain't gonna happen."

"Sounds expensive to me," said Freddy. "Besides which, the island belongs to Garret Webster."

Wayne said, "That ain't no problem. Probably could work something out with him once I raised the money."

"Nah. Garret's always been intent on keeping people off that island."

Quentin Moseley came in from the kitchen. "Way I figure it, you gotta assume the worst with these Indians. That way, you're ready for whatever comes."

Wayne Crenshaw frowned. "Jesus, don't let my boy hear a word of this. He thinks the Indians are out to take up all our land. He'd go off his rocker if he thought they was close to getting the island." He looked at Caitlin. "Even with the help you been giving him."

"Jesus, Wayne," said Freddy with a shake of the head.

"Wayne, Jasper's harmless," said Caitlin. "You know that."

He gave her an anguished look. "I know my son." He looked from Freddy to Caitlin. "And, speaking of which," he whispered, "It'd be a good idea if one of you tells Angelique Moseley over there not to go on longer than a hard winter about it being an Indian place."

~

Baptiste and three of his comrades set off to locate the Passamaquoddy. The rest of us settled in to wait. For three days we all suffered bitterly from the cold.

And on the fourth day, Grandmère Babineau died.

An hour later, and seeming to take example and courage from Grandmère Babineau, Madame Plamondon died.

We lay the bodies on the unyielding ground, far too frozen to dig graves, and I conducted a dual service pleading with God to take these poor souls into His everlasting embrace. All through the most holy service we were forced to endure the constant babil (blabbering, gibbering?—R.B.) *of Edmond's pagan death song. How the man kept it up day after day after day, I was at a loss to understand. Had the Passamaquoddy not arrived the following day, I am convinced Edmond would still be sitting under that spruce tree singing his death song.*

At last, after four days, the snows stopped. The skies cleared and the moon shone gibbous, imparting a soft, innocent, blue radiance to the deadly snow. I feared everyone (except Edmond who was too lost in his death song) was losing all hope of salvation. I tried to lead them in prayer to restore their spirits and their faith in the Lord, but despite my numerous entreaties (I certainly was not, as some said, nagging!) I began to suspect I had lost them to despair. Thus it was Divine intervention that allowed the Passamaquoddy and their Mi'kmaq escorts to arrive at that critical juncture. All at once spirits that had been completely squashed were revived.

Even Edmond, when he saw the Passamaquoddy, stopped his silly song, nodded, and smiled.

In their entirety, there were seven of them, all of whom I recognized as dear friends from the village I had known as home throughout most of my ministry for the Company of Jesus. I had expected a much larger number than seven so I inquired of Neptune, their sachem, about the others. He told me my village had been visited by the Indian sickness by which I understood him to mean the small pox. We call it the Indian sickness because only the Savages are afflicted, we Europeans having long enjoyed an immunity from the disease. I was deeply troubled, for the small pox can kill entire villages. It was important I get to the village as soon as possible so I could guide them to a French settlement for help. I knew of an island, not far from their village by the name of L'île des Perles Perdues (Island of Lost Pearls. Alabaster Island?—R.B.) *which had been settled by good French fishermen who in the summer fished cod and dried them on the rocks and in the winter engaged in fur trapping. Unlike most cod fishermen, they refused to return to France between seasons for fear the heinous English would try to take over the island. They were led by a gentle man by the name of Jean-Pierre de Custine and their company included a doctor, André Pajou, whom I counted among my dearest friends in New France. I determined at once that I would lead the party, with the help of Neptune and, if he were willing, the revivified Edmond, to L'île des Perles Perdues.*

I went to make this proposal to Edmond. He was surrounded by his Mi'kmaq Savages. I assumed they were welcoming him back to the world of the living. I resolved to have a good, long talk with him for putting such a fright into us all. But when I pushed eagerly past the men surrounding him, I saw that his eyes were wide open and motionless and the smile on his face was frozen.

In short, he was dead.

I was most confounded and dismayed. "But I just saw him smiling a few moments ago," I said to Baptiste. Baptiste nodded sagely and said Edmond smiled because he saw the Passamaquoddy and knew that his responsibilities were ended and he now had the freedom to die.

Once more I was forced to conclude the Savage is among God's most noble creations despite his frequent reversion to primitive and pagan beliefs. I only pray God looked into Edmond's heart and ignored his song when, in His infinite Wisdom, he decided whether to admit the man into Paradise.

And thus, once more bereft of spirit, my depleted party set out for the Passamaquoddy village and L'île des Perles Perdues.

When O'zalik reread that last entry while sitting against a rock near the beach, she put the manuscript down, gazed out at the reef and Snagged Anchor Island beyond. Her eyes filled with tears. She reached down, scooped up a handful of sand. She smeared it on her face, an old Passamaquoddy tradition for a rite of mourning. In a voice that started as a whisper and grew in volume but still seemed lost in the vastness of the day, she started to chant, using words her grandfather had taught her.

babbling...a silly song

~

Freddy returned from the bar with their before-dinner drinks—two celebratory Martinis. He couldn't remember the last time he'd had a Martini, but it was a special occasion. Caitlin somehow learned it was his birthday and she was treating him to dinner at the Boat Shed. The room was dark, lit only by indirect ceiling lights and candles at each table—the way honeymooning tourists liked it. He took a seat opposite Caitlin and slid her drink toward her. She raised it and held it out for a toast. "Happy birthday, Freddy."

They clinked glasses. "How did you find out it was my birthday?" Freddy asked, spearing the olive and swallowing it with one bite. Reflections from the flickering candle danced in their glasses.

She gave a delighted laugh. "I have my ways."

a laugh like wind chimes

"Folks're awful nosy around here. Probably Helen Underwood. She's into everybody's business."

"Well, I'm not telling."

"Eyuh...Helen Underwood."

Caitlin smiled.

"Or else Angus. He's knows more about me than I do and he ain't never been able to keep quiet about things. That I know for a fact."

"Why is it important?"

"Just like to know who's nosing into my affairs."

Caitlin reached into her purse and pulled out a small package. She held it out to him. "You're such a grouch, I shouldn't give this to you. But here, happy birthday."

Freddy felt his heart race. It had been a long time since someone had given him a gift. A blush suffused his cheeks. "What the hell's this for?" he asked. He hadn't meant for it to sound gruff. He wished he could take it back.

"Well if that's your attitude..."

"Sorry. Didn't mean it the way it sounded. It's just that..."

"Open it."

Freddy gazed at her a moment before tearing the wrapping paper with nervous hands. He removed a small wooden box, like a casket. He opened the lid. Resting on a specially molded bed of felt was a gleaming white meerschaum pipe in the style called a bent billiard. The bowl of the pipe was a carved representation of a bearded man wearing a cap with a large feather flopped to one side. Reflections of the candle flame gleamed in the pure white polished bowl and the ebonite stem.

A knot of panic rose in Freddy's throat. He thought of Jimmy.

"It's D'Artagnan," Caitlin said.

He looked at her with a blank expression, surprised, ambushed by the anger he felt.

"He was a clever and courageous chevalier," said Caitlin. "Like you."

He grunted an acknowledgement.

"A man who believed friendship was above all things." A frown appeared on Caitlin's face.

"Friendship...," Freddy repeated.

"...and who believed love is a treasure even if it leaves you...vulnerable." Caitlin paused. "Freddy, what's the matter?"

He shook his head.

"Oh, God. You don't like it."

"No, no. It's handsome. It's...Where did you get it?"

"I took the ferry to the mainland the other day," she replied. "Freddy, I've done something terribly wrong. What is it?"

What had she done? She'd disrupted the choreography of his remorse, his loneliness. How could he tell her she'd intruded on his most treasured memory? Did she expect him to give up his old meerschaum, the one Jimmy gave him? Was that her way of telling him he had to let go of Jimmy, get on with his life after twenty-five years? The same as with the comment about perfume losing its strength? "Like I said, it's real nice. I like it very much."

"But something upset you about it," she said. "Freddy, it's only a pipe."

"Goldang, I'm sorry if I seem ungrateful. It's just that...that I'm surprised."

only a pipe

Caitlin reached across the table and placed her hand over his. "I'm not suggesting you should give up the other pipe, if that's what you're thinking."

He didn't know what to say.

"Freddy, it's only a pipe but if you'd like me to take it back..."

His sense of panic grew as he felt his eyes water. "It's a wonderful gift. I don't want you to take it back. It just took me by surprise, is all."

"If I'd known it would shock you like this..." Caitlin said with an embarrassed laugh.

Her laugh sent a shiver of joy through him. Maybe it *was* only a pipe. "I want to keep it," he said. "Be nice having two pipes. Chance to rest the other one…from time to time."

"That's all I meant," said Caitlin.

"Be…interesting…breaking in a new pipe, watching it change color."

"So it's okay?"

Freddy nodded. "It's okay."

Caitlin held her glass toward him. "A toast?"

Sylvia, the maître d', arrived to say their table was ready. Freddy nodded, raised his glass and with a gesture toward Caitlin, lifted it to his lips. His emotions were still confused, but he would wait until he was alone later that night to sort them out. Might as well enjoy the dinner and Caitlin's company.

~

When she woke, O'zalik saw that Quentin had already left for his job at Pauline's. She rose and went over to the window. She peered out. The sky was just beginning to show a slash of red in the east, a swelling on the horizon.

people of the dawnland

A few masthead lights from visiting sailboats pricked the sky. The town crouched in darkness except for the big spotlight at Crenshaw's Marina and a sprinkling of other lights, one of them the night light at Pauline's.

She thought of the Jesuit's journal. Of Edmond. There was great honor in the way he died. And great sadness. It was a sadness that haunted her. For, in the space of his brief narrative, and despite his professed love for the Mi'kmaq and the Passamaquoddy, Father Dalou signaled the death of a culture by his European attitude. Edmond sang his death chant not only for himself but for the Indian way of life. Even then, he knew it would never survive the relentless incursions of the white man. Yes, he knew it even then. And O'zalik knew the rest of the story. She knew what would happen to Father Dalou and his Acadians, what would happen to his Passamaquoddy friends, her ancestors. And she knew what in years to come would happen to the Passamaquoddy people—the slow erosion of their spiritual life; the disappearance of the animals and the ancient forests; the corrosive seduction of alcohol; the ravaging epidemics of European diseases like smallpox, typhus, yellow fever, and influenza; the wholesale theft of Passamaquoddy lands; the imprisonment on reservations. The contaminating assimilation into a world of hatred and violence.

kji-nisgam...kji-nisgam...a death chant

She heard distant chants calling her. Perhaps it was time to join her ancestors, to leave the white man's world behind.

She slipped out the door and headed for the small outcropping at the end of Front Street. There was no sound in the harbor except a loose halyard slapping against a mast and the gurgle of water being expelled by an automatic bilge pump.

A swollen moon hovered in the southern sky. She reached the outcropping.

accihte, the changing color moon...grandmother moon

Its welcome roundness reflected in the water, shimmering in the ripples, throbbing, beckoning. A piety of light perling the water. With an agility born of purpose, she climbed onto the outcropping, balanced herself. Perched like a great bird on the rock, she spread her arms like wings. She stole a last glance at the moon. She launched herself, soaring out over the water.

~

However much she tried, Caitlin couldn't drive her experience on String of Pearls from her thoughts. When Jasper's knock came on her door, her hand was shaking as she twisted the doorknob and let him in.

It was their tenth meeting and they were growing close. He seemed to find in her a substitute for the mother he desperately missed and she finally sensed he was making progress. She'd persuaded him to apply himself and was looking forward to reading the essay he'd said he wrote.

Jasper entered with a big smile on his face and clutching a sheaf of papers in his hand. "I did what you told me. I wrote an essay about them that took my mother."

In desperation, and following the theory that if he wrote about his anger it would be drained of its virulence the way a boil is drained with the touch of a scalpel, Caitlin had asked him to write down everything he thought about strangers and his mother's death. She'd been at a loss for how to help him defuse his anger and turned to this theory—of which she was entirely unsure—as a last resort. She felt she was intruding on the territory of psychiatrists or social workers and had no business doing so. What Jasper needed was professional help, not a writing instructor. But when she proposed the idea to Wayne Crenshaw, he begged her to give it a chance to work. "Fancy doctors like that will only confuse him more," Wayne had said. "What he needs is somebody—a woman like you—to talk to. And he thinks the world of you."

So she agreed to keep trying—at least for a while.

As she ushered Jasper into the living room, she thought that, knowing the state of her own mind after her experience on String of Pearls, she perhaps should have delayed their meeting for a few days. But it was too late now, so she resolved to go through with it.

Yet when she read his essay, she became alarmed all over again. It was filled with references to Web sites of militia groups and others who promulgated every variety of conspiracy theory about Native Americans. Rather than lancing his anger, she was afraid the writing—and the extensive "research" he had obviously done—only served to inflame and confirm it.

She dropped the papers to the coffee table, looked up, and said, "Jasper, do you really believe all this stuff?"

"Eyuh."

"But surely you can see—"

"Researched it myself on the computer."

"Jasper, just because it's on the computer doesn't mean it's right," she snapped. "This...*material*...you found is gibberish."

At once, she knew she'd made a mistake. He narrowed his eyes at her. His lips were trembling and his neck flushed. "I worked hard—"

"I'm sure you worked hard, but you've got to be careful not to swallow everything you see on the computer," Caitlin said. She leaned forward and placed a hand on his wrist. "Look, I'm sorry I snapped at you. I didn't mean it, but—"

He withdrew his wrist from her touch.

She stared at him, appalled at what she'd done.

He stood.

"Jasper, I'm sorry," Caitlin pleaded. "Please forgive me. I'm only trying—"

Jasper walked to the door.

Horrified, Caitlin bolted from her chair and rushed to intercept him. "Stop, Jasper. Please. It was stupid of me." She placed her hand on his shoulder. "It was stupid and mean of me."

He gazed at her hand a long moment shaking his head slowly side to side. Gently, he removed her hand from his shoulder, opened the door, and said, "I'm the one that's stupid is what everybody thinks anyhow."

And he walked out the door.

Caitlin searched for something to say, but nothing came. She sagged against the doorjamb, tears welling in her eyes, and watched him climb into the Crenshaw Marina pickup truck and drive off. The large American flag planted in the bed of the truck whipped furiously in the breeze.

~

When she dove off the rock toward the reflected moon, Grandmother Moon, O'zalik was tempted to allow herself to sink beneath the surface. To open her mouth and swallow the sea. To escape Quentin's world. To join her ancestors. Yet even as she rejoiced in the thought, she understood she had a mission to accomplish. Without her, the Jesuit's journal, the crimes of the complacent islanders, would never be known. She couldn't allow that to happen. They must be made to see what they'd done, what their ancestors had done. They must be made to see themselves for what they were.

Also, she had to consider her grandparents who loved her.

After she swam to shore, she scrambled along the rocky shoreline, hidden by stands of spruce, until she came to a pathway leading to the road near her house. She crossed the road stealthily, slipped in through the back door.

She changed clothes near the front window, watching for signs of Quentin, then left the house and headed for the place where String of Pearls connected to Alabaster Island.

It took her nearly a half hour, clawing her way along the rocks, stepping around tide pools. Finally, she reached the reef. The air was heavy with mist from waves crashing against String of Pearls. In the distance, a wreath of mist girdled Snagged Anchor Island. She edged into a tall vertical crevice, like a giant stone vulva, sat with her knees to her chest, and thought about how the Jesuit described arriving at the Passamaquoddy village.

Our diminished party, suffering as we were from cold and the accumulated exhaustion of our journey, could move only slowly. The Savages wore their peculiar circular snowshoes and the rest of us followed in their path as if following some diabolical, many-legged beast. I prayed constantly, hoping for some sign from God telling me what I should do when we reached the village. I had seen what the small pox could do to entire communities and the thought terrified me. But I received no sign. God was silent. During the two days it took to reach the village, the deep forest was also silent in that profound way in which, only in winter, it can be. On the first day, we heard the long, chilling howl of a wolf, the song of the leader calling his brothers to the chase. Not long after, we saw at a distance, a deer flash silently across an open field, the pack close on its heels. Another time, we heard the unmistakable complaining bellow of a moose, a sound that always makes you wonder if it were wounded. But except for these, we heard no sound other than the soft fall of snow sifted from the spruce tops by the wind as if dropped on us by playful, negligent angels. Occasionally, we came across patches of distressed snow, diluted blood turned pink in the purity of snow, scenes of a mortal struggle between, if the tufts of fur be evidence, a fox and a snowshoe rabbit. And we came upon the carcass of a deer, no doubt the one we earlier saw chased by the pack of wolves. The kill was so fresh, its bloodied haunches still steamed with living body heat. Doubtless, we had interrupted the feeding and the silent wolves were watching us from behind trees. We paused only long enough for the Savages to claim the hindquarters and hoist them on their shoulders. For some time after that, the rest of us followed a trail of dripping blood like a spilled necklace of rubies.

Like Thomas, we often deny the truth we cannot see. As I trudged hour after hour through the snow, I allowed myself to imagine my Passamaquoddy village as I had last seen it several months before. It was a village of about a dozen cone-shaped birch bark dwellings and, in those warm months of the past summer, there was great industry and play. Amidst much shouting and laughing, the youths engaged in stick ball and stone throwing, once even inviting me to join them which I did until my breath succumbed. Older men smiled and sang as they mended hemp gill nets. At the edge of the village other men were constructing a canoe. They sang songs of praise to various animals intended to impart the qualities of that animal to the canoe. In their superstition, the Savages believe a song to the fox, for example, will lend swiftness to the canoe, or a song to the moose, strength, or a song to the heron, beauty.

In another part of the village, women chattered as they shelled clams and mussels. Naked children ran and laughed among them. One woman produced rhythmic, whispering sounds as she used a bow drill to pierce holes in periwinkle shells from which she would fashion jewelry. Near her, a pot steamed over a fire.

I embraced this happy image and urged it to stay as I struggled, exhausted, through the snow. Once or twice I even closed my eyes to hold the image more securely before I was startled awake by a clump of snow falling upon me. Later still, it was a cry of dismay from one of the Savages that pulled me from my reverie. We had come upon a deadfall baited bear trap, a large stone balanced on logs which were, in turn, balanced precariously on a cross log propped on two uprights. The bait was gone, yet the trap remained unsprung. The Savages took this to be a bad sign. I told them it was not the sort of sign God gives us, but I failed to allay their fears.

Late in the afternoon of the second day we stopped for a rest. I sat on an area of dry ground against a tall spruce tree following the curving flights of two hawks as they circled far overhead. I committed the sin of envy by wishing I could partake of their flight, their freedom, perhaps to be lifted up through the air by the hand of God and taken to His heavenly abode.

Someone started to wail. Hardly able to move my head, I turned my gaze to my children, the Faithful who had survived to this point. (I fear I neglected to mention that Aristide Babineau and his little daughter, Josette had been taken by the hand of God during the previous night. We woke to find them frozen together, she in his lap, he with his arms around her.) But none of the Faithful seemed to be the source of the crying. I heard the Savages murmuring among themselves. With great effort, I rose to join them. They were listening intently. The sound came again. Instantly I realized its source was from outside our own small group.

Neptune told me we had found the Passamaquoddy village. But such an announcement, which should have been accompanied by shouts of joy, was instead relayed with a countenance of deep sadness.

I was to see why when at last we entered the village.

The Jesuit's description of a happier time in the Passamaquoddy village had brought tears to O'zalik's eyes. How she wanted to be able to return to the past, to a time before the first contact with Europeans.

She had the strange sensation she was being lifted up out of her own body. She felt herself hovering over Alabaster Island and String of

Pearls. Perhaps a sacred eagle snatched her spirit in order to show her the world she lived in. And what she saw horrified her. It was not her world. It was not the world of the Passamaquoddy. It was a world in which the sacred earth below her suffered. And when she looked down to where she had been sitting, she saw she was no longer there. A shudder of fear passed through her.

When she returned to her house, she called her grandfather. She told him what she was feeling.

"O'zalik, we live now in the white man's world," he said. "It is no use resisting it, for you cannot change it."

"But is our world gone forever?"

"No. It's in our hearts and it will always be there. We struggle to preserve our language and our ways, but in the end we must live in this new world."

"I don't think I can."

He coughed. There was a long pause before he said, "O'zalik, it pains me to hear you speak like this. You must not let this Jesuit journal make you so unhappy."

"Grandfather, it's important I finish this work. The world must know. The people of Alabaster Island must know."

"Yes, O'zalik, but take care you don't destroy yourself in the process."

"I won't," she assured him.

They talked longer. She asked him to tell her an old Passamaquoddy story about the great bullfrog he told her many times when she was a child.

"In old times," he said, "there was an Indian village tucked away in the mountains and hidden from other men." He told her how the brook by the village dried up and the people found that another village had built a dam blocking their water. He told how the other village was ruled by a monster bullfrog and how the people sent a messenger to open the dam and that the man, knowing he was going to his certain death, was required to sing his death song on the way. But then, her grandfather said, Koluskap, who is the great and first being, was impressed by the messenger's bravery and decided to take things into his own hands. "So Koluskap went up to the other village and found the great bullfrog. Whereupon he thrust a spear into its belly and water gushed forth over the dam and into the brook. Koluskap rose high as a pine tree and picked up the giant bullfrog and squeezed it hard. And that's why the bullfrog has wrinkles on its back."

By the time her grandfather finished telling the story, O'zalik was crying. "Thank you, Grandfather," she said.

"Are your spirits cheered?" he asked.

"Yes…yes, they are."

"And no more talk of not being able to live in the white man's world. It is, after all, our world now."

She gave a short laugh. "No, no more talk."

"That's good O'zalik. We will pray for you."

"Will you teach me a prayer chant?"

"Now?"

"Yes…Please."

In a low, droning voice, he began to chant. She listened carefully to the words, mouthing them to herself as tears streamed down her cheeks. And when he finished, she thanked him.

But after she hung up the phone, she realized while she had been comforted she still felt herself an outsider in an alien land. She decided not to reread any more of the journal that day, to save it for the following morning. She knew what was coming. She knew it would be difficult.

She tried to remember what time Quentin got off work that day.

~

When Caitlin propped her bike against the wall of the building where Angus Macleod had his office, she saw Wayne Crenshaw going into Pauline's Coffee and Bake Shop. She turned to face the other way, not wanting to catch his eye. She felt she'd failed both him and his son. After giving him enough time to enter the shop, she ducked into

Angus Macleod's office.

Angus was with a patient so Caitlin took a seat in the waiting room. She forced herself to think of something—anything—other than her last meeting with Jasper Crenshaw.

She thought of Nigel. She recalled how they had honeymooned in Maui. It was a trip she'd been looking forward to for a long time and when they emerged from the baggage terminal at Kahului into the frangipani-scented air, fragrant leis around their necks, she thought they were in heaven. This was the true world God had created. And for the first two days at the Marriott on Kaanapali Beach it was just that. They strolled through the open-air lobby listening to the squawking of the hotel's pet parrot and admiring the koi fish in the lobby pool; they spent hours lounging by the pool, occasionally diving in and standing under the man-made waterfall to cool their sun-baked bodies; they drank mai-tais in the afternoon and fine wines with five-star food at night, after which they made love with moonlight and soft air coming in through the open balcony sliders. Even the raucous luau ten stories below their balcony couldn't disturb them.

They spent the afternoon of the second day shopping in Lahaina, and walking through an arts-and-crafts exhibit under the single banyan tree whose branches overspread an entire park. They came upon an old man, his dark, cratered face framed by a white beard. He sat cross-legged, chanting, keeping time on a gourd drum. A young, slim woman, with a glistening smile that raised Caitlin's envy, translated the words into English. She explained the chant was a *mele pule*, a prayer chant. Caitlin missed most of the Hawaiian phrases. But one she did get—immediately followed by the translation, "the sun appears"—was "*Puka 'ana o ka la.*" She presented her notebook to the woman and asked her to spell it out, which the woman did in neat handwriting. Caitlin took great delight in her discovery.

But that was nothing compared to Nigel's reaction. He was mesmerized. He insisted they stay until the chanter was finished. Caitlin knew he was using his prodigious musical memory to retain everything he heard. And when the chanter finished, Nigel asked the woman many questions including what the gourd drum was called *(ipu heke)*, where he could get one, and where he could buy recordings of chants such as the old man had sung.

For the next several days, Caitlin watched and listened in their hotel room as Nigel taught himself how to play the gourd drum and experimented with ways to merge Western composition schemes with elements of the chant. At one point, he excitedly said, "You know Caitlin, I can hear some similarities to plainsong in these chants." He had the hotel people send up some paper, which he lined off into staffs and began to develop a composition "...in free rhythm like plainsong and these Hawaiian chants" and not, as he explained, in the traditional major or minor modes but in the so-called church modes like the Phrygian and the Aeolian. To illustrate, he sang out a few measures of his emerging composition.

Caitlin understood very little of it but she took it all in. She was filled with joy at Nigel's childlike enthusiasm. What did it matter if she was spending her time alone at the pool and on the beach while he was deriving such great satisfaction from his discovery? What did it matter that even during al fresco dinners with views of the setting Hawaiian sun, he couldn't let his composition go? As long as he was happy, she was fulfilled. It didn't even bother her that he stayed in the hotel when she went gift shopping in Lahaina for both sets of parents. She went before dawn because somebody told her there were hundreds of mynah birds in the banyan tree and they all sing when the sun comes up. When she arrived in Lahaina, she saw no sign of the chanter and his translator. Except for one or two other jet-lagged early-risers, she was alone in the nearly deserted Front Street. Behind the small town and the sugar mill, the ridges of the hills were edged with early light. Gradually, they emerged, jagged, from the night. And all at once, as the sky brightened, the birds started to sing raucously. Caitlin had never heard so many birds at one time. She sat on a bench under one of the long arms of the tree and, after listening for a while, started to scribble out ideas for a poem. And as she wrote, she wondered, not for the first time, why she'd quit the creative writing program at Boston University or, for that matter, her archaeological studies, simply because she was to be married. True, they'd had to move to New York so Nigel could attend Juilliard, but she could always have found another writing program, other courses in archaeology.

Her near-trance lasted for two hours at the end of which she rose, tired and happy, and crossed the street to the Pioneer Inn for a long, leisurely breakfast to kill time before the shops opened. Later, after spending an hour or two at Hilo Hattie and buying the usual aloha shirts for her father and her father-in-law and the equally customary muumuus for the two mothers, she went back to the hotel where she persuaded Nigel to take a break and spend some time with her at the pool. She read her poem fragments to him. But he hardly seemed to listen and when she finished all he said was "That's nice, dear."

He lasted only an hour or so by the pool before he felt compelled to return to his composition.

Angus Macleod opened the door to his office and called in a woman Caitlin didn't know. She flipped through the old notebook she'd taken with her to the doctor's office to make use of the time. She searched for the fragments she remembered writing in Hawaii.

At the time it may not have seemed so to Caitlin, but from the perspective of more than twenty years, she knew the honeymoon had marked the beginning of her defining herself in terms of others—the daughter of an alcoholic evolving into the supportive wife of an aspiring musician and, later, the mother of the medical student and the mother of the dancer. Though it may have worked all those years, she now knew she could no longer continue defining herself that way. She found the fragments of that long-ago poem begun under the banyan tree in Lahaina. She started rewriting.

Not more than five minutes passed before she heard Angus Macleod's door open. He bid good-bye to the other woman and nodded to Caitlin, gesturing for her to enter his office.

Angus Macleod was a tall, balding man with a sharp nose and sad eyes. His voice fluctuated between coarse and smooth, like lumpy porridge, and he had a habit of protruding his tongue as if in thought. It took Angus years to lose the tag "from away." But after he intimately probed and examined most of the islanders, the natives finally figured they might just as well accept him as one of their own.

"What did you do to your knee?" Angus asked.

"Just scraped it a little. That's what I came to see you about."

"How?"

"I stumbled on some uneven rocks," she replied.

"How long ago?"

"A few days ago."

"You should have come to me earlier. That wound needs to be debrided." He rose from his chair and went to a metal cabinet.

She let him cleanse the wound.

She'd planned to ask the doctor about Agnes Orcutt dying only a short time ago, but in her anxiety about her meeting with Jasper Crenshaw she forgot.

~

Freddy and Caitlin were eating breakfast in Pauline's when Jasper Crenshaw walked in without his father. He took a seat at the table he and Wayne Crenshaw always used, next to Freddy's and Caitlin's table. All the other tables were empty. The lobstermen were already out and it was too early for people like Helen Underwood and the summer tourists. He cast an unfriendly glance toward Caitlin and Freddy.

"The usual, Jasper?" asked O'zalik from behind the counter.

"Eyuh."

She swung the door to the kitchen partially open. "Short stack, egg, sunny, *on top*," she called. She brought Jasper a coffee cup, filled it.

Some minutes later, the kitchen door swung open and Quentin Moseley appeared with a plate. He laid it before Jasper. "Short stack, friggin sunny-side egg on the friggin top."

Jasper jabbed the yoke with the edge of his fork and watched the liquid spread over the pancakes. He raised a jar of maple syrup and poured a huge amount over the mixture of egg and pancake until it pooled on the plate at the base of the stack.

Quentin leaned close to Jasper. "Your dad tell you what Angelique and her Indian friends are up to?"

Jasper gave him a look of concern. "What?"

"They figure on taking over Snagged Anchor Island. What's that do to the idea of building a new marina?"

"Quentin, you son-of-a-bitch," said O'zalik.

"Leave it be, Quentin," said Freddy.

Jasper let his fork drop on his plate. "Jesus Christ, I knew they'd come to get us. I just friggin knew it."

"Jasper," said Caitlin, sliding her chair back and placing her hand on his shoulder. "Quentin doesn't know what he's talking about."

Jasper leaned away from her. "And you do? You ain't even from here." He slowly shook his head from side to side. "Friggin Indians ain't gonna do that to my dad."

"They ain't gonna," said Freddy. "There's no proof there are Passamaquoddy remains out there. Relax."

"Think about it," said Quentin. "They'll make up proof."

"Shut up, Quentin," said O'zalik.

Quentin ignored her. "I think you and your dad better watch out," he said, leaning closer to Jasper.

"Jesus Christ, Quentin—"

"Quentin, leave it be."

"They'll probably build a settlement over there or something. Before you know it, they'll be all over Alabaster Island."

Jasper glowered up at Quentin.

"You're such a shit, Quentin," said O'zalik. "You know that?"

He turned and fixed her with an angry stare. Twin shafts of ice. He advanced threateningly toward her. "You started this, Sweetheart."

Freddy pushed his chair back and stood.

The screen door burst open. A loud, angry voice came from the doorway. "What's this talk about Snagged Anchor Island?"

Everyone turned to see Wayne Crenshaw glaring at Quentin. Quentin backed a few steps away from O'zalik. "I'm only repeating what I heard you and Morgan Fludd say."

"Is it true, Dad?" asked Jasper. "Is that what you and Morgan said? The Indians gonna take the island?"

"It was a stupid theory, Son. I don't believe it no more."

Jasper's neck flushed. "Friggin Indians."

"Now get a hold on yourself, Jasper," said Crenshaw. He took several steps toward Quentin who, his butt against a counter stool, couldn't back away farther. "You know something, Quentin, you are one piece of worthless shit. You know that? You have no business messin' with my boy's mind like that." Tears formed in Crenshaw's eyes. "No friggin business at all," he shouted in a strained voice. "Jesus Christ!"

Freddy put a hand on Crenshaw's shoulder. "It's okay, Wayne."

Wayne Crenshaw turned to face him, tears streaming down his cheeks. "No it ain't okay, Freddy. I spend half my friggin life trying to protect my boy from his own mind and some jerk like this has to go mess with it. It ain't fair."

Freddy's eyes misted with tears of empathy. He thought of a father's love for his son. He squeezed Crenshaw's shoulder.

Crenshaw slipped away from Freddy and knelt beside Jasper. He spoke softly. "Listen, Son, it ain't like that. It was a stupid idea and I realized it almost right away. Even Morgan Fludd recognized it. Ain't nothing gonna happen, so don't get yourself all riled up, okay? Please? Jasper?"

Jasper said nothing.

"Sometimes, people have stupid ideas," Crenshaw said, glaring at O'zalik.

Still, Jasper remained silent. He got up and walked toward the door.

"Jasper, listen to me. It's okay. If it wasn't, I'd tell you," said Crenshaw. "I'm your dad, ain't I?"

Jasper said, "I ain't gonna let them do it to us, Dad." He walked out the door.

Wearily, Crenshaw rose to his feet. His knees cracked. He looked at Freddy. "He ain't heard a thing I said. It's like that sometimes. The only thing I can do is wait and hope he gets over it."

"But Wayne," said Freddy, "he ain't ever actually done nothing has he?"

Crenshaw shook his head.

"Eyuh, so you see, it's all talk. Your son ain't gonna do nothing."

"I'd like to think that, but I ain't never sure." His shoulders sagged. "Jesus Christ, I ain't never sure. I wish his mother was alive. She'd know what to do." He moved toward the door. "I better go after him."

Caitlin went to the window. "No rush, Wayne. He's just standing out there."

Quentin slipped into the kitchen.

Freddy felt a shudder pass through him. He thought of Agnes and Jimmy.

Wayne Crenshaw looked at O'zalik. "You know, you don't help much with all this talk about Passamaquoddy remains. You're getting lots of folks riled up; it ain't only my boy."

"Sorry, Wayne," she replied. But there was no apology in her voice.

Crenshaw gave a sardonic laugh. "Funny thing is Snagged Anchor Island is on everybody's minds these days. Ernie Botham wants to have a meeting about it over to Burle's place."

"Ernie Botham?" O'zalik and Freddy asked in unison. "What has he got to do with it?"

Crenshaw shook his head. "Beats me."

~

As she merged into the crowd assembling to watch the annual Founders' Day parade, O'zalik was hoping to find Caitlin Gray. She was eager to talk with the woman. After reading the last journal entry of Father Dalou that morning, she was more than ever determined to persuade Caitlin to write the article for Jolene Baxter at the *Island Gazette*, otherwise it would never get written. Also, she knew she had to get away from Quentin. Maybe Caitlin could help. She'd been hoping to talk with Caitlin the previous day, but when she went to the cottage, no one answered the door. She heard the murmur of voices and a flutter of laughter from Freddy Orcutt's place. She'd debated briefly with herself before deciding she wanted to approach Caitlin privately. She'd left, returned home. She tried to take the edge off her impatience by pulling out Bob Blanchard's translation of the Jesuit's journal. She forced herself to reread the last entry, the one the Jesuit must have written some days after the previous entries, given the way the tone changed so abruptly. And so angrily.

And, not for the first time, she wondered, with a malignant smile, how big the explosion would be when it hit the *Island Gazette*.

Already, the parade was starting. O'zalik scanned the crowd for Caitlin but saw no sign of her. She positioned herself on the corner of Front and Main, where she would not only have a good view of the parade but would also have the best chance of finding Caitlin. The corner was also far from the spot near the viewing stand where the year-round islanders always gathered. Where Quentin was. Here, she was among the summer people who never glanced sideways at her with disapproving looks. After what she'd been reading in the Jesuit's journal, she wanted nothing more to do with the islanders. She'd seen representatives of the leading families taking their traditional seats on the viewing stand. There was Quentin, Garret Webster, Wayne Crenshaw—sitting in for his dead wife—John Peake, Helen Underwood, Freddy Orcutt, and Morgan Fludd.

They were all there, the names she'd read about.

The Grand Marshall's convertible turned the corner with Ernie Botham and Burle Ledyard sitting atop the backrest of the rear seat and waving to the crowd. The only reason the two men were not on the water with their lobster pots was because the town committee voted to bestow the honor of Grand Marshal on Ernie Botham since it would probably be his last parade. Of course, they also invited Burle Ledyard to sit beside him in the car. Behind the lead convertible came a float celebrating the ancestors of Alabaster Island. A construction representing one of the original settlers' houses occupied most of the float. Also, there was an old dory, freshly painted, with a fishing net and an American flag draped over it. Children dressed as the first settlers rode on each side of the float holding signs that read MOSELEY, ORCUTT, WEBSTER, UNDERWOOD, PEAKE, and FLUDD. People cheered as the float passed. Even from a distance, O'zalik could see the occupants of the reviewing stand rise in anticipation of their float.

Richie Comine followed in an open jeep bearing the legend, in bold letters, "Alabaster Island Police" with "and harbormaster" written below it in smaller letters. He waved and smiled at the crowd along with his three children, who were squeezed into the passenger seat of the jeep. Behind the jeep came a small marching band playing "America the Beautiful" out of tune.

The next float caused O'zalik to flush with anger. It depicted a small group of Passamaquoddy Indians, some being played by children with blond and light brown hair. Even the clothes were wrong, a Hollywood version of Native American clothes that bore little resemblance to what the Passamaquoddy traditionally wore. That the legend on the float proclaimed it honored the island's "Native American Heritage" didn't, in the least, appease O'zalik's anger, which was so great it brought tears to her eyes. For, she knew what they were doing. By pretending to honor the Passamaquoddy, they were co-opting their culture; assimilating them into their own white culture in a way that diluted the strength of the Passamaquoddy, neutered them. It was like sucking the venom from a snake bite. And she, O'zalik, was the snake.

The Passamaquoddy float was followed by several cars advertising island services, one of which was Pauline's Coffee and Bake Shop; a gaggle of clowns running from side to side; then the island's lone fire truck.

Fuming, O'zalik craned her head for some sign of Caitlin. She wanted someone to share her outrage with. How dare they?

The parade lurched to a halt. The marching band, which formed up in a half circle around the ancestors' float and in front of the viewing stand, stopped playing "America the Beautiful" and started playing the national anthem.

Shaking with rage, O'zalik pushed her way through the crowd. She could no longer tolerate being there. Once free of the press of people, she broke into a run.

She was sweating by the time she arrived at the deep cleft in the rocks near String of Pearls. After recovering her breath, she took from her pocket the folded pages that represented the Jesuit's last journal entry. Despite having been more than once annoyed at Father Dalou's airs of superiority when it came to the Mi'kmaq and the Passamaquoddy, she found herself sharing his excruciating pain, his sense of utter abandonment. His feeling of betrayal. His agonized spirit with which she could identify.

When I entered the village, there was no activity, only weeping and wailing. In one place, near the edge of the village clearing, a row of bodies, fully two dozen of them, lay covered by blankets. The blankets had been brushed by snow giving them the appearance of white winding sheets. All, that is, except for the body nearest the forest's border which lay in a pool of red more vivid than a Cardinal's vestments. For as we approached we saw a pack of snarling wolves tearing chunks of flesh from the thighs and buttocks of the poor soul whose body, yanked from under the cover of the blanket, was fully exposed to the snow and the wolves' jaws. With a cry of outrage, Neptune and two of his brothers rushed at the wolves who, momentarily emboldened or crazed by the blood that incarnadined their muzzles, stood their ground and stared with yellow eyes before bounding off.

I watched filled with sadness and compassion as Neptune knelt at the ravaged body of his mother and raised his arms to the heavens and let loose a howl of righteous rage at so great an indignity. I, too, raised my eyes to Heaven and asked what incomprehensible wisdom moved God to visit these pious, pure people with so great an injustice as to present them with the small pox and cause their bodies to be torn asunder by beasts.

I went from dwelling to dwelling and found another twelve dead. And of the living I found but nine, and of that nine, three died in the night so that in all, of a village of some fifty-two souls, counting Neptune and his companions, fully three out of every four were dead.

Was this God's most mysterious mathematics?

I had seen the progress of this disease before. I knew that if I did not get the remaining thirteen Passamaquoddy to L'île des Perles Perdues and to my friend, Doctor André Pajou, the remainder in all likelihood would also die. So I decided we would stay the night in the village and set off at first light to the island while we still had among us Savages healthy enough to paddle the canoes.

Twice that night we had to rouse ourselves and chase off the wolves who persisted in coming back and who betrayed their presence by snarling as soon as their teeth bit into flesh. What evil! Only partial bodies showed through the snow—half a face here, a single arm there, a hand, a leg.

Was God hiding them with snow?

Neptune and his companions forced themselves to remain on vigil throughout the cold night such that they were severely weakened for their great task of the next day. And I, wishing to show my solidarity also held vigil in the moonlight, that gave a soft radiance to the snow-covered bodies laid out before us, kept vigil with them. Such that I, too, was left not fully prepared to deal with the unimaginable hardships God would deliver up to us the following day.

The Bear was at the apex of the vault of the heavens when our sad, little party left the sad, little village behind and made for the shore from which we would paddle to L'île des Perles Perdues. The sea was unusually calm and the currents favorable. We beached near the long reef that runs out to a small island, the mate of L'île des Perles Perdues. As far as I know, it has no name except the Passamaquoddy name of Island of First Light where, in former times, they celebrated the pagan ritual of the Fifteenth Night of the Moon.

And upon that beach we were greeted not by Frenchmen but by satanic Englishmen. I had apparently not heard the island had fallen to the enemy. I was given no sign. The vicious Englishmen came to the shore, weapons drawn, and ordered us from the canoes. One of their number, a man named Webster, claimed to be their leader. He told me and my Acadian children to separate ourselves from the Passamaquoddy. He motioned the Savages to the far end of the beach, close by the reef. With our hapless party thus split, Webster called on four men by name. I made a point of remembering them. They were Orcutt, Moseley, Peake, and Underwood. He ordered them to destroy the canoes which, he insisted, were infested with disease. As the four men smashed boulders through the birch bark skins of the canoes, Webster approached me and asked what our purpose was. I replied we had sick among us and we were in need of the services of the physician, André Pajou, and I said that if, as it appeared, the good doctor was no longer on the island, we would appeal to his sense of mercy for the services of a doctor if they had one among them. To my surprise, Webster replied with a smile that on the contrary, André Pajou was still on the island and he would take me to the man. Upon hearing such good news, I was emboldened to inquire about the French leader, Jean-Pierre de Custine and was again assured that he, too, was still on the island and I was welcome to meet with him, also. I could only surmise that some sort of truce had been arranged and the French and English were no longer at war. This expectation was heightened by the pleasant conversation Webster engaged me in as we climbed the hill to the cluster of buildings I knew so well. He inquired about my journey and expressed great sympathy when I recounted to him the horrible difficulties that had beset us. Indeed, he even invoked Your name, did he not, when he said that it was only through God's grace that we survived.

As we approached the settlement, I was perplexed by the silence. If all the murderous Englishmen were at the beach, that still left unaccounted more than twenty Frenchmen who had dwelled here when last I visited the place.

But I soon had my answer. The bodies of twelve men were hideously impaled on stakes. From the wide-eyed, horrified, and contorted appearance of each and every one of the men, I could only surmise the vile procedure was performed while they were yet alive. Here was the body of the noble Jean-Pierre de Custine, stripped naked, dried blood smearing his body and caked around his mouth, his face half encrusted with snow giving him the appearance of wearing a mask. So, too, with dear, dear André Pajou. And so, too, with all the others. Was God hiding them with snow like the poor people in the Passamaquoddy village? Shall I sing God's praises for not submitting His own son to such cruel crucifixion?

Webster began to laugh at the tears that came to my eyes. And when he finished laughing, he pushed me before him back down the hill to the beach where my Acadian children huddled together on one side and my Passamaquoddy children gathered together on the other.

When we reached the Faithful, Webster went straight to Lisette Plamondon and pulled her away from us. He stood the unfortunate twelve-year-old girl before him and examined her with obvious lust in his manner. He laughed and pushed her toward the men he had called Moseley and Orcutt. They grabbed her arms and held her while a third man called Underwood (I must try to get the names right even if I never live to bear witness) while this Underwood felt under her dress between her legs. Little Lisette struggled and whimpered but there was nothing she could do. I advanced on the men and pleaded with them, in God's name I pleaded with them, to leave the poor girl alone. But it was to no avail. And then, in God's obscure, esoteric wisdom, He caused a fit of rage to enter me whereupon I turned to Webster and, wagging my finger at him, accused him of being of the same blood as one Captain Webster who violated this poor girl's mother, Madame Plamondon. There was nothing I could have said to more incite the man's rage against the Acadians and little Lisette and the Indians, for he had heard of the Madame Plamondon affair, and he knew her name, and he also knew of the death of his brother at the hands of the Mi'kmaq.

God must have known the man would become crazed.

Without a word, he turned his flintlock rifle on one of my Passa-

maquoddy children and blew a hole in his chest. He said he would do likewise with all of them until his brother was avenged. He ordered us to stay on the beach and he grabbed little Lisette and he marched up the hill with his men following close behind. Only a small guard was left behind, but what could we do in our weakened state? Where could we go?

They forced us to spend the remainder of that day and the entire night on the frozen beach with no shelter. All through the night we heard little Lisette's cries as, it seemed, the entire garrison of foul English had their way with her. In the morning, I awoke from an unwilled doze to learn that sweet Gabrielle Babineau had succumbed to the cold.

Not long after first light, Webster, followed by his men, came down the hill. He carried in his arms the limp, naked body of Lisette which he unceremoniously dumped at my feet.

It was the low water of a spring tide and the reef tethering L'île des Perles Perdues with its mate was fully exposed. The English stood in a half circle with their weapons while Webster ordered us to cross over the reef to the attached island. We had no recourse but to obey. Forlornly, we began our difficult trek. Neptune carried little Lisette on his back. Her arm swung lifelessly and drops of blood still issued from her private area to be diluted in the tidal pools scattered along the reef. We were but a few paces out when Webster called to me that this was the last day of the spring tide. I, of course, knew what this foretold. The reef was fully exposed and capable of being crossed only a few days of each month. After this day, another month would pass before it was crossable again.

They meant us to starve to death.

What irony it was that at that moment God caused the sun to briefly emerge from a cloud and the reef to sparkle like a street scattered with pearls, like a road to Heaven.

Only Madame Babineau failed to make the crossing. She was swept away by an especially large wave and we could only watch as her dress blossomed like a water lily and she floated helplessly away, arms spread wide as if in praise of God's most Holy Mercy.

So here I sit and complete my journal. It is starting to snow.

Have you penetrated the treasures of snow? Have you seen the treasures of hail that I reserve for times of distress, for the day of battle and of combat?

(I can make little sense of the above sentences, so I have provided a strictly literal translation. The sentences in French read, "As-tu pénétré jusqu'aux trésors de neige? As-tu vu les trésors de grêle, que je réserve pour les temps de détresse, pour le jour de la bataille et du combat?" Perhaps others can ferret out its true meaning—R.B.)

But why do I write if God will be my only witness. Would it be better, then, to address Him directly?

I ask, would it be better to address You? Certainly not to inform You, for You know everything. You know what I found when I entered the village of my beloved Passamaquoddy children. You know because You permitted it just as You permitted what soon followed and just as You permitted everything that occurred before. You beheld a devoted servant doing his utmost to honor Your name by endeavoring to rescue and bring to safety a number of Your Faithful and, upon seeing this selfless and pure act of piety, You chose in Your infinite and most inscrutable wisdom to send one trial after another against me until I lost fully one half of the people—Your children—that I was trying to save. And then You presented me with several dozen more suffering souls to try, with my meager and diminishing strength to save.

You knew what I would find when I entered the beloved village of my Passamaquoddy children. Yet, despite the knowing of it—the all-knowing of it—You, in your most unfathomable wisdom, planted in me a vision of the happier days of last summer and allowed that vision to fill me like a good meal until it blotted out all other thoughts. Was it Your unknowable wisdom that by so doing You would be able to punish me the more severely with the comparison? Did You plant images of Paradise in the minds of Adam and Eve after their fall?

What, I am humbly compelled to ask, have I done or left undone that I deserve such harsh punishment? What, I ask? Please, I beg You, tell me!

Was it that I took under my protection Madame Plamondon, a vio-

lated woman who, through no blame of her own, was left impure in Your all-knowing eyes? Was it that I persisted in the crossing of the turbulent waters and thus brought young Guy Plamondon and Auguste Leclair to their deaths? Was it, in Your all-knowing eyes, that I hurried through the Requiem Mass for sweet, little Georges Babineau on that frozen land because my concern was for the others of the party who were still living? Perhaps it was because I proved unable to pry open the head of the Savage, Edmond, in order to move his tongue with my hand that he might cease singing his pagan death song and instead offer his final prayers in praise of Your most impenetrable wisdom? Or was it that I was so focused on the mystifying suffering of my hands, and so sleep deprived because of that suffering, that I failed to notice You, in Your inexplicable wisdom, had reached down and snatched up Aristide Babineau and his young, innocent daughter, Josette, into Your all-knowing presence or that, mindful of the desperate condition of the others, I chose to press on without celebrating a Mass for the frozen father and daughter?

Were You angry that my Passamaquoddy children used to celebrate a primitive rite they called the Fifteenth Night of the Moon on this little island connected to L'île des Perles Perdues, the one they call Island of First Light?

I pray You say what baffling and ungraspable wisdom, moved you to complete the story in this way.

But You do not answer. Are You hiding?

My journal is a work that, though I will protect it, and bury it, and mark its presence, none but You will probably ever see. Which is why I felt it proper and fitting to address these last paragraphs to You. The entry is one that, as You know, I composed in its entirety on this our first day of banishment since I doubt I will have the strength to write more in the coming final days of our ordeal that will, as it happens, coincide with my own final days before coming into Your Divine presence.

If that is, indeed, what is to happen.

So, I am finished. I will close my book and bury it under a cairn of boulders. Already I have marked the spot with a crude cross scratched in the rock of this overhang. It is a weak cross because I am weak. It is for You to decide if my mark will survive; if my journal will survive.

Into Thy hands I commend it.

The snow continues to fall.

Her face fixed in an angry stare, O'zalik looked out at Snagged Anchor Island—Island of First Light. The last, lingering rays of sunset lit the tops of the spruce, that serrated, like a carving knife, the red sky. She crouched in the cave for hours as the sky turned red then ink blue then black. Stars appeared, her ancestors. The moon rose in the east. *Grandmother Moon.* It shone over the lurking outline of Snagged Anchor Island, washing the tips of the spruce.

island of first light

A wind rose, blowing through crevices in the rocks like a flute. It probed.cold fingers into the cave. O'zalik hugged herself tightly but couldn't stop the shivering. The flute was like a chant.

edmond's death chant...sung in the comforting presence of grandmother moon

her death chant

But not until she finished what she had to do.

In the middle of the night her grandfather visited, his arm around Father Dalou. Their faces were bone white under the gaze of Grandmother Moon. Her grandfather said, "Be patient with the Jesuit. He never fully understood our ways, but he tried to help. Only, they wouldn't let him. And his god wouldn't let him. Now he is condemned to wander between the world of the living and the world of the dead without a voice, without peace. Have pity on him. Give him back his voice. You have it within you."

Later, an eagle landed at the mouth of the cave. It stood at her feet staring at her. It never made a sound. After a while, it flew off and she felt her muscles quiver, every nerve in her body stretch out for flight, every cell. But her body was heavy and wouldn't leave the earth.

A parade started to the tune of a flute played by Grandmother

Moon. It danced around faint Polaris. The Boy Spirit led. He was followed by Pisces and Pegasus and Cassiopeia. Orion was also there, as was the Big Dipper. They moved in perfect order, slowly, with great dignity. As morning approached, Saturn came to join the parade. O'zalik watched with tears of joy in her eyes. She watched until at last the sun appeared blood red and hungry on the horizon and lifted Snagged Anchor Island from the gloom.

island of first light

She waited until the sun rose three hands into the sky before she stood, on shaking legs, and started back to her house.

Quentin would be on the mainland today.

It was time. But first she had a mission to complete.

~

Caitlin was the only customer in Pauline's Coffee and Bake Shop. She sat at a window table, chin propped on steepled hands, staring through the rain-streaked window at summer people bustling into and out of the gift shop. As they came and went, they snapped umbrellas closed or open. The morning started out bright but it soon clouded over, bringing rain. Laura in the gift shop would do a good business today.

The lobstermen who were in earlier left behind little puddles on the floor of Pauline's. The atmosphere was dank. With every opening of the door a quantity of sea air, laced with low tide odors, was let in. It now saturated the space.

All morning she'd been plagued with thoughts about Nigel, Dylan, Ellen…and Jasper Crenshaw. She was constructing new stories, trying them out. Maybe she did all she could with Jasper and he would be fine. Maybe Dylan and Ellen weren't as condescending and as dependent as they'd seemed. Maybe Nigel wasn't having an affair with cavatina-Ekaterina. What is real, anyway? Life is nothing more than the stories we tell ourselves. She marveled at how in the night, in the dark loneliness of bed, the stories were different from the daylight stories; how they were always more stark, more sinister, more convincing. Didn't that prove they were only stories? If they were the truth would they change so easily with a difference in daylight? Why, then, not try different stories that didn't leave her so filled with anxiety and self-loathing?

"What're you thinking so seriously about?" asked O'zalik, wiping the adjoining table with brusque sweeps of a cloth as though trying to strip it of its finish. It was mid morning and she was cleaning up after the breakfast rush, getting ready for the lunch crowd. There was an unfamiliar flatness to her voice.

"Just thinking about my husband and kids."

O'zalik gave a disgruntled look. "Feeling guilty?"

"Not exactly guilty..." Caitlin saw Jasper Crenshaw leaning against a telephone post on the opposite side of the street. He gripped a can of soda as he gazed in the direction of Pauline's.

"Not exactly?"

"All right, maybe a little bit. Perhaps I should give them a call."

Jasper raised his head, drained the soda, and crushed the can, throwing it into a trash container.

"But you told me you didn't want a phone in your cottage because you didn't want to be tempted...and so they wouldn't pester you."

"Yes, I suppose."

"And now you're getting all weak inside." O'zalik shook her head sadly. She moved to the table on the other side of Caitlin and started to rearrange the salt and pepper shakers, the menus, the napkin-wrapped silverware. Caitlin noticed a discoloration on O'zalik's cheek.

"What happened to your cheek?" she asked.

O'zalik's eyes darkened. "He hit me."

"O'zalik! Why?"

"He was pissed off because I showed up at Garret Webster's lobster bake and raised the issue of Snagged Anchor Island again."

"You can't let him do that to you, O'zalik."

"Don't worry. He won't get away with it."

"You should report him."

"To who? Richie Comine? This is their island. They've been friends since childhood and I'm just an *injun* woman."

Caitlin glanced toward the kitchen. "Where is he?"

"He had to go to the mainland today."

"O'zalik, you just can't let him get away with it."

O'zalik gave a wooden smile. "I told you...he won't. None of them will."

"What do you mean?"

"Do you remember our little discussion about writing?"

"Yes."

"It's all connected."

"How?"

O'zalik stared at her a moment. She sat at the table. "It's the Jesuit journal." She told Caitlin in low tones and in exhaustive detail about what it contained.

When O'zalik finished, Caitlin said, "My God..."

"The journal makes quite a story—one Jolene at the *Island Gazette* wants badly."

"Why are you telling me this?" Caitlin asked, reaching out and touching O'zalik's reddened cheek. "Does it hurt?"

O'zalik placed her hand over Caitlin's. "Because you should write that story."

"Me?"

"You're a writer, aren't you?"

"But it's your story. Why do you want me to write it?"

"Three reasons. One, since I'm Passamaquoddy, people will think I have an ax to grind. Two, you can write and you're looking for something you can sink your teeth into. And three, I can't write worth shit."

"O'zalik, I came here to write my own stuff."

"That's what you say," O'zalik snapped, "but now you're sitting here thinking of calling your family. So which is it? Are you going to write or are you going to go crawling back home?"

Caitlin glared at O'zalik but said nothing.

O'zalik took several deep breaths. "Listen, I'm sorry. I didn't mean to jump down your throat like that. I know you're not being weak just because you want to call your family…see how they are. It's that this journal thing has me so wound up, so furious. I just think…"

"What about Quentin?"

"I can't wait to see his face when it's published."

"No, I mean how can you go back to living with him?"

O'zalik shrugged.

"O'zalik, come stay with me at the cottage…for your own protection. I'm sure Freddy won't mind."

O'zalik's eyes filled. She nodded. "If it's okay with you. And I really want you to write the article."

"Can I have some time to think about it?"

O'zalik said, "Sure. But if you don't do it, their story will never be told. I can't do it and I don't trust anybody else." She lifted Caitlin's arms from around her shoulders, got up, and started wiping the next table. She looked across at Caitlin and said, "And there's one other thing I need to say."

"What?"

"You said you were Acadian, the same as the people the Jesuit tried to save. You have a stake in this, too." O'zalik moved to the counter and started rearranging sugar bowls and creamers. After a few moments she said, "I'm going to have to quit my job. I can't work here with him."

"Of course not. And you must come live with me."

"I won't be able to pay you anything."

"We'll manage."

Ten minutes later, Caitlin was sorry she called Nigel. Dylan and Ellen were with him and she ended up talking with all three of them. She couldn't fail to notice the concern in her children's voices and the sadness in Nigel's voice. It re-aroused the guilt in her and left her defenseless and without an answer when Nigel suggested he, Dylan, and Ellen drive up to Maine and take the ferry over to Alabaster Island for a few days. "You wouldn't mind, would you?" he asked.

Caitlin hesitated before saying, "No…No, of course not." She hated herself for giving in so easily. She turned to face the wall and hunched her shoulders, hoping her body would block her words from reaching O'zalik's ears.

"Because we all would love to see you."

"And I want to see you, too," Caitlin answered weakly.

"We miss you."

"Yes, of course. I miss you, too."

"How's next weekend?"

It was Tuesday. That would give Caitlin several days to prepare. "That sounds fine."

She heard Nigel lower the phone and talk with Dylan and Ellen for a few moments. He came back on the line. "It's all set. We'll come up Saturday morning. Any idea what time the ferry runs?"

Caitlin's shoulders sagged as she studied the ferry schedule posted on the wall beside the phone. "There's one at ten-fifteen," she said.

"Hmm. Well, we'll have to leave at ah…hell, the wee hours of the morning." He paused. "But Dylan and Ellen say that's okay. We'll grab something at Dunkin' Donuts and eat on the road."

"Then I'll meet you at the ferry a little after eleven," Caitlin said, trying not to sound…what? Trapped? After exchanging good-byes, she hung up the phone.

"The weekend?" asked O'zalik as she ran a mop over the floor with rapid, brusque motions.

Caitlin nodded.

"Well it's only two days. It's not your whole life—unless you let it be."

Caitlin gave her a weak smile. "Yes, I suppose." After a pause, she asked, "What do you know about Garret Webster at the Spruce Cove Inn?"

"Him? Nice man, but stubborn in his ways. Why do you want to know?"

"Just curious," Caitlin said as she headed for the door. "I knew his mother many years ago and I just thought I'd ask." Though she had not spoken with Garret Webster in all the time she'd been on the island, she thought it was time to have a private conversation with him—to make sure the past remained the past, especially with Nigel and the kids arriving in a few days.

Later that day, the tires of Caitlin's bike crunched the gravel of the inn's driveway, causing two elderly women to look up from their knitting, needles poised before them. They both seemed lost in the wooden embrace of huge Adirondack chairs. Caitlin smiled at them, wondering how they would manage to haul themselves out of the chairs whose seats sloped backward. Seemingly in response to her smile, all four knitting needles started to fly again.

Caitlin propped the bike against a utility shed and started up the wide porch steps. But her resolve weakened. She decided to wait, to gather herself. She came back down the steps and, aware of the two women glancing at her over their knitting, walked quickly to the edge of the lawn where a bench had been placed to overlook the ocean and Snagged Anchor Island. Judging from its weathered appearance, it was the same bench that was there twenty-seven years before when she'd last been at the inn. She sat, gazing out at String of Pearls and the island. She judged it to be mid tide because the reef was covered for almost its entire length, a long belt of white foam where the waves broke over it. Except for the two pearls, only a small section was exposed over which a flock of seagulls hovered, making occasional dives for whatever creatures lay exposed.

She'd been sitting for about fifteen minutes, debating with herself about going into the inn, when a voice behind her said, "You've been looking out at that island for some time now. What's got you so interested?"

She turned. It was Garret. He showed no sign of the anxiety he displayed that time on the ferry and occasionally at places like Pauline's. "Did you recognize me when you first saw me?" she asked.

"After all, it's been almost thirty years."

"Twenty-seven, to be exact." He said it with a blank expression and with a peculiar flatness, like oil on water, that raised a small alarm in her.

Trying to sound cheerful, she asked, "Really?"

"Twenty-seven years in August."

She didn't know what to say. "Have you been living on Alabaster Island all that time?"

He nodded.

She recalled how those many years before he talked avidly of going to art school, of living in New York. "Why did you never leave to pursue your sculpture?"

"I had to give all that up. My mother got very sick and I had to take care of her and the inn."

"I see." Caitlin said. "I'm sorry. I—"

"When she died, it was too late. There seemed no point."

"Again, I'm sorry." Caitlin didn't know what else to say.

He shrugged and smiled. "So?"

She frowned, unsure what he meant. "So…?"

His smile brought her back more than two decades. "What's got you so interested in that island?"

"Nothing in particular."

"No, really. I want to know."

She wasn't sure what to say. After all that time, it was an odd question but he seemed genuinely interested. "O'zalik Tomah thinks there are Passamaquoddy remains out there." She smiled, added, "I'm thinking of going out there and seeing for myself."

"I know what Angelique thinks. Don't."

"I beg your pardon?"

"Don't go out there." Though he was still flashing his personable smile, she sensed an underlying hostility in the way he said it. In an apparent attempt to offer an explanation for his brusque command, he added, "It's dangerous. I'm just concerned for your safety."

She laughed. "That's what Freddy Orcutt keeps saying."

"He's right."

"Perhaps, but—"

"Listen to him."

She'd not known what to expect, but she was wholly unprepared for the mixture of his old charm and the strange new hostility she now felt. She stood. "Look, perhaps this was a mistake. I should be going." She started to walk toward her bike.

"You didn't return the following summer like you said you would."

She stopped, turned to look at him. "Plans changed. That was a long time ago." She didn't tell him she'd met Nigel the following winter, or that when she last saw him he'd acted so strangely about the incident with the sketchbook, she had no desire to return.

"So why have you come back now?"

"I wanted a place to write."

"Is that all?"

"What do you mean?"

"You've never seen the sculpture I made of you." He offered his hand. "Come with me. I want you to see it."

"I'm…I'm not sure I should."

"It'll only take a few minutes." He started toward the inn.

Caitlin hesitated a few moments, then followed him, a feeling of lightness in her chest. Once inside the inn, they mounted the two flights of stairs to where she remembered his attic studio was located. He opened the door and stepped aside to let her in. Again, she hesitated before slipping past him. Their bodies touched. She felt a flush rise to her cheeks.

The room had an unused look to it. Dust covered the desk and the bookcases. "You haven't been sculpting lately," she said.

"Not for years. Too busy with the inn."

Several sculptures sat on the desk. One was of a young woman, nude except for a pendant in the shape of the moon that contained the word "ACCIHTE." She remembered that word from the sketch pad she saw many years before. Garret lifted another sculpture and held it out to her. "Recognize yourself?"

She blushed. It was the figure of a young woman with shapely breasts, long legs, well-rounded hips. Beautiful in every way. "Did I look like that?"

"You still do," Garret answered from behind her.

She couldn't take her eyes off the statue. She felt Garret's hands on her shoulders and let out a small gasp. He moved his hands to the edges of her breasts. She wanted to get away from him, turn, leave the attic, run down the stairs, run out of the inn. Instead, she leaned back into him. He seemed to take encouragement and turned her so she was facing him. "I think of you a lot," he said. "Even after all this time." His fingers started to work the buttons of her blouse. Caitlin closed her eyes, sucked in a breath. It was as if no time had passed since they last were together like this. He was much gentler than Nigel. Much more attentive.

She pulled herself away. "No, Garret. No, we can't do this." She re-buttoned her blouse. "I'm sorry. I just can't."

He said nothing. He only smiled.

Minutes later, they were downstairs in the lobby.

Garret took her hand and said, "You're welcome to come over any time. We've really upgraded the restaurant. You can be my guest. All in innocence, I assure you."

She said nothing.

"Besides," he said, looking at her left hand, "you're married. Bring him along."

She withdrew her hand. "He's not here. He's a conductor and he's preparing for a concert." Why did she tell him that? She needed to make reservations for her family for the weekend. Perhaps she was hoping she could do it through his staff and he wouldn't need to know about it.

"Then bring Freddy Orcutt."

She nodded. "Maybe I will. But I'll insist on paying. I owe him anyway for all the help he's given me."

"And the good advice," replied Garret. He lowered his voice as would a priest admonishing a child. "Don't go out to Snagged Anchor Island."

Twenty minutes later, she was descending the road into town when she heard a car coming up fast behind her. She pulled onto the shoulder, stopped, and stood holding her bike until the car passed. Garret Webster was behind the wheel. He didn't look at her. She watched as he drove down the hill and stopped at a small house on the outskirts of town. She remounted her bike and coasted down the hill. Just as she was passing the house where Garret stood on the porch, the door opened and Quentin Moseley appeared.

She hoped O'zalik had the presence of mind not to return to her house after work.

~

On Saturday morning, an hour before the ferry was due to arrive, Caitlin stopped in at Pauline's. As soon as she sat down, O'zalik appeared at her side with a pot of coffee and said, "You look like your favorite dog just got run over twice." She turned Caitlin's cup right side up and filled it with coffee.

Caitlin frowned at her. "I'm not feeling my best today."

"Sorry to hear that."

"Is it safe for you to be here? Where's Quentin?"

"Making a ferry run," O'zalik replied. "Morgan Fludd hired him for a few days to replace a sick crew member. It's safe for now. Have you given some thought about that Jesuit article?"

"A little," replied Caitlin. "But I haven't decided anything yet. I've got to get through these next few days first."

"Is this the day your family's coming?"

Caitlin nodded.

"How long are they staying?"

"Just the weekend," replied Caitlin.

"So your family's coming. Why does that upset you so much?" asked O'zalik in a flat voice.

Caitlin cradled her coffee cup in both hands, feeling the warmth. "Because they'll patronize me and they'll try to persuade me to go home with them, that's why."

"Just don't go."

"You don't know how they can play on my guilt. Like a violin."

perhaps more like a cello

O'zalik gave a sardonic nod. "I understand. Quentin can be the same way. He makes me feel guilty for being Indian then he uses it like a weapon or something."

"By the way, speaking of Quentin, I saw him talking with Garret Webster the other day. I think it was at your place. Are they close friends?"

"Uhm-hmm," replied O'zalik, "I'm told by Freddy Orcutt they go back a long way."

Caitlin glanced at her watch. "The ferry's due soon. I guess I'd better go." She took two more sips of her coffee and left the rest. She stood, paid O'zalik, and headed for the door.

As she left, O'zalik said, "Be strong, Caitlin."

Caitlin smiled at her and nodded. "You, too."

Ten minutes later, she had just leaned her bike against the ferry terminal building when Caitlin heard the deep-throated blast of the ferry's horn. It meant the ferry was entering the outer limit of the channel and would be at the dock in less than twenty minutes. While waiting, Caitlin debated with herself where to stand. If she stood at the edge of the loading ramp, she would appear too eager, giving them encouragement if, as she thought, they planned to pressure her to return with them. On the other hand, if she waited inside the terminal building, she would give them the impression of being indifferent to their arrival and that might hurt them, especially Dylan and Ellen. In the end, she decided on a middle ground, leaning against the post-and-rail fence that ran off to the side of the loading ramp to keep spectators from interfering with the cars and pedestrians using the ramp.

The ferry, a cloud of seagulls hovering over it, slid into the slip with a jolt. The massive pilings groaned. Caitlin saw Quentin Moseley lower the loading ramp with a rattle of chains then turn to direct cars off the ferry. He glanced at her, an unfriendly look.

They were in the first car off which meant they had arrived early since the ferry operated on a first-on-first-off basis. As they passed her, waving, she was surprised to see four people in the car. Ellen had brought Turrel Tyler along. That presented a problem—there wouldn't be room in the car for her. No matter, she thought. She could ride her bike to the Spruce Cove Inn, where they had reservations. That would give her more time alone and, besides, the trunk was probably filled with luggage and there would be no place to put her bike.

Nigel parked the car on the side of the road and stepped out. He threw his arms around Caitlin, pulling her to him. Unexpectedly, his embrace felt good to her. It reminded her of the way it used to be. She tried to concentrate on the pleasure, but she also found it constricting. She thought of Garret Webster. And she remembered Ekaterina Valerovna. After a long hug, Nigel stood back and said, "You have a tan. Island life must be agreeing with you."

"It's quite pleasant," she replied. "And how are the rehearsals going for Tanglewood?"

"I'll tell you all about it over lunch."

of course he would

Ellen joined them and hugged Caitlin. Dylan followed. Turrel Tyler extended his hand and said, "Good to see you again, Mrs. Gray."

They all started to talk at once. Nigel said, laughing, "Whoa, everybody. You'll all get your chance. Let's save it for lunch." He turned to Caitlin and said, "Come on, hop in and show us the way to the inn."

"Oh, no. There's not enough room for five."

"Nonsense. You'll sit in my lap and Dylan will drive."

"But I have my bike."

"We'll put it in the trunk."

"Don't you have luggage?"

"It's okay, we'll make it fit." Nigel inserted the key and popped the trunk open. Four large backpacks and one suitcase occupied most of the space.

"No," said Caitlin, "it won't fit."

"Of course it will," replied Nigel. "Go get your bike."

Reluctantly, Caitlin went to the terminal building, retrieved her bike, and walked it to the car. Dylan lifted it into the trunk, arranging the pedals so they wouldn't puncture the luggage. However, when he tried to close the trunk, it wouldn't latch.

"That's okay," said Nigel. "We'll just drive with it open. Right, then, everybody in."

As they left the parking lot, Caitlin saw Quentin Moseley directing cars onto the ferry for the return trip to the mainland. She knew the ferry would make several more round-trips and O'zalik wouldn't have to worry about Quentin for a while.

The drive up to the Spruce Cove Inn, although short, was uncomfortable. Caitlin was forced to sit like a child in Nigel's lap. He wrapped his arms around her like he'd never let go. With every bump, the trunk lid bounced off the bike's frame. Caitlin pictured the paint being chipped off and resigned herself to having to pay Freddy Orcutt for having the bike repainted. Also, she was worried about being at the inn with her family and with Garret Webster present. There was the chance he would let on they knew each other and that would arouse Nigel's easily aroused suspicions. She didn't need any scenes.

As they pulled into the long driveway of the inn, Caitlin looked around for a sign of Garret Webster. She saw none. But that meant nothing; he was probably inside at the registration desk or in the dinning room charming people. She was bound to see him no matter what she did.

After piling out of the car, Caitlin leaned her bike against the porch while the others carried their luggage inside. She followed them.

When she was there only a few days before, Caitlin hadn't really looked at the lobby. Garret had gone to some expense to redecorate. She was surveying the huge oriental rug and the Chippendale furniture when she saw something she instantly recognized and that made her suck in her breath. Garret had taken the sculpture from the attic and placed it along with others on a sideboard. She was confident Nigel wouldn't recognize her as the model—she'd put on too much weight over the years. Though if he looked at it closely, he might notice the resemblance. After all, he knew her then, too. How good was his memory?

When the receptionist asked Nigel if they still planned to stay two nights, Caitlin listened carefully.

"That's the plan now," Nigel answered. "But it could change, depending. We'll let you know in good time."

Caitlin wondered, *depending on what?*

Garret made only a brief appearance when he delivered menus to their table and told them, smiling brightly, who their waitress would be. As he left, he gave Caitlin a long, frank look but, to her relief, none of the others seemed to notice.

After they ordered, and throughout the entire lunch, first Nigel, then Dylan and Ellen, talked nonstop about the things they were doing. As the lunch wore on, she began to grow more and more annoyed. Not once did they ask her how her writing was going or what else she might have been doing. They talked only of what they were doing. It felt just like being back in Waltham. It was as though her sole purpose—the one they found difficult to live without—was to be a mirror to their accomplishments and they had come to partake of it, to fill themselves up with it. It occurred to her they'd come for a transfusion. To nourish their own self-worth with the blood of her creative caring, because their creative instincts had gone anemic.

Only as they were leaving the table did Turrel Tyler ask, "So, Mrs. Gray, have you been able to get much writing done?"

She saw the others look at her, waiting for her answer. "Yes,

Turrel," she said, finally. "Quite a bit. It's been going well."

She waited for Nigel or Dylan or Ellen to probe a little further, but nobody said a word. Finally, Nigel said, "I wonder if they have a piano in this place. I'd love to play for you the first movement of the new piece I'm working on. I finished it just last week."

It went the same way over dinner that night and for the entire weekend. It was only over lunch at the Boat Shed on Sunday, several hours before they were due to board the ferry, that her family did what she had been expecting all along—make a concerted effort to talk her into returning home with them.

"You know, Caitlin," Nigel said, "I've been thinking. We could build an addition on the house that would be your exclusive domain, your writing studio."

"What are you saying?"

"You should come home with us."

She felt a heat rise to her cheeks. "You know I need this time, Nigel. It's unfair of you to ask me that. Besides, I'm thinking of doing an article for the local newspaper that will require me to do some research here."

"I…we…miss you terribly. We want you with us."

"And what about me? Doesn't what I need count?"

"Of course it does," said Nigel.

"Then don't ask me to come home. Not just yet, anyway." She looked from one to the other. Only in Turrel's eyes did she see any sympathy. "Do you understand what I'm saying, Turrel?" she asked, feeling ashamed of manipulating him into the family argument.

"Yes, Mrs. Gray, I do."

Ellen shot Turrel an angry glance. However his simple assertion seemed to deflate their will to argue. They passed the rest of the lunch mostly in silence punctuated only by occasional idle observations about the food or the weather. As soon as they finished lunch, it was time to go to the ferry terminal.

As they walked, Nigel placed a retraining hand on Caitlin's arm.

"Let them get ahead of us," he said. "I want to say a few words in private." There was a hostility in his voice Caitlin hadn't detected before. Finally, when the others were well ahead of them, he stopped, turned to her and said, "Listen Caitlin, I'm getting just a little fed up with this act of yours."

"What act?" she asked, her cheeks feeling hot.

"You know bloody damned well. Your act of being the long-suffering, supportive wife and mother who gave up her own ambitions to dedicate herself to her loved ones. It sounds noble and generous, but it won't wash."

She felt an urge to hit him. "What are you talking about?"

"I'm talking about your blaming us for holding you back when all along you know perfectly well you could have done all the writing you wanted with full support from every one of us."

"Damn you, I—"

"Caitlin, you're not the victim you make yourself out to be." In a softer voice, he added, "None of us is."

Caitlin stared at him, fuming. Everything he said made her blood boil. But at the same time she knew instinctively there was at least some truth in what he said and that made her all the more angry. She searched for words. "Now you listen to me, Nigel. I am staying on this island and I'm going to write and that's all there is to it. In fact, I've agreed to do an article for the *Island Gazette*."

"Well, brilliant. So you've finally decided to have a bloody go at it. What are we supposed to do, applaud?"

"I'm only saying it's about time I look after my own needs."

"And I'm only saying it's too bad you didn't figure that one out long ago."

"Meaning?"

"Meaning it was you holding yourself back, not us. We never asked for a goddamned saint who—"

"I'm not trying to be a saint." A gust ruffled Caitlin's hair. She brushed it away from her forehead.

"Perhaps, perhaps not. But you're perfectly willing to blame your devotion to us for your failure to do what you wanted to do. And now look what you've done. You've let this thing fester so long you have to leave your family to deal with it." He looked away. "It just doesn't make sense to me. You would have been far more useful to us if you did what you wanted to do long ago instead of resenting us for your not doing it."

"Useful?" Caitlin's anger flared. "Useful?"

"Okay, maybe that's the wrong word. I'm a musician, not a writer. But I think you get what I mean."

"No, Nigel, I don't get it at all."

"It's just...," He stammered. "It's just that...Christ, I don't know..."

She stared at him, waiting.

Nigel continued. "We would have all been happier, including you, if you weren't afraid of your writing and just did it like the rest of us did what we were driven to do."

Caitlin said nothing. Everything she could think to say seemed futile. She was confused and wanted nothing more at that moment than to be somewhere else. To be alone. By this time, they had arrived at the terminal. To Caitlin's great relief the ferry, for once, was a little early and already sitting in its slip. She saw Quentin Moseley staring at her.

"I'm writing an article for the *Island Gazette*," she repeated as if to reaffirm the decision she'd made only moments before in the heat of the moment.

Nigel pulled her aside, away from the car. "Does this have anything to do with the innkeeper?"

"The innkeeper?"

"Yes. The sculptor."

"I don't know what you're saying."

"Only that I happen to know you posed for one of those nude sculptures."

Caitlin stared at him incredulously. "What?...How?"

"I asked at the desk about buying one. They have a portfolio with more details about each piece. That one, the one that looks like you, is titled 'Caitlin Aroused'." Nigel's eyes burned with accusatory anger.

"Bastard."

"Who, me or him?"

"Yes, goddamn it," Caitlin snapped. "That was almost thirty years ago, for God's sake."

"I thought we weren't supposed to have any secrets. We said—"

"You mean like your little secret concerning Ekaterina Valerovna?"

Nigel flinched. He stared at her dumbfounded. He said nothing.

She felt as though she'd been hit in the stomach. "Jesus Christ, it *is* true isn't it?"

Nigel shifted his gaze from her.

"Look at me," said Caitlin with a hiss. "You're screwing her aren't you?"

"Caitlin, I—"

"Get off my island."

"Caitlin, just listen to me. I—"

"Get off my island. Now!"

He stared at her for a long moment. He glanced at the car, the ferry, returned his gaze to her. "Can't we—"

"There's nothing to say. You've said it all."

Nigel started to stammer something. He stopped. He nodded. "Call me later. We can talk."

She said nothing.

He climbed into the car and maneuvered it into the line waiting to board. Giving her a hard look that clashed with the sweetness in his voice, he said, "I'm sorry we put such demands on you. Of course you should stay and give your writing a real go."

She knew he said it only for the benefit of Dylan, Ellen, and Turrel Tyler.

"Yes, Mom, we're rooting for you," Ellen added, giving Nigel a curious look.

"Yuh, hang in there," said Dylan.

Nigel said something, but it was drowned out by the small detonations of flags flapping in the stiffening breeze.

Quentin was already waving cars over the loading ramp. Caitlin was thankful she wasn't forced to struggle through long and awkward farewells before her family disappeared into the belly of the ferry. She looked up at the wheelhouse and saw Morgan Fludd looking at her. She gave him a weak smile.

Soon the ferry's horn sundered the air and its propellers churned the water, raising muddy sediment. Slowly, the ferry slid out of the slip. As she watched it maneuver through the sinuous channel accompanied by a flock of seagulls dipping and swirling, Caitlin seethed with anger. More than ever now, she was committed. Even before the ferry disappeared around Sheep's Pasture Point she was making plans for her journey out to Snagged Anchor Island.

cavatina ekaterina

As she started to walk along Harbor Street toward the coast road, Freddy's truck approached her. He gave a little toot and pulled over in front of her. He leaned across and opened the passenger door.

"Fancy meeting you here," Caitlin said with a suspicious smile, struggling to bury her emotions.

"Just happened to be passing by."

"Just happened to be passing by?"

"Eyuh. And saw you walking."

"And you figured you'd give me a lift back to the cottages."

"Eyuh, 'bout like that."

Caitlin climbed into the truck. All the way back to the cottages, neither of them spoke. As they passed the cemetery, Caitlin thought to ask Freddy about his wife dying only three years before, but the time didn't seem right. She decided to wait for one of their frequent chats on his porch. When they pulled into the gravel driveway and stepped down from the truck, Caitlin asked, "Can I offer you a beer or something?"

"No. I expect you're itching to get to your work seeing as how you lost an awful big chunk of your writing time."

Caitlin smiled. She hugged Freddy and murmured, "Thank you."

A blush suffused his cheeks. He backed away from her. "It was only a ride home. No need for thanking me."

Later, Caitlin was scarcely aware of the passage of the sun overhead as she wrote into the late afternoon. And when she came out of the trance she looked out to see String of Pearls once again exposed for most of its length out to Snagged Anchor Island. She stared at it for a few moments before taking up her new poem and reading it through again.

Now in the last decaying hour before dawn I heard
A congregation of myna birds electrifying the banyan tree,
Their singing freeing nightmares from the stables of mind,
Urging the salving sun from high Haleakala even as the harvest
Moon settled heavy in the west to seesaw the sun
From Haleakala's kiln. I felt the startled Earth tremble with joy
As plumeria scented the scene from the thuribles of a thousand
sun-drawn stems.
And after the birds I faintly heard an ancient chant, muffled by years,
singing that the sun appears…Puka 'ana o ka la!

She was pleased with her work, though she had that familiar nagging sense she often got with her writing that she could do more, refine it further. But she decided it would be best to put it aside and pick it up again in the morning. Then, if she still felt it needed more work, she would be fresh.

After the visit, writing the poem was, in some way, a necessary thing. A reestablishing of herself.

cavatina ekaterina

Now that the truth was out, there was a relief in it. Infinitely better than not knowing, was knowing. Now she could make her choices without groping through a fog of uncertainty.

She went to bed contented.

~

When Freddy stepped outside with his second cup of coffee at first light, the sun, just now rising over the saw tooth outline of Snagged Anchor Island, caught him full flush in the face. He shielded his eyes. A great blue heron—long legs and S-shaped neck—was feeding on the ebbing tide at String of Pearls. Freddy sat in his chair and began to rock slowly. Across the way, Caitlin emerged from her cottage. She stretched, yawned.

"Mornin'," Freddy called.

Caitlin turned. "Good morning, Freddy."

Freddy motioned for her to come over. He continued to rock slowly with the casual ease of one who'd already reserved a plot in the cemetery and was in no hurry.

"What's the weather going to do?" Caitlin asked, mounting the steps to the porch. It had become a morning ritual with them. It amused him.

"Fog most of the day on George's Bank," Freddy answered. "Clear here, though. Southerly breeze kicking up this afternoon." He gestured toward her cottage. "She sleeping?"

"O'zalik? Yes."

He told Caitlin to go into his kitchen and pour herself a cup of coffee. When she returned, she sat in her rocker. They sat in silence as they sipped their coffees and stared out to sea—another morning ritual. He was glad O'zalik had a habit of sleeping late. It gave him more time alone with Caitlin. Finally, he asked, "Recovered from your family visit?"

The heron lifted off on its great wings and flew with slow, steady wing beats toward Snagged Anchor Island trumpeting a deep-throated, hoarse, *fraaahnk... braak*.

"I don't think they realize how much I want to write."

Freddy gestured toward the heron with his coffee cup. "Been watching him the last half hour. Don't often see them in daytime." He turned to look at Caitlin. "You seem to want it—writing, that is—something awful."

"I do."

"Wanting something real awful is a powerful thing."

Caitlin chuckled. "I guess I got married too young. Before I really knew what I wanted to do."

"Eyuh, most everyone is too young when they marry."

Caitlin gave a rueful smile. "I suppose."

"...and too young when they die."

"Have you ever wanted something so badly you thought you couldn't live without it?"

For a long while, Freddy said nothing. He was testing the proposition the way he tested almost everything she said. With a sad smile, he said, "Eyuh...wouldn't mind having them back, them that's gone. But that ain't the way things work."

"No, guess not."

"You never told me what happened, Freddy. If you don't mind talking about it, I'd like to hear."

Freddy took a deep breath and paused to consider whether to tell the story or not. Sometimes it was best just to let things be. But, in the end, he decided to tell her. "He left for a few days out on George's Bank, just some hook and line fishin' since I wasn't there to help. Goldang radio was broke, but I was too busy with Agnes to get it fixed. She was sick at the time." He stared out to sea. "Gets harder and harder to work George's Bank. Most of the ground fish—cod, haddock, halibut, yellowtail flounder—they're damn near fished out. Then the goldang factory ships get most of what's left. Besides, that day he left—it was fine weather for as far as the eye could see. Several days' worth with the sea smooth as a baby's backside. Leastwise, that's what God was showing us. Guess you can't trust him nohow."

"So a storm came up?"

"A real baster. Came up out of nowhere like it had a purpose. Like it had a mind it was going to take my boy. Swept overboard. Never did find his body. The boat, she washed up on String of Pearls out there."

"Is that why you always have the marine forecast on?"

"Eyuh. Never make that mistake again."

"No, I suppose not."

"A body needs to be prepared for what's coming." He looked out toward Snagged Anchor Island for some sign of the great blue heron. There was none. "Seems kinda late, though," he said.

"I'm sorry, Freddy."

"Eyuh."

They fell silent for a while before Freddy, grateful for the opportunity to talk, said, "When Jimmy died—my boy—I looked into the bottom of my soul and it warn't pretty. All that bitterness and guilt and whatnot. Seems to me this thing you were taking such a fit to do—go out across String of Pearls and such—might just make you look into the bottom of your own soul." He turned, looked into her eyes. His brow was furrowed. "Are you prepared for that?"

"I don't know."

"Seems to me you'd be taking a mighty big risk. It ain't pretty looking inside yourself." He started to rock more vigorously. "Nope. Ain't pretty."

"But maybe that's the point, Freddy," Caitlin said, placing a hand on his wrist. "Maybe that's what I need to do."

Freddy smiled. "Now, how about accompanying me to Burle Ledyard's house? There's some kinda mysterious meeting Ernie Botham's called for."

"What's it about?"

"Snagged Anchor Island."

"What about it?"

"That's what I'm dying to find out," Freddy replied. "O'zalik be okay on her own?"

"I'll make sure the door's locked."

A half hour later, Freddy and Caitlin knocked on the door of Burle Ledyard's small, ramshackle cottage. After Ernie Botham was diagnosed with cancer, Burle insisted the man move in with him instead of keeping his single room at Angus Macleod's house. Burle's theory was, with Angus having his doctor's office on the first floor of the house, Ernie didn't need to be reminded of his own medical condition every time he went out or came in through the waiting room. "Who wants to be seeing sick people all the time when you have the option of looking at me?" Burle asked with a smile, to which Ernie answered, simply, "Eyuh, guess you're right."

While waiting for someone to come to the door, Freddy surveyed the plot on which the house stood. In years past, Burle Ledyard always kept a neat garden of mixed perennials and annuals. Freddy used to judge when it was time to plant impatiens by watching to see when Burle planted, for the man was always earlier than everybody else on the island—so early that several times he had fallen victim to late frosts. But now the garden was turned over to weeds because Burle spent nearly all his time out on the water with Ernie. They combined what formerly had been separate lobster territories and now fished nearly twice the traps with a single boat since, with his growing weakness, Ernie was no longer able to fish alone. But that, of course, required many more hours on the water, especially since Ernie needed all the money he could get because he insisted on paying off his share of the boat before he died.

The door opened. Burle Ledyard stood smiling at Freddy and Caitlin. "Come on in," he said. "The others are here, so we can get started. Me and Ernie want to get this over with so we can get out on the water." He led them into the small living room where Garret Webster sat on a chintz sofa facing Ernie Botham who was sitting upright in a high-backed chair taken from the kitchen. Helen Underwood was nestled in an easy chair. Burle motioned Caitlin to the remaining easy chair while Freddy sat in one of the two additional kitchen chairs. Burle went into the kitchen and emerged with a tray of muffins and a coffee thermos. He placed them on the coffee table where cups were already laid out. "Muffins and coffee are from Pauline's," he said. "Guess we ain't got no milk or cream or sugar 'cause I forgot. Me and Ernie never use the stuff. How about you, Mrs. Gray, you use cream and sugar?"

"Well, normally, yes. But black is just fine."

Everybody else agreed black was okay and they made idle conversation until the muffins were gone. "So what's this all about?" asked Freddy.

"It's about Snagged Anchor Island," Ernie said.

"What about it?"

"I need to decide what to do with it," said Ernie. "That's why I invited you folks. I figure it's a matter for all the residents of Alabaster Island and what with you all being on the town committee and all."

Freddy saw a look of alarm on Garret's face.

"But, Ernie, Garret here owns the island," said Helen Underwood. "What's it got to do with you?"

"But that ain't true," said Ernie. "At one time the island belonged to Garret's grandfather, but sometime later it was willed to me."

Garret Webster shifted nervously on the sofa.

"But I don't understand," said Freddy. "I thought everybody knew old Otis Webster left the island to his sons and—"

"Freddy's right," said Helen. "Being in real estate, I certainly know these things. Otis Webster—there never was a more ornery old cuss—left the island to his sons Melvin and Clive, then when Melvin died first, it all went to Clive who was Garret's father, and of course when Clive died, it went to Garret. Isn't that right, Garret?"

Garret remained silent. He stared at the floor.

"Garret?" Helen prompted in her twig-snapping voice.

"Ain't the way it happened," said Ernie.

Helen turned to him. She stared open mouthed. Finally, she asked, "How *did* it happen, Ernie?"

"Old fart was some pissed off at his sons for marrying girls from away. Cut them off and left the island to me."

"Why you?" asked Helen, a look of stunned incredulity on her face.

Ernie shrugged. "Guess I was the only one could tolerate the old fart and he was appreciative. Figured I was his only friend." Ernie turned to Freddy. "Secret was, I never listened to the man; just shut my ears up. Reason you and him was always fightin' is you listened to him too much, 'specially when he went on longer than a hard winter about Jimmy's accident."

Freddy felt a surge of anger even after twenty-five years.

Helen Underwood rose and walked to the window as if this revelation was too much to take sitting down. She turned to Garret Webster. "So now I see why you didn't want to partner with me about a resort on Snagged Anchor Island."

"Why did you never tell nobody?" Freddy asked Ernie.

Ernie shrugged. "Why bother. Warn't going to do nothin' with the place anyhow. Too busy fishing."

"So you let Garret pretend he owned the island?"

"Why not? I figured I'd just give it back to his family someday anyway."

Garret sat upright. He and Helen exchanged glances. Garret stared at Ernie. Helen said, "Your plan was to will it to Garret, here?"

"Eyuh, but that was before I got cancer. Now, seems fittin' to give the place to Burle, here, for all he done for me."

Burle seemed stunned by this. "But, Ernie…"

"Now don't get all mushy about it, Burle. You deserve it."

"But why bring this all up now?" asked Freddy.

"Good a time as any," said Ernie. "I won't be here much longer, so we might as well figure it out now." He looked around. "Way I see it, Burle here won't have any more use for the island than I do. As soon's I'm gone, he'll give it away, but if I know him and his generous soul—and I sure as hell do—he'll want to give it to *all* the people of Alabaster Island."

Burle nodded, smiled. "Eyuh, sounds fittin' to me."

"So, you see," said Ernie, "that's why I asked you people to be here. Whatever happens to the island, it should be decided by a town meeting."

"That the way it's gonna be with you, Burle?" asked Freddy.

"Eyuh. If he gives the island to me, I'll just turn around and give it to the people of Alabaster Island."

Freddy turned to Ernie. "So why don't you just give the island directly to the people?"

"'Cause I want Burle to get the credit. He's a good man and he deserves it. Besides, I shouldn't get no credit because all this time I had the island it never occurred to me till just now the people of Alabaster Island could've benefited. That's a lot of wasted time."

"So where does that leave us with regard to Angelique Moseley's interest in the island?" asked Helen Underwood.

"You mean about there being Passamaquoddy remains out there?"

"Yes."

"Seems to me she ain't got no proof," said Burle.

"And what about Wayne Crenshaw?" asked Freddy. "He's talked some of building a marina out there."

"Seems to me if he's got the money, the people of Alabaster Island would be happy to lease him some land," said Ernie. "Be good for everybody."

Everybody nodded in agreement.

"What do you figure that'd be worth?" Freddy asked Helen.

"Just the land? Figuring the revenue he'd be likely to generate, I'd say a hundred thousand or so. But if we were to subdivide the island so rich folks could build summer homes…I'd say we're talking a good two or three million, maybe more."

Burle Ledyard let out a whistle. "Dang, I knew I shoulda got cream and sugar for the coffee."

~

O'zalik gazed at the approaching fullness of the moon. She knew, as all islanders knew, that it was tracking toward perfect alignment with the earth and the sun and also that it was edging ever closer to the earth like a shy but beguiled lover. They were nearing the ideal conditions for a spring tide—a perigean spring tide.

Grandmother Moon.
accihte...changing color moon

Several days before, O'zalik received a phone call from her grandmother telling her that her grandfather was dying. She had to go to his side. But she didn't want to go alone. She asked Caitlin to accompany her. When Freddy heard about it, he insisted on going, too. The three of them took the ferry to the mainland, rented a car, drove to the Pleasant Point Reservation on Passamaquoddy Bay and the Canadian border. O'zalik's grandparents lived in a small house overlooking Half Moon Bay on the eastern side of the peninsula locally known as Sipayik. When they pulled up to the house in the middle of the night, O'zalik's grandmother came out to meet them.

"O'zalik, it's so good you could come." She gazed at O'zalik with sad, tired eyes.

"How is he, Grandmother?"

"Waiting for you."

O'zalik quickly introduced Caitlin and Freddy. Then she said, "Please, take me to him."

While Caitlin and Freddy waited in the small living room, her grandmother led her to the bedroom. He was lying on his back, head propped on pillows. His eyes were closed, his head was motionless, but his lips moved. O'zalik recognized the barely audible murmur issuing from his lips as a death chant. She moved closer. His nose, lit by a soft light and silhouetted against the white wall, appeared like a bony ridge. She hadn't known he'd lost so much weight. His voice always seemed strong over the phone. Incongruously, her attention was fixed on his long nose hairs. She thought she saw them move with his breathing.

He fell silent. A moment later, he opened his eyes, slowly turned his head toward her. In a labored voice he said, "Soon it is the feather shedding moon, *Apsqe.* I will be happy to join her."

"Grandfather..."

He reached for her. When she placed her hand in his, he turned it over and examined her wrist. He nodded. "You have been our daughter and we are happy. Now you must be strong on your own."

"But there is Grandmother."

"No, O'zalik, you must be strong on your own. You must always remember you are Passamaquoddy."

"I never forget it."

"We live in a different world, we live among strangers, but our ways never die. They are of the earth and the sky. That is our power. Remember that."

"I will remember."

"Can you be strong now?"

O'zalik nodded. "I can be strong."

"And will you honor those who have gone before? It's our way."

"You know I will, Grandfather," she said. "That's why I'm going to make sure that Snagged Anchor Island is turned over to us."

"That will be difficult. People don't like us taking over land they figure belongs to them."

"They stole enough of our land."

"They will fight you."

"All the same, I'm going to do it. It will honor you and Grandmother as well as our ancestors. It will be a place for your spirits to go to when the time comes."

He gazed into her eyes for a long moment, smiled. Then he rolled his head, stared at the ceiling, and resumed his murmured chant. His hand stayed in hers. After a while, he reached his left hand to the other side of the bed. O'zalik's grandmother moved to that side and took his hand in hers.

Arms stretched as if in flight, holding his granddaughter's hand, holding his wife's hand, he let out a long wheezing breath.

With a sigh that was a soft whimper, O'zalik's grandmother rose. She crossed his arms over his chest. She leaned over and kissed him on the forehead. She closed his mouth and kissed him on the lips.

O'zalik followed her into the living room. When they told the others, Caitlin, then Freddy, embraced her and her grandmother. Her grandmother went into the kitchen, emerged moments later with a tray on which were three cups of coffee and an assortment of cookies. She set the tray on the coffee table. Without a word, she disappeared into the bedroom.

O'zalik, Caitlin, and Freddy drank coffee and ate cookies in silence.

Ten minutes later, O'zalik's grandmother reappeared. She had changed into her best Sunday clothes. "O'zalik, you should take your friends to the park."

"But I want to stay here with you."

"It was his wish. He wanted you to see what you will see."

"But..."

"It was his wish, O'zalik. Please do it for him."

O'zalik continued to protest but it was to no avail. Given the circumstances, what could she do but honor her grandparents' wish? Caitlin, Freddy, and O'zalik piled into the car, drove to Gleason Point Park. In the wash of moonlight they saw, near the shore, the vague outlines of the herring weirs. Farther out was the hulk of Deer Island, New Brunswick, barely discernible in the gloaming. They sat in silence, O'zalik playing over and over in her mind her grandfather's words.

you must be strong on your own

honor those who have gone before

She was so absorbed in thought, she failed to notice what was happening. Only when Caitlin and Freddy gasped did she look up. The ground had started to emit a greenish phosphorescent glow. Deer Island, formerly lost in the murk, now shone dully with a ghostly radiance. She turned her gaze to the horizon in the north, where a swelling green incandescence bloomed. It seemed to throb, expanding and shrinking slowly. She heard a faint crackling, a slight hiss like the sound of granular snow falling through trees. Softening the earth. Some people said you couldn't hear the Northern Lights, but she knew otherwise. The globular light receded then came back as an arch of light that began to drift across the sky. A second arch luminesced, then a third. They followed each other, waves and curls of light dancing about each arch. Within minutes, rays of brilliance shot down from the sky, flickering curtains, draperies of light with woven strands of red and violet. Some were bluish-red, like bruise blood. More shafts of light rained down from the sky. They formed veils of flickering, shimmering radiance. The wake of the earth riding through space. She remembered her grandfather telling her of an old Inuit belief that the sky is a huge, solid dome overarching the earth. In the dome are many small holes and through these holes you can see the light from the other world and also through these holes pass the spirits of the dead to and from heavenly regions. The spirits who are already in heaven light torches to guide the feet of new arrivals. And that is what the light is.

O'zalik closed her eyes. She wanted to cry, but no tears would come. She tried to summon the face of her grandfather but it was difficult. Only the detail of his nose silhouetted against the wall would come to her.

After an hour, they left the park. When they returned to the house, O'zalik expected to find her grandmother in the kitchen. Even in the presence of the death of her husband, the woman would be sure to put food out for her guests. But her grandmother wasn't in the kitchen. Nor was she in the living room. O'zalik went into the bedroom.

Her grandmother lay on the bed next to her grandfather. Their hands were joined.

Later, the doctor said he could see no reason. They found no marks on her body; there was no empty bottle of pills; there was nothing out of the ordinary in the medicine cabinet; nothing she might have used in the kitchen. "It appears she just decided to die," he said, bewildered.

"Is that possible?" asked Caitlin.

"It's possible," Freddy answered.

Caitlin and Freddy agreed to stay with O'zalik over the next few days for the burial ceremony. Throughout the event O'zalik stood rigid, not saying a word.

Several times on the way back to Alabaster Island, they tried to engage O'zalik in conversation, get her to talk about it. But she remained silent. When at last they arrived at the cottages, she settled onto Caitlin's sofa and was soon asleep.

It was a week later and the tears that wouldn't come before now streamed down O'zalik's cheeks. She watched the sky over Snagged Anchor Island for some sign the spirits of her grandparents had traveled to her, had come to Island of First Light. And she saw, high above the island, a tiny speck. From the way it hovered on currents of air, she knew it was a raptor. She decided it was Thunderbird, the sacred eagle. She decided it was the joined spirits of her grandparents.

She lowered her gaze to String of Pearls, which glittered in the wash of moonlight. In five days the reef would be more fully exposed at low water than it had been in a long time. How fitting, she thought with a wry smile, since the weekly issue of the *Island Gazette* was due out the day before.

~

When she read through the Jesuit's journal, Caitlin became increasingly angry. And when she got to the final entries, she thought of Freddy. Robert Blanchard had been confused about the sentences: "Have you penetrated the treasure of snow? Have you seen the treasure of hail which I reserve for times of distress, for the day of battle and combat?" But she wasn't confused. Because of her study of the Book of Job, she recognized the words instantly. They were part of God's answer to Job. The New King James Bible rendered the word as treasuries, or storehouses. A little research told her the French version came from the Olivetan Bible as translated by David Martin in the early 18th century, the Bible Father Dalou would have used.

God was asking about storehouses of snow and hail.

What did Freddy say about the half-buried bodies at Dachau? "...like as if God was trying to hide something but ran out of snow."

She put the journal down and started immediately to write with a passion she'd never felt before. She shared O'zalik's outrage and was resolved the whole island should know what happened despite the consequences. She felt she owed it to her friend who suffered so much. And to Father Dalou. And to her own ancestors.

It took her three days, starting at dawn and working into the night, to complete the article. She called her grandmother and learned that, indeed, the Babineaus were among the original families living in Grand Pré, Nova Scotia, and, to the best of anyone's knowledge, were among the families deported in the mid eighteenth century.

Now, as she paused in making final edits to the article, she looked out the window to see the moon. It was nearly full and as large as she'd ever seen it.

It was the same kind of moon that had witnessed the agonies of the Acadians and the Passamaquoddy those many years before. Its lambent light gave String of Pearls the appearance of a road to hell.

~

Surreptitiously loosening his belt buckle after finishing the dinner Caitlin had cooked and taken over to him, Freddy strode from one end of the wrap-around porch to the other and studied the sky. In the west-northwest rode Jupiter and Mars, both near the horizon, and a little higher, Venus. The moon, fat and full, glided high above Snagged Anchor Island to the southeast. He knew that, to the north, the only direction not visible from the porch, Cassiopeia, sitting upright, would be about twenty degrees above the horizon. And more to the northeast, at about forty degrees, the Northern Cross would be on its side. Later, he would go out front and gaze up at the northern sky. A building wind ripped through the harbor causing halyards to slap against masts like so many flat-toned wind chimes.

He sat in his rocker, lit his new pipe, and started to rock. "Now ain't that beautiful?" he said to Caitlin, pointing the stem of his meerschaum toward the moon.

She was sitting in her customary rocker, the one Agnes used to use, and rocking in unison with him. He was happy to see her in a such a good mood after working so hard the last several days writing something.

"It sure is," she replied. "You know, it will soon be the fifteenth night of the moon. Many societies have special celebrations on this night."

"You don't say. Now why is that, d'you 'spose?"

"Something about the full moon representing life at its fullest in the cycle from birth to death to rebirth."

"Rebirth?"

Caitlin smiled, rested her hand on his wrist. "Don't you believe in rebirth, Freddy?"

"Can't say I give it much thought."

"It's said the moon on the fifteenth night represents the thirty-fifth year of a human life—the peak."

"If thirty-five is the full moon, then I guess I'm just about a sliver."

"A wonderful sliver. And one that'll be around a good long while."

String of Pearls seemed to come alive under a drizzle of moonlight. Millions of mica crystals flared electrically, providing a twitching, rhythmic counterpoint to the slow shimmer of light on the surrounding water. Freddy studied the show, unable to think of a response to Caitlin. "Spring tide in a couple of days," he finally said.

Caitlin nodded. She was quiet for a moment or two before saying, "Many Native American cultures think the moon represents the impermanence of human life—it sheds its shadow, waxes to full, then wanes and eventually dies into its own birth cradle where it's born again. At the same time, the sun, which doesn't wax and wane, represents eternal life. That's why Native Americans celebrate the dawn."

Freddy said, only, "Eyuh." As he slowly rocked, struggling to find an appropriate answer, his chair creaked Goldang, he thought, she could talk on something awful once you wound her up. It was good.

"So you believe that might be true?" asked Caitlin.

He didn't answer right away. He was still contemplating the proposition, testing it to see if he agreed. Finally, he said, "Eyuh, seems like." He looked over to Caitlin. She was smiling and gazing at Snagged Anchor Island. He, too, looked at it. It seemed to glow with an inner, milky radiance under the fullness of moonlight. After a long pause, he said, "Still feel like the waning moon myself. Almost done waning, in fact." He turned to give her a smile. "So you saying I'm coming back?"

Caitlin looked at him and laughed. "I hope so, Freddy. We'd all be the poorer for it if you didn't."

wind chimes

"Eyuh."

She turned to stare at Snagged Anchor Island again. "Do you believe there are Passamaquoddy remains out there like O'zalik says?"

Freddy shrugged. "Could be, but she ain't got proof."

Caitlin stared at him for a moment before saying, "Maybe they used to go there to celebrate the fifteenth night of the moon and something happened and they could never get back again."

"Could be."

Caitlin nodded. "Could be." Then she leaned toward him and said, "You know, Freddy, I used to say all I want is five hundred pounds and a room of my own."

For a long time he thought about that, but could make no sense of it. "Eyuh," he said. "Five hundred pounds of what?"

Caitlin laughed. "No, no. I mean British pounds...money. I suppose that's two or three thousand dollars."

"Well if that's what you want, why didn't you say, 'I need two or three thousand dollars'? Why confuse the issue?"

"I was only speaking metaphorically."

He knew what she meant, but he thought he'd make a joke because he didn't know what else to say. "That something like in church?"

Again she laughed. How he loved to hear her laughter. Agnes, when they first met, had a laugh like that. But it disappeared over the years.

"Never mind, Freddy," she said. "It's not important."

"It's important to me if it's important to you."

She smiled at him. "You're sweet."

"I have it if you need it."

"What?"

"The two or three thousand dollars. It's yours if you need it."

"But I wasn't asking you for money."

"I have no use for it anyway," he said. That old pain, like something clawing at his insides, hit him. He'd never touched the money he got from the insurance company for their boat after it ran up on String of Pearls and Jimmy died. Somehow there never seemed to be a right use for it. This was the first time he'd found something for which he would be willing to use the money; help Caitlin find whatever it was she was looking for.

Caitlin placed a hand on his wrist. It roused a vestigial pleasure in him. "Freddy, now listen to me. I was only quoting Virginia Woolf. It's what she said about the things a woman needs in order to write."

Freddy felt the conversation slipping away from him. He suspected Caitlin was trying to tell him something but was being indirect about it. Sometimes it had been like that with Agnes. It was a thing about women, he supposed. "Don't know Virginia Woolf. Know a Trevor Wolf. Sailor over to Jonesport who sailed around the world." It was all he could think to say.

"I doubt they're related. Virginia Woolf was a British writer."

"Anyhow, this here Trevor Wolf took a fit to sail around the world all by himself. Took him three years and when he came back he gave a lecture at the church here on Alabaster Island. After his talk I went up to him and introduced myself and asked him why he took such a fit to sailing around the world alone."

"What did he say?"

"He said he didn't figure that one out until he was in the 'Roaring

Forties.' That's a stretch of heavy winds forty degrees south of the equator. Said he finally figured it had something to do with learning things about himself, what he was made of. And then he leaned close to me so others couldn't hear and kinda smiled and said, 'And it ain't all pretty, I gotta tell ya.' But I guess he was happier for doing it anyway."

"So you think that is what this is all about, my wanting to write?"

"Eyuh. 'Cepting I don't think it's a case of *wanting* more than a case of *needing*. I'm guessing you ain't never done nothing like this and you need to know something about yourself the same as Trevor Wolf."

She laughed.

Keeping the conversation going was becoming more and more difficult. "Wolves pretty much gone from these here parts," he ventured. "See a lot of coyotes..."

She looked at him, puzzled. "Coyotes?"

"Eyuh...But no wolves."

"No, I suppose not."

They fell silent. Freddy wondered if he should say the thing that had come to his mind. Finally, feeling his heart race, he said, "Jimmy and me, we used to sit out here and talk like this while Agnes made dinner. Afterwards, it was just me and Agnes. Got to kinda missing it some."

Caitlin leaned forward. "Do you mind if I ask you something, Freddy?"

"Ask away."

"I got the impression from talking with you before that Agnes died many years ago. But I saw her tombstone at the cemetery. She died just a few years ago."

"Eyuh."

"I don't understand."

"There's two kinds of dying," Freddy replied.

"What do you mean?"

"She stopped talking back in '87, stopped listening a little time after that. She was only sixty-two; it shouldn't of been like that. Began in '80 or so when she started to forget things."

"Alzheimer's?"

"At least that's what the doctors said. They called it early-onset Alzheimer's. But don't need no doctor's degree to know she was only trying to forget...about Jimmy and all, I mean. What's so hard to understand about that? Dying of heartbreak, that's what she was doing."

"Then she stopped talking?"

"Started wandering around first. As though she was looking for something. Caught her out on String of Pearls once. She damned near drowned. Looking for Jimmy, I 'spose. Then she stopped talking. Guess she felt there was no use, no point to it."

"I'm sorry, Freddy. It must have been terrible."

What is it about this woman makes a man want to talk?

"That ain't the whole of it. Soon after she stopped talking, she stopped taking care of herself. Wouldn't brush her teeth, wash up. Wouldn't even eat. I had to wash her and feed her."

"You took care of her for almost a decade like that?"

"Eight years." He didn't tell her of the times O'zalik came over to help him bathe Agnes; how they would strip off her clothes, Freddy tying to ignore his embarrassment; how they would haul her limp body to the bathtub like a sailor's duffle of dirty clothes; how Freddy would cradle Agnes in his arms, murmuring a song for her—her favorite Platters' song, "Twilight Time"—while O'zalik washed her private places; how they would haul her out and dry her off; how Freddy would dab a bit of Fidji by Guy Laroche above her breasts before they dressed her again and put her to bed.

heavenly shades of night are falling, it's twilight time...

"My God, Freddy."

"Well, what's a man s'posed to do? She died but her organs kept on going."

"There are nursing homes."

He gave her a hard look. "Warn't about to put her in no nursing home. It wasn't where she belonged." *Besides, she wasn't the one to forget about the weather forecast.*

Caitlin placed her hand on Freddy's wrist again. "You really miss them," she said.

"Eyuh." He took a deep breath and turned his face from her. He followed the running lights of a boat turning the point and heading for the harbor. He wondered what it was doing out so late. Faintly, he heard the thrum of its engine. He supposed it was Ernie Botham and Burle Ledyard just making use of the remaining time. He wanted to change the subject. He turned to Caitlin and said, "So, guess what I'm sayin' about this what-a-woman-needs-to-write thing is, if you need the money to stay here and write…it's yours. I'd be pleased if you stay."

"Freddy, it has nothing to do with money. I don't suppose you'd know what I meant if I said I just don't want to be Shakespeare's sister?"

He shook his head. There she goes again, he thought. He was more convinced than ever she had something on her mind, something to tell him, and she was just circling round it like a boat around a bell buoy that's invisible in the fog. Almost as if she were afraid to come right out and say it. All he could do was wait and see where she was headed.

"In Shakespeare's time, women were mostly uneducated. They never had a chance to use their creative gifts. Can you imagine what Shakespeare's sister, if she had the same genes, might have written—if she was allowed to write, that is?"

"No." He didn't want to admit he'd never read Shakespeare himself.

"That's my point. All that potential wasted."

"Eyuh." He looked at her. Her eyes had an intensity he hadn't noticed before. It alarmed him.

"I'm not saying it's like that now. But for my own reasons, and much of it being my own fault, I feel like Shakespeare's sister."

"Eyuh."

Again, Caitlin leaned forward and looked into Freddy's eyes.

"Freddy, I have a confession to make."

"Eyuh?"

"I wrote an article for the *Island Gazette*. It appears tomorrow."

"Well, there. So, you see? You're writing."

"You don't understand. It's going to cause ripples. It concerns ancestors of Garret Webster, Helen Underwood, Quentin Moseley, and others and a terrible thing they did a couple hundred years ago."

"A couple hundred years ago?"

Caitlin nodded. "Also, one of your ancestors was involved."

He paused, looking at her. "What did they do?"

Caitlin described the article to him. She told him it was the least she could do for him, that she wanted to warn him. "I remembered what you said about Dachau. If I didn't write it, it would have been like trying to hide it."

He gave a sardonic smile. "You mean sorta like burying it with snow?"

"Something like that."

"People around here, they're pretty proud of their ancestry."

"I know, but it's the truth and I had to write it. I hope you understand."

"That'll also give O'zalik some ammunition. You and her ain't gonna be very popular on this here island."

"Surely, no one's going to blame today's islanders for what their ancestors did?"

"Like I told you before, ain't one of us is a saint. Not a damned one of us. It's in our natures."

"But what happened on Snagged Anchor Island has nothing to do with the people who are alive today."

"Ain't the way they're gonna see it. All they're gonna see is the Passamaquoddy have a claim to the island and they got it by digging up stuff about our English ancestors."

"Freddy, I'm sorry."

Freddy said nothing. Only for the second time, he felt a twinge of anger toward Caitlin and he didn't know what to say. He wasn't even sure if he was angry that she was saying this about the islanders' ancestors, including one of his own, or about the fact that she was exposing herself to the hostility of so many people. He gazed at the moon, higher in the sky and toward the south. By this time, the Northern Cross appeared standing upright well above the moon, both over Snagged Anchor Island. He stood and walked to the eastern end of the porch. Starlight seemed to sizzle on the water. He looked down at String of Pearls. Because the tide was out—he recalled low tide had been at 10:37—much of the reef was exposed. It seemed to glow with an inner luster under the wash of starlight and moonlight. He knew the moon was sliding into position close to the earth and in perfect alignment with the sun.

"Spring tide soon," he said. "Dangerous time."

He thought of Jimmy...and Agnes.

~

O'zalik stood beside Caitlin in the office of the *Island Gazette*. She was nervous. Jolene Baxter had just offered Caitlin a final opportunity to pull the article before it went to press and Caitlin hadn't answered immediately. Was she thinking of backing out? O'zalik had seen how Caitlin gave in to her family. She wondered about the woman's staying power. She watched Caitlin walk to the window and look out. O'zalik waited, her gaze fixed on Caitlin's back. She tried silently to communicate her determination...her strength...to the woman.

Finally, Caitlin turned and said, "I told Freddy about the article."

"What did he say?" asked Jolene Baxter.

"He said the people of Alabaster Island were proud of their ancestors. He of course was implying the article would cause a lot of anger."

"Does that mean you want to pull it?"

Caitlin said, "It pains me terribly to hurt Freddy."

O'zalik felt a sinking sensation. She was convinced Caitlin was getting cold feet. She was losing her one ally other than Jolene Baxter.

"It sounds to me like you want to forget the article," Jolene said.

O'zalik was at least happy to hear the disappointment in the woman's voice. She looked at Caitlin who lowered her head and closed her eyes. *Damn.*

Caitlin raised her head and looked at Jolene, then at O'zalik. "No. I want to go ahead with the article. It's the truth and it should be known."

O'zalik smiled, placed a hand on Caitlin's shoulder. "Good going."

"Maybe it'll do some good," Caitlin said.

"The truth never hurts," said Jolene Baxter.

O'zalik smiled. *Oh no, this truth is going to hurt big-time.*

~

Freddy was nervous as he approached Pauline's Coffee and Bake Shop. Earlier that morning he'd read Caitlin's article in the *Island Gazette*. It was much worse than he'd expected based on Caitlin's description. She had clearly softened it for his benefit. Damdest thing was, he found himself empathizing with Father Dalou—the Passamaquoddy bodies half buried by snow, the torture and killing of the Jesuit's friends, the obscenity of what happened to the girl. More than ever, Freddy was convinced of the evil Snagged Anchor Island harbored which the article now exposed for all to see.

He was afraid both Caitlin and O'zalik would bear the brunt of the hostility they'd ignited among the long-established island families. No one likes to have the reputation of ancestors besmirched, especially when those same ancestors were revered as the founders of a way of life. For the residents of Alabaster Island, the founding families were akin to the framers of the American constitution and to have them accused of rape, murder, and mutilation (in the telling of it to him, Caitlin had left out the rape and the mutilation parts) would surely charge the air with hostile electricity. Even he, as much as he loved Caitlin, had grown increasingly angry as he read the article. And sad.

And if *he* was offended, what of the others? All that hate-filled voltage would have to be discharged and Freddy worried that Caitlin and O'zalik, along with Jolene Baxter, would be the lightning rods.

As he'd feared, the atmosphere inside Pauline's was somber. Many of the permanent residents were there and the conversation, far from its usual gaiety, was subdued and sullen. When he took his seat after a few peremptory greetings, Helen Underwood asked him if he read the article. When he answered yes, all he received were dark nods.

"What's gonna happen with Snagged Anchor Island?" asked Morgan Fludd.

Helen spoke. "It turns out that Ernie Botham owns the place and—"

"Ernie Botham? I thought Garret Webster owned it."

"We all did, but it's Ernie's."

"How the hell—?"

"It's a long story. You'll hear all about it at the special town meeting tonight."

"I ain't gonna let them Indians take the place," said Jasper Crenshaw.

"Nothing like that's been decided yet," replied Helen. "Seems to me we all have a say in it. That's what we'll discuss tonight."

"You ain't gonna believe O'zalik, are you?" asked Quentin Moseley. "What's to say she didn't make this whole journal thing up?"

"Yuh, you ain't gonna believe an Indian, are you?" repeated Jasper.

"I don't know what to believe," said Helen.

Freddy expected Wayne Crenshaw to try to allay his son's suspicions, but the man said nothing. He only sighed deeply.

The door opened. Caitlin walked in. Everyone fell silent. Caitlin moved to the table where Freddy sat and took a seat beside him. Freddy put a hand over hers, noticing the many hostile glances.

Jasper glared at Caitlin as he said, "The Indians are *outsiders*. They don't belong here."

Freddy looked to Wayne Crenshaw, hoping he would say something. But the man maintained his silence, his shoulders sagging. Caitlin looked at Freddy with a furrowed brow. He squeezed her hand.

"The whole thing's made up," Jasper said. "It's that Indian woman...and that woman, there." He pointed to Caitlin.

Caitlin was about to say something when Freddy stopped her with a squeeze of the hand and a harsh look. With a slight gesture of the head, he indicated that they should leave. He stood. After hesitating a moment, Caitlin rose and followed him to the door. Freddy was acutely aware of the silence and the eyes following them.

He heard Jasper Crenshaw's voice. "You said one of them was Peake." He was speaking directly to Caitlin. "That was my mother's family."

Freddy urged Caitlin out the door onto Front Street. He waited for some tourists to pass before saying, "It's getting plum ugly in there with Jasper going on longer than a hard winter about Indians and such. You've made them circle the wagons against all outsiders, you and O'zalik."

"It was over two hundred years ago."

"It was about their ancestors...their *blood.* Time don't matter. It might as well have been about them."

"Is that how you feel, too, Freddy?"

"Well, I wasn't exactly tickled with joy."

Caitlin closed her eyes. "God, Freddy, I'm sorry."

"Well, I can see how you had to do it. All along I figured you'd start writing when you got your teeth into something you felt strong about." Freddy laughed. "Can't say I figured it would be this, though."

"I feel responsible," said Caitlin.

"You are," replied Freddy. After a slight pause, he added, "But that don't mean you're wrong."

Caitlin said nothing.

Freddy continued. "Guess I just figure the truth's gonna come out anyway. Always does." He thought of Jimmy and Agnes and a wave of sadness broke over him. "But right now I'm thinking you and O'zalik should come to my place. Wait for people to simmer down. Is she at Jimmy's cottage?"

"I think so."

"Good."

Caitlin said, "I'm saddened the article hurt people's feelings, but I have no regrets. I think O'zalik was right. It had to be written. What upsets me, though, is I think I failed Jasper Crenshaw. His hatred is as strong as ever."

"I don't expect you ever had much of a chance with him. Even Wayne seems to have given up. Hate—it's in his nature. Hell, it's in all our natures. Ain't none of us are saints."

"All the same, I was making progress until I let my own problems get in the way. If I had given it more time—"

"Caitlin, that's spilt milk now. Let's just hope talk is all he does."

~

It was in a spirit of near defiance that O'zalik went to Town Meeting that night. When she descended the steps into the basement of the Congregational church and entered the meeting room, it seemed the entire island was already there. And, it seemed, everybody turned to look at her. She saw Jolene Baxter sitting alone near the back of the room and made her way to the adjoining chair.

The church basement was a large room with a low ceiling and fluorescent lighting. The three walls, except for the front where the stage was, had narrow-board wainscoting thick with layers of peeling paint. Most of the metal folding chairs were arranged facing the stage. The rest, along with a few folding tables, were stacked against the walls. It was a chilly evening, so the steam radiators had been fired up. They hissed and clanked.

"I get the feeling people don't much like us here," said Jolene with a wry smile.

"Welcome to the club. I've felt like that all my life."

"Think they'll run us out of town?"

O'zalik smiled. "Nah, more likely they'll put us in stocks in the town square. Or maybe burn us as witches or force us across String of Pearls as the tide's coming in." She was aware people were staring. She stared right back at them, catching the eye of Helen Underwood. She bared her glistening teeth in an exaggerated smile.

"How's Caitlin doing?" Jolene asked.

"She's upset about hurting Freddy," replied O'zalik. "And also about the experiment with Jasper Crenshaw that didn't work out. Wayne was crazy if he ever thought anything would put Jasper's mind at rest. He lives for hate and conspiracy; sees it everywhere he looks."

Jolene nodded. "He worries me."

"Do you think they'll listen to me now about Snagged Anchor Island?"

"We'll find out soon," Jolene replied, gesturing to the front of the room where Helen Underwood, Freddy Orcutt, Garret Webster, Ernie Botham, and Burle Ledyard mounted steps to the stage and took seats behind a long table.

Helen Underwood spoke. "Good evening everybody. I guess word's been going around the island, so you know what we're all here about. Seems what we all thought—that Garret Webster here owned Snagged Anchor Island—ain't true after all." She turned a sideways glance toward Garret, who had his head lowered, staring at the table. "Seems old Clive Webster left it to Ernie, here, and Ernie plans to leave it to Burle, who, in turn, plans to give it to the people of Alabaster Island. Now Ernie and Burle say they're ready to follow through immediately and—"

"Eyuh," said Burle Ledyard. "Don't want nothin' to do with it. Me and Ernie just want to go fishin'."

A ripple of laughter rose from the audience.

Smiling, Helen continued. "As I was saying, it can all happen right away, which means we all need to decide what we want to do with the island."

"You're in real estate. What do you suggest?" somebody asked.

"Seems to me we got two choices. We can lease some of the land to Wayne Crenshaw so he can build a new marina. I figure that'll take in maybe one, two hundred thousand. Or we can subdivide the land so rich people can build summer homes. In that case we get to split one, maybe two million."

"Couldn't we do both?"

"We could, but my thinking is a marina would devalue the rest of the land. People won't want all that activity, the noise of power boats and all, around their homes."

"What about the Indian claim?"

Helen looked at O'zalik. "By the time all that goes through the government bureaucracy, there could be a couple dozen homes out there. That's another reason to subdivide. Homes will go up much quicker than a marina when you consider Wayne would have to eat up a lot of time raising the money."

Jolene leaned toward O'zalik. "You better believe she's figured a way to get agent's commissions out of this."

O'zalik frowned. She could feel her dream slipping away.

"I think I could work much faster than that," said Wayne Crenshaw.

"You'd need to build a breakwater," said Morgan Fludd. "That's awful expensive."

"Also, it would involve the government," said Helen. "They might be reluctant to move if there's an Indian claim on the land."

Wayne Crenshaw stood. "But what if we did it ourselves? What if we levied a special tax?"

"Still need the government. Building permits. Coast Guard would be involved if you're changing things about navigation," said Morgan.

O'zalik glanced to her right and saw Jasper Crenshaw sitting across the aisle from her. His gaze was fixed on her.

"Besides, how does a marina help the people of Alabaster Island?" asked Helen Underwood.

Wayne, still standing, said, "Bring lots of boaters who'll spend money on Alabaster Island." He turned to Garret Webster. "Garret, you'd be full up in your restaurant every night."

"I'm already filled every night," Garret replied.

"Furthermore," said Helen, "I don't think there's a chance in hell you can raise the kind of money you'd need, Wayne. And who needs more taxes?"

"Oh, now listen, Helen—"

"No, Wayne, she's right," said Garret. "I, for one, have no interest in a marina and, frankly, without me you haven't much of a chance raising the money here on Alabaster Island. And if you go outside the island, well, you know Town Meeting would have to vote on it and if you're partnered with people from away..." He didn't have to say the rest. Not only Wayne Crenshaw but also everybody else in the room was certain to get his implication. Wayne sank to his chair.

O'zalik turned to look at Jasper Crenshaw. He was still staring at her.

Someone in the middle of the room stood and said, in a loud voice, "I think we oughta divide up the island for houses and be done with it. Hell, a couple million bucks divided by one or two hundred folks is a lot of money."

"About twenty thousand each," somebody called out.

Garret Webster stood. "Now wait a minute. We haven't heard all the alternatives yet." O'zalik thought he looked shaken. His hands were trembling. "I, for one, think we should leave Snagged Anchor Island just as it is."

His comment raised a rumble of objections from the audience. Helen Underwood glared at him. Even Freddy Orcutt, who until now was sitting quietly with his arms folded across his chest, looked up in surprise.

"I agree with him," said Quentin.

"Since when have you two become environmentalists?" asked Helen.

"Give it up, Garret," called Morgan Fludd. "It ain't gonna fly."

The room went silent. For a long while, nobody spoke. Garret sank into his chair and poured a glass of water from the pitcher in front of him. The pitcher clinked against the rim of the glass. He drained the glass with one gulp.

Jolene leaned close to O'zalik. "Where's he coming from?"

"He's snatching at anything," O'zalik replied.

"But why?"

"For as long as I can remember, he...and Quentin...have tried to keep people away from Snagged Anchor Island. But I, for one, ain't falling for that bullshit anymore." She stood.

"Be careful, O'zalik," said Jolene in a whisper.

O'zalik ignored her. In a loud voice, she said, "It seems to me there's an option you're not even discussing, and you all know what the hell it is."

Quentin rose from his seat in the first row and turned to face O'zalik. "Angelique, sit down and shut up."

"The name's O'zalik, and I won't sit down. I—"

"Ain't you done enough damage already?" Quentin shouted.

Murmurs of agreement rose from the people.

O'zalik continued. "I never thought the truth could do damage." She felt Jolene kick her lightly on the ankle. It only served to make her raise her voice. "Snagged Anchor Island is a sacred place for the Passamaquoddy. If there's anything to be done with the island, it should be dedicated as such."

"Sit down," shouted Quentin.

"Go to hell," O'zalik replied.

Quentin started up the aisle toward her, but he was restrained by Wayne Crenshaw. It occurred to O'zalik that if she made too much of a scene it would not go well for Freddy since the islanders all knew how protective he was of both her and Caitlin Gray. She decided, for Freddy's sake, to leave. "Well, I've said my piece. I think you all owe it to my ancestors. And once I have proof they're out there, you won't have a choice in the matter." She made for the door and quickly mounted the stairs.

When she stepped outside, it was into a wash of moonlight. She looked up. The full moon hung low on the horizon. She was trembling. She leaned against the side of the church and took several deep breaths. She tried to think what to do. After confronting Quentin the way she had in front of everybody, she was certain it would be far too dangerous ever to stay with him again. He was not the forgiving kind. She decided to go to her house while the meeting was still going on and pack some things she didn't have a chance to retrieve before. After that, she would return to Caitlin Gray's cottage.

When she arrived at her house on the outskirts of town, breathing heavily from running much of the way, she quickly threw some clothes into a pair of pillow cases and started out the door. Then something else occurred to her. She went to the closet and pulled out Quentin's shotgun and a couple boxes of cartridges. There was no telling what he might do, so it made no sense leaving him access to his weapon. Emerging from the house, she headed for the car but stopped, realizing that if she took the car, Quentin was sure to come after her. She tried to think. On a sudden impulse, she headed for the office of the *Island Gazette*. Jolene Baxter undoubtedly would return to write an article about Town Meeting.

By the time she got to the building housing the *Gazette's* office, she saw people start to emerge from the Congregational church. She slipped into the alleyway beside the building and waited.

Ten minutes later, Jolene appeared. After the woman went into the office, O'zalik slipped out of the alley and tapped lightly on the window. Jolene came quickly to the door. She pulled O'zalik inside and shut the door. "What's that?" she said, pointing to the gun O'zalik cradled in her right arm.

"You don't think I'm gonna leave Quentin with it, do you?"

"No, perhaps not. Good thinking."

"Can you drive me up to Jimmy Orcutt's cottage?"

"You gonna hide out with Caitlin?"

"Already have been."

Jolene nodded. "Makes sense. I think you two could help each other. Nobody's going to do anything with Freddy around. My car's in back. We can go out the back door."

Soon they were driving along Front Street with O'zalik spread out on the floor behind the seat, the gun cradled on top of her.

"They decided to subdivide the island," Jolene said.

"Shit."

"You should have seen Garret Webster. He was white as a ghost. Quentin, too."

"Surprise, surprise."

"And Jasper Crenshaw was so hot I thought he was gonna explode," said Jolene. "We're out of town, now. You can sit up."

O'zalik carefully slipped onto the rear seat.

Within minutes, they pulled into Freddy Orcutt's driveway. The lights in Caitlin's cottage were on. O'zalik stepped from the car and went up to the door. She knocked.

Caitlin appeared quickly. She looked at the gun. "What are you doing with that?"

"I'll explain later."

Jolene Baxter stepped forward. "I need to get back and write the article about Town Meeting. I'm putting out a special issue of the *Gazette*. When Freddy gets back, make sure he knows you're both here."

"He'll know," said O'zalik.

After Jolene left, O'zalik followed Caitlin inside. She dropped the two stuffed pillow cases on the hallway floor and leaned the rifle carefully against the wall. "How about a beer? I've got a helluva lot to tell you."

Over beers, O'zalik described the meeting to Caitlin. She talked about the confrontation she had with Quentin, then ended by telling Caitlin what Jolene said about Jasper Crenshaw's response to the decision to sell Snagged Anchor Island to outsiders.

"Damn," Caitlin said. "I could shoot myself for giving up on him."

"Now, don't get all in a tizzy about it. Probably there was nothing you could do, anyway. I doubt anybody could."

"All the same, I worry."

"They probably figure the journal was made up."

"You knew they might."

"But they won't be able to say bones are made up. I've got to get out to that island."

~

Freddy drove slowly back to his cottage trying to think of a way to protect Caitlin and O'zalik from the anger of the islanders. After Town Meeting he'd heard a great deal of talk about the Jesuit article and was alarmed by the vehemence of the anger it stirred. He speculated that the islanders had idealized the past, one in which people led hard-working, simple, Christian lives filled with love for one another and with strong family ties. A time in which the outside world didn't intrude. It was a past celebrated by the annual tradition, on Founders' Day, of leading the parade with a float with actors depicting the ancestors as pioneers in a modest eighteenth century home in the center of a sea of tranquility. It was a past in which the ancestors who founded Alabaster Island were larger than life and pure. Caitlin and O'zalik had wreaked havoc with that vision and he worried the islanders would make them pay for it. The best Caitlin and O'zalik could hope for was some kind of social ostracism. And that would be bad enough. But there were a lot of hotheads on the island and Freddy feared some sort of violence against Caitlin and O'zalik. Certainly, Quentin Moseley, for one, had violence on his mind where O'zalik was concerned. Then there was Jasper Crenshaw. Freddy hoped O'zalik was smart enough to return to Caitlin's cottage after the meeting.

He gazed up at the moon. Seldom had he seen it so bright and so big. It was clearly nearing perigee and the spring tide the next day would be greater the usual. He also noted the stars in the west were blotted out, a sign that bad weather might be on its way.

He pulled into his driveway. The lights in Caitlin's cottage were on, so he went straight to the door and knocked.

After a few moments, he heard Caitlin's voice. It was low and hesitant. "Who is it?"

"Freddy."

The door swung open. Caitlin faced him. "Oh, thank God it's you, Freddy. We were afraid it might be Quentin."

"Eyuh. Is O'zalik here?"

"Yes. Come on in."

Freddy entered and saw O'zalik standing at the far end of the room. There was a look of determination on her face. A shotgun was propped against the wall. "By the looks of it, I guess I'm lucky I'm not Quentin," Freddy said with a smile. "Am I safe?"

O'zalik said. "You're safe."

"Good. Wouldn't want to get shot. Make a mess of this here rug."

"O'zalik had a run-in with Quentin at Town Meeting," said Caitlin.

"Eyuh. I was there. Seen it all," Freddy replied. He turned to O'zalik. "How'd you get here?"

"Jolene drove me." Freddy noticed a peculiar dullness to her voice.

"You folks have started a real ruckus. Guess it ain't gonna be comfortable for Jolene, neither. But at least she's considered an islander, not an outsider like you two. I expect they'll hold it against you more."

"I figured it would stir people up," said Caitlin, "but I had no idea they would react this strongly."

"Wasn't very good thinking on your part. You messed with their idea of the past and they ain't gonna forgive you for a long time…if ever. O'zalik, I'm thinking you better plan on staying here with Caitlin for a while. See how things work out."

"That's what I was saying," said Caitlin.

"Eyuh. Now if you'll excuse me, I have a deadbolt over to my cottage. Never had a use for it. Don't even know why I have it. I'm gonna get it and install it on this door."

"Now?"

"Seems fitting," Freddy replied, heading out the door.

He located the deadbolt, collected a screwdriver, a power drill, and an extension cord, and crossed the driveway to Caitlin's door. He started immediately installing the deadbolt. He worked quickly. After a half hour he had the deadbolt installed and tested. "Ain't the prettiest job I ever done, but it'll do. Guess I'll leave you ladies now to get some sleep." He gathered up the tools, nodded toward the rifle leaning against the far wall, and asked, "That thing loaded?"

"I don't know." answered O'zalik. "I'm just making sure Quentin doesn't have it."

Freddy lifted the shotgun and checked the chamber. "It ain't loaded, but all the same I'd be mighty careful, I was you. I'll be just across the way. I'll keep an eye out for a while. Also, my window's open and I'm a light sleeper since Agnes died. I'll hear anyone tries to come up the driveway."

When he entered his own cottage, he turned the weather radio on.

"*...increasing winds from twenty to twenty-five knots, higher in gusts. Wave heights from three to five feet, occasionally higher...*"

~

Caitlin slept fitfully, waking often to find a veil of moonlight draped over her face. The wind, which seemed to increase during the night, rattled the windows with a sound like distant gun shots. She heard O'zalik snoring and was happy her friend at least was able to sleep. Sometime in the middle of the night she rose to gaze out the window. Despite the wind, the sky was still clear. The moon sat heavy and low near the horizon, drizzling light on the reef. String of Pearls gleamed like Caitlin had never seen it before. She saw waves breaking over the reef, their spume lit to a spectral glow in the moonlight. A perling light.

When dawn finally arrived, she willed herself out of bed and began to prepare coffee. A blue heron, probably the same one she'd heard almost every morning, gave its harsh "braaak, braaak" from somewhere in the cove. Early shafts of sunlight slanted through the big window, falling on O'zalik who was sleeping on the sofa. O'zalik stirred and rolled onto her back. Caitlin drew the curtains to block the light from her friend's face.

While the coffee brewed, Caitlin went to the door and stepped outside. A gust of wind ruffled her hair. The sea was filled with whitecaps, giving it a piebald look. Streams of spindrift, looking like thin, shredding cotton, stretched downwind. String of Pearls was exposed for much of its length and she remembered low tide would be at nine-thirty that morning. According to what Freddy said the previous night, in a few hours they would see more of the reef than had been seen in more than a year.

Between the gusts of wind she heard Freddy's weather radio:

"...a perigean spring tide will occur today. That, along with a confused sea and wave heights of six to ten feet from an approaching storm will produce hazardous conditions along the coast and outlying islands when high tide occurs shortly after four o'clock daylight saving time. A small-craft advisory is in effect from the Canadian border to Portland Light..."

Caitlin smelled Freddy's pipe and went over to his porch to say good morning. He was rocking, as usual, in time to the rhythms of the waves. He smiled at her. "No sign of anyone all night long."

"You didn't stay up all night, did you?" asked Caitlin.

"Nah. Got all the sleep I need."

But Caitlin suspected he was lying. "Me, too," she replied.

Freddy pointed the stem of his meerschaum pipe toward the sea. "Was a surprise storm just like this came up the day Jimmy was lost. They're the worst kind."

"But the sun is shining."

"Won't for long. Go out back you'll see a storm building on the horizon. Be here maybe this afternoon sometime."

"How bad will it be?"

"They're saying winds of forty knots or more. Lightning. The whole works. Probably come at around high tide, which means the shore and especially the reef will take a real battering."

Caitlin stood at the porch rail looking out to String of Pearls. Even though it was nearing low tide, torrents of water swept across the reef.

"Little later I'll go into town and gauge the mood of the folks," said Freddy. "My advice is you and O'zalik stay put for the day."

Caitlin nodded. They talked for a while longer until Caitlin, calculating the coffee was ready, went across to her own cottage. O'zalik was already up and had poured them each a cup of coffee. "How's Freddy?" she asked.

"I think he stayed up the whole night watching out for us."

O'zalik shook her head in amazement. "Wish they were all like that."

"He's really worried," replied Caitlin, "which has me frightened."

~

Freddy pulled the truck into the marina's parking lot and stepped out. Boats in the harbor were nodding up and down to the waves that fretted the harbor, waves bigger than Freddy could remember seeing in a very long time. Even the floating dock was rocking. If it was this rough in the harbor, Freddy imagined conditions outside on the open sea must be especially turbulent. Yet even as he thought it, he saw Ernie Botham and Burle Ledyard motoring out toward the cove's entrance. He smiled, shook his head, and headed for Pauline's.

Most of the regulars were already in the shop. Freddy greeted everybody, got a cup of coffee at the counter from a sullen Quentin, and took a seat at his usual table. He was surprised to see Pauline herself working the tables, but then he remembered O'zalik was at Caitlin's cottage. He could only guess how angry Quentin, and even Pauline, had been when O'zalik didn't show up for work. He listened to see if the conversation was about Caitlin, O'zalik, and their Jesuit article. Instead what he heard was Morgan Fludd complaining about the weather.

"Gonna be a bitch on the ferry today."

"Nah, Morgan," said Wayne Crenshaw. "You've handled worse than this."

"Eyuh, but still don't make it easy. Passengers will be complaining I got the boat rocking too much...as if I had some control over it."

"Be good if one of those passengers was that Caitlin Gray woman," said Tommy Jenkins almost under his breath. "And that Angelique Moseley."

Freddy looked at the man, who turned his gaze away.

Jenkins's comment silenced the crowd for a moment. Nobody seemed to want to talk about it, especially with Freddy present.

To relieve the tension, Freddy asked Morgan, "Any new boats over to Crenshaw's?"

"A few," replied Morgan. "A Buck Harbor Forty came in last night. Real pretty. Built by the Dupuy Boatyard down to Sedgwick. By the way, heard that old man Jordi Dupuy retired."

"Nothing bigger?"

"Nope. That's about the biggest boat in the harbor."

"That's good. Don't think the moorings could handle it."

Angus Macleod said with a smile, "Morgan, tell Freddy about your calendar idea."

There were chuckles from many of the men. Freddy got the impression Angus was trying to relieve the tension. A few days before, he'd talked with Angus and the man said he was worried about the anger that surfaced every time talk returned to the Passamaquoddy claim O'zalik was pushing. The doctor said he thought the islanders needed a diversion.

"See, it's like this Freddy," Morgan said. "I got to thinking how we could help Ernie Botham pay off his share of *Taunting Tammy*, him being so generous with the island and all."

"Don't know how he keeps up with the payments."

"That's my point. I was reading about these calendars folks are making. There's one called "Women in Wool" down to Ellsworth.

Bunch of women—all ages—decided to pose nekkid for a calendar, raise money. Also, there's a garden club somewhere else in Maine."

"And there's a group of farmers down to Brattleboro, Vermont," said Richie Comine. "They all posed nekkid."

Freddy raised his eyebrows. Angus Macleod was smiling.

"So Angus got me to thinking," said Morgan. "What if we was to put out an Alabaster Island Calendar—the men and women of Alabaster Island all nekkid and such?"

"You're not serious."

"Eyuh, I'm serious. Them other calendars raised a lot of money. Folks like to get to know folks."

"Well, there's other ways of getting to know folks."

"We could call it 'See almost all of the people who see the sunlight first.'"

"I'd do it," said Richie Comine.

"Me, too," said Angus Macleod. "Hell, I already seen all you uglies nekkid. Might as well reciprocate."

"With all the money Helen Underwood plans to make for us, what do we need no calendar for? Seems we'd all have plenty to contribute to Ernie."

"If the sale goes through and if the title clears," said Morgan.

"Besides, it ain't as poetical," said Angus Macleod.

"Or as much fun," added Richie Comine.

Freddy looked around. "Where's Wayne and Jasper?"

"Ain't seen them yet."

Morgan Fludd said, "And we can get the ladies. I bet I could persuade Gladys."

Freddy gave him a skeptical look.

"And Helen Underwood," said Richie Comine. "We gotta get Helen Underwood."

"Oh, God..." someone moaned.

Freddy asked, "What would Ernie think, you was to help him like this?"

"He was here earlier this morning and heard all about it. Said Burle should pose nekkid with Taunting Tammy, that inflatable sex doll."

This drew a squall of laughter.

Morgan asked, "What about you, Freddy? Would you pose for this here calendar? I can see you now all nekkid except for your pipe."

Freddy laughed. "That would destroy sales."

"Maybe you could pose with Helen Underwood," said Richie Comine.

Freddy made a stagy frown. "Bury me first." He paused. "Odd, that Wayne and Jasper ain't here. They're always here at this time."

"Still think the calendar's a great idea," said Angus.

Wayne Crenshaw burst through the door.

"What the bejesus?" said Morgan. "You look like the marina's on fire or something."

"Has anybody seen Jasper?" Wayne asked.

"No, we was just asking about that."

"He's disappeared. I looked in on him this morning and his bed was still made up. He wasn't home all night."

"Where could he have gone?"

"Damned if I know."

"Is your truck still there?"

"Eyuh. First thing I checked."

Freddy rose. "Come on, he's got to be around somewhere." He thought of Caitlin and O'zalik alone at Jimmy's cottage.

They walked across the street and into the parking lot of the marina. "Any of your launches missing?" Freddy asked Wayne.

"Nope. We've got to find Jasper. I'm afraid of what he might do." He entered the marina's office.

"Ain't no way he could've gone far," said Freddy, following him.

Wayne shook his head, slumped to the chair behind his desk, and put his head in his hands. "Kid can run like the wind when he wants to," he said, his voice muffled by his hands.

Freddy remembered the look of hatred in Jasper's face when he told Caitlin his mother was a Peake. He tried to remember if they had secured the dead bolt when he left the cottage just an hour before. "I need to use your phone, Wayne. Okay?"

Wayne nodded.

~

Over coffee, Caitlin and O'zalik were talking about the town meeting. When O'zalik repeated her description of Jasper Crenshaw's expression, Caitlin said she still worried about what he might do and regretted not giving the writing experiment more of a shot.

"You can't persecute yourself over it," O'zalik said.

"You should have seen the look of hatred he gave me at Pauline's. One of the ancestors we mentioned in the article was Peake. He said that was his mother's family."

"Shit, I didn't know that. All the same, I've got to get out to the island. I've got to find some evidence of my ancestors so they'll know the journal's not a lie."

"You mean now?"

"Can you think of a better time? It's spring tide. The reef is fully exposed."

"You mean walk across String of Pearls?"

"We can't very well go into town and beg for a boat. People will want to know why."

"But how will we get back?"

"Another low tide will occur in twelve hours."

The thought sent a shiver of fear through Caitlin. All the same she said, "You're right. It's the only way. We better get started immediately. It's just about low tide now."

Judging they wore the same size, Caitlin loaned O'zalik her spare hiking boots. She put on her other pair and moved toward the door.

They heard a phone ring.

"Where's that coming from?" asked O'zalik.

"It must be Freddy's. He always leaves the window open."

They left the cottage and descended the wooden steps leading down to the rocky beach. Caitlin saw that String of Pearls was fully exposed and seemed to be higher out of the water than ever before. Waves crashed into the reef and sheets of spume shot across the rocks. Both Big Pearl and Little Pearl, even jutting as far as they did out of the water, were drenched in clouds of spray. The wind whistled in Caitlin's ears. At the bottom of the steps they walked over the clattering stones toward the rocky finger. The reef stretched out before them.

They stepped onto it.

~

That there was no answer to his phone call alarmed Freddy. He decided to go back to the cottages to check on Caitlin and O'zalik. He drove faster than usual, not even slowing at the cemetery to catch a glimpse of Agnes's tombstone. All he saw of it was the tall maple that overspread her grave. Its branches were swaying in the wind like a grieving woman.

He pulled into the driveway, skidding the last few feet. He rushed to Caitlin's door and knocked. No answer. He knocked again. When still no answer came, he tried the door. To his dismay it opened easily. "Hello," he called.

Tentatively, he went into the cottage, calling "Hello" several more times. With a sinking feeling, he realized nobody was there. He checked the bedroom then returned to the living room. A gust of wind fanned the curtain over the partially opened picture window. He went over to close the window. He looked out to sea where the waves were piling high and breaking before the rising wind.

He saw them.

Two tiny figures a third of the way out on String of Pearls. He knew instantly they were Caitlin and O'zalik. "Goldang it to hell," he muttered.

He knew it would be impossible for him at his age to catch up to them. He thought of who he might ask for the use of a boat. Ernie

Botham and Burle Ledyard were already out tending their lobster pots. He was unlikely to find anyone at the marina because they would all be looking for Jasper. Then it came to him: Garret Webster. The inn had two launches that it used to ferry visiting boaters to and from the inn's restaurant. He ran out the door and climbed into his truck.

As he drove, he tried to think what he would do if he could get the use of one of the inn's launches. In the current state of the sea, there would be no possibility of making a landing on String of Pearls. He would end up the same way Jimmy ended up twenty-five years before. The thought of Jimmy sent a wave of grief and guilt over him. About all he could think was he would patrol off the reef watching Caitlin and O'zalik and, if they were swept off the reef by waves, go in to pluck them from the water. However he would likely have to be on the leeward side of the reef, which meant he would have to entirely circle Snagged Anchor Island since Spruce Cove opened only to the windward side. By that time, they would have either made it to the island or they would have been swept away.

It wouldn't work. The only option was to beach on Snagged Anchor Island itself and hunt for them.

Assuming they ever made it to the island.

And assuming Garret Webster would let Freddy use one of the launches. He couldn't see why not. Freddy had known Garret since he was a little boy hanging around with Jimmy and Quentin Moseley. Unlike Quentin, however, Freddy thought highly of Garret and had been happy to have him associate with his son. Freddy never forgot how gracious Garret had been at Jimmy's memorial service, how he persuaded his mother to hold a reception for the mourners at the inn without charging Freddy and Agnes for it. And again, when Agnes died, Garret was more than generous. As far as Freddy was concerned, he was a good man and Freddy repaid him by doing odd carpentry jobs around the inn and never accepting money for it. He was confident Garret would let him use a launch.

When Freddy arrived at the inn, Garret was on the expansive lawn giving instructions to the landscapers. When he saw Freddy approach, his face brightened. He rushed to Freddy. "Mr. Orcutt, what a pleasure it—"

"Listen, Garret, I'd like the use of one of your launches."

Garret appeared startled. "Why?"

Freddy told him about Caitlin and O'zalik on the reef.

"They're going out to Snagged Anchor Island?" Garret asked with obvious alarm.

"Appears that way."

"That reef is dangerous, especially in weather like this."

"Which is why I'd like the use of one of your launches."

"Where's Quentin Moseley?" asked Garret.

"Probably looking for Jasper along with everybody else—unless he couldn't leave Pauline's. Why?"

"Well, after last night…We better be sure he's still at Pauline's. I wouldn't want him going after O'zalik." Garret turned toward the inn. "I'll call to make sure, then we can take the launch out."

"We?"

"I'll go with you to help. Sea's pretty rough out there."

Freddy was annoyed by the delay. He said, "Okay, okay. But please hurry."

Garret went into the inn and, after what seemed an eternity to Freddy, returned. "Okay, let's go. Quentin's still at Pauline's."

Freddy followed Garret down to the inn's dock. While Garret jumped aboard to start the engine, Freddy untied the bow and stern lines. The engine started with a deep-throated rumble, spray spitting from the exhaust pipe just above the water line. Freddy climbed aboard and they eased away from the dock. As soon as they had maneuvering room, Garret shoved the throttle forward and the launch dug its stern into the water of Spruce Cove.

Planing on their bow wave, they sped toward the cove's entrance.

~

It was with an odd mixture of trepidation and excitement that Caitlin made her way along the reef toward Little Pearl. With the huge waves crashing against the reef throwing curtains of spray, it was a dizzying sensation. The sun broke through the roiling clouds. All at once, millions of flakes of mica embedded in the granite backbone of String of Pearls caught the sunlight and flickered iridescent. The water in cracks and crevices of the rocks, where it was less tossed, seemed to respirate—a gentle inhalation and exhalation of seawater.

The breathing of the sea.

With O'zalik moving ahead of her, Caitlin continued along the spine of rock. She hurried to keep up with O'zalik, who was much more agile, and who seemed to be moving with some purpose. She stepped gingerly, concentrating on every sensation of balance, testing herself. When she needed to, because of the footing, she walked more slowly, gradually gaining confidence. Up ahead, she saw O'zalik waiting for her at the base of Little Pearl. She passed the small depression where she'd stumbled the last time and caught up to O'zalik.

"It's not as bad as I thought," said Caitlin.

"We ain't there yet." Without waiting for a reply, O'zalik started up Little Pearl.

With just a brief pause to gather her breath, Caitlin began to scramble over the rocky protrusion. It took only minutes before she was on the other side, again much more quickly than she could have hoped. She leaned back against Little Pearl and rested, a sense of triumph welling in her. She looked to her right. The sea was a roiling cauldron, ranks of breaking waves throwing off spume. Salt-laden spindrift hissed by her ear. She saw a boat far off String of Pearls. One of the lobstermen from Spruce Cove? Ernie Botham and Burle Ledyard? But the hull was not dark enough. The boat was bobbing violently in the tossing sea. From it came a series of rhythmic flashes, almost like a signaling lamp. Something made of metal or glass must be catching the sun, she thought, some piece of equipment the lobstermen were using, perhaps even a watch as hands busied themselves with traps. She scanned the sky in all directions. In the west a brooding band of clouds, like tarnished pewter, sat on the horizon. Swollen, blackened udders bulged from the bellies of the clouds.

She set out again. To her left, on the protected side of the reef, was a small patch of sand on which a crab scurried sideways toward the water. For some reason, the sight of the crab filled her with an inexpressible, empathic joy, an assurance she and the crab were co-travelers, two creatures with a purpose in the world. She became aware of an excitement of seagulls swirling and skimming above her, raucously calling *kree-kree*. One dove toward the crab but was too late. It had already entered the water and disappeared in the depths. Caitlin continued on toward Big Pearl. When she reached it, O'zalik was already on the other side and calling for her to move faster. "The waves here are getting pretty bad. We need to move before the tide starts turning."

Caitlin paused before Big Pearl. A cormorant, fighting the wind, floated down toward the apex of the rock but, apparently startled by the presence of humans, took off again with a flapping of wings. Again, she looked out to sea. The boat was still there, easily spotted because of the rhythmic flashes of light.

Caitlin glanced at her watch. They had been on the reef little more than an hour and already she was at Big Pearl. Their progress was much better than when she tried it alone. With renewed energy, she started to scramble up Big Pearl. Near the top, she had to reach blindly for a handhold and felt something wet. She took her hand away to find it was smeared with bird dropping. She laughed aloud. "Well, if that's the only problem you have, sweetheart, you'll be one happy camper."

"Come on, Caitlin," called O'zalik from the other side.

Finding another place to grip, Caitlin hauled herself onto the summit. Snagged Anchor Island was now easily visible and close at hand, its swaying spruce trees darkly piercing the graying vault of sky.

She descended Big Pearl, rejoining O'zalik, and they set out to cover the final stretch of reef before the island. Within fifteen minutes, they were standing on Snagged Anchor Island.

She stood upright. With her hands on her hips in the manner of a conquering explorer, she surveyed her immediate surroundings. The rock-strewn beach where she stood sloped gradually up toward a thick stand of trees—mostly spruce with some birch scattered here and there. The trees extended up a small hill, growing ever more stunted, until they petered out leaving a bare summit. Caitlin thought it must have been because the higher trees were more exposed to the salt-laden lash of the ocean winds.

"Where do we start looking?" asked O'zalik.

Caitlin looked at the hill again and decided the bare summit would make a good vantage point to survey as much of the island as possible. "How about the top of that hill?" she asked O'zalik.

Without a word, O'zalik started toward the hill. The rocks were covered with lichen and green algae and, here and there, small colonies of mussels, barnacles, and periwinkles. The ground at her feet was pocked with several tide pools. O'zalik stopped and Caitlin came up to her side.

"How do we get up there?" asked O'zalik.

Caitlin searched for a gap in the trees through which they could begin climbing the hill. Finally, she pointed far to their left. "Over there."

They moved to their left and started up the hill.

~

Freddy squinted into his binoculars. He had no difficulty following Caitlin and O'zalik along String of Pearls. They seemed to be moving well and without hesitation. He was glad for that. A large swell rolled under the launch and the view field of the binoculars moved wildly up and down. The magnified motion brought a stirring of nausea to Freddy. He lowered the binoculars and stared at the water until the sensation passed.

"Looking through those things in this kind of seaway can be tough," said Garret Webster. "Do you want me to spell you for a while?"

"No, I'm fine. Always did have an inclination to get queasy."

Garret laughed. "Not a good thing for a life-long fisherman."

Freddy shrugged. "You take what life gives you." He raised the binoculars to his eyes again, scanning right then left until he located the pair. They were already past Big Pearl.

"I'm going to ease her back a bit," said Garret. "We're taking these waves too hard."

Freddy lowered the binoculars and grasped the rail as the boat lurched over another wave with a shuddering thump. With the naked eye, he sighted the lighthouse at Sheep's Pasture Point and the bell buoy, which was about a mile off the point. Earlier, they were lined up in an almost perfect range. Now, from his new position, he saw the bell was far to the right of the lighthouse. They had been drifting away from String of Pearls with the current that, opposing the waves, made them steep and choppy.

Freddy listened to the squawk of the weather radio he had brought on the launch with him. "*. . . a line of thunderstorms moving rapidly from west to east across Englishman Bay in advance of a cold front.*"

Garret said, "Sounds like they're in for it."

Freddy raised the binoculars again. "And they're gonna get to the island before us. They're almost there now."

Garret said, "Shit."

Freddy looked at him, puzzled.

~

The climb up the hill took them longer than Caitlin anticipated. She was sweating by the time she reached the top. Breathing heavily, she stood beside O'zalik and surveyed the island. Clouds already overspread the sky and she felt a few drops of rain on her arms. She used her open palm as a visor to protect her eyes, scanning the island and the encircling sea in every direction. The waves were already higher than when she and O'zalik started across String of Pearls. They heaped in angled rows toward Snagged Anchor Island and the reef, the wind decapitating them in shreds of spindrift. A gust of wind whipped her clothes, making her adjust her balance. She saw a small, stationary power boat a mile or so off String of Pearls. It was bobbing furiously in the building seas. Further out, a sailboat, under bare poles, was making its way toward Alabaster Island, some trapped sailors desperately making for safe harbor. To the west, an angry looking band of clouds was advancing closer. Through a cat's-claw tear in the wadded clouds shot a shaft of smelted sunlight like the rays sometimes intended to represent God in religious paintings.

"We're going to be hit by a storm," she said to O'zalik.

"Looks like it." O'zalik's voice was still strangely flat.

"What do we do?"

"Not enough time to go back. Already green water is going over parts of String of Pearls."

Caitlin looked at O'zalik to try to understand the peculiar quality of her voice. Then she looked to where O'zalik was pointing. Indeed, in the low spots that ordinarily would still be fully exposed in the spring low, water from the monstrous waves was sweeping across the reef. Had the waves been as high when they crossed, they never would have made it.

They studied the island, looking for where to begin their search. Snagged Anchor Island was almost uniformly covered with trees, mostly spruce and a scattering of birch, except for the beach where they had stepped from String of Pearls and a larger clearing on the opposite, southwestern, end of the island.

O'zalik said, "I think there might be small caves on that shore. There are on most of the islands where the windward shore is exposed to the open sea like this."

"And you think we should start looking there?"

O'zalik shrugged.

They plodded toward the shore which was perhaps a half mile away. They were forced to lean into the growing wind screeching past their ears. Caitlin heard the surf pounding against the rocks like distant artillery. The air reeked—a foul, putrid odor.

"What's that smell?" asked Caitlin.

"Death."

Caitlin looked at her companion. "Death?"

"Probably a beached whale rotting away."

As they neared the shore, Caitlin heard strange grunts and moans, bellowing trumpet sounds, and a rapid, rhythmic growl like a distant chain saw. Feral, primitive sounds that could have been from souls trapped in bestial origins. They frightened her. "What can that be?" she asked.

O'zalik shook her head, saying nothing.

"Should we…?"

Without answering, O'zalik resumed walking toward the shore.

The sounds grew louder. They were accompanied by the thunderous crash of waves. Caitlin saw columns of salt spray shooting high into the air.

They came round a large rock. Before them, spread across a large flat area of granite, was a colony of Atlantic puffins. Caitlin recognized them easily from pictures she'd seen—large orange triangular bills, pale gray clownlike faces, black backs, white underbodies. A great commotion was happening with lots of low growls and higher-pitched skirls. About a dozen or so puffins, their feathers stirred by the wind, gathered around two individuals struggling on a rocky perch in apparent combat, their beaks locked, their wings and feet flailing. Caitlin watched spellbound for several minutes as the fight continued unabated until both puffins rolled off the perch to the excitement of the others.

On the beach was the carcass of a whale.

The scene disturbed Caitlin. She turned away, looking out to sea. A broad sheet of cloud, deep gray at the ragged edges, turning toward black in the center, hovered only a few miles away. A tongue of lightning shot down from the cloud, linking it for a split second to the sea. She counted silently until she heard the deep rumble of thunder. The storm was only a few miles away. The air temperature dropped perceptibly. A chill ran through her. Even as she watched, the waves seemed to be getting higher, more violent.

"There," said O'zalik, barely audible. "A cave."

Caitlin looked to where she pointed and saw a tall, narrow cleft in the granite. Cautiously, they crossed a sloping slab of rock from which streams of water boiled back into the sea. Caitlin heard nothing but the caterwauling of the wind, the sluicing hiss of seawater.

They stood before the opening trying to decide what to do next. Caitlin looked to her right and saw the puffins had disappeared from their rock. She guessed they must have retreated from the building storm.

~

Freddy felt the wind shift even before the first flash of lightning. It was cold and menacing on his cheek. "Storm's coming our way," he said.

"This boat is getting hard to handle."

Freddy looked at Garret. The man was no seaman. Anyone with the slightest familiarity with boats wouldn't be having difficulty, at least not in conditions like the ones they now faced, rough as they were. Nonetheless, the waves were building and becoming more lumpy as they rolled against the outflowing current. If things got much worse, they would have to find shelter. "Want me to take it?" Freddy asked.

"No…I'm okay. So far."

"Eyuh. Well, just let me know."

Freddy looked to leeward. He judged them to be a least a mile and a half off String of Pearls and Snagged Anchor Island. That gave them plenty of sea room. However, he also knew they wouldn't be able to make a landing on that side of Snagged Anchor Island. Their only option was to circle the island and approach it from the northeast where the island itself would act as a barrier to the onrushing waves. He lifted the binoculars and scanned the horizon to the southwest. It was a habit he had adopted since nearly being capsized by a rogue wave on George's Bank more than forty years before. But he saw nothing unusual, only rank after rank of steep waves, all roughly the same height and most with their tops being blown off. The air was filled with spindrift that stung his face with its needle-sharp salt crystals.

"No way we can get in on this side," he said to Garret. "We're gonna have to go 'round the island and approach it from the northeast."

Garret nodded and shoved the accelerator forward. He steered toward the southwest tip of Snagged Anchor Island.

"Ain't a good idea to approach that close," said Freddy. "Want to give her a wide berth."

"But I want to see if they're on this end of the island before we go around to the other end."

"Maybe so, but if a big wave comes, we're gonna need as much sea room as we can get. I'd stay at least a mile or so off."

Garret hesitated. He continued driving the launch toward the point, a frown of indecision on his face.

"Ain't you heard me? We happen to catch a big wave near that point and we'll be driven onto the rocks."

"I heard you."

"Then change course, damn it."

Again, Garret hesitated. The launch, with the waves on her quarter, hurtled toward the point. Freddy scrambled forward and grabbed the wheel. He jerked it to the right.

"What are you doing?" cried Garret, struggling to turn the launch back to port.

"Ain't gonna let you drive us on the friggin rocks."

The launch yawed violently as the two men fought for the wheel. Finally, Garret yielded to the stronger man. Freddy altered course to starboard and pointed the launch for a spot about a mile off the southwestern tip of the island. Before them, a zigzag of lightning electrified the horizon. Moments later the air buckled with a whiplash of thunder.

"Now keep her on this course," Freddy said harshly. "Once we clear the point, we can go in closer along the western shore."

"Damn!"

"What's got you so hot to be near the southwestern point anyway?"

Garret didn't answer.

Freddy stared at the man. Glancing at the compass, he said, "Hold a course of Oh-two-oh degrees and I don't want you changing course until the island bears dead north of us. Until then, I'll lay the binoculars on the point. See what I see." He raised the binoculars to his eyes, pressed them painfully into his eye sockets, to steady them.

Nothing.

The boat lurched in a trough and Freddy had to lower the binoculars to grab the rail. He checked their course. Garret still had the launch pointed toward the imaginary spot Freddy selected more than a mile off the point. He gave a nod of satisfaction. Once more, he lifted the binoculars. Snagged Anchor Island rose and fell in his view field. He thought he saw some movement near the rocks on the point, but he couldn't be sure. He sensed the boat, waiting for that momentary pause at the crest of a wave when the boat would, for a brief instant, hang still.

The launch rose onto a wave, hesitated. Freddy steadied the binoculars. He saw them. Two figures approaching what looked like a large cleft in the rocks. "Got 'em," he said.

"You see them?" Garret's voice was pitched artificially high.

"Eyuh. On the point."

"What are they doing?"

"Nothing much. Just walking. Looks like they're coming up to some sort of cave."

"Shit."

Freddy lowered the binoculars and stared at the man. Suddenly, Garret yanked the wheel to port. The launch caught the crest of a wave and started to shoot toward the point. Freddy rushed forward.

He grabbed Garret's arm and squeezed with all his strength, slowly pulling it to the right. Garret let out a cry of pain. The launch gradually turned back to starboard.

"You try that once more and it'll be your friggin neck I grab," Freddy said between clenched teeth.

Garret, rubbing his arm, gave Freddy a look filled with equal parts fear and hatred. Freddy had never seen such an expression on the man before. "You okay?" he asked.

"Yuh," answered Garret with a sullen tone.

"Sorry if I hurt you. You gonna stay on course now?"

"Yuh."

"Sure?"

"Yuh, goddamnit."

"Okay. See to it."

The muscles in Freddy's forearm ached from the sudden, violent contraction when he gripped Garret's arm. Once more, he raised the binoculars. He located Caitlin and O'zalik. They were still approaching the cave.

~

"Oh my God," Caitlin cried.

A wall of green water, more than twice as high as the other waves and with spume curling from its teetering top, rushed toward them. She shouted, "Quick. Into the cave." There was nowhere else to go. She scurried into the dark opening, peering back over her shoulder to see the mountain of water looming above them. There was a roar and clatter as it sucked up stones from the shore. "Climb up here," she cried, her voice tremulous.

~

Freddy turned to scan the horizon once again. What he saw took his breath away. "Oh shit," he muttered.

"What?"

"We got a big one coming." He braced himself against the gunwale and steadied the binoculars. A wall of roiling green water was rolling toward them. He quickly stored the binoculars and scurried forward. "Give me the helm."

"What is it?"

"A big friggin wave."

Garret gasped and relinquished the wheel.

"You got harnesses on this here boat?" asked Freddy, knowing it was too late anyway.

"No."

"Then hold onto something real tight."

Freddy turned the launch to port. His plan was to run with the wave and when he felt it lift them, slow down and hope the wave rolled under them without breaking and that they had enough sea room before being thrown onto the rocks of the point. The boat hurtled before the waves. He glanced over his shoulder. The wave was almost upon them. Sheets of green water plummeted from the crest. Freddy tensed his hand on the gear shift, waiting for the right moment. He eased the throttle back. Once more he looked back, determined to get his timing right. Everything depended on it. The giant wave seemed to have trapped all the sound of the universe in its maw. The roar was deafening. Suddenly, the wind went slack, blocked by the wave. He slowed the launch even more. The boat began to rise like an express elevator. Freddy held his breath. He threw the engine into reverse, simulating the sea anchor he would have used on his old fishing boat. The boat rose frighteningly fast. All at once he was slammed by the returning wind as they teetered on the crest. He heard the scream of the engine as the propellers, no longer pushing against water, cavitated in thin air. Its engine freewheeling, the boat shuddered violently and hovered for an instant before plunging toward the trailing trough as if from a tall building.

"Hold on!" Freddy yelled. He tightened his grip on the wheel and braced himself. He held his breath.

~

On one side of the cave was a small shelf, waist high. Caitlin scrambled onto it and stood with her back pressed against the wall.

O'zalik followed.

When Caitlin leaned into the rough granite, she felt a sharp protrusion against the small of her back. She tried to ignore it. She clawed at the wall with her fingers, trying to find a handhold. The muscles in her forearms strained. The advancing wave came with a deafening roar. It pushed before it a heavy, compressed gust of wind like a train in a tunnel. The cold, wet wind struck Caitlin in the face, taking her breath away. The water burst into the cave. Caitlin felt her body being tugged from the wall. She tightened her grip until her muscles screamed. The water raced up the wall, sluiced at her ankles, then her hips, then her shoulders until she was thrown back into the cave against O'zalik. She felt herself dragged from the narrow shelf. She flailed her arms, felt a sharp blow across her forehead and knew it was O'zalik's arm. She was lifted in a giant heave and her body pressed against the ceiling of the cave. It knocked the breath from her. Everything went black. She tasted salt water.

All at once she had a sensation of sliding down a long chute. They were being flushed out of the cave in the roiling backwash. Her back hit the sloping granite slab leading from the cave with a shock. Desperately, she grasped for something, anything, to arrest her wild plunge toward the sea. Her body slowed, dragging along the slab. She came up against something hard and crumbled against it, gasping for breath. The seawater gushed by her on both sides back into the ocean. There was sky above her. She was no longer inundated by the sea. Gingerly, she rose to find both she and O'zalik had been slammed against an outcropping, stopping their plunge.

~

The launch hit hard. Freddy was thrown against the wheel,

bruising his ribs. He waited for a long moment. Surveying his body, he decided nothing else hurt. He saw Garret sprawled on the floorboards, gasping and squirming. Apparently the man had the breath knocked out of him. Gingerly, Freddy stood. He glanced all around him. The sea appeared as it was before, no more giant waves. With a sinking heart he thought of Caitlin and O'zalik. The wave would have broken on the shore like a tidal wave; it did that with every storm from this direction.

Garret fell silent for a moment, then he muttered, "Oh shit…"

"What?"

"We're taking on water."

~

Caitlin struggled to regain her breath. Finally she asked, "O'zalik, are you all right?"

"I think so," answered O'zalik weakly.

Caitlin turned to gaze at the sea. Though it still tossed and heaved with huge waves, there was no sign of another wave like the one that just hit them. "Looks okay now," she said.

O'zalik nodded absently. She was looking back toward the cave.

Caitlin followed her gaze. "Oh, God!"

Scattered along the slab were bones, dozens of them. Caitlin saw two skulls—one lodged in a crevasse and one rolling slowly toward them.

~

Freddy looked to where Garret pointed and saw water starting to seep above the floorboards. "Must have sprung some seams," he said. He studied the seeping water for a moment. "I think we can keep up with it between hand bailing and using the bilge pump." He flipped the switch for the pump.

"We need to get back," said Garret, panic edging his voice.

"Eyuh." Freddy had already debated in his mind whether to go around to the northeastern end of Snagged Anchor Island where there was a chance they could beach the launch, or head back to Alabaster Island. He decided on the latter. There was no guarantee they could beach the launch in the existing conditions because, even though that end of the island would be sheltered from the direct brunt of the waves, he had no way of knowing if there would be confused seas where the wave train, split into two by the island, converged again at oblique angles. Such a convergence zone could be extremely dangerous. Besides, Alabaster Island was closer.

"Find a bucket. Start bailing," Freddy said to Garret. "We're making for Spruce Cove."

Garret did as he was told.

~

Caitlin jumped to her feet, scrambling to avoid the rolling skull. It came to a stop against the rock that arrested her slide. She stared at the skull in silence. A long moment passed. Finally, she said, "These aren't the people from the Jesuit's journal."

"How do you know?"

"Think about it. How often are there storms like this where waves come into that cave?"

"Probably every year."

"That's what I figured. No way they would have survived over two hundred years."

"Then these bones are recent?"

Caitlin shook her head. "If I remember my archaeology, they have to be at least seven or eight years old."

"Why?"

"No soft tissue."

"Then how did they survive in the cave?"

Caitlin thought for a moment. "They didn't. They must have been moved here. And only since the last storm. Wasn't there one back in June?"

O'zalik nodded. "But who? Why?"

"Your guess is as good as mine. But let me ask you a question: Who's been trying to keep people off this island?"

O'zalik stared at her.

Caitlin said, "If the bones were moved recently, they must have been exhumed from somewhere."

"Meaning?"

"Meaning there should be disturbed earth somewhere on this island."

~

Freddy set course for Alabaster Island. He glanced over his shoulder. He saw two tiny figures moving on the rocks near the southwestern tip of Snagged Anchor Island. He frowned because he knew they would have to spend the night alone out there in the storm that was now almost fully upon them. He couldn't push the launch any harder for fear of opening up more seams, and by the time they made it back to Spruce Cove, there wouldn't be enough time to find another boat and return to Snagged Anchor Island before dark. In such seas, approaching the island in the dark would be suicidal.

It would have to wait for morning and the women would have to fend for themselves.

~

"Where do you suggest looking?" asked O'zalik wearily. She felt drained in body and spirit.

"If you were trying to hide bodies, where would be the best possible place?"

O'zalik shook her head.

"What about an existing burial site?" asked Caitlin.

O'zalik stared at her. "You mean the people from the journal?"

"Can you think of a better place?"

"But—"

"Look, given what the Jesuit wrote, it's likely they died of starvation or exposure. Which means some would have survived longer than others simply because they were stronger or healthier. As long as they had enough strength left, wouldn't they honor their comrades by burying them?"

O'zalik nodded.

"So if you were with them and you were one of the last survivors," asked Caitlin, "where would you have buried them?"

When O'zalik didn't answer, Caitlin said, "O'zalik, concentrate. This is important to you. If you were one of the Passamaquoddy survivors, where would you have buried your brothers?"

O'zalik gave her a blank stare. "Where the sunlight first hits the island."

people of the dawnland

"And that would be?"

O'zalik raised her eyes, pointed. "The eastern side of that hill."

"Let's go."

By the time they reached the summit of the hill, O'zalik was exhausted. She told herself to move more slowly, to pace herself, to save her energy for the long night ahead.

For the task she'd given herself.

island of first light

She scanned the summit for signs of a burial ground. She saw nothing. The summit was covered with low-lying bushes. She began to search the ground, pushing aside the bushes with her feet. It was tiring work. After a short time, she stopped to rest. She looked down from the summit and saw String of Pearls was already partly awash and the next low tide would occur during the night when it would be insane to cross, especially since there would be no moonlight to guide them. It was clear they would be forced to spend the night. But what did it matter to her if they could cross the reef or not? It would give her more time to search in the morning...or by moonlight if the weather cleared.

grandmother moon

Accihte, the changing color moon; *Apsqe*, the feather shedding moon; *Toqakiw*, the autumn moon...*Kelotonuhket*, the freezing moon. She recited the names over and over in her mind.

She thought of her grandparents. Tears came to her eyes.

Here, on this island, she felt their spirits and the spirits of her long-ago ancestors; here she felt their agonies, their unrest. It was the heartache of a people oppressed. But she would bring rest to them, she would quiet their pain. She would sing a song of prayer. The world of the white people was not their world. Their world ceased to exist centuries before. She would make it right.

She had decided.

honor those who have gone before

She looked over her shoulder. The storm was drawing nearer. The underbellies of the clouds bloomed with lightening. The light had a jaundiced look, like a nicotine stain. The roots of her hair tingled with electricity. She looked down at String of Pearls. It was a confusion of spray with the turning of the spring tide. Big Pearl and Little Pearl wore sheaths of mist like shrouds.

A flash of lightning, followed almost instantly by a deafening crack of thunder. O'zalik felt the earth tremble under her feet.

"We've got to find shelter," she heard Caitlin say. "Down this side." Without waiting for a reply, Caitlin set off down the eastern side of the hill.

O'zalik followed. Rain slashed at them every time they passed through a small clearing in the trees. The tops of the spruce trees swayed like dancers in a frenzy. She thought: this has become an island of evil and it must be purified. She would purify it. She had decided.

island of first light

No longer would she allow them to dishonor her ancestors, to dishonor her. The world of the white people of Alabaster Island was not her world. Her world was this sacred island where the wind sang through the trees, where the ocean played with the shore, where animals scampered through the underbrush. It was a world where the whale,

Putep, swam in the sea and the eagle flew overhead—the sacred eagle Thunderbird who flies in the realm of lightening and thunder and on whose wings the rays of the sun shine. This island—where on many nights the moon, Grandmother Moon, poured down her light on her daughter, Earth, until she retired with the brightening dawn—this island belonged to her and her ancestors and she would claim it not by the laws of the white people, but by her own law. It was her power.

people of the dawnland...her people

She started to chant softly to herself. A chant her grandfather taught her. A song of the people. It contained no words, only thoughts.

"What are you singing?" asked Caitlin.

O'zalik ignored her and kept on chanting and kept on walking. Her lips become dry, cracked. Trickles of blood formed at the edges of her lips, but she continued to chant. She started to bound down the hill.

you must be strong on your own

~

Caitlin worried about O'zalik. The woman seemed to close herself off from everything, to be following some internal urge, some purpose, only she understood. And whatever purpose it was O'zalik had, it made her move swiftly and with an agility Caitlin couldn't hope to match. She struggled to keep up.

And she remembered Father Dalou's journal. Edmond's death chant.

The light was failing. Black-bellied clouds covered the sky, lightning swarming from them like raptors at an alewife run. Thunderclaps shook the ground.

O'zalik stopped abruptly.

Caitlin caught up to her. They had come into a small clearing. At the back of the clearing, facing east, was an overhanging ledge. And under the ledge Jasper Crenshaw lay on his side, his knees tucked to his chest.

"My God, Jasper," cried Caitlin.

Jasper didn't respond.

Caitlin ran toward him.

~

Freddy guided the launch through the narrow opening to Spruce Cove. The steering was sluggish because of the water sloshing in the bilge. They had taken turns with the bailing bucket, but after nearly an hour both men were exhausted and the seeping water was becoming deeper. Every ten seconds the beam from Sheep's Pasture Light swept across them, momentarily transforming the gloom. In the bright swath of light Freddy saw sheets of rain, nearly horizontal. A slash of lightning lit the harbor. In the blinding flash Freddy saw several boats jerking at their moorings. In an instant they disappeared.

Easing back on the throttle, Freddy slowed the launch. The bow settled down. The bilge water sloshed forward and the bow dug deep. Dangerously deep. He turned the wheel to point the boat toward Crenshaw's Marina. "Ain't no sense in bringing her back to her mooring," he said to Garret Webster. "She'd just sink. Best if we can get her to Crenshaw's travel lift and pull her out."

Garret nodded absently.

Slashes of rain streaked across the lights at the marina dock. Freddy saw Wayne Crenshaw standing on the floating dock, waiting for them. He pulled the throttle back so they were barely making headway and nudged the launch against the dock. Wayne took the lines Freddy and Garret threw him and wrapped them quickly around cleats.

"Ain't no sign of Jasper anywhere," Wayne said. "Where the hell have you guys been?"

"Snagged Anchor Island," replied Freddy. "Caitlin Gray and O'zalik went out there."

"Snagged Anchor Island?"

"Eyuh."

"Jesus."

Garret jumped out of the launch. He said nothing.

Freddy spoke. "Fell off a big wave. Sprung some seams, looks like. Need to get her out right away."

Crenshaw called for some men to prepare the travel lift with its giant sling of canvas straps. Within minutes, they rolled it forward on its tracks, lowering the sling over the deep slip. Freddy guided the boat carefully into the sling, adjusted the straps so they were in the proper place, cut the engine. He climbed out of the launch and up a vertical ladder on the side of the slip. He stood beside Wayne Crenshaw.

"What do you figure those women are doing?" Wayne asked.

"Looking for Passamaquoddy remains. My guess is O'zalik wants to find proof before any deals for the island are made."

Wayne said. "You know, Jasper has this crazy idea his mother's spirit is out there. Sometimes he goes out to the island when things get too much for him."

"And you're thinking he might be out there now?"

"All this talk of the Passamaquoddy taking over the place has him mighty upset."

"What if he runs into the women?"

"That's what I'm thinking," said Wayne.

"Shit."

"We gotta get out there."

"Can't do it until morning. With those seas and in the dark, no way we'd be able to run up on the beach."

"Damn, you mean we gotta sit here with him and the women out there?"

Freddy placed a hand on Wayne's shoulder. "We'll go out at first light. It's a big enough island. There's always a chance they won't run into each other."

Wayne looked at Freddy but said nothing.

Freddy said. "I know how you're feeling, Wayne, but ain't nothing we can do about it."

Wayne nodded.

Freddy saw Garret Webster standing to the side, looking at them. Listening.

~

When Caitlin reached him, Jasper Crenshaw looked up at her with a haunted expression. He remained on his side, his knees to his chest.

"Jasper, what are you doing here?" Caitlin asked. "You must be miserable."

In a halting voice he said, "I came to be with my mother."

"Yes… Yes, I know."

"She understands."

"Have you talked with her?"

Jasper nodded. "She says not to let the Indians take her island." He shot a hate-filled glance at O'zalik.

"Jasper, even if they did dedicate the island to their ancestors, it wouldn't mean your mother couldn't be here."

"He told me I should scare you…and her."

"Who told you."

"He said if you was scared real good, you wouldn't come out here—"

"Who, Jasper?"

"You wouldn't come out here to upset my mother."

"Was it Quentin?"

Jasper nodded. Caitlin looked at O'zalik. The woman turned her back and spit on the ground.

"Only scare you and you wouldn't take this island," Jasper said.

"How were you supposed to scare us?"

"He said to burn your cottage down."

"Jesus!"

"He said you would leave us alone then."

Caitlin stared at him for a minute. "But you didn't do it. Why?"

"It belongs to Mr. Orcutt's son."

Caitlin closed her eyes and sat back against the rock wall. "Oh, Jasper..."

A flash of lightning illumined the clearing followed instantly by a clap of thunder.

you took our jeremy from us

~

O'zalik sat against the rock wall deep under the overhang and far from Caitlin and Jasper. She knew, with a knowledge that came from deep inside her, that her ancestors' spirits were on this island. And she knew it was where her own spirit belonged.

island of first light

In the frequent flashes of lightning, she imagined she saw pairs of eyes. Foxes? Squirrels? Creatures who, like her, like her ancestors, crossed String of Pearls on a spring tide, creatures who came and stayed. Like her ancestors.

As dawn approached the lightning and thunder ceased and it stopped raining. O'zalik stepped out from the overhang and looked up to the western sky. Stars had appeared through the shredding clouds. Grandmother Moon appeared. She shone a bone-white incandescence on Island of First Light, home of the People of the Dawnland.

She rose and started to climb the hill. She had no trouble finding her way in the bright light of the moon. Ten minutes later she reached the summit. Immediately, she set about searching the underbrush. A strong sense of her ancestors' presence came over her. She was convinced they were here. It was difficult going. Twice, she had to stop to recover her breath, sitting on a boulder.

And then she saw it. Something glinted in the moonlight. She approached it. It was a large metallic cross, mostly dull and corroded, almost hidden by the low-lying bushes. It appeared that it would fall apart if lifted. But one corner had been scraped, perhaps by a rock, perhaps by a boot. It was this corner that the moonlight revealed to her. Afraid to touch it, she carefully moved aside the underbrush.

Deeper into the underbrush there was a small clearing where she came across freshly disturbed earth. She knew instantly it was where the bones they found in the cave had been exhumed. If Caitlin was right, this was the spot, on the summit of the hill, facing east, where her ancestors were buried. She fell to her knees. After a while, she rose, searched for some branches, found three that would serve her purpose, and jammed them into the ground in three places at the edges of the disturbed earth. It was a temporary solution, but never again would she lose her ancestors.

~

Before dawn, Freddy met Wayne Crenshaw at the marina and they set out immediately for Snagged Anchor Island in the marina's small, flat-bottomed utility boat. As they neared the mouth of Spruce Cove, they came upon Ernie Botham and Burle Ledyard motoring slowly out on a parallel course. Freddy hailed them and Crenshaw steered to bring the utility boat alongside.

"Where're you fellahs going?" asked Burle.

Freddy told them. "If Jasper's out there with the women, we might need some help."

Ernie and Burle nodded and spoke simultaneously. "Eyuh, we're right behind you."

Conditions were nothing like the previous day. Though the waves were still high, they were longer and rounded, more of a rolling swell, the underlying respiration of the ocean, over which the boats rode easily.

Freddy spoke. "Yesterday, before that friggin wave hit us, I saw the two women on the rocks of the southwestern tip. But they were alone. My guess is they've moved. That end of the island is too exposed."

"Makes sense. So what do you suggest?"

"We go to the northeastern end. Better holding ground for Ernie and Burle, too. We'll ferry them into shore with this boat. Flat bottom will let us run right up the beach."

"Let's do it," replied Wayne. "Jesus, I hope Jasper's not gone off the deep end."

"Eyuh. I understand how a father feels about a son."

Wayne glanced sideways at him. "Expect you do."

As they neared the southwestern tip, Freddy put the binoculars to his eyes just in case he was wrong and the two women had stayed there. He saw nothing. Because of the easier waves, they passed much closer to the point than Freddy had dared the day before. All the while, he scanned the shore with his binoculars but still saw nothing. "Guess I was right. They're on the other side."

With Ernie Botham and Burle Ledyard following close behind, they turned to port and followed the shore of Snagged Anchor Island. Fifteen minutes later, they cleared the northeastern tip and turned in for the beach. Fifty yards off the shore, they came to a stop and waited for Ernie and Burle to pull alongside.

"You guys drop anchor here. We'll run up the beach with this boat."

"Eyuh."

Burle went forward to lower the anchor. When he gave the signal, Ernie put the lobster boat in reverse to set the anchor. He turned the engine off. Burle helped Ernie climb into the utility boat, then followed him.

Crenshaw slipped the engine into gear and headed for a flat, shingled area on the shore.

The sun was just beginning to appear, a rim of blood red blistering the horizon.

~

O'zalik remembered exactly what sweetgrass looked like—her grandfather had taught her when she was a child. Sweetgrass, which sent its fragrant smoke as a sacred offering. Sweetgrass, which her Passamaquoddy ancestors wove into baskets and ornaments of all kinds. And as she hunted for the sweetgrass, she looked also for red ochre, the substance of Mother Earth that cast out evil spirits. Grandmother Moon lit her way with a soothing radiance, guiding her.

Eventually, she found a clump of sweetgrass sheltered from the slashing rain by a large outcropping. In the soft, lambent light she fell to her knees. She started to tug. The stubborn grass, with its deep roots, resisted her efforts but at last she was able to collect enough for her purpose. She carried it to the overhang and spread it out on the ground to dry.

Caitlin and Jasper were still asleep. In the east, the sky was brightening.

O'zalik set out in search of red ochre. She'd been searching no more than ten minutes when she made a discovery that brought joy to her heart. An eagle's feather in a wash of milk-white moonlight. She picked it up and felt heat coming from it, the heat of the sun. She tucked it inside her shirt.

Moments later, she found some red ochre which she scooped up and smeared on her cheeks to cast away the evil spirits inhabiting the island. To help her ancestors find rest. To purify herself for the task ahead.

you must be strong on your own

She made her way back to the overhang and began her preparations.

Of all the emotions she'd expected to feel when she discovered the burial site of her ancestors—fear, loathing, anger—the one she least expected was the one she first felt. Guilt. She wondered how she could account for that. The guilt of the living toward the dead? The guilt that comes with the knowledge of what lurks in the human soul? Of what lurks on this island disturbing the spirits of her ancestors? But now there was no longer guilt. There was only a sureness of purpose, a conviction deep within her that what she was doing was the right thing, the only thing. It was a purification.

She needed kindling, but after the rain there was little left dry. So she stripped off her outer clothes, removed her underwear, and put her outer clothes back on again.

She saw Jasper, now awake, watching her. What did it matter?

She spread her underclothes on the ground and distributed the sweetgrass over it. Reaching into her backpack, she removed a waterproof tin of matches. She struck a match and held it first to one corner, then another, of the underclothes. A fire sputtered to life. The clothes flared and burned quickly, but the moist sweetgrass was stubborn. She quickly removed her shirt and placed it on the fire. After a few moments, the sweetgrass caught and smoke rose and fanned out along the underside of the overhang, releasing a sweet, vanilla-like fragrance.

Jasper sat up, staring at her naked breasts.

"What are you looking at, White Man?" she asked. Her voice was strangely soft and soothing, contradicting the anger her words implied.

Jasper looked away. Caitlin began to stir.

O'zalik spread some of the red ochre on her breasts. She sat back against the wall of the overhang, holding the eagle feather. She began a chant. Its wordless meaning was this: in fire is purification...in fire Mother Earth is healed...in fire the evil spirits are expelled. She watched the eastern sky and waited for the dawn.

Soon, the eagle's feather took life. It transformed itself into Thunderbird. Beckoning O'zalik to follow, it spread its wings and lifted from the ground. O'zalik found herself suddenly aloft, ascending into the night sky. Thunderbird flew beside her, guiding her. They flew past Grandmother Moon and climbed higher and higher. They came to an area of light, a swelling green light, and here she met her grandparents, who smiled and took her hands, one each. They lifted her through the heavens, escorting her on her night journey. They passed under a great arch of light and into an area where waves of brilliance—shimmering white, green, blue—filled the sky. Here, they encountered Edmond and Father Dalou. They, too, smiled at her. They motioned for O'zalik to follow them, turned, and sped toward a different area of sky where they passed through flickering curtains of light, draperies of radiance with woven strands of red and violet. At last, they reached the outer limit of the sky, a huge dome pierced by holes through which shone rays of brilliance. They passed through one of the holes and O'zalik entered a region of unbelievable brightness—a pure, pious white light—where she saw thousands upon thousands of her ancestors. She heard a chant, innumerable voices raised in praise of Father Sun. Close by, she heard her grandparents' voices and the voices of Edmond and Father Dalou and the voices of the Acadians and the Mi'kmaq and, of course, the Passamaquoddy—all who perished on their journey through the snows or on Island of First Light. She raised her voice and joined them. She was moved to tears by the indescribable harmony. She wanted to stay, she wanted desperately to stay, but she knew, beyond knowing, that her time was not yet. Thunderbird told her she had a mission to accomplish first. Her grandparents told her, as did Edmond and Father Dalou. Reluctantly she yielded herself up to Thunderbird for the journey back to Mother Earth. But even as Thunderbird enfolded her in its wings and escorted her back, she heard the voices of the multitudes and merged her voice with theirs.

And she found herself once again sitting half-naked under the overhang and holding the feather still radiant with heat. And as she completed her chant, she watched Grandmother Moon move slowly between the tips of the spruce trees. She was slipping out of alignment with the sun.

The spring tide had run its course.

And the sun was soon to appear. She rose and climbed to the summit of the hill again.

~

Caitlin woke to find Jasper sitting beside her. O'zalik was nowhere to be seen. At the far end of the overhang a fire smoldered, its smoke sending a sweet smell, like vanilla, to her nostrils.

"Where's O'zalik?" she asked Jasper.

He shook his head.

"Did she say where she was going?"

Again, Jasper shook his head. He appeared dazed. "I want to speak to my mother," he said, "but she won't answer."

"Perhaps she's sleeping. Do you want to speak to me?"

Jasper said nothing.

"Please, Jasper, speak to me."

He remained silent.

Caitlin scanned the clearing for a sign of O'zalik. She turned to Jasper and said, "Come on, Jasper. Let's go down to the shore. Maybe your mother's there." She was hoping somebody might have come looking for them.

Saying nothing and moving like an automaton, Jasper rose and started for the beach. Caitlin came up beside him and linked an arm into his. "It's going to be okay, Jasper," she said. "It's going to be okay."

They walked slowly. Through the trees before them, Caitlin saw a penumbra of brilliance. The sun was starting to flood the island with light. They came to the edge of the woods. The sea, drenched in golden sunlight, spread before them, heaving gently.

"Will my mother be here?" asked Jasper.

"Perhaps," Caitlin answered just as she saw a boat with four men approaching the shore. She recognized the men. "Perhaps, Jasper. We'll ask your father."

~

O'zalik sat cross-legged on the summit of Snagged Anchor Island. She faced east, watching the sky brighten. An eagle flew across her vision and her heart soared. She spread her arms as if to fly with the eagle. The flaming edge of Father Sun appeared over the sea. Slowly, it rose golden-red, a fireball. Its first rays shot across the undulating sea and she felt them on her face, on her red-ochered breasts. She was warmed. She looked back to see the branches she implanted had caught the light. She was filled with joy. She began to chant a welcome to the dawn as shafts of sunlight moved across the rocks and the trees of Island of First Light, soothing fingers of warmth. She rose and started to twirl slowly, arms outspread, chanting softly.

people of the dawnland

Slowly, she turned and turned, feeling the warmth of the sun on all parts of her body. She closed her eyes and her lips formed into a broad smile. Behind her eyelids, she saw a flash—the sun. She smiled and continued to turn.

Another flash of light confused her, for she had only completed a half revolution. She opened her eyes. Below her, not far off the southwestern tip of the island—her island—a boat bobbed in the large swells. Its windshield caught the sun and hurled its brilliance back at her. She recognized one of the inn's launches and she knew, she knew without needing to see them, that Quentin and Garret were in the boat.

And she knew as surely as she knew anything that they were too late. It would be the final act of purification.

honor those who have gone before

~

As he and the others approached the beach, Freddy saw Caitlin and Jasper emerge from the forest. He nosed the boat into the shore with a crunch of pebbles. Wayne Crenshaw leaped out of the boat and ran to Jasper. He took the boy into his arms.

"I want to talk to Mom," said Jasper.

"Yes, of course."

Freddy came up to Caitlin. "Are you okay?" he asked.

Caitlin nodded. Freddy watched Wayne Crenshaw and his son, a feeling of profound sadness sweeping over him.

Wayne led Jasper to the utility boat. "Come on, son. It's time to go back. It'll be okay." Over his shoulder, he said to Freddy. "We'll take him back in Ernie's and Burle's boat. Will you take my boat back?"

"Eyuh. Meet you at the marina."

"Thanks, Freddy."

"One father to another," replied Freddy.

Everyone except Caitlin piled into the utility boat. Freddy drove them out to the lobster boat. Ernie fired up the engine while Burle hoisted the anchor. Wayne Crenshaw stood in the stern holding his son close to him. Slowly, the lobster boat pulled away from the shore and headed for the point. Its wake sloshed on the shore, stirring pebbles. Freddy returned to the beach for Caitlin.

After she helped him step from the boat, Freddy asked, "Where's O'zalik?"

"I don't know. She's acting strange. I'm afraid of what she might do."

"We have to find her." He swept the island with his gaze.

Caitlin said, "I don't know where to begin. I think she—" She paused. "Wait, look." She pointed to the hill where a solitary figure stood on the summit. "That's her."

"Let's go," said Freddy.

It took them a half hour to reach the summit. Freddy, breathing hard, had to stop several times. When they finally arrived, there was no sign of O'zalik.

"Where could she have gone?" Freddy asked.

They circled the summit, peering down through the spruce trees for a sign of O'zalik. Freddy saw the upright branches. "What's this?" He pushed through the undergrowth to find an area of disturbed earth.

Caitlin came up beside him. "I'm afraid it's a burial ground," she said.

"The Passamaquoddy?"

"Yes."

"But this earth is freshly turned."

"There were others buried here. Their bones are down by the cave on the southwest tip of the island."

"Whose bones?"

"I'm afraid, Freddy, they're more recent. I'd guess ten, twenty...maybe thirty years."

Freddy stared at her, afraid of what she might be telling him. "What makes you say that?"

"They are relatively intact," answered Caitlin. "That wouldn't be the case if they were the bones of the people in the Jesuit's journal. Those remains would be what my archaeology professor would call 'bone kibble.' They'd be almost totally disintegrated."

"Then who was buried here?"

"Oh, I think we'd find bone kibble here. This is where the Jesuit's people are. But there were others—two, from what I could see of the bones at the cave—who were buried here."

"Who would bury them here?"

"Someone who thought if they were ever found, they would be mistaken for ancient bones. Someone who wanted to hide them."

Freddy thought for a long moment. Finally, he said, "Sometime between ten and thirty years? Jimmy disappeared almost exactly twenty-five years ago."

"And that girl. What was her name?"

Freddy felt his heart sink. "Chatfield. Cindy Chatfield." He paused and said, "But who would do that?"

Caitlin shook her head.

"Let's find O'zalik and get back to Alabaster Island," said Freddy. "We gotta get Richie Comine out here."

"No need to look hard for O'zalik. There she is now." Caitlin pointed toward a figure making for the southwest tip of the island. "She's going back to the cave."

"Let's go. We'll take the boat. It'll be quicker."

It took them only a short time to bound down the hill. They moved quickly to the utility boat and shoved it from the beach with a scrape until they were knee deep in the water. They climbed into the boat and Freddy lowered the outboard engine. With one tug of the starter cord, the motor sputtered to life.

Traveling at full throttle, it took them less than a half hour to reach the southwestern point. They turned the point and headed for the shore. As they approached, one of the Spruce Cove Inn launches plowed past them. Quentin and Garret were in the boat.

"What in hell are they doing?" asked Freddy.

"What if they were the ones who tried to hide the bones?"

Freddy looked at Caitlin a long moment. "Let's find O'zalik and get the hell back to Alabaster Island. I want to have a word with them."

He drove the boat toward shore. At the last possible moment he cut the accelerator and slammed the motor into reverse. Caitlin lurched forward as the boat hit the pebbles with a scrape and shuddered to a stop. Freddy cut the motor and scrambled from the boat, Caitlin following.

The air was putrid with the rotting whale carcass.

On a nearby slab of rock a colony of puffins raised a cacophony of grunts, moans, and growls. Laughing gulls swerved and darted overhead with a mocking cackle of yawps and cries. And on another rock, several storm petrels rose long, stridulent, deep-throated chirrs that ended in high-pitched squawks. It was as though the whole island pulsed with primeval sound. As though here was the raucous soul of creation. He hated this island.

Freddy stopped. He'd seen the bones. For a long while he knelt, gazing at them. A flood of thoughts swept through his mind—the years of loneliness and heartbreak on his back porch; the lost grandchildren; the long years of Agnes's decline; the frantic days looking for Jimmy; the piles of ashes and bodies at Dachau; the German soldiers slumping in sprays of blood; rib-ravaged Miesko. The partially snow-covered bodies in the gondolas of the death train.

Was Jimmy here?

like as if God were trying to hide something but ran out of snow

"Killing them Germans wasn't a right thing to do," Freddy said. "I guess I had to pay for it."

"Freddy, this has nothing to do with what happened at Dachau. The world doesn't work like that."

"Don't it? There's gotta be a reason for everything."

"It's not connected, Freddy."

"All those years…everything lost. Agnes. Jimmy. What was the point in it?"

like as though God were trying to hide…

"Freddy, these aren't all the bones," Caitlin said, puzzled.

"What do you mean?"

"I mean I saw more bones yesterday. At least twice as many."

Freddy turned to watch the inn's launch speeding away from them. "I'm gonna call Richie Comine on the radio." He went back to the boat, switched the radio on, and turned to channel 16. "Crenshaw Marina to Alabaster Island harbormaster. Come in please."

He had to repeat the call twice before Richie Comine came on. "Harbormaster to Crenshaw Marina, what's up Wayne?"

"It ain't Wayne. It's Freddy. I'm in one of Wayne's boats." He went on to tell Richie about the bones and the Spruce Cove Inn launch.

"Goldang, Freddy. Are you sure?"

"All I'm saying is it'd be good if you could meet them. See if they're carrying anything."

"Will do."

"Thanks, Richie. Crenshaw Marina launch out."

"Freddy, look," said Caitlin.

Freddy turned to see O'zalik standing in the mouth of the cave. She emerged from the cave into the sunlight. Freddy couldn't believe what he was seeing. O'zalik naked from the waist up and smeared with dirt. Her eyes were wild. There was a sudden frenzy of bellowing yowls from the colony of puffins. The excitement rose a flurry of caws from the laughing gulls. A flock of gulls rose in confusions of flight. On the nearby slab, the puffins scattered, grunting and moaning.

"O'zalik, what the hell?"

O'zalik said nothing.

Freddy took off his jacket and wrapped it around O'zalik's shoulders. "Come on. It'll be alright. We're going back to Alabaster Island."

"I found my ancestors," she said.

"I know."

"And they killed Jimmy, Freddy," she said. "Quentin and Garret killed Jimmy and that Chatfield girl."

"How do you know?"

"I know."

Freddy and Caitlin tried to get her to talk more, but she refused. She climbed into the launch and sat staring at Snagged Anchor Island. Freddy started the engine and pointed the launch toward Alabaster Island. To their left, caught in the slanting rays of the rising sun, String of Pearls flared into a glittering iridescence.

All the way back to Alabaster Island, O'zalik said nothing. When they arrived at the marina, Richie Comine and Wayne Crenshaw were waiting for them. Wayne took the bowline and tied the launch to the dock. O'zalik stepped out and, without saying a word, climbed the metal ramp and disappeared down the street.

"She's been like that since we left Snagged Anchor Island," Freddy said as he stepped onto the dock.

"Freddy, I've got some bad news for you," Richie Comine said.

"I suspect I know what it is. Where's Quentin and Garret?"

"I got them locked up. Guys from the mainland will be here tomorrow to cart them away."

Wayne Crenshaw stepped forward. "Freddy, why don't we go up to my office. We'll tell you what we learned."

Freddy and Caitlin followed the two men up the ramp and into Wayne's office. There was no sign of Jasper. "How is your son doing, Wayne?" Caitlin asked.

"He's resting. I figure I got to get him some professional help. Been putting it off all this time, but can't put it off any longer. Angus recommended a doctor. I'll call him tomorrow."

Freddy turned to Richie. "Eyuh, so what have you got?"

"See, it's like this Freddy. We figured if those guys were carting off something like you said, they wouldn't just come honking in here like nothing was wrong. They'd head for the inn's dock. So we went out and hid ourselves behind the point. When they came into the cove, we was on them before they knew what was happening."

"You shoulda seen Richie gun that old boat of his," said Wayne.

"They didn't have time to do nothing. I saw Quentin move like he was gonna throw something overboard, but I got on the megaphone. Told him it wouldn't do him no good. But he just stared at me. Looked like he was gonna go ahead and throw it overboard anyway—it turned out to be a sail all tied up to make a sack—so that's when I rammed them. Knocked them both flat on their asses before Quentin could react, and me and Wayne was on their boat faster than a lobstah'll get your thumb if you ain't careful."

Wayne said, "First thing Richie says was, 'Excuse me Garret. If I'm wrong, I apologize for any damage I done to your boat.' Then he says, 'Now show me what you got there'."

"All they did was back away," said Richie. "They didn't say nothing. So I untied the ends of the sail…" He exchanged glances with Wayne. "Freddy, there was a bunch of bones in there." He reached into his pocket, held his hand out to Freddy. "And this here ring. I cleaned it up because it was all gunked up with dirt and corrosion and stuff."

Freddy took the ring and examined it. It was a wedding band. On the inside was inscribed "JFO—DMO 8-5-72".

"It's Jimmy's all right," said Freddy.

"Figured as much. I knew his middle name was Frederick."

Freddy sighed deeply. He shook his head. "It don't make no sense. Why wouldn't they get rid of it?"

"Only in the movies are murderers smart. In real life they're pretty friggin dumb."

"They was probably all panicked," said Wayne.

"Goldang, I'm sorry, Freddy," said Richie. "I guess we can't be certain without some tests, you know, DNA, that sorta thing. A medical examiner is coming out with the law tomorrow. But it sure looks like those two guys murdered your son."

"And the girl, Cindy Chatfield, who disappeared about the same time?" asked Caitlin.

"Looks like. Enough bones for it anyway. But we'll know more when the medical examiner does his stuff."

"What are Quentin and Garret saying?" asked Caitlin.

"Not a goldang thing. But they sure are shaking in their boots a lot."

~

That night, Freddy knocked on the door of Burle Ledyard's house. After a few moments, Burle came to the door. "Freddy, come on in. Goldang, I'm sorry about Jimmy."

"Eyuh."

"Who would have thunk it?"

Freddy shook his head. "They were a lot of years of not knowing. At least now I know."

"Eyuh, but still it must be tough."

"Like Ernie says, we gotta roll with it."

"Eyuh. That's what he says. And he's a man oughta know."

"Is he in?"

"I'll get him." Burle went to the bedroom door and called out, "Ernie, Freddy's here."

Ernie emerged from the bedroom looking worn.

"You feeling all right, Ernie?" asked Freddy.

"Just a little tired. Get that way these days," Ernie replied. "How 'bout you. You feeling okay?"

"Guess I'll survive."

"Eyuh, guess you will."

"Listen, Ernie. I came to talk with you about Snagged Anchor Island. Seems to me O'zalik has proof there're Passamaquoddy remains out there."

"And you was thinking it might be fitting if I donate the island to the Passamaquoddy tribe."

Freddy gave him a surprised look. "Well…yuh, that's what I'm thinking."

"Me and Burle already talked about it. We figure it's the right thing to do."

"You've already decided?"

"Eyuh."

Freddy hesitated. He didn't know what to say. "Well, then…"

"There being Passamaquoddy remains out there warn't the only thing that decided the issue for us."

"What do you mean?"

"It's near where your boy's boat washed up. We figure it'd be a fitting thing to do for him, too."

Burle stepped forward. "The way we see it is: whatever you want to say about them Indians, they know how to honor them that's passed away."

Later, when Freddy told O'zalik the news, she said nothing. She only smiled.

~

All night O'zalik thought of Edmond, how he waited until his mission was completed before he felt the freedom to die. At first light, she rose from bed and walked down to the shore where String of Pearls joined to Alabaster Island. The shore was deserted. She turned to face east. A flock of gulls rose from the water and spiraled against the backdrop of the rising sun.

first light

She smiled. When she turned again, she saw two groups of people huddled on the shore. They were the Acadians and her Passamaquoddy ancestors. She joined them on the shore of L'île des Perles Perdues. She stood with them, waiting. They said they had been standing like that, guarded by the English, ever since Father Dalou went up into the town with Captain Webster. It was cold. She folded her arms across her chest and shivered.

At last she saw Father Dalou descending the bluff. Captain Webster was behind him. He went straight to little Lisette Plamondon and pulled her away from the Acadians. He forced her to stand in front of him while he ran his hands over her body. He tore her overcoat open, ripped off the buttons of her blouse, and reached inside. Laughing, he pushed her toward the men he had called Moseley and Orcutt. They grabbed her arms and held her while a third man felt under her dress between her legs. Little Lisette struggled and whimpered but there was nothing she could do. O'zalik started toward the men but one of her Passamaquoddy brothers held her back with a stern look.

Father Dalou didn't hesitate. He went up to the men and pleaded with them, in the name of God, to leave the poor girl alone. The Jesuit then said something to Webster that O'zalik couldn't hear. Whatever it was, however, it angered the man so much that he leveled his flintlock rifle and fired. The man standing next to O'zalik let out a cry and fell to the ground, a gaping hole in his chest. Then Webster grabbed Lisette Plamondon and marched up the hill. His men followed. Only a small guard was left behind, but O'zalik knew there was nothing they could do in their weakened state. She knelt and soothed the dying man.

It seemed to O'zalik that only moments had passed. But somehow she felt she'd spent the remainder of that day and the entire night on the frozen beach with no shelter. All through the night she heard the little girl's cries. She could only imagine what the men were doing to her. Sometime in the middle of the night, O'zalik heard whimpering coming from among the Acadians. She went over to find the one called Madame Babineau holding her daughter in her arms. The girl was dead. The cold had been too much for her. O'zalik tried to comfort Madame Babineau. She put her arms around the woman and then leaned down to kiss the forehead of the dead girl.

Not long after first light, Captain Webster, followed by his men, came down the hill. He carried in his arms the body of Lisette. He dumped the girl at the feet of Father Dalou.

It was the low water of a spring tide and the reef tethering L'île des Perles Perdues with its mate was fully exposed. O'zalik and the others were ordered onto the reef. Neptune carried Lisette on his back. Her arm swung lifelessly and drops of blood still issued from between her legs. As O'zalik followed, she saw the blood diluted in the tidal pools. All at once, the sun emerged from a cloud and the reef started to sparkle. And she felt a peace descend upon her.

They were halfway across the reef when a large wave advanced toward them. The others scrambled for handholds, but O'zalik stood and faced the wave. It swept into her. She felt it lift her feet from the rocks. It was as though she were flying. The shock of the cold water hit her. She was in the sea, she was merged into the sea. Her clothes blossomed out like a water lily. She smiled and spread her arms like an eagle in flight.

~

The following morning Caitlin and Freddy sat in Wayne Crenshaw's office listening to him and Richie tell them what the police from the mainland learned.

A careful search of the inn's launch turned up another object in the bilge. When Richie Comine cleaned it off, it turned out to be an amulet depicting a moon with the letters ACCIHTE inscribed across its face. Caitlin told Richie of the statue in Garret's attic studio and of the sketchbook that had the name Cindy in it associated with the amulet.

"I guess that about says it," said Richie. "They ain't gonna get out of this one."

The mainland police spent several hours questioning Quentin and Garret. Finally, confronted with the evidence of the ring and the amulet, the two men confessed. They said that they went out to the island with that Chatfield girl and they all become drunk. Garret and the girl exchanged caresses while Quentin watched. But it soon got out of hand and the two men ripped off her clothes and started to take turns with her. She screamed. They tried to muffle her but she screamed and screamed. They were too busy with the girl to notice that Jimmy

Orcutt, apparently having heard the girl, had beached his boat and was rushing toward them. He started to pull Garret from the girl when Quentin stove in his head with a boulder. Jimmy died instantly. In their panic, knowing the girl was a witness, they killed her, too. They buried the bodies in the ancient burial ground Garret discovered but kept secret so no one would challenge his ownership of the island. (He always figured he could eventually wrest it from Ernie Botham.)

Richie Comine asked them why they moved the skeletons to the cave and they said it was because O'zalik was making such a stink they figured she'd eventually bring experts out there who would be able to tell the difference between old bones and recent ones. Originally, they were just going to take the bones with them and figure a way of disposing them. They wrapped everything in a sail and dragged it to the launch. But then they saw Ernie Botham and Burle Ledyard out tending their lobster traps not more than fifty yards off shore. The men waved at them and called out to pull alongside so they could give them some lobsters. Quentin and Garret waved and said they would be out soon. Then they panicked and dragged the sail around some projecting rocks and hid the bones in the cave. Their plan was to return when Ernie and Burle weren't around. That's what they were doing when they saw Freddy and Caitlin approaching the shore.

"So if we didn't show up, they might have gotten away with it," said Caitlin.

"That's about the size of it." Something made Crenshaw glance toward the window. He rose and went to stand before it. "Well I'll be...It's Ernie Botham and Burle Ledyard comin' in early."

"At this time?" asked Freddy. "They ain't due for hours."

"I hope Ernie's okay," said Caitlin.

"Something's up," said Richie. "'cause they're coming here instead of their mooring."

Caitlin and Freddy bolted from their chairs. "We better see what's going on," said Freddy, heading for the door. Caitlin, Richie, and Wayne followed him. By the time they made their way down the ramp to the floating dock, Burle was easing the lobster boat alongside. Ernie stepped out and tied the boat to the dock.

"You guys are in early," said Crenshaw.

"We found Angelique Moseley floating out near Snagged Anchor Island."

"What?"

"Afraid she's drowned." They pointed to a form wrapped in oilskins.

Caitlin sagged against a piling. Freddy put his hands on her shoulders.

Later, they were sitting together on Freddy's porch when he asked, "You remember us talking about how things sometimes just don't make sense?"

"Yes." Caitlin answered.

"Well, I'll tell you what does make sense. It's you sitting here with me looking out to Snagged Anchor Island and talking about the weather…and other things."

"Yes, Freddy, that makes sense."

"So I guess I'm wondering if you'll be willing to stay in Jimmy's cottage? Keep an old man company."

She smiled. "I'll stay."

He gave a satisfied nod. "Snow comes usually in December. You'll like it. It's real pretty."

When she returned to her cottage, Caitlin found a note left by O'zalik. It said if anything happened to her, she wanted to be cremated and have her ashes spread on the island of her ancestors.

~

A week later, Caitlin and Freddy visited Wayne Crenshaw at the marina. They found him sitting behind his desk drinking a cup of coffee. Now that most of the visiting boats were crossed off his mooring list, the green marker stains on his fingers had faded. His face was drawn, dark shadows under his eyes. A picture of him, his wife, and Jasper sat on the bare desk. It was turned toward him. He stared at it as he talked. "The way it is, they've committed Jasper to a mental hospital in Bangor for observation and evaluation."

"It's the best thing," said Caitlin. "He needs to find a way to get over your wife's death."

"Eyuh. Seems like a lot of us need to get over things."

"How long will he stay there?"

"Don't know. But they take care of him pretty good. Food's not bad, neither. I tried it to make sure." Crenshaw sighed deeply.

"If I'd only kept trying…" said Caitlin.

"Now don't you go blaming yourself. You did everything you could. Ain't nobody was going to get through to him." He gazed at the framed photograph and shook his head.

And I'm here to tell you, Wayne," said Freddy, "you done everything you could, too. You been a good father to him. A damn good father."

"Thanks, Freddy." Wayne rose and went to the coffee machine. "You folks care for a cup?"

They both nodded. Caitlin said, "When do you see him next?"

"Gonna go to Bangor Fridays for as long as he's there."

"Do you mind if I go with you?"

"Be glad of the company. My guess is Jasper—he'd be pretty pleased, too. 'Bout the only thing he said that day we found him out on the island was how nice you were to him…like his mother woulda been. Told the psychiatrist about you, too."

"Would three of us be a crowd?" asked Freddy.

"Be glad to have you along, too, Freddy," said Crenshaw. "You're a man knows how it is between fathers and sons."

"Eyuh, guess I do."

"Sorry what you found out about Jimmy."

"Eyuh, but it's nice to know what happened to him anyhow."

"He was just trying to rescue that girl. You oughta be proud."

"I am, Wayne. I'm proud."

~

A week later, the entire island attended a memorial service for Jimmy. A day before the service, Burle Ledyard cornered Freddy and Caitlin at Pauline's. He said, "I was worried about Ernie attending so many funerals and memorial services, what with his own coming up. But you wanna know what Ernie says? He says, 'It's just the way things work, Burle. Ya gotta roll with it.' That's what he says. Ain't that something?"

Freddy shook his head. "We could all learn a goldang lesson from that man."

Caitlin surprised Freddy by making several phone calls to New York and arranging for Miesko Heilprin to come help officiate at the service. He arrived with his wife, Rhea, and stayed several days with, as he put it, his "adoptive father" Freddy.

On the day of the service, she went down to the ferry terminal to greet her other surprise guests. Together, they drove up to Freddy's cottage. When they arrived, Caitlin heard conversation coming from Freddy's porch and knew he was there with Miesko and Rhea Heilprin. She motioned for her guests to wait at the bottom of the steps. She went up to the porch, exchanged greetings with Miesko and Rhea Heilprin, and said good morning to Freddy.

"Where you been?" asked Freddy. "We're having lemonade and I was looking for you."

"I was down to the ferry terminal meeting some people who wanted to come to Jimmy's service."

"What people?"

She turned, made a gesture.

The three people mounted the steps to the porch.

Freddy bolted from his rocking chair. "My God! Jimmy... Catherine...Diana." He crossed the porch to embrace them. They hugged for a long time, tears welling in Freddy's eyes. Finally, he turned to Diana, "Jimmy looks just like his father."

Diana laughed. "And Catherine looks like Agnes, don't you think?"

Freddy stood back and gazed at Catherine. "Yes...yes, she does."

Catherine hesitated a moment then came forward and took Freddy in her arms. "Grandpa, it's so good to see you." Her eyes were wet.

Freddy held her tight to him. He seemed unable to speak.

Jimmy extended his hand. "Grandpa," he said.

Freddy shook his hand vigorously.

Caitlin saw that Miesko Heilprin had tears in his eyes. She wondered if he was thinking of his parents and his sisters.

They spent the rest of the morning talking. Freddy couldn't hear enough about what his grandchildren were doing. In the afternoon, at Jimmy's service, they stood on each side of him listening to the words Miesko spoke.

"It may be unusual for a rabbi to participate in a Congregational service," Miesko said, "and I want to thank Reverend Collins for including me and Caitlin Gray for inviting me. For, you see, I have a special reason to be here...Freddy Orcutt is my father. He is the father of my spirit. When my birth parents and my sisters were killed by the Nazis at Dachau, when I saw all the pain and suffering, when I saw the inhumanity with which people can treat others, I came close to losing my faith in God and the human race. But when the Americans came to liberate the camp, my faith was restored. Beyond all the death, beyond the killing that went on that day, I saw a man profoundly moved by what he was witnessing and doing. I saw a man wrestling with his soul. As he said to me that day through a translator, "Ain't none of us is a saint, not a damned one of us." And I was almost prepared to believe him until I saw that here before me was a man, a human being, who earnestly struggled with his own human nature, who sensed that despite all the hatred, all the killing, a little love could make a difference. Maybe that isn't sainthood. But maybe that's as close as we can ever get, anchored as we are in our natures. For a young boy who had seen hell firsthand, who had witnessed day after day after day the greatest sin of all, indifference to human suffering, this man's display of conscience made all the difference for me. He may tell you all he did was give me some food. That, he did. But he gave me much more. He gave me back a faith in humanity and he gave me the will to live and to do what little I could to help bring more love into the world. That man was Private First Class Freddy Orcutt and I'm here today to honor him as well as to celebrate the wonderful life of Jimmy Orcutt, another man who tried to do what he could. He tried to rescue young Cindy Chatfield from a terrible evil. He gave his life doing it. You're wrong, Freddy, there are some of us who are saints. You brought one into the world."

KILOTONUHKET

Freezing Moon

On Caitlin's suggestion, they chose the fifteenth day of November for the ceremony dedicating Snagged Anchor Island as a Passamaquoddy sacred burial place. O'zalik's note specified that her ashes should be spread on the island only after it became a Passamaquoddy site.

For days after O'zalik's suicide Caitlin berated herself, wondering if there hadn't been something she could have done to prevent it. Finally, it was Freddy who said, "Ain't nothing you could have said. She was fixing to do it all along because she never felt she belonged here. Hell, she didn't even think she belonged in this century."

"All the same, there must have been something."

"Nope. Not a thing you could do. There's things that happen make us feel guilty but come to find out, they was gonna happen no matter what. Ain't no sense in feeling guilty for the things you can't do nothing about. That goes for all of us."

Accompanied by Robert Blanchard, a large delegation came from Pleasant Point to lay claim to the island and to perform a dedication ceremony. Caitlin talked with them beforehand and won their enthusiastic agreement to include in the ceremony the unveiling of a small monument to Father Dalou and the Acadian families who died, as well as to the Passamaquoddy who died with them. Working quickly, and using her own funds, she commissioned a stone cutter on the mainland to create the monument in time for the dedication ceremony. She wrote out the inscription.

On the evening of the ceremony, a fleet of boats brought the Passamaquoddy and some of the inhabitants of Alabaster Island to the island. They gathered around a huge bonfire that created moving shadows on the rocks. Several of the Passamaquoddy elders said the shadows represented the ancestors who were present for the sacred occasion.

At six o'clock, with the Northern Cross directly overhead, arms spread like a being in flight, the moon rose fat and full on the eastern horizon. It was the signal to begin the ceremony.

Emmanuelle Tomah, a distant relative of O'zalik's, performed a welcoming song. At the conclusion, she gave a short speech. "We gather on this island to honor our ancestors and to dedicate this place as a Passamaquoddy burial ground. We are the people of the dawnland and from this time forward this place will be called Island of First Light. Those of you who stay with us through the night will witness Father Sun rising in the same place as we now see Grandmother Moon. Before we begin the ceremony, I want to thank Mister Ernie Botham for his wisdom and courage in donating this island to the Passamaquoddy people."

Her words were greeted with warm applause. Ernie shyly raised his hand to acknowledge the applause. He turned to Freddy and said, "Ain't no need for her to say that. Was just the right thing to do." Burle Ledyard slapped him on the back.

Emmanuelle Tomah sang an honor song accompanied by the rhythmic beating of a drum sounding like the heartbeat of the earth. At the end of the song an old man, one of the tribal elders, stepped forward to recount a dream he had in which he saw, across the waters, many canoes coming to Island of First Light. He said they were ancestors who had no burial place coming from all points of the compass to join those whose spirits already inhabited the island.

As the moon started to follow Cygnus across the vault of sky, two men came forward to perform a pipe ceremony. They pointed their pipe toward the four directions of the medicine wheel—north, south, east, and west. Speaking Passamaquoddy words that were a prayer to the spirit who protects land and sky, they offered the stem of the pipes to the earth and the heavens.

Caitlin was pleased to see Freddy puffing on his new meerschaum, D'Artagnan, as he watched.

When the two men finished, others advanced into the space. They waved pungent smoke wafting from a smudge pot over themselves for purification, then they each smoked the pipes used by the previous men.

By now, the moon, Grandmother Moon, was well along in her journey across the sky. Passamaquoddy children, in single file, performed a pinecone dance. After a while, others joined them until, in the end, everybody, islanders included, was dancing.

Island of First Light now dedicated, consecrated, and purified, it was time to return O'zalik to the place she loved. Carrying an urn, Caitlin moved to the edge of the circle of light where the monument to Father Jérôme Dalou, the Acadians, and the Passamaquoddy sat. It was a simple, rough-hewn stone bearing the inscription:

Father Jérôme Dalou, Jesuit priest
b. circa 1715, d. 1756
who tried to do good but found
the devil loosed a little season
lies here with the remains of the Acadians
and Passamaquoddy he loved
and tried to save.

She removed the cover from the urn and allowed some of O'zalik's ashes to fall on the stone. Then, with a great heave, she cast the remainder of the ashes into the sky, into the place where the eagles fly.

The ceremony over, warmed by the bonfire and by each other, the people passed the night in celebration, song, and a feast. Sometime in the middle of the night, Caitlin saw Orion appear in the east. It comforted her.

Though everyone slept in sleeping bags for portions of the long night, nobody was sleeping when dawn appeared. It came as a swelling of molten gold on the eastern horizon, sending long shafts of light that inflamed the tops of the spruce.

puka 'ana o ka la

One of the tribal elders sang a chant to the rising sun, Father Sun. In the middle of the chant an eagle, its wings irradiated with a soft, rose glow, flew overhead. Above it, an airplane caught an eruption of sunlight.

~

Later that month, Caitlin and Freddy sat on the porch bundled against the November cold. They were waiting for their guests to arrive.

The day was crystalline with a vanishing-point sky—a vast, reflective sheet of blue streaked by high stratus radiating out from an infinitely distant point of singularity.

Caitlin watched the steady drip from icicles hanging at the edge of the porch roof. Fusillades of ice and confettis of snow fell from the trees out back. The branches of the spruce, heavy with snow, looked like ermine-clad kings. Caitlin heard a sharp ping when a chunk of ice hit the bird feeder she'd installed between the cottages. It delivered a shiver of joy to her. Earlier, she'd tramped through the snow to fill the feeder and to poke snow with a broom from the bent branches of the new maple she'd planted. When the released branches sprang up, they showered her with snow.

The smell of Freddy's pipe mingled with the savory aroma of the Thanksgiving turkey Caitlin had roasting in the oven. Below them, the harbor was mostly empty of boats. The water in Spruce Cove was unruffled, rocking slowly to the heaving of the tide.

Every now and then, Freddy glanced through the kitchen window at Catherine and Dylan who were preparing some of the trimmings to go with Caitlin's turkey. Each time he looked, a smile appeared on his face. "Too bad your daughter couldn't make it."

"Maybe next year," said Caitlin. "I'm sorry your grandson and daughter-in-law aren't here."

"Eyuh. As you say, maybe next year. Be glad for what we got." He turned to her and asked, "What did you say the Passamaquoddy call this month's moon?"

"*Kelotonuhket.* The freezing moon."

"They got that right," replied Freddy wrapping his arms around himself.

Caitlin laughed, a sound like wind chimes. "It's warm inside. Are you finished with your pipe?"

Freddy withdrew the pipe from his mouth and studied the bowl. "Eyuh, suppose so." He held the pipe out to Caitlin. "See that? It's beginning to color with age already."

"It happens."

"Eyuh," he replied. He rose from his rocking chair, took a last look out to String of Pearls and Island of First Light, and said, "Well, best to go inside where it's warm."

They walked into the kitchen where Dylan and Catherine were talking animatedly.

An hour later, their guests started to appear. Ernie Botham and Burle Ledyard came together.

"Good day to be thankful," said Ernie by way of greeting.

"Eyuh," said Burle, "Good day to be thankful."

Caitlin opened the oven door to inspect the turkey. Waves of warmth engulfed her. The juices sizzled, sending a savory aroma throughout the kitchen. It was done. Feeling the heat of happiness, she removed the turkey from the oven and carried it, balanced on the roasting pan, to the counter. When it was ready for carving, Freddy took up his knife. He handed her the first slice. It tasted good—moist, warm, tender. Redeeming.

When Wayne Crenshaw arrived, he said, "Guess I'm a lucky man getting two Thanksgiving dinners in two days. Folks at the hospital are putting on a spread tomorrow for Jasper and the others. Family invited."

"In that case you can count on Freddy and me to be there," said Caitlin.

"Eyuh," said Freddy. "Sure as fish jump."

Shortly after, Angus Macleod arrived. "Uhmm, smells like old times. I haven't had a family-type Thanksgiving like this since...Oh, hell, I don't remember."

When at last the dinner was spread about the table, they all sat down. Caitlin saw the happy faces of their guests, the perpetual smile on poor Ernie Botham's lips; listened to praise about her turkey; offered her own praise for Dylan's and Catherine's sweet potatoes and squash; watched Freddy's eyes glisten as he studied Catherine; smiled at Dylan; poured more wine; and was warmed to the core of her being. Out the window over Freddy's shoulder, she saw String of Pearls and Island of First Light. High above the island, she saw a speck. Caitlin wanted to believe it was an eagle. She told herself it was an eagle. She returned her gaze to the island and saw its contours unlike she'd ever seen them—soft, rounded. Peaceful. A cold sun glinted off the snow, imparting an inner radiance to it.

For the snows came early that year. They came in time for Thanksgiving, sifting from the sky in large, gentle, consoling flakes lit by lights from shop windows on Front Street. In the boreal forests the branches of the spruce bowed low under the weight of the snow. And up on Cemetery Hill the snow swaddled the stones in the Founder's Section—clinging to the branches of the large maple overspreading the adjoining graves of Agnes and Jimmy Orcutt; burying the withered flowers on Doris Peake Crenshaw's headstone. The snow mixed with the fallen, dead, wind swept maple leaves, then buried them. Snow dust, sifting from the trees, flared in the winter sun. Snow drifted in the ten-second sweep of Sheep's Pasture Light, gracing the gunwales and decks of Ernie Botham's and Burle Ledyard's lobster boat. The snow mounded the summits of Big Pearl and Little Pearl, softening the sharp edges of rock and melting in the tidal pools of String of Pearls. It sifted into the cavities of the whale carcass. It softly crowned the rough-made memorial to Father Dalou, the Acadians, and the Passamaquoddy, mingling with O'zalik's ashes.

And the Thanksgiving snows blanketed Island of First Light like a comforter.

ACKNOWLEDGMENTS

As always, I must first acknowledge and thank my wife, Susan M. Reynolds, for her unfailing support. It can't be easy living with a novelist.

For their generous help in a variety of technical matters I thank (in alphabetical order):

Rebecca Cole-Will of the Abbe Museum for help in matters concerning the Passamaquoddy; Dr. Stephen M. Dickson, State Marine Geologist with the Maine Geological Survey for advice about coastal-conditions in Maine; Robert Leavitt of the University of New Brunswick for help with the pronunciations of Passamaquoddy words; Dr. Ann Marie Mires in the Office of the Chief Medical Examiner of Massachusetts for help in matters of forensic pathology; Todd Pattison of the Northeast Document Conservation Center for help concerning the conditions allowing for the survival of a 250-year-old journal; Dr. Neal R. Pettigrew of the University of Maine School of Marine Sciences for help with the island geology of Maine.

A special thanks to my agent, Kimberley Cameron, for her continued patience, encouragement, and persistence.

Thanks also to Aoise Stratford and John Gray for their valuable suggestions.

And, finally, thanks to all the fine people at MacAdam/Cage, especially Tasha Kepler for her constant help; my editor, Pat Walsh, for his sage advice; and my publisher, David Poindexter, for his continued faith.

DATE DUE		
SEP 12 2007	8-22-14	
FEB 14 2008		
APR 03 2008		
MAY 31 2008		
JUL 08 2008		
JAN 27 2009		
FEB 28 2009		
JUN 26 2009		
JUL 24 2009		